RAISING THE STAKES

Anne Marie Becker

COPYRIGHT

This is a work of fiction. Names, characters, places, and incidents either are the product of the author's imagination or are used fictitiously, and any resemblance to actual persons living or dead, business establishments, events, or locales is entirely coincidental.

STACKING THE DECK by Anne Marie Becker

Cover Design by The Killion Group

www.AnneMarieBecker.com

DEDICATION

For people who not only try to see the good in the world,
but be the good in the world.

ACKNOWLEDGMENTS

Andrea Edwards, Kim Law, June Love, Rita Henuber, & Autumn Jordan – I extend my sincerest and deepest gratitude. Without you, this book would not have reached completion.

Emme Adams, thank you so much for lending your editing expertise. Deborah Nemeth, your help with the overall Redemption Club series was, as always, invaluable.

Daniel W., your help understanding the world of security contractors in Afghanistan was so helpful to laying the background for my hero. I greatly appreciate the insight. (And any errors are my own.)

And finally, to my wonderful family... Tim and the kids, I love you so much and am thankful every day that you're in my life.

Books by Anne Marie Becker

MINDHUNTERS SERIES

Only Fear

Avenging Angel

Deadly Bonds

Dark Deeds

Acceptable Risk

End Game

REDEMPTION CLUB SERIES

Stacking the Deck

Sleight of Hand

Raising the Stakes

PROLOGUE

"He's going to find out everything." Linda Castillo stood at the sink, wringing her hands.

Ivy Stone crossed the small kitchen that had always seemed homey and safe. Today, it was overcast by the long shadow of the infamous underground crime ring known as Redemption Club—and her father's possible connection to it.

Ivy clasped her ex-nanny's fingers to calm the older woman's agitation. "We're not certain yet that his case will go to trial. According to Dad, they don't have a leg to stand on. Besides, you haven't had any contact with him in over fifteen years."

Not that it mattered. Anyone who'd been associated with Robert Stone during his fifty-eight years on this planet was at risk for being placed under the microscope. Both sides of the legal battle gathered ammunition, determining who was friend and who was foe.

"These are just routine questions," Ivy assured Linda. "And if there's anything to worry about, I'll protect you."

Linda reached over to cup Ivy's cheek. "I know you will." Linda had kept Ivy's secret, and Ivy would keep hers. Briefly, Ivy allowed herself to lean into the comfort of the soft, paper-thin skin before pulling away.

Moving to the kitchen table, where coffee and freshly baked cinnamon rolls awaited, Ivy glanced across the threshold toward the living room of the modest three-bedroom home Ivy paid for in central Las Vegas, Nevada. Her gaze touched on the six children who were part of Linda's in-home daycare service. It was a school holiday, so today's group ranged in age from two to seven years old. They watched PBS and played on the floor. The January day would grow warm enough to play outside later, but it was too early yet. Ivy envied them their innocence and freedom. Her childhood had been extremely different.

Linda sensed the direction of her thoughts. "You've done what you could to keep attention away from me, but I'm afraid nothing you can do will stop the questions. I've told them nothing, but if I'm subpoenaed, what will we do?"

"If they put you on the stand, you answer truthfully."

"Okay." But Linda still looked worried. She didn't deserve to be scared. She'd raised Ivy since she was four years old, had nurtured her when nobody else had—until she'd left suddenly when Ivy turned thirteen. Ivy had lost touch with her beloved nanny until they'd reconnected years later.

"We'll worry about that if it comes to it."

"It may already have come to it."

"Is that why you asked me to come over this morning? Have Dad's lawyers been bothering you?"

"They aren't the only ones calling." Linda gripped her mug tighter.

"The task force?" Ivy silently cursed. "I should have known. They're leaving no stone unturned to build a case against Dad." When corruption and Redemption Club influence had been exposed within the LVPD and even the local office of the FBI, a special task force had been created that merged trusted agents from various law enforcement branches in a joint effort to bring down the Club.

"There's a man who insisted on coming by this morning. I can't risk testifying against your father. I'll lose everything." They exchanged a knowing gaze.

There was too much at stake. "I think it's time, *mija*."

"I'll start making the arrangements, just in case." Better to be prepared for any eventuality.

Ivy cast a glance toward the living room. One dark-haired boy stretched out on the floor on his stomach, his eyes glued to Elmo. The kids seemed bigger, longer and wiser every day. Time flew by so fast, and she wished she could hit pause or rewind.

Linda caught Ivy's unguarded expression. "If this goes to trial, it'll drag you down with him. Get away from your father while you can. There's plenty of room for you here."

"I know, but he needs me." Her father needed her PR skills now, more than ever. So, she'd stay. And she'd fight, as her father had taught her to do.

A knock sounded and Ivy jumped. Several of the kids glanced toward the door, knowing it wasn't common to have two visitors in one day. She sent them a reassuring smile and they immediately settled again.

The deep rumble of a male voice came from the entryway, but Ivy couldn't make out the words. A moment later, Linda showed her guest to the kitchen. A familiar, wide-shouldered frame clad in an impeccable suit darkened the archway. The man's smile was slow and deliberate as it moved from Linda to Ivy, his surprise at finding her in Linda's kitchen evident.

"Ivy," Linda began, "this is Devlin—"

"Grimm," Ivy finished, ignoring the flutter in her stomach as she stood to face the man who ran Global Security Solutions.

"Please, call me Dev," he said. He probably wanted to create a false sense of comfort where there was none. Knowing better than to trust anyone, Ivy only frowned.

Linda cast a curious look between them. "You seem to know each other."

"We run in the same business circles," Ivy said.

"But haven't talked much," Dev added, eyeing

her. "Not about anything of importance, that is."

"You're not the only one he's contacted about Dad," Ivy explained, moving to Linda's side in a gesture of solidarity. "Although why you'd contact Linda is a mystery. She hasn't spoken to my dad in years."

"As part of the task force, I try to be thorough," Dev said.

"We have nothing to say," she told him.

He arched a brow. "Too bad. I came all this way."

"Sorry to inconvenience you."

Dev turned the full force of his charm on Linda. "I was hoping you could help the task force put away the worst criminal Vegas has seen in decades. Besides, you've already got others wanting to talk to you." He gestured toward the window that faced the front yard.

"What?" Ivy asked, drawing his attention back to her.

"Two men in a dark SUV across the street. I have a feeling they'll want to know what your old nanny—a woman who was deep within Robert Stone's household, possibly privy to his secrets every day for nearly ten years—had to tell me."

"She told you nothing!" Ivy moved to the window. Sure enough, a nondescript car sat across the street. And her father's right-hand man Archer sat in the driver's seat. "They're probably keeping tabs on you and the task force's investigation. It's only smart to know what the enemy is doing."

"Princess, they were here when I got here." Dev seemed to be analyzing every nuance of emotion that crossed her features.

Which meant they'd followed *her*. It was almost as if her father didn't trust her, which hurt her more than she'd care to admit. "You need to leave now."

"We can protect you. My agents at GSS—"

"Won't be enough to take down Redemption Club."

Dev studied her for a long moment, then turned to Linda, who avoided his gaze. He handed her a business card. "If you remember anything that could be helpful to our investigation, contact me. Make no mistake, there will be a trial. Stone will pay for the crimes he's committed."

"Allegedly committed," Ivy said.

He sent her a grim smile. "Nothing alleged about those men camped outside this house. My guess is they're Redemption Club members, wondering what the two of you are sharing with me. Think very carefully about who you're going to trust—and who will keep you and your loved ones safe."

CHAPTER ONE

Three months later

I am invisible. I am untouchable. I am secure in who I am. I am...

Delusional.

Ivy Stone released a slow breath as she exited the women's restroom at the Eighth Judicial District Court in Clark County, Nevada. No matter what she told herself, a challenge awaited her, and she may as well face the hurdle so she could move on.

Picking up the pace, she hurried from the courthouse and into the blinding Las Vegas sunlight. Even at five o'clock in the evening in early April, the air was warm. Still, the rays didn't permeate her ice-cold skin. Perhaps that was for the best. It kept her face frozen in the permanent, empty smile required of her, despite the shouts of the crowd that waited below, angry about the outcome of the trial.

Ten minutes ago, her father had been found innocent of numerous counts—everything from embezzlement to murder—but suspicion about Robert Stone's involvement in the Vegas-based organized crime group known as Redemption Club would remain in the public's mind.

The troublesome doubts about her father's involvement, despite his consistent denials, lingered in Ivy's mind, too.

But he had been cleared of all charges and her job was to polish the tarnish off her family's image. For the past several months, she'd rubbed at that stain until her hands were raw, and she'd continue to do so, because this was her life, too, damn it.

She descended the steps into the chaos. Reporters and cameramen clustered in little groups near the busy street lined with news vans and protestors, a media circus with acts in all three rings. Sadly, Ivy had left her lion tamer's whip at home.

Instead, she gripped the strap of her Louis Vuitton bag, but not so hard that her knuckles would turn white. After all, she mustn't let them see her inner struggle for optimism. Resisting the urge to smooth her free hand over her stone-gray suit, she kept her fingers loose at her side, the picture of calm. Combined with her white blouse—the color of innocence her father's lawyers had mandated she wear to the stand—her outfit was like a castle wall that could not be scaled.

I am untouchable.

"Mr. Stone was found *not guilty* on all counts," Christine from Eyewitness News reported at Ivy's right. Christine's makeup was caked on so thick she could have been the clown act.

To Ivy's left, another woman faced a camera, pausing to listen via her earpiece to questions from the main studio. "Yes, that's correct, Jim. Not guilty of any involvement in any of the dozen murders he'd been loosely linked to over the past twenty years. Not guilty of racketeering, or numerous other vicious acts traced back to Redemption Club. The pages recovered by the task force on organized crime, which allegedly detailed these acts, weren't enough to convict Stone. Without the intact journal, the prosecution stumbled and fell flat on its face."

"The man's slicker than a stripper on a pole," someone from the crowd shouted.

"And even wealthier, too," the reporter replied without missing a beat. Clearly, Live at Five's lovely reporter was the high wire act, astonishing everyone with her balance of wit and hard-hitting news. Or maybe she was the juggler.

A laugh went up from the people, but there was an angry, frustrated edge to it that shot fear through Ivy. Many of them held signs that advertised their low opinions of her and her father, and their demand for justice. How much longer would they be content with just expressing opinions? The threats she'd received could easily become action, and real danger.

But the craziness around her only confirmed and inflamed the desolation that had been burning a hole in her chest. Her father, once highly esteemed around the world, was a joke. Her entire family had become Public Enemy Number One since last July, when her brother Ryan had committed everything from embezzlement to blackmail to murder in his greedy grab for power. And then Ryan had died, leaving this mess in his wake.

Again, Ivy resisted the urge to rub the angry ache in her chest. It was her burden to bear after what she'd put her body and soul through for the past eight months.

I'll make it right, she promised herself yet again.

But maybe it was time to reprioritize, to put herself first.

Unfortunately, old habits reared their heads when the circus strongman—Ron Bloomberg from Channel 12—cornered her as a murmur from the crowd alerted him to Ivy's presence.

"Miss Stone!" Ron called out above their voices. "Give us a sound bite." She ignored his demand and prepared to keep walking but he followed, pushing closer to edge out the other reporters who were now rushing toward her. "We'll make up our own if you don't give us something," Ron threatened at a level only she could hear. Clearly, his breath mint had lost the war against the raw onions he'd apparently consumed on his street-vendor hot dog at lunchtime. She held in a wince, knowing the cameras were waiting to capture any hint of emotion. They'd easily— *eagerly*—misconstrue her misery at Ron's rancid breath as a sign of guilt. Her father's team of lawyers had coached her for hours about body language, as if she didn't already understand how her body could betray her feelings. She hadn't been dubbed an ice queen for nothing. "Come on. Just a few words, Ivy."

Oh, she had plenty of choice words to throw at him. The media had been slinging mud left, right and center for months and her father hadn't done a single thing to change his image. In his usual way, he'd rather forge onward and shove his success down their throats as an example that he'd done everything right. All of her hard work hardly made a dent in preserving the Stone name, or the legacy her father was always going on about. Exhaustion pulled at her. She shouldn't be here, shouldn't have to face the heat for something she'd had no involvement in. She'd done nothing wrong.

But as she looked for her hired car along the curb outside the cement security barriers, and didn't see it— *couldn't she count on anyone?*—her gaze landed on another source of hostility.

Devlin Grimm. A shiver of awareness wove through her like heat, threatening to thaw parts of her that had been frozen long ago.

Co-founder of an elite security company called Global Security Solutions, Dev had served many of her high-profile guests at Legacy Hotel and Casino, and they'd had nothing but glowing praise for the man. With broad shoulders, immaculate suits, and an omnipresent sense of self-confidence, he certainly looked the part of protector to the wealthy.

Unfortunately, she'd had occasion to bump into him over the past year under more unpleasant circumstances as he helped the task force assigned with bringing down her father—such as when he'd shown up at Linda's home. Since then, Dev's agency had led the charge in swaying public opinion against her family. Whether he'd meant them to or not, his actions had indirectly attacked Ivy and Legacy.

Even from across the street, his scowl communicated his displeasure with the trial's outcome. And probably with her, as well, for not turning against her father. That didn't stop the frisson of awareness that snaked through her body.

And so, when Ron wouldn't stop pestering her, she dug deep into her reserves, letting anger and frustration fuel her.

"Silence, Miss Stone?" Ron said. "Probably because nothing you say could defend your father's actions, or your acceptance of them."

She turned a brittle smile on him and counted to ten in her head. Her father's lawyers had sent her out here for just this reason—because she would deflect attention from Robert Stone, his legal team and security detail while they snuck out the back entrance after the unpopular verdict had been read. Hell, her illustrious father was probably clear across town already, snug in his Legacy penthouse suite. The hotel and casino she managed for his international entertainment- and hospitality-centered corporation, Stone Corp, was only a few minutes away. He'd probably reached safety while she'd escaped to the solitude of the courthouse bathroom for several precious, composure-gathering minutes following the close of the trial.

Or maybe, while she'd been reapplying her makeup and preparing herself for an onslaught, he'd retreated to his private mansion in Henderson, where he could close the gates against prying cameras and reporters.

"Miss Stone?" Ron persisted, shoving the microphone in her face. "How do you respond to the public's outrage over your father's *not guilty* verdict?" The cameraman took a step closer, his weapon aimed at her as other television channels and various news sources closed in.

I am secure in who I am.

She slowly inhaled and exhaled. For once, Ron waited patiently, sensing her acquiescence. She could buy her father a few more minutes if she replied. And damn it, she was tired of everyone thinking the worst of her. Her life had been impacted, too. It was time she showed the world she would no longer tolerate the innuendo and personal attacks that had blanketed social media these past several weeks. Besides, it was hurting her business.

"My father was found innocent," she began. All true words, but she wasn't particularly proud of them, in light of recent suspicions. She tried to inject confidence into her tone. "Our family is going to put this witch hunt behind us and we'll be stronger than ever."

Clearly meant solely for her, Ron's answering smirk wasn't captured by the camera's angle. "Is that what your *charity* work is? An attempt to make the public look the other way and restore the crumbling Stone legacy?"

"No," she answered simply. But at the mention of her other passion, a pain stabbed at her breastbone. Her work with Hope's Light Children's Foundation had been one of the few happy places she'd escaped to for years. But it was also her private oasis. Nobody had known about her contributions. Only recently had her father leaked her connection—she hadn't even known he'd known about it—to benefit Legacy. And himself.

But Ron wouldn't let it go. He wanted his damn sound bite for the evening news and was rapidly running out of time. "That's it? Come now, Miss Stone. You're letting the public jump to conclusions."

"I'm sure the public is smarter than you're giving them credit for. They can choose to believe whatever you, the media, says is the truth." She paused and let her most imperious, assessing gaze sweep over his body, from scuffed loafers to the first-rate head of hair and gleaming smile that had landed him this position. She took several long beats to complete her study, savoring the way he twitched as he resisted the urge to squirm, as well as the dead air his supervisors would not be happy about.

"Or," she finally continued when Ron opened his mouth to fill the silence, "the public can choose to decide for themselves. My involvement with Hope's Light dates back years, not that I'm inclined to prove my motives to you." She hadn't been the one on trial this past week. "Perhaps you should attend the casino night charity event tomorrow and see what the Stone family name truly stands for, and what we support."

Ron's tone became snider. "Recent evidence indicates the Stones support criminals. First, your brother Ryan was tied to several murders. Then, your father's name was discovered in a ledger full of crimes dating back decades, and he was rumored to have started the organized crime ring known as Redemption Club—"

"Of which he was just pronounced innocent by a jury of his peers," she interrupted to point out, but Ron continued talking right over her.

"Suddenly, the Stones are hosting a large charity event at Legacy. They've never done that before. The timing seems a little convenient."

She forced a smile and chose to capitalize on the positive portion of his statement. "There's a first time for everything. I'm glad you're giving the charity some exposure here. Hope's Light—not this fiasco the justice system put my father through, and certainly not me—should be the focus of all of your attention. My goal is, and always has been, to make Las Vegas stronger than ever." From the corner of her eye, she spied the black car she'd rented for the day pull up to the curb a few feet away. *Thank God.* "Excuse me." Without waiting for the seas to part, she nudged her way through the throng.

"Poison Ivy!"

"Ice Queen!"

"Frosty bitch!"

"Give us justice! Clear the stink of organized crime out of Vegas!"

Several people waved signs on sticks, shouted rude comments and even called her names, but she blocked it out. She tried to, anyway.

I am invisible.

The driver didn't emerge as she approached the car, so she grabbed the handle. Feeling like prey running from hunters, she jerked open the rear door and slid inside. She yanked the door closed the moment her three-inch heels cleared the opening. Her tinted window flashed with light as the cameras outside continued to record video footage or snap photos.

She swung her head the other way, but her gaze landed on Dev, still standing across the street like a sentinel. There was no sympathy from that direction, either.

Taking a deep breath, she closed her eyes, shutting it all out. "Legacy," she ordered the driver. The next time she opened her eyes, she hoped she'd see the familiar lines of the seventh largest casino and hotel complex in Las Vegas. Home, sweet home.

They pulled away from the press of people. A few seconds later, Ivy braved a peek. The courthouse was a miniature in the rearview, the mob like specks of sand. Hopefully, she'd never have to see the place again. Listening to several long weeks of testimonies and legal arguments was enough to last her a lifetime.

She let her head fall back against the seat, enjoying the way the cool, smooth leather shocked her neck, the skin there bared by the updo she'd rigged to complete the look she called *frigid bitch*. Her early years of dabbling in theater had come in handy today. Her ensemble had done the job, giving her a uniform to remind her of her task as well as a suit of armor to hold the wolves at bay and keep things impersonal. She'd done her part.

But sometimes her job was so damn lonely.

From across the street, Devlin Grimm watched the crowd outside the courthouse. Disgust and frustration pulled the corners of his mouth downward as reporters swarmed Ivy Stone. He could have sworn she'd met his gaze, and that she'd sent him a matching look of disappointment. Not that he cared. He'd given her a chance to work with the task force to bring down her father and she hadn't accepted. She'd sealed her fate. Besides, he had little doubt the woman could hold her own in a zombie apocalypse, let alone when confronted by a few predictable reporters.

His dark mood reflected the shit-sundae of a month he'd had, which had just culminated in the ultimate cherry on top—Robert Stone was a free man. The charges of murder, embezzlement, and other nefarious activities—the indictment a result of nearly a year of investigation—had been blown away like dust in the breeze. Just once, Dev wanted the good guys to win a battle in the war against Redemption Club.

Across the street, people hoisted signs and shouted malicious comments at Ivy, but now that her father was cleared of criminal charges there was no outlet for their anger. Details about the secret club's existence had come into the public eye in recent months and crime was at an all-time high as delinquents flocked to the dark organization, eager to trade their skills for an evil favor or two. Redemption Club bartered in alibis, resources, and connections, and there was no shortage of willing participants—or injured victims.

The general population of Vegas was outraged and scared. The LVPD, FBI, DEA and Dev's own security firm, Global Security Solutions, had formed a multi-agency task force and worked overtime to put an end to the violence and mayhem. But the head of it all was untouchable. With Robert Stone's status and wealth, he had resources beyond the common man's reach. Heading up Redemption Club only amplified his power.

One of those resources was Stone's daughter. By all appearances, Ivy Stone was a cold-hearted, female version of her father—a father who'd just gotten away with murder and left his own flesh and blood to deal with the blowback. Stone was always a step ahead of the law, always had a plan to escape through the backdoor. Which must be exactly what he'd done today, leaving his progeny to go out the front to defend him.

When Dev's head started to throb, he realized he'd been gritting his teeth. He forced himself to consciously relax every muscle in his body, from head to toe, until the tension left him—most of it, anyway. It was an old trick he'd learned from his days working in Afghanistan as a security contractor. It had been hard as hell to relax in that environment, but he'd learned to cope with whatever life threw at him.

He pulled out his phone and punched in a text. *You okay?*

The reply came back almost immediately. *Of course. Got the fences repaired today. You? Heard the news.*

Despite his frustration, more of his tension eased. His mother was always putting him and his brothers first. *Fine.* Or he would be, when he finally put Robert Stone away for good.

Good. See you for Sunday supper. It was a weekly gathering, when he and his brothers could manage it. Since Aidan's arrest six months ago, they hadn't gotten together as often as they'd have liked, but Brady and Colt would be there this weekend. A family meal might be just what they needed to feel unified again.

The family ranch, half an hour north of Las Vegas,

specialized in boarding horses. Rose Curry had always had a special touch with animals, and she'd found a place in her heart and in her home for four feral foster boys who'd been passed around and passed over for most of their lives. At age fourteen, Dev had been taken in by Rose. His three foster brothers had had similar experiences. She'd given them love and stability, even when they'd been difficult.

Guilt stabbed at him. He owed her so much, even more so because his pursuit of justice, of Robert Stone, may have led to problems at the ranch. The fence she'd repaired had been deliberately cut overnight, and a couple horses had escaped the property. Thankfully, they'd been recovered before any further damage or harm could be done.

But that hadn't been the first odd occurrence in recent weeks. Something added to the horse feed had made some of the animals sick. Luckily, the horses affected recovered under a veterinarian's care.

The following morning, a rattlesnake in the barn had spooked the remaining healthy horses. Hell, the thing had nearly bitten Rose when she'd arrived to check on the commotion.

Taken together, the incidents reeked of sabotage. If Redemption Club was behind this, if members had been encouraged to go after Dev's family, he was damn well going to return the favor. No matter what Stone thought, the Stone family wasn't infallible.

When he looked up from his phone, the black sedan and its occupant were gone, and most of the reporters were settling for interviews with the crowd or were packing up their gear. They'd apparently realized what Dev had already surmised—Robert Stone had used the rear exit to slip away unnoticed, using his lovely daughter as a decoy. And why not? Likely, Ivy was just as dangerous and devious as the rest of her family.

CHAPTER TWO

The doubts were creeping in again. Ivy tried to focus on the quiet calm of the luxury sedan, with its plush, black leather seats. She inhaled deeply, centering on the faint, pine-woodsy scent from the air freshener dangling from the rearview mirror. But the reporters' questions and protestors' shouted insults still rang in her head. She almost said something to the driver just to hear a kind—or even neutral—voice that might block out the remembered insults, but she didn't know the man. He was just a temporary hire for the afternoon, since her father had claimed the company limousine as his escape vehicle. Her driver might not be kind or neutral at all. Or worse, he was probably one of her father's men, since she'd had their receptionist make the arrangements. So, instead of striking up a conversation, she kept the wall of silence between them unbroken.

Absently, her gaze flicked across familiar Las Vegas landmarks as the car progressed, growing closer to Legacy. The sun was setting, and the iconic lights of the Strip were already bright, warming her soul. A cobalt-and-magenta neon sign looked like a speck in the distance but marked Legacy's location, and relief poured through her. She'd grown up at the hotel and now ran the entire 90,000-square-foot complex that was part of her lifeblood. Though it was only a small piece of the Stone Corp pie, it was home.

She relaxed into her seat, pressing her hand against the ever-present ball of nerves that had sat coiled in her stomach for the past several months. The trial was over. Everything would return to normal now. Maybe the threats on her life would stop, too. But part of her knew they wouldn't. In fact, they'd probably get worse now that her father had been cleared in the eyes of the law but remained tainted by the charges. He'd been likened to the mobsters of old-time Vegas, and that would be a hard image to shake.

And part of her, a part that was growing more insistent every day, knew it was time to move on before the evil touched her in an irrevocable way. What kind of daughter did that make her?

To avoid the negative emotions crowding in, her mind ran through the list of items to address and appointments to make after the weekend was over. She accessed her calendar app on her phone, intending to tackle what she could this weekend during non-business hours to make up for the weeks she'd lost attending her father's trial and lending her support. Her body relaxed further into the seat as the familiarity of managing her world infused her with calm.

A minute later, the car rolled to a stop and she tucked her phone away. Expecting to see the familiar rear entrance to Legacy when she looked up, adrenaline flooded every cell as she spied only an empty parking lot outside an abandoned theater. Boards covered what had once been glass and the poster cases lining the front wall advertised plays that had closed their doors years ago.

"What's going on?" she asked, trying to still the fear that churned inside.

"Don't you recognize the place?" The driver sounded as if he smoked two packs a day and her heart pounded in her ears, but she had no trouble hearing his low-spoken words in the quiet car.

Still, she was Ivy-freaking-Stone. Even after what her family had been accused of, that counted for something in this town. "You were hired to do a job," she reminded the driver, dismissing his question. "I told you to take me to Legacy, and that's what I expect. No side trips."

He answered her high-handed tone with narrowed dark eyes that could have been brown, but might have been black. Really, it was all of him she could see in the rearview mirror, since he hadn't once turned to face her. Another ripple of anxiety ran through her as she realized he was hiding his identity, but she'd long ago learned not to show fear. Besides, if he were planning to kill her, he wouldn't bother to hide himself, would he?

"Do you recognize the building?" he asked again, controlled rage rumbling beneath his carefully enunciated words.

She glanced at the decrepit theater as if studying it, though she was well aware of where they were. "It's the old Alpha Omega Theater." The beginning and the end. She'd certainly had some amazing beginnings here. And they'd come to a tragic end.

"Correct. Do you know why I brought you here?"

"To see a play?" She hated the tremor of unease that belied her snarky tone. Beneath the surface, her mind whirled. How could this stranger know what this place had meant to her? Was he behind the odd emails she'd received in recent weeks—the ones that had involved a past she'd long ago buried?

"There've been no plays here in years. But then, you know that. Your father bought the place and shut it down. Left it to rot. And you know why."

Her skin went ice-cold and she reached for the door. The locks snapped shut with a click as loud as her swallow. She jiggled the handle, but her door wouldn't open and her attempts to unlock it were futile, stoking not only her fear but also her anger. "Hurting me would be a bad idea."

"I'm not planning to hurt you. Yet." His words, followed by a rusty chuckle, were anything but reassuring.

Mentally, she assessed her options. He

apparently wasn't out to murder her—*yet*—so that greatly increased her odds of survival. She considered the contents of her purse, which was weapon-free since she'd been practically living in the courthouse for weeks. She didn't have the pepper spray she normally carried, but there was the cell phone she'd just put away. If she could reach it, she could dial 9-1-1. Her fingers inched across the seat while she held his gaze in the rearview mirror.

His attention flicked to her hand. "Stop right there," he ordered.

Her questing fingers halted as he raised a gun to the level of the steering wheel. Had there been anyone besides them on this sad abandoned lot, they wouldn't have been able to see the weapon, but to her, the threat was all too clear.

"Doesn't surprise me that Robbie's daughter would try to stab me in the back the first chance she got," he said. "Apple doesn't fall far from the tree."

Her chin raised a notch in defiance, but she pulled her hands back into her lap. "What do you want? Is this about my father?"

"I want to know if *you* know why I brought you here." There was a sharp edge to his voice that sliced at her already raw insides.

Yeah, she knew. But why would this man care? She cleared her throat. "It was once special to me."

"To you?" Her abductor's gaze, reflected by the mirror, was penetrating. Expectant. Everything around them seemed to go still, almost as if he were holding his breath.

"Not just me. There was a man I dated, about eight years ago. We were... close."

The driver's features—what she could see of them in the mirror and in profile—tightened in anger. She didn't care if her answer hadn't been what he'd wanted to hear. It had been the honest response.

"And now?" he pressed.

"He will always be special, but he's gone." He'd

left her when she'd needed him most, just as everyone else in her life had. All she had were memories, and she'd cursed them more than once. She'd gotten used to the pain of abandonment, and learned how to survive on her own.

"Not just *gone*. He's dead." Not a question this time. Again, she wondered how her driver knew so much about that time in her life. She attempted to study him more carefully, but he turned away, looking out the window at the structure. "Wiped off the face of the earth, along with the rest of his family."

"You knew Nathan?" The name cracked as it squeezed through her throat. She could count on one hand the number of times she'd said his name aloud since he'd died. One had been in a eulogy. Her throat closed even more at the memory and she nearly gasped for breath.

The man's sharp gaze met hers again in the rearview. "I work for someone who did. And that someone wants you to know he's watching. He *knows*."

"Knows what?" God, she'd been so careful. Or she thought she had, but she'd only been twenty-one, and so naïve it hurt now to look back on the whole experience.

"What you did. And you'll pay for your sins."

Her chin shot up in defiance and anger. "And the first step is scaring me?"

"You got it, sweetheart."

"Is this man you work for the one who's sent me emails, pretending to be Nathan?" She'd dismissed them as nonsense, knowing Nathan was dead.

"He deserved better."

Which didn't answer her question.

Suddenly, he shifted the car into gear and sped through the parking lot. The tires squealed and her body lurched sideways as he turned sharply. Just as suddenly, he slammed on the brakes. The momentum nearly tossed her from her seat.

"Get out," he ordered, panting as if he'd just

sprinted through the parking lot on foot.

"What?" Her survival instinct quickly superseded her shock that he'd kick her out onto the street. She'd walk to the moon if it meant getting out of this car and away from the odd stranger who knew too much and might decide at any moment to *make her pay.*

"I can't look at you anymore," he roared. "Go, before I change my mind!"

A click indicated he'd disengaged the locks and she scrambled to grab her purse strap and the door handle all at once. She was on the sidewalk in seconds, stumbling to regain her balance in her high heels. She kicked them off, ignoring the bite of crumbling concrete on her soles as she braced herself to run. She needn't have bothered. In front of her, the innocuous-looking sedan sped away, leaving behind the acrid stench of rubber kissing pavement.

Behind her, the theater where she'd stolen away the happiest, most content moments of her young adult life taunted her. At the onslaught of memories, and the fear that lingered, she bent over at the waist and gasped for breath, suddenly unable to suck in enough air.

No going forward. No going back.

She'd *pay*? What the stranger didn't know was she'd paid a high price long ago. She had nothing left to give.

By necessity, Victor del Fuego was a patient man, but seeing Ivy Stone had tested his limits. The need for retribution churned in his gut, and dumping her on the street was as much to save himself from acting without forethought as to save her from his wrath.

She'd been so close. One quick slice of the hunting knife—currently strapped to his ankle—across her slender throat, and he'd have executed his revenge.

He could have dumped her mutilated body at Robert Stone's front door. But ending up in prison for murder before he could accomplish the most important part of his mission wasn't today's objective. The victory would have been temporary, hollow without the rest of the components in place.

Hands shaking, he sped away until the theater was a speck and Ivy was a silhouette backlit by the setting sun. A few minutes later, he pulled into the enormous parking lot of one of the nearby casinos to gather his composure. Besides, a crowded lot was as good a place as any to dump the car.

He yanked the silver wig from his head and tossed it to the floor of the passenger seat. Retrieving a ball cap from beneath his seat, he tugged it low over his brow, hooked his jacket collar up around his lower jaw, and wiped down anything he'd touched.

Merging with the pedestrians walking the Strip, he walked like a tourist until he reached the fountains at The Mirage, better known as The Volcano, which was dormant at the moment. There, he took the opportunity to observe his surroundings under the guise of gawking at the sights. He released a slow breath as he checked his six and realized nobody was following.

He'd done it. His skills might be rusty after years of disuse, but he'd succeeded in accessing and threatening one of Robert Stone's biggest assets—his daughter—without consequence. Stone wasn't as fucking untouchable as the man would like to think.

Victor had a long way to go yet to get everything he wanted, but it was a promising start. Later, when all his ducks were in a row, he'd confront his enemy more directly. He just had to keep his fiery need for vengeance under control a little bit longer.

But when the time came, he'd burn Stone, and all he stood for, to the ground.

CHAPTER THREE

On the desk beside his laptop, Dev's cell phone rang and he cursed as he spied the caller's image on the screen. He debated whether to answer for a few long seconds, but he owed it to Jared Bennigan—Dev's best friend and co-owner of Global Security Solutions—to pick up. Unfortunately, he had nothing good to report.

With a sigh, he answered. "I guess you've heard?"

"What the hell is happening to the world?" Anger seethed beneath Jared's question. "I leave for one week and all sanity is lost. I thought we finally had him."

Tension crept back into Dev's shoulders and fisted into tight little knots. "Bad news travels fast."

"I had an Internet alert set up so I'd know the moment anything was decided," Jared admitted. "Thank God Skye wasn't by my side when it popped up." His lowered voice told Dev that Jared still hadn't shared the bad news with his new wife.

Skye was a force to be reckoned with. She fought for those she cared about no matter what the cost. Unbidden, the image of Ivy came to mind and he immediately dismissed the comparison. There was strong like a willow and there was strong like a cold, stone fortress.

"So what are we going to do about this?" Jared asked, pulling Dev from his thoughts. "My sisters have already called. I need to give them some hope." Chelsea and Haley had been impacted by Redemption Club actions as much as anyone. Like hundreds of other people, they wanted justice.

But Dev wasn't sure they had any options left. After leaving the courthouse, he'd retreated to his office at Global Security Solutions, poured a shot of whiskey, and then spread the Stone files across his desk. It took a lot to shake Dev after all that he'd been through in his thirty-four years, but watching Robert Stone walk away from every allegation of wrongdoing, unscathed, had driven him to drink.

"I'll check in on your sisters," Dev promised. "Aren't you supposed to be on your honeymoon, chilling, focusing every thought on your new bride?"

Jared cursed. "How am I supposed to relax when the man responsible for Redemption Club, whose members tried to kill both my wife and my sister, is free to hurt them again? What about all the other people Club members are still free to harm? That shit's not going away."

"No, it isn't." Dev had no proof Stone's lackeys had ordered the fence line cut at Curry Ranch, or had done any of the other things that had threatened the ranch, but he'd find out. And if Stone came close to Rose Curry, he'd kill the man with his bare hands. "I'm working on it. You go back to the sun and surf."

"Right. Skye will be on the first plane back after she hears this news. She didn't even want to keep our reservations after she heard about the trial dates. And the disappointment when our statements were ruled inadmissible... Fuck, man."

"There's nothing you could have done here to sway the verdict." Which made Dev feel fucking helpless, too. The hard work of GSS, in coordination with the multi-agency task force led by DEA agents Adam Wilde and Mason Gray, hadn't been enough. They'd tracked down a couple of ledger pages obtained via the Red Market, an underground auction where pages from the notorious Redemption Club ledger had been sold for hundreds of thousands of dollars apiece. The notations had led to identifying several victims of the Club, as well as their families. Unfortunately, the witness testimonies presented in court, about events going back twenty years, had counted for nothing at the trial.

Zilch.

Stone had likely paid off or threatened the jurors. Over the past few weeks, several of the witnesses had recanted their stories or been discredited. Dev had tried to convince the district attorney to hire GSS, or anybody else who could be trusted, to guard the sequestered jury or witnesses, but he'd been denied. Stone probably had the DA in his pocket, too.

"It was out of our hands," Dev reminded his friend. The helplessness had him pouring another shot.

Jared released a puff of air. "I know, I know."

"Good. Then stay and try to enjoy yourself. You only have another couple days, anyway."

"We'll see what Skye says. I have to go. She's coming out of the shower."

As he disconnected, a chime sounded from the lobby down the hall, indicating someone had just entered the offices. No clients were expected at eight o'clock on a Friday night, and the adrenaline that flooded his system was a regression to more dangerous days when he had to be on alert twenty-four-seven. He'd dismissed his receptionist two hours ago and each of GSS's dozen agents was working in the field, assigned as bodyguards or doing legwork on investigative cases.

He pressed a button on his laptop and the website he'd been viewing was replaced with live footage from the security camera in the GSS lobby. Displayed on his screen was the one woman he'd never expect to cross his threshold.

"Hello?" she called out, peeking her head around the corner at the end of the hall that led to his and Jared's offices. "Dev?" She disappeared from the camera's view.

He was still trying to figure out if he'd somehow consumed more alcohol than he'd thought when Ivy Stone appeared, in the flesh, in his doorway.

"Remember me?" she said when he didn't greet her. He was too busy working at concealing his surprise.

"How could I forget?" He closed his laptop with a snap. "What I can't figure out is why you're here. The trial's over. Your family won."

"I want to hire you."

"Me?"

"Yes. To kidnap me." Her chin rose a couple inches as if daring him to laugh.

Dev, never one to back down from a dare, let out a sound of disbelief. "Kidnap you?" An unusual request for a Friday night, or any night—or day, for that matter—even at GSS, an agency dedicated to providing the best in protective services to the Las Vegas area, and to clients from all over the world.

The request was all the more amazing because this woman had, just a few short hours ago, faced a pack of hungry reporters without flinching. By the looks of her now, however, she'd done some serious flinching since fleeing the scene at the courthouse. The fancy twist that had held back her hair earlier had come undone and long, ebony waves hung about her face. Her high, flushed cheekbones and emerald eyes, which turned up slightly at the corners to create even more mystery—as if the woman needed any more secrets—were striking in their vulnerability. The slim skirt that had once been pristine on camera was now wrinkled. Instead of calm and collected, she seemed revved up and ready for action. There was a wild light in the green depths of her eyes that indicated she wasn't kidding about her job offer.

Stunned by the quiet intensity in her gaze, he looked away, his attention landing on the silent television on one wall of his office. Two hours ago, he'd switched it off in disgust after watching the evening news. Ivy hadn't looked or sounded clinically insane on TV. The camera had captured her stoic confidence and pride as she'd stood in front of the courthouse and coolly answered the reporter's barbed questions. She'd cleverly turned the topic to her charity work with Hope's Light Children's Foundation. Dev had felt sick to his stomach. It took a lot of guts to hide the evil truth behind a children's charity. But Ivy's request that he *kidnap* her seemed to indicate she had taken a graceful swan dive right off the Cliffs of Insanity.

Her determined gaze never left him. "I'll pay whatever you want."

"What happened to you?" he asked, wondering at the change in her appearance. The GSS offices were at least ten miles from the courthouse, and five miles from Legacy. Last he'd seen her, she'd been climbing into a perfectly viable escape vehicle.

For a split second, humiliation pinched her features, but she quickly smoothed away any sign of tension. "That's not vital to this conversation. I'm offering you a job."

Dev scrubbed a hand across his jaw, absently noting the five o'clock shadow had thickened to an eight o'clock scruff. He also noted that her gaze locked on and was tracking the movement. Something else flickered in her eyes but was gone before he could analyze it.

"Why me?" he asked. "You rejected my requests to talk, told me in no uncertain terms that you didn't intend to work with the enemy against your father."

"This has nothing to do with my father."

Wrong. In Dev's experience, every illegal, immoral, or just-in-general *bad* thing in Las Vegas could be traced to Redemption Club, and therefore to her father. And Ivy was never far from Robert Stone's side. Guilt by association.

Besides, *kidnapping* wasn't a service GSS offered. Still, the idea of taking her held definite appeal. She had to know how Dev felt about anyone related to the Stone family. It was no secret one of his agency's missions was to destroy Redemption Club and put anyone linked to it behind bars—an exercise that had proved fruitless.

But now, it appeared a fallen angel could lift them up again. And she'd fallen right into his lap.

A little too convenient? There had to be a catch. Ivy had the same cold business sense as her father, without the drive to be a social icon who would go down in the history books. Nowhere had the press hinted that her deck might be short a card or two, so there had to be a hidden agenda that brought her to his doorstep.

She charged on before he could question her, as if he'd agree to go along with whatever crazy plan she came up with. "It wouldn't be a real kidnapping, of course. I'd go willingly. I just want it to *look* real. Nobody can know it's not. Later, we'd make it look like I went willingly or spin it whatever way works for you and you'd be free and clear if my father decided to press charges."

All he needed was to be on Stone's radar again. Individuals in that man's crosshairs usually ended up destroyed or dead. Or their ranches were attacked, innocent people and animals placed in danger.

Dev steepled his fingers and considered Ivy as she began to pace like a caged panther—sleek, beautiful and deadly. Her father's file was spread across his desk, forgotten, though she didn't seem to notice.

"Forgive me," he began, "but this feels like a trap. Why would you want to fake a kidnapping? That seems extreme—even for a Stone."

Something in her eyes sparked. "Someone wants to hurt me, and I refuse to let them. I believe testing the security at my home and office is the best way to identify and strengthen any weaknesses."

"The trial is over. If you were ever at risk, you should be safe now." Although he, of all people, knew that was blatantly untrue. There were plenty of people who'd still be looking for the justice they'd been denied.

"If you believe that, you're an idiot." She stopped pacing and braced her fingers on the desk, leaning into his face and calling his bluff. "Or maybe you're afraid to get involved."

Damned if her words didn't stir him to accept the challenge, but his sense of self-preservation was strong. Something about her offer didn't ring true. "It would probably be best if you and I didn't get *involved.* We're on opposite sides of the fence on so many things."

Her wide mouth curved. "Which is exactly why you're the perfect choice."

"No."

Her smile faded. "That's it? Just no?"

"If rumors can be believed, your family has an entire army of mercenaries at your disposal. And they work on the barter system, so it would be relatively cheap to find someone to perform any manner of strange requests—including kidnapping. Hell, those guys who were camped outside your old nanny's house three months ago would probably jump at the chance to build up a little Club credit. However, I suppose you would be required to do something equally distasteful in return. Isn't that how the Club works?"

Her wide mouth pressed into a flat line as she pushed off the desk and stalked away two paces before swinging back to him. Her eyes shot shards of green glass. "Rumors often contain only a kernel of truth, Mr. Grimm. The rest is fantasy or gossip. I would have thought you, of all people, knew that."

He arched a brow at her subtle insult. She'd probably read the media's version of his time as a security contractor in Afghanistan. How much did she know about his background? And how much of it would she use to push him to do her bidding? He should just send her away, but he found he was more curious about her than was good for him. And there was the matter of keeping the Stones away from his family. He needed to put Robert Stone behind bars. Maybe he could use Ivy

Stone to achieve his own agenda.

Maybe they could use each other.

He stood and rounded the desk, amused when she stepped back to keep some distance between them.

He dropped his voice to a seductive tone. "A Stone who wants to quash rumors by speaking the truth? I may be in shock." Her chin shot up a notch and his gaze traced the edge of her jaw. "So, your brother wasn't the leader of an illustrious crime ring for the past several years? And your father hasn't picked up the reins again at Redemption Club?"

"I said *rumors* held a kernel of truth," she said, her expression shadowed, and a bit vulnerable. "Those stories about my family, unfortunately, probably hold more truth than I'd like. I honestly don't know. That's why I didn't help you before."

She was good. Not a twitch or a blink out of place, and with only three feet of space between them, he could see everything. She didn't look away from him, either. He'd always been good at reading people, but he couldn't tell if she was lying. "And now you have doubts."

"Maybe." Her poker face was back, but only after a flash of uncertainty crossed her features.

"Why fake a kidnapping?"

"Take me on as a client and I'll share that." She'd share her version of the truth, no doubt, and then only to the extent she deemed necessary.

"I demand complete honesty from my clients."

"And we don't always get what we want." Instead of retreating from him, she took a step forward.

She was only a few inches shorter than his six-foot frame. If he reached out, he could place his hands at her waist and tug her even closer, aligning their bodies. The unexpected thought shot a hot thrill through him, which he ignored. Her expression wasn't revealing any of those same warm, tingly feelings. In fact, her eyes were narrowed on him.

"I met your partner last year," she said. "During

that horrible situation that revealed the possible existence of Redemption Club—"

He scoffed, interrupting her. "Oh, it exists. Plenty of people have been hurt by it. And several people got a good look at the ledger before it disappeared. Then there were the pages that led to the charges against your father."

"—And I came here because Jared seemed to treat me fairly, and because I do my homework. Your agency is the best in the security business, at least in the immediate area. But maybe you're not up to the challenge." Two dark eyebrows arched in question.

Damn, he respected a woman who could give him hell. In this moment, she reminded him of his mother, and the comparison stunned him. Steady and no-nonsense, Rose was a touch of the devil, and the rest was pure saint. She'd had to be in order to foster and eventually adopt a fourteen-year-old boy with enough negativity to generate his own perpetual storm system. And she'd done that three other times with his brothers. But Rose was also warm and good-hearted.

As for the woman standing before him, he didn't know what to make of her. In the media, she was portrayed as a cold bitch. In living color? He couldn't deny the warmth and passion he sensed pulsing beneath the surface, especially when it was so close he could touch it. He'd seen that same passion in Ivy's eyes the day he'd shown up at Linda Castillo's home.

Usually, he was all about giving people a second chance. Sometimes, even a third. After all, he'd been given multiple chances to reinvent and prove himself over the years. People went through rough patches. They made mistakes. He acknowledged that. And Ivy had obviously been through something between leaving the courthouse and coming here that made him soften slightly toward her. If he was totally honest with himself, there'd always been something about the woman that had intrigued him.

The Stone family had been connected to so many

misdeeds over the past twelve months, yet they'd dodged and diverted justice and manipulated media to come out looking squeaky clean. He couldn't help but be suspicious of her motives. Ivy was the driving force behind cleansing the Stone name in the media. She was firmly ensconced in her father's camp.

And then there was his partner and employee to consider. Dev wouldn't forget that the Stone family had been connected to what Jared and Skye had survived. If he took this job, he could only imagine what they would say when they returned from their honeymoon.

"I don't trust you," he told Ivy. "Or your father. And in my mind, you two are forever linked."

She accepted this with a nod, though disappointment darkened her expression. "I understand. I don't entirely trust you, either, but I can work around that. This would be a business relationship. It has nothing to do with my father. It isn't personal."

"Like hell." At his tone, she flinched, but he didn't bother to bite back the curse that leapt to his tongue. "I won't dance around the issue. I know your father's guilty. Know it in my gut, which has rarely been wrong. I've spent a lot of hours over the past year dedicated to helping prove his guilt, listening to the stories of people who were impacted by Redemption Club's actions, people who lost jobs or money or even loved ones. How can accepting a job offer from a Stone *not* be personal?"

"I know you have it in for my family, after what they've done to your friends." What *they'd* done. She hadn't included herself in the terrible acts her brother and father had perpetrated over the years, distancing herself from their behavior. "And yes, that's why, after wandering for hours, I ended up here. I need someone I can trust not to pull any punches, and not to back away if things get rough."

As he silently contemplated his options, her chin went up again in defiance and he spied a smudge of dirt along her jawline. A touch of imperfection, that hint of vulnerability was enough to soften him. If anyone was reluctant to ask for help, it was Ivy Stone. And yet, here she was.

"You said your gut's never been wrong," she said. "What's it telling you now?"

He sighed, admitting defeat. "It's telling me you need help. But I can't accept your offer."

Ivy stared at the man who blasted her family name one minute, and showed her tender sympathy the next. And then rejected her.

After her strange abductor had turned her loose and fled, she'd hid out in crowded casinos for a bit, until she'd needed quiet and space to think. She wouldn't find that at home, so she'd walked the streets for hours, not wanting to return to Legacy until she was sure of her best course of action. Besides, her so-called hired driver could have changed his mind and been waiting for her there.

It was time to disappear.

And yeah, maybe a little part of her was as crazy as Dev suspected, because her plan involved putting herself in her enemy's hands, but she was just desperate enough to do the unthinkable.

She cleared her throat. "*Grimm.* I had hoped your name might be symbolic, like the authors of those fairy tales, but I'm starting to wonder if it's more like the Reaper."

"I suppose I'm a bit of both." A spark of dark humor flashed in eyes that were hazel mixed with a warm brown, but then his expression hardened like ice. "Unlike you, I didn't come from anywhere or anyone. The woman who raised me encouraged me to choose my own last name when I was of age. I selected one that wouldn't let me forget the grim past I survived, but also encouraged me to forge my own path, even if it wasn't going to be a fairy tale."

"What a gift."

He searched her features as if looking for sarcasm, but she was honestly in awe of the concept of becoming whoever you wanted to be. A blank slate was exactly what she wanted. "We aren't always free to choose our path, or our names. I admire that. Did you choose Devlin, too?"

Something painful lit his hazel eyes. "No, that was the only thing my biological parents gave me. My friends and most of my clients call me Dev. Or Devil."

"Devil?" Instead of feeling intimidated, as he'd clearly intended by the comment, she was intrigued. The devil was the perfect candidate to get her out of this mess. Going up against her father wouldn't be easy.

His mouth curved in a wicked smile, and for a moment, her breath was caught in her chest. "It's been a while since I've been called that, but yeah."

"Since Afghanistan?"

His smirk dissipated and his eyes narrowed. "You've been doing some digging."

"I told you, I do my homework." By all accounts she'd read about him—research she'd done since he'd shown up at Linda's home, looking to pry something from them that could be used against her father—he'd survived hell while working as a security contractor in Afghanistan, and had emerged from the brimstone a new man. The *Devil* nickname had been apropos.

"I'll have to remember how thorough you are." He tilted his head as if studying her from a different angle. There was probably little she could do to shake her association with her father from his mind, but she supposed the distrust in his gaze was better than the caution and disdain she'd seen earlier.

"Don't forget selective."

One side of his mouth kicked up. "So many positive attributes. So why do I feel like you're going to use those against me?"

"Because you're careful, thorough, and selective,

too. And you think your *positive attributes* will protect you." She stepped closer, entering his personal space. She wouldn't let him intimidate her with his glowers and his barbs about her family. Besides, she was certain he was testing her. "But they won't. Nothing is completely bulletproof, but it's okay to be afraid."

"I'm not—"

She interrupted by taking another step, until she could see the gold flecks flash in the green depths of his eyes. "There's nothing wrong with a little fear. But I'm not afraid of you coming after my father. He can handle himself."

"And you?" His gaze flicked for a moment to her mouth, only a few inches away now. If he bent down, if he touched his lips to hers, he'd taste her uncertainty.

"Normally, I can handle myself, too. But I know my limits."

"Another attribute?"

"I believe so, yes. I need help." She felt rather than heard his exhaled sigh. This close, she was engulfed by his masculine scent, laced with a touch of the whiskey he'd been drinking. He wasn't unaffected by today's events. Both of them had missions to accomplish—Dev wanted to take down Redemption Club and she wanted to make her dream life a reality— far away from the reach of despicable people like the one who'd tried to scare her today. "I think we can help each other."

"What happened tonight?"

"Let's just say it was a wake-up call." She was feeling particularly fragile and needed to bolster her confidence before she told him everything. Thankfully, he didn't press. "I've received threats prior to this, and tonight, I realized those threats I'd dismissed are very real."

He searched her face as if he could read the entire story there. Then he surprised her by reaching up and swiping gently at her chin with his thumb. "You had a smudge of dirt," he explained, his voice soft.

She froze, unaccustomed to a man's touch, especially one so gentle and selfless. She could barely hear his words over the roar in her ears and let out an unsteady breath. But whether her nerves were still rattled from her near-abduction or had been shaken anew by Dev's sudden surprising kindness, she wasn't sure.

Before she could recoup her composure, he dropped his hand and moved past her to a mini-fridge in the corner. He returned with a water bottle, which he handed to her. "We'll come back to what happened tonight. For now, tell me about the previous threats."

With relief that maybe he was finally taking her seriously, she twisted off the cap and took a long pull from the bottle. And then another, dehydrated after two hours of walking. Besides, it gave her a moment to steady herself. "Death. Dismemberment. Arson. You name it, the hotel has received threats about it."

"The hotel, or you?"

"More than a few were directed at me. Until now, I didn't take it personally. Besides, one of the sources was a dead man." She saw the doubt and surprise flicker across Dev's features and sensed a rejection coming.

"Miss Stone—"

She held up a hand. "I know this sounds weird. Hell, me being here is odd enough. If my father knew where I am, he'd disown me."

Something predatory flashed in his eyes. "No, I don't suppose your father would approve of you meeting with the enemy. Isn't that why you turned me away before and convinced Linda Castillo not to talk to the task force?"

She took another long swallow from the water bottle, sensing she was losing ground somehow. She wasn't pleading her case very well, but pleading for anything had never been easy for her. "You're saying I deserve this, then? That when I thought I was getting into the car I'd hired, and instead was nearly kidnapped, that it's my penance because my last name is *Stone?*"

Dev's gaze swept over her again, this time more neutrally assessing, as if seeing her as a potential victim instead of the daughter of the enemy. "The car that picked you up at the courthouse... the driver took you against your will?"

"Yes. Pulled over in a deserted parking lot and held up a gun. Warned me he'd be watching, ready to make me pay for my sins at some point." She shuddered at the memory, but there was also anger. How dare the stranger assume she hadn't paid enough already?

Dev was studying her, probably trying to assess the truth of her story. "You didn't recognize him?"

"No. He kept his face averted. Said he's been watching me on behalf of Nathan, a man I was involved with eight years ago. But Nathan's dead, so there has to be someone else behind this. Whoever's behind it, this man seemed confident he could take me at any time, which is why I don't trust any of the men around my father. I need to know that's not possible."

"Have you reported this to the police?"

"The police aren't exactly on my side since—"

"Since your lawyers launched a smear campaign in the media against the LVPD's and FBI's investigations?" His scowl showed just what he thought about how her father had handled his case.

"Not *my* lawyers. I've tried to focus on the positives, showing how Legacy is a premiere hotel and how the Stone money has been donated over the years to various causes. The negative campaigning was my father's doing, not mine. I've never felt the need for a bodyguard." She was ashamed by the tremor that shook her body when she recalled feeling trapped in the car, alone and at a stranger's mercy. "Until now."

She met his powerful gaze, reading suspicion there, but also interest. "Look," she continued, "I assumed you were a professional, which I also assumed meant you could work without bias. I'm hoping that's true, since I was also told that you were the best in town. Was I wrong?"

His jaw tensed. She'd apparently hit some kind of hot button that triggered his sense of pride. "But you're not looking to hire a bodyguard. You asked me to kidnap you."

"It's the same thing." At his upraised brows, she hurried to explain. "I need my security breached. Tested. I want the weaknesses shored up."

A corner of his mouth kicked up. "As much as I'd probably enjoy *breaching your security*, I'm too busy to take on another case."

She gestured to the papers scattered across the desk behind him. "Too busy trying to revive the investigation against my father?"

"Actually, yes. Make no mistake, sooner or later justice will catch up to Robert Stone. Why don't you go to him? I'm certain a powerful man like Robert Stone has the resources to find someone he trusts to try to kidnap you. Working with me would be a conflict of interest."

How could she explain that she didn't trust her father without making herself look like an idiot for being the devoted daughter all these years? She'd done everything she could to please Robert Stone, but always seemed to fall short. She was on her own. She stood a little straighter, girding herself against a wave of dismay. Her plan wasn't going to work after all. "You're right. I'll find someone else who will get the job done."

"Some mercenary, possibly a thug involved in Redemption Club, who might take advantage of your wealth or vulnerability." Dev muttered the words, and Ivy wasn't entirely sure whether she was meant to hear them. He was obviously waging an inner war. "Or worse, who might not be as good as me. You'd truly be a victim. Assuming you're an innocent bystander in all of this, that is." He straightened from the desk where he'd been leaning, his dark scowl coming across angry and turbulent. "You came to me."

"I did," she said, not sure what he was after. She'd laid all of her cards on the table. It was up to him to see the value in them.

"Earlier, you indicated you were willing to pay me whatever I required."

"That's right." A twinge of anxiety spiked her in the breastbone as his eyes lit with a calculated glint.

"If I take you on as a client, you're going to help me take down your father. Those are my terms."

CHAPTER FOUR

At first, Dev didn't receive an answer to his counter-proposition, other than a scowl. Ivy turned to grab her purse.

She paused at the door. "I'll have to think it over."

"You can't just leave," Dev said. "Not if someone's really after you," he couldn't resist adding, poking at the potential holes in her story.

Her fingers shook as she pulled her cell phone from her purse. "Right. I'll call a cab." She really did seem upset at the prospect of getting back into a stranger's car.

"I'll take you home," he offered before he could judge the wisdom of his decision. "You look as though you've been through enough tonight." While appearances could be deceiving, the gentleman and bodyguard in him insisted he walk her to her doorstep. And the not-so-gentlemanly side of him was eager to discover all of her secrets—so that he could use them to take down Stone. Only then would his mother and Curry Ranch be safe. Only then would all of Las Vegas be safe from Stone's ego and the destruction it wrought.

He only needed Ivy to agree to his terms. And taking her home would give him time to convince her.

But the ride to Legacy was a quiet one. The only evidence she was considering his offer was the way she gnawed on her bottom lip as she used the small mirror on the inside of the visor to straighten her hair and clothing.

"Thank you for the ride," she said as he pulled up to Legacy's valet. "I'm sorry, but I don't think this bargain is going to work. As far as I know, the Club's activities ended when my brother died."

"You believe that?" Dev watched her carefully for any sign of malice or deceit and saw none. His gut was telling him she regretted her family's actions, and that she wouldn't have condoned them if she'd known about them. But despite his earlier assertion that his gut had rarely been wrong, he didn't trust his instinctual responses to this woman. Ivy had a strange way of slipping past his usual defenses. After all, he shouldn't even be at Legacy with her, and yet, here he was at his enemy's doorstep.

She sighed and looked away. "Not really. But I can't help you." She stepped out of the vehicle when the valet opened her door, preventing Dev from responding to her reluctant admission. Instead of driving away, he handed the keys to the attendant and hurried to catch up to Ivy as she went through the glass doors at the main entrance.

She looked up in surprise as he reached her side. "What are you doing?"

Conscious that he wasn't exactly welcome on this property and that eyes were probably already on him, he leaned down to speak into her ear. "Your father didn't pay for the crimes he committed. We're going to see that he does."

"There's no proof he's done anything wrong."

"Yet."

She shot him a look of disbelief. "You think you can succeed where countless others have failed?"

"With you on our side, yes."

"I told you I don't know anything. We can go our separate ways and forget I ever had this crazy idea. I'll be fine now that I'm on my home turf," she added as he continued to follow her through Legacy's cavernous lobby. A glass dome towered over the rotunda, which served as the hub of Legacy and held twelve large stone pillars around the circumference. Between the pillars were openings to different areas of the complex. A grand archway led to the casino on the right, with another farther up leading to a theater that hosted shows six nights a week. The restaurant and entertainment lounge were to the left. Straight ahead, in the direction Ivy was headed at a brisk clip, was the sleek, curved check-in desk for the hotel portion of the complex.

Dev easily kept up with her long strides. "You mentioned one of your father's men might be behind your near-kidnapping," he said.

Ivy barely spared him a glance. "Yes, but this is home, and I'm always surrounded by people here." She gestured to the busy lobby. "A person can only get to the penthouse floor where I live via a special keycard." She held up the keycard to illustrate her point.

"I may as well make sure you get all the way home safely, now that I've come this far." *And I'm not giving up now that I have a plan.* He snatched the card from her hand and strode to the bank of elevators beyond the check-in area. She followed, trying to keep up with his brisk pace and muttering a curse. He enjoyed keeping her off-kilter and breathless. This was all to take Stone down, he reminded himself. He needed to take every opportunity to find out what the man was up to so that they could catch him. And this time, they'd make the charges stick.

"I'm not sure I want you to take the job anymore," she grumbled behind him as he slid the card into the slot.

"I think I can make you reconsider. But at the very least, I need to check out your place—for my own peace of mind."

"Fine." She shot him a suspicious glance. "But only for a moment. After all, you don't need to know the layout if you're not going to kidnap me."

"Oh, I've known the layout for months," he said as the elevator door slid open, and he held it for her.

Her jaw dropped. "What?"

"Like you said, I'm the best at my job. I make it a point to get to know everything I can about my enemy. And Robert Stone does live, part of the time, on the same penthouse floor as you, does he not?"

She strode past him onto the elevator. On the thirtieth floor, the doors slid open and a long hallway hosted only six doors. He handed her the keycard and she opened the first door on the right.

"I feel so privileged, seeing the exclusive part of Legacy," he said.

She pushed the door open. "If you're implying I'm snooty or entitled, you can save it. This is my home and I was born into it, but I also work hard to earn it every day."

Ah, a hot button. She was proud of her work at Legacy, just as much as the heritage that went with it. Which was why it was going to be hard to convince her to accept his terms and help take down her father. Not to mention, she apparently carried a hell of a chip on those beautiful, slender shoulders. However, pride goeth before the fall.

He filed the information away and surveyed his surroundings. Elegantly appointed in neutral colors with splashes of brighter hues placed strategically throughout, the penthouse suite was surprisingly warm and inviting. It wasn't the normal, sterile or neutral hotel room. "Nice place."

Her chin went up as if she thought she might have to defend herself to him. He thought of the smudge he'd seen on her jawline earlier. That mark of imperfection that made her somehow vulnerable. Touchable. Human. It had reminded him that even a Stone had flaws. Behind her family name was a normal woman—a beautiful, intelligent woman, at that.

"Relax, princess," he said. "I only meant that you obviously take pride in your home." And in a lot of things.

She sent him a curious glance. "You don't?"

"Absolutely, I do." But he wasn't thinking about the condo he occupied during the workweek across town. That was just living space. Home was the log cabin he'd designed and built on two quiet acres of Curry Ranch. Ivy's father had attacked that sanctuary. Dev using Ivy would help defend his homestead, which eased his guilt about involving her. Besides, she'd come to him. And he wasn't contemplating any action the Stones wouldn't commit themselves to protect their interests. "I'd like to take a quick look around, make sure there's nobody lurking."

She nodded, her proud stance crumbling in an instant. "Of course."

When he returned after a thorough circuit of the four-bedroom luxury suite, he found her sitting at the breakfast bar, her eyes narrowed at her laptop's screen.

"All done," he said when she didn't look up at his approach. "No boogeymen under any of the beds or monsters in the closets." And she had plenty of room for them to hide. It was a lot of space for one woman, especially a woman rumored to spend most of her days and nights in her office. When he saw she was still shaken and distracted, he dropped the teasing tone and stepped closer. Her fingers, hovering over her keyboard, were trembling. "Hey, what's wrong?"

Green eyes sparking with anger and, worse, fear met his. "He emailed me again."

Dev moved closer to read over her shoulder. "*It won't be long now, angel. We'll be together again, on the other side.*" The brief message was signed *Nathan*. "It's from *NWilson*. Could that be Nathan's email address?"

"No." She closed the computer with a snap. "He's the only one who ever called me angel, but I know it's not him. He's dead. Isn't he? God, this can't be happening." She pressed her fingertips to her closed eyelids. Dev fought the urge to comfort her. After all, this could be part of some act to suck him into her web.

"Maybe it's your kidnapper pretending to be

Nathan?"

She opened her eyes again and nodded. "That's my thought. They have to be connected. It's the only thing that makes sense, right?" She met his gaze with a pleading one of her own, silently begging him to explain something he had no explanation for. "It seems unreasonable that two people might be trying to gaslight me at the same time about something that happened years ago. Has to be the same guy." She shook her head and rose from the barstool. "But we don't need to discuss it. You've done your chivalrous act for the week and seen me home. It's safe here. I'll be fine. I'll hire a bodyguard in the morning. I don't know anything about my father's business that could help you connect him to Redemption Club, anyway, and that's what you want as payment, so—"

"I'll take the job."

She'd been heading to the door to see him out, but her step faltered at his words and she swung back to face him. "What? I just said I don't have information to repay you with."

He stepped forward and shoved his hands in his pockets to keep from sweeping aside a hair that had fallen against her cheek. "Then there's no risk to you. You simply won't find anything to report. The risk in taking this job is all mine." Perhaps, he'd find the information he sought just by being close to the inner circle. Access to her security, the hotel, and her emails would be a good start. "I'll test out your security. I'll kidnap you."

Triumph flashed in her eyes and she sent Dev a smile that was like a secret weapon—a nearly lethal one. It took him a moment to catch his breath.

"I have the perfect time," she said, shifting gears like a racecar driver as her thoughts sped ahead. Of course, taking charge and planning was this successful businesswoman's forte. In fact, Stone's frequent parties were a hit because of Ivy's careful preparation. "I'm hosting a charity casino event here at Legacy tomorrow night, in the grand ballroom at the conference center annex."

He smirked. "Miss Stone, a kidnapping isn't something you can schedule—even if it is a fake one. This endeavor will be totally under my control. And I promise, you'll be mine before you know what hit you."

Despite his recent chivalrous behavior, Ivy saw the devil in Dev's smile. It should have warned her away—she had enough assertive men trying to take over her life. Instead, it weakened her knees and made her stomach do flips. Thankfully, he only aimed that weapon at her for a few brief moments before shifting into action mode.

"Tell me about your relationship with Nathan," he said, moving back to her computer. "I need to think like your potential stalker," he explained, shifting his glance from her screen, where he was scrolling through her emails, to her when she didn't answer right away.

"His father and mine were business associates."

Recognition dawned in his hazel eyes. "*Wilson*. Nathan was the son of the late David Wilson, one of the three men who founded Redemption Club twenty years ago?"

She nodded. "Neither of us knew what our fathers were up to, of course." Annoyance flashed when Dev didn't respond to this assertion. Let him continue to believe the worst of her, as long as he did his part in helping her start her new life, far away from the danger. "But Nathan and his parents died in a car crash, a horrible accident."

"And you're sure—not about Nathan's death, but that it was an accident?" Dev's expression turned thoughtful. No doubt, he wanted to exploit the possibility and find out more about her father's involvement with Wilson. She'd dangled a particularly juicy carrot and she couldn't blame him for wanting a bite.

"Yes." She'd once loved Nathan with her whole, naïve, twenty-one-year-old heart, and she'd never doubted those feelings were returned. "Nathan would never have left me like that. And now, eight years later, I'm in danger because of my association with him. It's like someone blames me for what happened, even though his death was an accident."

He cocked his head, suspicion in his gaze.

"What?" she demanded.

"It's not like murder is beyond the realm of possibility for your family. And evil typically begets evil."

The thought of her father killing Nathan, Joanna and David Wilson made her sick to her stomach. "The Wilson tragedy was just a stupid, horrible accident. Nathan and his parents had gone on a trip together. He was driving too fast on a winding road. The authorities said his new sports car had a defect in the braking system."

"And I have to wonder if Robert Stone created that defect. Or bribed the authorities to write up the report that way."

Her jaw dropped. "That's quite a leap. Why would he kill three people, one of whom was a close friend?" But a nagging feeling pulled at her.

"He likes to be top dog. Getting rid of a partner isn't outside the realm of possibility. And getting rid of your boyfriend was probably a bonus to an overbearing father who wants to be the only man in your life."

Tendrils of a remembered conversation she'd overheard between Archer and her father, not long before the Wilson tragedy, drifted through her consciousness, leaving her cold and shaky. Had what she'd overheard that night meant so much more than she'd guessed?

"I won't let her throw her life away!" Her father's angry shout resounded from within his den and Ivy came to an abrupt halt in the hallway, out of sight just beyond the open door. The anger in his tone

reverberated all the way to her marrow, and she could imagine his dark expression, though she couldn't see him or his companion. "Wilson is the worst kind of man, a friend who would stab you in the back. Anyone who would give a Wilson the time of day is just as worthless."

Archer's voice replied more matter-of-factly, "She's young. She thinks she's in love. We'll make sure she makes the right choices."

"Damn right we will. If she'd choose a Wilson over me, she'll be disowned."

But Ivy had never had to make a choice when it came to Nathan Wilson. A week later, he'd been killed.

Now Ivy truly was feeling ill. "I think you'd better go," she told Dev.

He shot her a sympathetic glance. "You've had a long, eventful day." He shocked her by reaching out to brush a strand of hair from her cheek. It was just the lightest touch of his fingertips, and gone in an instant, but it seemed like more. It seemed like an act of protectiveness. "Forward me the emails from *NWilson* and I'll go through them and be in touch tomorrow. In the meantime, don't go anywhere alone."

"Won't that make your job more difficult— kidnapping me, I mean?"

His grin stole her breath. "I love a challenge."

A moment later, Ivy closed the door behind Dev and sagged against it. Strangely, she'd felt safer with him—a near stranger and probably an enemy who wouldn't hesitate to use her to his advantage—than alone in her home. But then, she'd been alone for far too long. And she hadn't felt at home here in several weeks. Not since her doubts had set in, an insidious beast eating her up from the inside, destroying her sense of who she was and where she came from.

Getting rid of your boyfriend was probably a bonus to an overbearing father who wants to be the only man in your life.

Was Dev right? Was her father responsible for

isolating her eight years ago, when she'd finally found the life she desired? Her mind went back to the memory of a day not long after Nathan's funeral, when her father had been his usual commandeering self.

"You were always too good for him," he'd said. *"It's time to stop wasting your time pining for a boy who would never have measured up."*

The problem was, nobody measured up in her father's eyes. She wasn't sure *she* even did. And she'd become more and more certain over the years that her father manipulated people and situations to suit him. She'd often wondered if he'd pushed her mother away to eradicate Gloria Westwood's influence. Gloria had left for an acting job in Los Angeles when Ivy was four years old and had never looked back. It had made a younger Ivy fight even harder to keep her father's love. But she was tired of fighting for something that a child should simply have as a birthright.

And then there was Linda. Her nanny had left suddenly when Ivy was thirteen. When Ivy had tracked her down several years later, Linda admitted she'd been let go without explanation, but Linda had always suspected it was because Ivy had become more dependent on their relationship as she'd entered the teen years. And the firing had occurred not long after Linda had stood up to Ivy's father about a decision he'd made regarding Ivy. Robert Stone had threatened to blacklist Linda and Linda's husband Miguel if she ever tried to make contact with his precious daughter again. If they wanted to continue to make a living in Vegas, Linda had to let Ivy go.

Ivy moved to a bottom drawer in her gourmet kitchen, shifted aside a baking sheet and removed the yellow legal pad she'd started making lists on months ago, after Dev and Archer had shown up at Linda's home. Her plans for a new life looked back at her. At first, they'd been the scribblings of an angry, frustrated woman who'd been pushed to the edge by the growing number of threats—which had become deadlier—from the faceless public, as well as the demands of her father. Slowly, they'd become a plan, a final option should her life continue the downhill slide it had begun when her family had been linked to Redemption Club. Now, with a very real danger on her doorstep—or in the driver's seat of her hired car—she was forced to consider her escape plan a viable alternative.

Step One: Obtain new identity documents. She'd received them just days ago, and quickly squirreled them away somewhere safe.

There were a few more steps, with detailed notes about who, what, where, and how much money each might require, but she hadn't taken them yet. Near the bottom was the step that had given her the most pause.

Disappear. Don't look back. Ever.

It looked like she was finally going to be able to check that one off her list.

And yet, it was hard to sever the ties she'd had all her life. Was her father really as bad as everyone said? She'd seen glimpses of temper over the years, sure. She'd even been the target on a few unlucky occasions, especially if she ever dared to do anything he didn't agree with. But she'd usually tried to do her best to please him, so she hadn't really tested the limits there.

Maybe she should give him another chance before there was no going back. Maybe he could explain why someone would be after her, wanting her to pay for her past sins.

But then she'd have to be completely honest about the extent of those sins. The steps she'd taken at that time had been taken to ensure her safety. She regretted nothing. Unless... could Robert Stone really have been involved in Nathan's death? If so, he'd set into motion a tragedy that not even he would have fully understood.

CHAPTER FIVE

Robert Stone was sipping scotch and making a note beside a name in the leather-bound Redemption Club ledger when the sound of footsteps on marble alerted him he had a guest. With anyone else, he would have scrambled to hide the blood-red book, but he recognized the measured cadence as that of one of his closest allies.

"The power of money in action." Archer sounded triumphant as he waltzed into the den of Robert Stone's penthouse suite on the thirtieth floor of Legacy.

Archer had no first name, as far as Stone knew. Or maybe Archer was his first name and he had no last name. Despite the shortage of monikers, the man had a wealth of experience and a lack of morality that was the perfect combination in a right-hand man, which Archer had been for a quarter of a century, as well as one of the earliest members of Redemption Club. His confident swagger combined with his stocky build gave the impression of a streetfighter, but he always wore the most fashionable suits. The resulting image intimidated the biggest of thugs as well as the wealthiest of men.

Stone locked the ledger in a drawer. He would return it to a safer location tomorrow. He'd wanted it close to him during the trial, and it had come in handy as Archer played puppet master behind the scenes.

From his pocket, Stone withdrew a torn playing card with the name of his head lawyer—Douglas Rains—on it, and handed it to Archer. "See that Doug gets his debt card back."

"He fulfilled his obligation today," Archer said, tucking the card into an inner pocket of his jacket.

"That he did. Everyone did their part well and now we celebrate."

Archer slid behind the bar in the corner and snatched a bottle of Stone's most expensive liquor. Mimicking his cordial persona, Stone grinned and resisted comment, even when several drops spilled on the wood bar top as he poured and Archer didn't wipe them up. Stone took a gulp from his own glass to make his annoyance easier to swallow. After all, Archer was the primary reason Stone had returned to his own accommodations this evening, absent the threat of imprisonment that had been hanging over him for months. Stone was a free man. He could afford to be gracious. Apparently, Archer was of the same opinion.

"After what I just pulled off for you, I should just move in," Archer said. "Or maybe I could live in one of those half dozen other houses you have sprinkled throughout the world." He leaned forward and dropped his voice. "Or the other half dozen you own under an alias that nobody knows about. Nobody but me, of course." He slugged back the fifty-year-old vintage without appreciation for its velvety texture.

"You do know me so well," Stone said. And Archer should know better than to test his limits, even in his current convivial mood. The problem with good help was they often knew too much. Eventually, they either wanted to take advantage or became a liability when the cops came sniffing around. He needed Archer to remain firmly invested in Stone's wellbeing.

"Better yet, maybe you have some kind of elite gold status card that would allow me to sail the world on Stone Corp's luxury cruise line indefinitely or stay without limit in your worldwide hotels."

"Maybe," Stone murmured, noncommittal as he stared at the amber liquid in his glass.

Archer detected his lack of enthusiasm and his

celebratory mood faded. His cold, black eyes glittered like black diamonds. "Without me, you'd be in jail." He'd administered the appropriate bribes and pressure with the utmost discretion. Archer was irreplaceable.

To smooth things over, Stone grunted in agreement. He lifted his drink. "To loyal, profitable, symbiotic friendships."

Archer clinked his glass to Stone's before consuming the rest of the expensive drink in one long bob of his Adam's apple.

"I may have to look into that gold card idea," Stone said.

"Another club?" Archer's eyes twinkled with dark humor. "People would pay big money to be a gold-card member of the Stone Corp entertainment industry."

"Titanium's stronger, though. Or maybe platinum. Or something more precious?" Stone tipped his head, pretending to study the other man. "Nah. I don't see diamond-encrusted as your type of card."

"Too flashy." Archer laughed and snatched the bottle for a refill. "But I wouldn't mind the acknowledgement of the status I deserve."

"You know you're irreplaceable." Stone's comment only earned a nod from Archer. "How much did this bump in the road cost me?"

Archer pursed his lips as he tallied in his head. "I paid off most of the witnesses and the jurors from the account you set up. Used some of the Club's connections to collect favors, too, but there's very little money left since a couple of the holdouts had to be brought around." Which meant Archer had either hired additional men to scare them or used his intimidation tactics on loved ones connected to those involved in the case. Murder hadn't been an option this time. If even one witness had died, it would have generated even more rumor and suspicion.

"As we both know, this isn't over," Stone said. A silent understanding passed between them. There would be more to pay before the account was settled.

They had yet to figure out who had leaked the ledger pages to the authorities.

"I assume other methods are allowed, now that the trial is over."

"If you're discreet about it. Do what you have to do, but keep me posted."

Archer's brows went up. "You sure you want to know?"

"This time, yes. It's personal." He wanted to savor every delicious detail of their demise. "Find the person who turned over those pages and destroy him."

"And the little accidents at Grimm's ranch?"

"That damn task force." The Club had arranged for little, subtle distractions. They hadn't been enough, but they'd been his only recourse. Threatening task force members outright would have only rained more heat and pressure on Stone. He sighed. "Put out the word with the Club that we're in a holding pattern until I see what the task force's next move is."

Archer grinned and saluted him with his glass. "Will do. But if this drags on much longer, you'll be the one owing me." Archer was working off a debt to Redemption Club as well as earning enough coin to tuck away a sizeable retirement savings account. The man seemed just as greedy and hungry for power as Stone, but he knew his place.

"It's worth it. We need to make an example of whoever gave the authorities those pages. The Club doesn't view betrayal lightly." He looked up sharply as the sound of heels clicking against marble echoed again from down the hall. Another set of footsteps he knew well. Lighter, more purposeful. There was only one other person who had access to every place in Legacy, including the private penthouses.

"Expecting company?" Archer's brow was raised.

"Ivy." He'd forgotten.

"I suppose she deserves to celebrate your freedom, too, after running decoy for us."

"I mentioned I might come here instead of the

Henderson estate. Told her to come by when she could."
He glanced at the clock. It was growing late, but maybe
it had taken her longer than he'd expected for her to
ditch the reporters. Or maybe she'd had some work to
do in the office downstairs. His daughter was a hard
worker, and he felt a spark of pride that was quickly
squelched when the recent doubts reared their ugly
heads again. Had she been the one to turn over the
evidence that had almost landed him in jail? She was
friends with Emily Moore and had insisted on keeping
the woman on as a bartender, even after Emily had
gone against their family. But Stone hadn't argued. He
hadn't wanted to have to explain his objection. Besides,
at least this way he could keep an eye on the Moore
woman.

And, in the months leading up to the Club's
discovery, Ivy had been seen talking to Jared
Bennigan. Both Jared and Emily had tried to rip apart
the Club and were at least partially responsible for the
suspicion that had been cast Stone's way.

And then there was the fact Ivy had been tailed
going to her old nanny's house, when he'd strictly
forbidden further contact. It seemed his loyal daughter
was suddenly defying him, left and right, but how far
had she gone? Had she found access to his ledger,
taking a couple pages without him knowing?

Archer dropped his voice as the footsteps grew
closer. "Does she know?"

"She knows only what I tell her, which is very
little." He hoped.

He set his drink down with a loud snap, irritated
that Archer would have the audacity to ask him such
impertinent questions. There was a limit to his polite
acceptance. Archer needed to remember his place, just
as his daughter did. She'd been distracted lately. If
she'd somehow seen the missing page that detailed
some of his most infamous betrayals—the ones that
impacted her the most—would she turn against him?

"Sorry I'm late," she said as she entered.

"I see you made it out in one piece." He kissed her cheek, breathing in the citrus scent of her soap and stepping back to take in her more casual, but still fashionable attire. He appreciated that she was always ready to be the fresh face of Legacy.

Her lips quirked, but the humor didn't reach her eyes—eyes the same vivid green as his. She was annoyed, but today's victory was worth a little irritation. While he hadn't wanted her harmed, he hadn't exactly protected her when his lawyers had suggested the strategy. He'd wanted to test her loyalty.

"It wasn't too horrible," she said.

"I'll add a little something to your bonus this year for the extra effort. Or maybe a week of vacation this summer at one of our other resorts?" She nodded, but seemed distracted and wouldn't meet his gaze. "Archer just arrived, too. Join us in a drink to celebrate our victory." Her mouth tightened as her gaze landed on Archer. "What's wrong?"

"Nothing," she said. She didn't like Archer. Never had, though Stone wasn't sure why. For all she knew, Archer was head of his security and nothing more. "I was going to talk to you about something important."

"We're here to relax. Can't it wait until morning?"

She made an effort at a more genuine smile. "Sure."

"That's my girl. Besides, things are finally looking up for me." And he was going to make sure it stayed that way.

"If you want to have a family powwow, don't let me stand in your way," Archer said, but made no effort to leave. In fact, he moved behind the bar and began mixing a drink. "How about a little Redemption?"

Ivy stepped forward as Archer poured Legacy Lounge's signature cocktail, a Redemption, into a martini glass and added a cherry, then slid it toward her.

"You do that with such ease," Ivy said, distrust in her gaze.

Archer smirked. "I guess you didn't know I started out as bartender here, before my other talents were discovered. Of course, you were just a child at the time, safe in your nanny's care."

Ivy's gaze shot from Archer to Stone and back again. Had that been a quick flash of guilt in her expression? "Yes, well, I've grown up."

"Doesn't mean we don't still make mistakes." Archer poured the royal blue drink into a martini glass. "I'm the one who created the drink."

She arched a brow. "That's a bit of Legacy history I didn't know. Maybe you can help me with my question, after all."

"Try me."

"Know anyone who might want to kill me and who would refer to Dad as *Robbie*?"

Stone's hand froze with his glass halfway to his mouth. From behind the bar, and thankfully outside of Ivy's view since she was eyeing him instead of Archer, Archer shot him a significant look.

"Nobody calls me that," Stone said. Not anymore. Not in a long time. His whore of a mother and drunk of a father had, once upon a time. He'd left them in his rearview long ago. He'd made something of himself, a real legacy, while they'd rotted away in some trailer park in Florida, unaware their runaway son was filthy rich.

"You're sure?" she asked. "This guy definitely seemed like he had a score to settle. It seemed like he knew you."

He pointed a finger as if just remembering. "You know, your mother used that nickname when we were first dating, but I quickly broke her of the habit. Robert sounds so much more professional. But you say a man wants to kill you? What makes you think that?"

She opened her mouth, then shut it and shook her head as her gaze slid to Archer. "Never mind," she finally said. "I get a few emails a week from people wanting to express their opinion on everything from the way I run Legacy to how I let my father ruin this town. I'm sure it's nothing important."

His face grew tight with anger. "Forward those emails to me. I'll reply. Or better yet, ignore them. People will always be jealous of what we have, Ivy." He looked at Archer. "I want you to look into this first thing tomorrow."

"I'll make it my priority," Archer replied.

"Really, it's not necessary," Ivy said. "I've already got someone digging into it."

"You have Archer. They go after my daughter, they go after me. Nobody gets away with hurting me." And anyone who called him Robbie was being intentionally disrespectful. They'd pay for that misstep.

As Victor dialed his partner, he grimaced at the peeling wallpaper of the rundown, cramped motel room. Worse, the green, leafy pattern within the stripes reminded him of Ivy, the duplicitous bitch. But she was her father's daughter. Perhaps she couldn't be blamed for the hand genetics and environment had dealt her.

Once, he'd had only the most luxurious accommodations. Robert Stone had taken everything from him, and Victor would now return the favor. But he needed his partner, the one who knew the history of Ivy and Nathan well enough to send the vaguely threatening emails, and whose calls he'd been avoiding for the past several days. Together, they would raise the stakes, exposing the truth and forcing Stone's cards until the bastard lost everything.

"It's about damn time," came the abrupt answer to Victor's call. "What in the hell have you been doing out there? I thought we agreed to keep each other posted." As if his partner did anything productive to advance their agenda. Victor did all the dirty work—not that he minded. It was good to feel useful again.

"I saw her," Victor said.

"Ivy? I thought we agreed you should stay away."

"She didn't recognize me. I used a disguise."

"Then there's no reason for you to kill her. I told you as much."

"And I told you I'd decide how to handle this venture. If Ivy's helping Stone, then she deserves to die. But first thing's first." First, they had to find the ledger that detailed all of Redemption Club's actions. The thing was worth its weight in gold—and then some. "I'm betting the ledger's back in Stone's possession, or he wouldn't have pulled off his victory in court so easily today. He had to be calling in favors and twisting arms behind the scenes." It's what Victor himself would have done.

"Or he had his men doing it for him. I really thought sending those other two pages to the task force would be enough to ruin Robert's reputation. I should have known he'd weasel out of his punishment."

Victor grunted in agreement. But putting Robbie in prison wouldn't be enough. He wanted the man dead. Handing over those pages had been a miscalculation. "Thankfully, we still have the one page."

"And we should use it."

"We need more. The case the DA built against him based on *two* pages wasn't enough. Besides, I want him to suffer first." Victor had approached his partner a few months back, when he'd learned that a man was auctioning off pages from the Redemption Club ledger on what, in underground circles, was being called the Red Market. Victor supposed the name came from the book's blood-red leather cover. Together, they'd managed to get their hands on three pages and plan Stone's downfall.

"How?"

"The man's driven to build a legacy, so we take that option away. His daughter is his weakness."

"It's Stone we want," his weak-willed partner insisted. "No innocents should be harmed."

Ivy Stone is no innocent. "I'm not doing anything to her for the moment. Her primary value is her relationship with Stone. Better yet, I can use her as a bargaining chip to get the ledger. That's still the goal, right?"

"Of course. He deserves a fate worse than death. And if we control the ledger, too, that's even better. We'll turn the whole Club, the whole world, against him."

"And Ivy is the key. Her loyalty to her father can be used against them both. Those emails you sent weren't enough to rattle her into going to Stone, so I had to do something in person. I want her to run to her daddy and tell him what happened. I want him to be scared for his child." The thought sent a happy thrill through Victor's body.

"I'm not sure he feels that deeply for her. She's more like a possession than a daughter."

"Maybe," Victor conceded. "But she's his legacy. And his ego demands he leave behind a legacy to remember." Robert Stone had come from nothing, arisen from poverty in a home as dysfunctional as they came. He seemed to have a burning desire to leave his own distinct imprint on the world by building up his family's power. It was the only thing the megalomaniac truly cared about. "I need to take that away from him, take *everything* from him. And then I'll kill him."

There was a long pause before his partner replied. "You're harder than I remember."

"I'm the monster Robert Stone created." A monster who'd been hibernating, gathering his energy to strike. And now that he'd awakened from his long sleep, the monster had to be fed.

After leaving Legacy and making a quick stop to check on Jared's sisters, Dev picked up a late dinner and headed to his condo. His food remained untouched as he soon became absorbed in the emails from

NWilson Ivy had forwarded him.

Then he'd turned to researching the public's view of her, which had led to the slurs. He'd spent hours reading up on not only the truth he could pick out from between the lines, but also the blogs and social media sites, where people felt free to hide behind their online identities as they slung hurtful names, attacks, and libel at Ivy Stone with both fists.

Ice Princess. Rich Bitch. Chip off the old Stone block. Devil's spawn. Stoneheart.

Dev's stomach churned with anger on her behalf. Privately, she'd endured varying degrees of threats to her or the casino. Publicly, the social media sites had crucified her. He wasn't defending her, wasn't saying she hadn't presented an image that might be labeled in those harsh ways by unsympathetic commentators. Her actions during the weeks of her father's trial had certainly reinforced the view that Ivy was a stoic but steady voice that gave the media the bare minimum and knew how to spin an opportunity.

But he sincerely doubted these people knew the real her, either. Probably, nobody did, and he found the mystery behind Ivy was way too intriguing. Recalling the hints of vulnerability, softness, and passion he'd detected this evening beneath her tarnished veneer, he wasn't sure she deserved any of those harsh descriptions. The woman who'd walked into his office, flush with worry born of fear, with eyes as wide and turbulent as the Colorado River, was an Ivy Stone nobody had seen before. Had it been an act, or had he been gifted with a rare glimpse at her true emotions?

Needing to get away from his computer and clear his head, he bypassed the car he had parked under the carport and walked to one of the small storage units each condominium was assigned. Inside his unit was his Harley, customized courtesy of his brother Brady, who owned a bike shop across town.

Wanting the cool night air against his face, he steered the bike onto the interstate that ran parallel to the busy Las Vegas Strip. This area had always felt like it was backstage, where you could see the Strip from a different perspective, pulsing with the energy of the throngs of people who lived and worked behind the scenes. He swung into the fast lane, but couldn't go as fast as he wanted, which was faster than the thoughts racing through his head. Fast enough to escape the memory of Ivy's troubled eyes.

Damn. He knew he should walk away from this one, or let one of his colleagues handle it. But it wasn't just ego that had him thinking he was the right man for the job.

He found himself in front of Alpha Omega, the abandoned theater just a couple miles from the Strip where Ivy had been left by her abductor. Dismounting his bike, he took out his phone and used it as a flashlight. Sure enough, it illuminated a set of black tire tracks that looked fresh among the crumbling concrete and weeds. Someone had accelerated in a hurry here, which jived with Ivy's story.

As he searched the perimeter of the building, he dialed Jared's number, needing someone with common sense, but hoping the honeymooner wouldn't pick up. Of course, the fool did.

"Hello," Jared answered, sounding both tired and harried. Certainly far from relaxed. The mishmash of sounds in the background, coming from Jared's side, sounded like numerous footfalls and voices. One of them sounded as if it was coming over a loudspeaker.

"Where are you?" Suspicion added sharpness to Dev's question. "Please tell me you're not stateside." But the voice in the background announced baggage for Flight 102 from Honolulu could be found on carousel thirteen. "How the hell are you already in LA? I told you the world would survive a couple more days without you two."

"Well, see, my wife has her own opinions on that. On everything, actually. Ow! Damn, woman, you have sharp elbows," Jared muttered, obviously to Skye. But then there was a softer sound that Dev guessed was a quick kiss, followed by a murmur. "Skye's opinions aren't against you or your skills," Jared said when he spoke to Dev a second later. "She has complete confidence in you. She wants me to be clear about that."

"And yet she didn't trust me to handle this on my own."

Skye's voice came on the phone next. "Don't blame Jared. I changed our flight home the minute I heard the outcome of the trial. We can't let the Club hurt anyone else." Skye would fight for the underdog until her last breath, and Dev wasn't surprised she'd been watching for the news, prepared to change her own plans to be here. But they'd be shocked to learn that Ivy Stone might be the underdog they'd be protecting next.

"So you're nearly home." Arguing with Jared would be a waste of time, and trying to talk sense into Skye would be even worse. She was stubborn, but skilled. Besides, if Dev was going to war, he'd want this pair at his back. GSS employed a dozen security agents, and contracted with more as needed, but Jared and Skye had a personal stake in seeing Stone and Redemption Club go down. Besides, he could use their input on Ivy.

"We'll be in the office first thing in the morning," Skye said. "I'll give you back to my husband." Her voice softened with the last word.

"Sorry about that," Jared said a moment later. "I'm sure you had a reason for calling other than checking up on our whereabouts?"

"We may have a new client." Dev continued his trek around the building, pausing as he eyed a padlock on the rear door. At first glance, it appeared all was well. Up close, it was apparent the lock was broken.

"Yeah? Please tell me he wants to hire us to take down Stone."

"Actually, *she* may be able to help us with that.

Our new client is Ivy Stone." Silence stretched out between them. "I don't believe she's as bad as people seem to think," Dev added, cursing himself for defending a woman he barely knew.

"If she's like her father or brother or any of these freaks who enjoy hurting others and calling it a *club*, it would be a piece of cake for her to make you think that she's soft and vulnerable. Especially if it served her purpose."

"You met her when you and Skye were working the Hunting Grounds case. I seem to recall you were surprised at how cooperative she was, and it was your opinion that maybe she didn't know anything about her family's crimes."

There was some muffled side discussion between Jared and Skye, but Dev had little patience for their rebuttals after the week he'd had.

"She came to me," he continued before they could argue. "She wants to hire me to kidnap her. How would that serve her father's purpose?" Still, something didn't sit right with him. There was another layer to her story, but he'd never hear it if he didn't give her a shot. Besides, the emails she'd forwarded indicated there was a valid threat to consider.

"Who knows? But I guarantee it serves the Stone agenda, somehow. Why you?"

"Because I'm that good." But he'd had the same thoughts himself when Ivy had first walked into his office.

Jared snorted. "Sure you are, but it's no secret GSS has been investigating Redemption Club. Maybe this is a distraction, or a small part of a bigger plan to take us down before we can take down the Stones."

"Tell him to talk to Emily," Skye said from the background. Emily Moore was the bartender at Legacy Lounge, inside Legacy Hotel and Casino. Her fiancé Adam Wilde was one of the coordinators of the task force. The woman might know how much Ivy was involved in the Club.

"That's not a bad idea," Dev said.

"Skye made a connection with Emily while we were working the case," Jared said. "She'd be happy to talk to her. Why don't you wait for us? We're renting a car to drive the rest of the way from LA, since Skye can't wait to get back and we only managed to get onto standby lists on the flights out of here."

"You'll be exhausted by morning," Dev pointed out.

"We'll be more rested than you, I'd bet. We're the ones who laid on the beach and drank mai tais for days on end." There was a murmur from Skye that Dev couldn't make out, followed by Jared's low chuckle. "He doesn't need to know that."

Dev grimaced. "Fine. I'll wait, but not for long." After all, he had a kidnapping to plan. But first, a little B & E. Since Stone owned the theater, and Dev was acting in the interests of Stone's daughter, Dev decided a little crime might pay this evening.

CHAPTER SIX

Early the next morning, Ivy's gaze was everywhere as she emerged from the elevator onto the first floor and headed for her office.

She wasn't sure if her nerves were due to the remnants of last night's rush of adrenaline during her conversation with Dev, the fear that an attack might come at her at any moment courtesy of her mysterious stalker, or the memory of Archer and her father, so cozy together in her father's suite. The pair had always been thick as thieves, and she'd never liked the way Archer looked at her—sometimes as if he wanted her, and other times as if he wanted her gone. Thankfully, Linda hadn't seen him parked outside her place since that day in January. It seemed his objective had been to follow Ivy, so Ivy had taken extra care on future visits to be sure nobody was following. And he'd been the one to create the Redemption cocktail? Both the timing and the name implied early connections to Redemption Club.

Whatever Archer's motives, she was more certain than ever that she couldn't trust the people around her father. Hell, she wasn't sure she could trust her father anymore, either. Had he had something to do with Nathan's death? She'd buried the memories from that time down as deep and often as possible because the pain would steal her breath away. Yet, something had kept her from asking her father directly about a possible connection between Nathan and the man who'd threatened her. The quick look between him and Archer told her there was more to the story behind *Robbie*.

She passed the check-in desk and continued down the hall to the business offices. By design, her office was a mirror image of her father's, but the décor was slightly more feminine in color and design. Both looked out over the hotel's pool and garden area a floor below. At night, the lights of Vegas were visible in the distance. Her father had purposely built Legacy a mile from the busy Strip to provide the feeling of an exclusive resort experience.

Megan, the personal assistant Ivy and her father shared, looked up from the notes she was reading. She didn't always work on Saturdays, but this was a big event, and a first for Legacy, so she'd agreed to be on hand for any last minute needs.

"Ready for tonight?" Megan asked.

Ivy's first thought was of Dev, and a potential kidnapping. Would she be starting her new life tonight? He'd said he no longer required Ivy to spy on her father in return, but his hope that she would do so, repaying Dev with information that would condemn her father, had been evident.

"Just a few last minute things," Ivy replied, hoping her nerves didn't show. She collected her messages from Megan's desk and was happy to see there were no fires to put out. Her gaze moved to the closed door to the office adjacent to hers. "Dad's in?"

"He is. Came in whistling and eager to get back into a regular office routine, even though it's Saturday. But you may want to give him some space. He received a phone call, and then Archer arrived. I heard raised voices a little while ago." There had been a lot of those mood shifts since Ryan's death. Her father had become harder, more jaded and controlling.

While she hated what had happened to her brother, she couldn't say she missed Ryan. He'd barely given her the time of day when he'd been home from boarding school. He'd viewed Ivy as the reason his father left his mother, which was mostly true, since Robert Stone had impregnated Gloria, a young and beautiful aspiring actress, while he'd still been married to Ryan's mother.

In the end, Ryan hadn't thought twice about dragging their family through the mud. If she stayed and maintained the status quo, she could foresee only years and years of continually cleaning the mud off the family name, since her father didn't appear to want to change his ways.

But it wasn't the bleak family future that had Ivy wanting to run. The threats had grown more numerous and dangerous as the weeks passed. She feared last night's near-kidnapping was only a prelude of what was to come.

"Maybe I'll wait to speak to him, then," she told Megan. "Could you get me the supervisor from the company where you hired my car on the phone?"

"Sure thing."

Ivy entered her office and closed the door, relishing the quiet. She wanted to revisit her checklist and prepare for the future. Unfortunately, in the present, she needed to switch gears in preparation for tonight's charity event. She'd quietly been involved with Hope's Light for years, but her father had demanded she pull out all the stops to improve their family's image. While she'd do anything to distance herself from the tainted legacy Ryan had left them when he'd died last summer, she wouldn't support any cause she didn't actually believe in.

She had a lot to do before the casino night event began at seven. There were calls to be made to confirm catering, music, floral arrangements, floor setup, and speakers. The more generous donors would be staying at the hotel overnight and Ivy wanted to arrange for gift baskets of wine, fruit, cheese and chocolates to be waiting for them upon arrival.

"Mike Lowell from the rental company's on line one," Megan said over the intercom.

Ivy used her crisp business voice to deal with Mike, who apologized profusely when she explained that someone had basically hijacked her last night in their company's car.

"Our driver has been fired for drinking on his lunch hour," Mike assured her. "Apparently, someone slipped him a mickey as well. He woke up hours later in the alley behind the bar."

"And the car? The man who stole it? What happened to him?"

"The car was found in the visitor parking lot at The Mirage. Unfortunately, the police tell me the video surveillance of that area only showed a man in a ball cap walking away. He never lifted his face to the cameras." Her stalker probably knew they were there.

Ivy felt a chill. Her abduction hadn't been a sudden act of insanity. Someone clever and devious had thought things through. She wasn't sure if that made her feel better or worse.

"There's nothing to indicate who did this?" she asked.

"The police are looking for prints, but other than a wig—"

"A wig?"

"Police found it on the floor of the car. Gray, a little on the long side."

So she was even further away from being able to identify the man stalking her. Unless they could recover a hair from inside the wig, maybe run a DNA sample. But that would take weeks.

"I'm sorry I can't be of more help." Mike was back in apologetic mode and Ivy was out of patience.

"Just keep me posted." She hurried to stave off his assurances. His words were useless to her. She needed results.

She quickly hung up as her cell phone rang. She was surprised when she looked at the screen. Her mother. Gloria was rarely up before nine, and almost never took time out of her busy production schedule to give her daughter the time of day. It had always been that way. "Hello," Ivy said in greeting.

"Darling, I'm so glad I caught you." Gloria Westwood was a critically acclaimed actress who spoke and moved as if she were in a 1950s classic movie— smooth and silky. And she'd never been comfortable with the title of *Mother*, so she'd insisted Ivy call her Gloria, like everyone else. "I need to speak with you."

"I'm free now."

"Can you come to California?"

"Are you okay?"

"I have some news, but it would be better shared in person."

Ivy looked up as her door opened without a knock. Her father and Archer strode in, followed by a barrel-chested man who filled her doorway, who wasn't so much tall as stocky. "I'm going to have to call you back. Something just came up."

"Darling, please. It's vitally important."

"Can't you just tell me your news over the phone?" It wasn't like she wasn't busy, too. Her mother could drop everything and come to Ivy for once.

"It's sensitive information."

"Sensitive?" She blew out a breath. Everything was sensitive when it came to Gloria Westwood. "I don't think I can get away for at least a week." And by then she might be gone for good. Not that her mother would notice. Still, Gloria rarely initiated contact, had never once requested to see her, so the oddness of this sudden phone call had her considering the trip.

Out of the corner of her eye, her father cleared his throat and scowled with impatience.

"I really do have to go," Ivy said to her mother. "I'm swamped at work."

"Because your father keeps you on a damn leash." The loathing in her mother's tone was a shock. Gloria Westwood and Robert Stone had been divorced since Ivy was four years old, after which her mother had promptly packed up and moved to Hollywood to make her mark, remarrying soon after and seeming to never look back. But Gloria had rarely shown emotion when it came to Ivy's father. In fact, during Ivy's infrequent visits to California, her mother never spoke of him. Ivy had followed her cue and avoided that particular topic of conversation.

"Look, I'll see what I can do about a trip to California," Ivy said. "That's all I can promise right now." After a quick good-bye, she hung up and turned her full attention to the trio still darkening her doorstep. "Can I help you with something?"

"This is Manny," her father said, introducing the tough guy. At least he lacked the piercing, unsettling gaze Archer currently had trained on her. Her father's bodyguard always seemed to have a knowing smirk. She wondered what Archer thought he knew. Manny, on the other hand, had a more vacant stare, avoiding eye contact.

"Hello, Manny." Ever polite, she came around her desk to shake the man's hand, though he looked uncomfortable with the gesture. "Are you interviewing for a job with Security?"

"He's your new bodyguard," her father said. "After our discussion last night about the troubling threats you'd received, Archer suggested that you be looked after at all times."

Looked after? As if she needed a babysitter. And *troubling* didn't begin to cover it.

Besides, she already had Dev. Then again, he was supposed to be testing her security efforts with a surprise kidnapping and therefore wouldn't be around to protect her, and the man from the car could come back for her in the meantime.

She felt a twinge of guilt about not letting Dev in on all of her plans. But it had to be this way, or every item on her checklist would be for naught. Suggesting a kidnapping was an odd enough request, but if he'd found out she wanted to use him to help her disappear—especially before he could convince her to inform on her father—he probably would have thrown her out of his office so fast her head would still be spinning.

Oh, there were certainly other ways to vanish. As recently as last week, the U.S. Marshals office had offered to put her in witness protection if she'd testify against her father. But she had many reasons for not going up against her father. Part of her loved him, despite her fears he was involved in Redemption Club. She didn't fool herself into thinking she meant as much to him. For Robert Stone, Ivy was a means to an end, a symbol of the legacy he wanted to leave, the empire he wanted to build. But he never saw *her*—not the real person who served as his underling.

"Archer will look through your email history to determine where the threats originated," her father added. More than one source, he'd soon see. But maybe Archer could help find a lead as to who was looking to make her pay for whatever she'd supposedly done to Nathan. It couldn't hurt to have another set of eyes searching for clues.

"As long as they both stay out of my way," she said. She had a lot to do to be sure all was ready for the charity event tonight. It might be her last hurrah as Ivy Stone, and she wanted to be remembered for something good she'd done for the world.

"Good," her father said, looking somewhat surprised by her easy capitulation. "And one more thing. Devlin Grimm is not welcome in this building."

She went still. "What?"

"I saw you with him on last night's video surveillance of the elevators," Archer said, his lips curving into a sly smile.

"After you came to me last night I had Archer start investigating any threats to your safety," her father explained. "Grimm is our enemy, and doesn't belong here. Why were you with him? How could you trust him after all he's done to destroy me?" The smoldering anger in her father's expression was disturbing. But what was worse was the distrust she read in his gaze. She'd lost nearly everything, because she'd always done what he wanted her to do, no questions asked.

"I was thinking about hiring Dev," she said, knowing her father's sources—namely, Archer—would uncover any lies she told anyway. "We were discussing my options for dealing with the emails, and he escorted me home to ensure I arrived safely." Again, she left out the part about a man trying to take her. She had a feeling her father would tighten security even more if he knew the full truth, and then Dev wouldn't be able to get close to her and her dream for a new future would never become a reality.

"Going to him was a mistake, but I'm willing to overlook your lapse in judgment."

How nice of you. She bit the inside of her cheek to keep from escalating the argument.

"Now you have Manny," her father said as if he were bestowing the greatest gift upon her, "at least from the time you come to the office until he tucks you in at night."

"That won't be necessary," Ivy said. "I'll only need him when I leave the property."

"I could tuck you in," Archer offered with a grin.

Ivy repressed a shudder of revulsion. "Again, not necessary. Besides, Legacy has its own security department. They'll do just fine." She moved around her desk and turned back to her work to end the discussion. Thankfully, they took the hint. All except Manny, who remained posted by the door. She arched a brow, giving him her most imperial look. "I need privacy to work. Wait in the lobby." Megan could babysit him out there.

His scowl deepened. "I'm not supposed to let you out of my sight until you're in your suite for the night. Then my shift's over and you're someone else's problem."

She was always someone's problem. Her mother

had left to start a new life and hadn't looked back. Nathan had been reckless and abandoned her in his own tragic way. Her father only showed his love and approval when he needed her or she succeeded in something business-related, which usually meant he expected her to be at his beck and call. She'd made her biggest life decisions based on his advice, and his so-called guidance.

Well, no more. Soon, she wouldn't be anyone's problem.

For noon on a Saturday, Legacy Lounge was surprisingly empty. Dev was only there to talk to Emily, but sitting in Robert Stone's territory made his skin prickle like a limb awakening too slowly from sleep—painful, yet necessary. Without Ivy there to run interference, he fully expected to be approached by security and escorted to the door at any moment. So far, his presence had gone unnoticed. Of course, most resources were being funneled toward making that evening's charity event a success—and boosting Robert Stone's image at the same time.

The lounge's cobalt, magenta, and dark wood accents made the place both dark and cool in a comfortable way. It beat the hell out of many of the places where he'd done recon. The siren's song of slot machines coming from the casino area a hundred yards away was faint but audible over the soothing jazz music playing over the speakers.

Emily set the soda he'd ordered in front of him. Her blonde hair had been pulled back into a short ponytail and the tattoo of a phoenix rising from the flames shifted on her shoulder as she moved.

"Pretty empty today," she said. "Perfect for talking. Skye said you had some questions?"

All he had were questions, and no answers. Even his visit to the luxury car rental company had only revealed that Ivy's story could be true, that a man had very likely drugged one of the regular drivers and the car had shown up at The Mirage, with a wig on the floor by the passenger seat. But that didn't rule out the possibility that Ivy had staged the situation to make it look like she was in danger.

Still, Ivy was the key to bringing down Redemption Club. Dev would bet his life on it. And after meeting with Jared and Skye early that morning at GSS to review their options, he'd been more convinced than ever that working with Ivy, even if she had ulterior motives for enlisting his help, was an opportunity he couldn't pass up. He would use her strange job request as a way to get behind the scenes in the Stone family. Meanwhile, Jared and Skye planned to follow up with the jurors and witnesses, searching for evidence of tampering, and to continue aiding the task force in seeking out the missing ledger.

"Skye said you'd be the most likely to know about Redemption Club's recent activities, or the Stone family's involvement in them," Dev said.

Emily frowned. "Stone knows about my connection to Adam and his connection to the task force, which is probably why, other than a few rumblings, I haven't heard anything lately."

"I'm surprised Stone didn't let you go."

"Ivy runs things around here. She must have insisted on keeping me here. Besides, it would look suspicious if he fired me for telling the truth about his son. It's been relatively quiet for months, but the ledger's still out there, as are several loose pages sold on the Red Market. I have no doubt the Club is still active." Concern laced her words. "I had hoped taking down Ryan would cut off the head of the beast but Adam's convinced, no matter what the jury decided, that Stone's doing very bad things."

"I agree. In fact, recent events at my family's ranch make me think Stone has a personal vendetta. My guess is, after Ryan's death, he picked up the scepter—or ledger—and ran with it."

She grimaced. "If that's the case, it'll be tougher than ever to rip that organization apart. Stone's smart. I'm just grateful it's Ivy who really runs this place, and not him." She slid Dev an assessing glance. "Skye mentioned you might be working with Ivy?"

"I've accepted a job from her, yes. Thought we might be able to help each other. You seem to trust her."

"And you obviously don't."

"Should I?"

"She comes across tough as nails, but—" Whatever Emily had been about to say was cut off as the woman in question entered the lounge. *Ivy.*

"Did the alcohol delivery for tonight arrive?" The warm female voice pulled at something inside Dev, though Ivy's question was aimed at Emily. And then Ivy's gaze landed on him and something electric sparked and charged the air between them. "Oh, hello." Her eyes softened. Or maybe he was imagining that the ice was thawing. "Didn't expect to see you here."

"I'm full of surprises," he said.

Her eyes widened imperceptibly, lit with an unspoken question, and he subtly shook her head. *Not yet.* He wasn't ready to *kidnap* her until he had every ounce of intel he could gather—such as why she really wanted to hire someone to take her. He didn't buy the *testing my security* line. He wasn't walking into a trap—at least not blindly.

Despite the way she'd rushed in as if she had a million things to check off on that electronic tablet she held like a shield, she was calm and cool, the picture of beautiful efficiency. Her dark hair was held back from her face in another businesslike twist. Dev had the urge to step up to her and pull the pins from her hair, just to see the long waves tumble about her shoulders like they had last night. Was the pink tinge to her porcelain skin from her hurried pace, or had seeing him put that blush on her cheeks?

A corner of his mouth lifted, surprising him.

Nothing about this job should be remotely amusing. Or arousing. And yet, he was drawn to her in some inexplicable way.

"The order arrived first thing this morning," Emily said in answer to Ivy's original question. "And it's been quiet here, so I already inventoried and had it moved to the grand ballroom." Her gaze shifted beyond Ivy's shoulder to a man standing just inside the archway, his stance almost military-like. "New friend?"

A tiny furrow formed between Ivy's verdant green eyes and the invisible string connecting her to Dev snapped. "That's Manny," she said, frustration heavy in her voice. "As of this morning, I've been assigned a bodyguard, since my father believes I'm in danger." Had she told her father about the near-abduction? When Dev had left her place last night, she'd seemed reluctant to trust Stone with the information, as someone close to him could be involved.

Emily's expression turned alarmed. "Are you in danger? I thought the world would be targeting your father."

"Turns out people lump us together." Ivy waved it off, but Dev felt the barb. He'd been one of those who'd lumped her with her father. She glanced briefly toward Manny, who was shooting Dev dark looks as he spoke into his cellphone, probably alerting security to his presence. "I think Dad's going with the *better safe than sorry* policy. We're getting more hate messages than ever after yesterday's verdict. My inbox was crammed full of venomous comments this morning."

She seemed to be avoiding Dev's gaze, which was probably a good thing because he wasn't hiding his anger. Why hadn't she called him about the influx of new emails first thing this morning? The least she should have done was forward them to him. Yes, her job offer was for a kidnapping, but that was ridiculous. His primary goal was her safety. That she didn't trust him to do his job rubbed him the wrong way.

"I'm sorry, Ivy." Emily reached across the bar to

grip her hand in sympathy and Ivy squeezed back. Clearly, the pair shared a friendship as well as a working relationship. He was intrigued by this new side of the ice princess. "You don't deserve that. I guess that's why you're working with Dev?"

Ivy shot a surprised glance toward him. She'd asked to keep their arrangement a secret, and for the most part, he had. But he needed Emily's input.

When he remained quiet, Ivy replied to Emily's comment. "Yeah, well, like I said, people tend to lump me and Dad together. Now that he's free and clear, the easiest target for their anger is me. I'm the face of Legacy—at least for now."

Curious about the cryptic codicil to her comment, Dev eyed her, but Emily was already on to the next topic. "Your father needs to cut you a damn break. You deserve a vacation or something. Maybe go on a date. Someone who will help you relax."

Ivy laughed. "Just because you found the love of your life, and he takes good care of you, doesn't mean everyone is so lucky. Some people are meant to be alone."

Emily frowned at that, and Dev found himself doing the same. Twenty-four hours ago, he would have agreed wholeheartedly with Ivy's comment, but something about the way she accepted the lack of loving relationships in her life as normal didn't sit well with him. Hell, even a disagreeable foster kid like him had eventually found a family who surrounded him with affection. Where would he have ended up if he hadn't had Rose Curry and his brothers in his life?

According to last night's research, Ivy didn't date, rarely went out, and was a slave to her work at Legacy, where she ran a tight ship. She'd always been that way, in fact. The only time she'd been linked to a significant other was during her time with Nathan Wilson eight years ago. The only time she'd done something uncharacteristic was when, immediately after his funeral, she'd traveled Europe for several months rather than finishing her senior year of college. When she'd returned to the States, she switched majors from theater to business. Still, she'd finished *summa cum laude* a couple years later and become a successful businesswoman, probably the most successful in Vegas at only thirty years old, so maybe it had simply been a matter of her finding her calling.

Ivy suddenly shifted her hips, drawing Dev's attention there as she pulled a vibrating cell phone from the pocket of her slim skirt. "Hello?" she answered.

"All work and no play," Emily murmured with a shake of her head as she moved away to take care of some customers who'd just arrived.

The furrow in Ivy's forehead deepened as she listened to her caller. Dev's gaze trailed downward, landing on the tightening of the tiny muscles around her lips. He'd been annoyed by the fantasies about that mouth that had crept up on him last night.

Whatever Ivy was hearing on the phone, she didn't like it. Her gaze shot to him, and a jolt of something passed between them, stunning him with its intensity. He couldn't look away. Her eyes widened and her lips parted with surprise as she looked from him to the surveillance camera mounted in the upper corner of the bar, to Manny standing in the archway looking smug, and then back to Dev.

"Okay," she said into the phone, then slid it back into her skirt pocket. She licked her lips nervously and took a step closer to him. His heart rate sped and mouth watered as he caught a whiff of her light citrus-and-woman scent. "My father cordially invites you to visit with him in his office. If you don't agree, you'll be escorted to the parking lot and banned from the premises. I'm not allowed to take no for an answer."

CHAPTER SEVEN

Ivy resented being relegated to the role of fetch-dog for her father, but his whims ruled her life and always had. All of that would change—provided her father didn't scare Dev away. She needed Devlin Grimm to make her dreams a reality.

"Sounds more like a summons than an invitation," Dev said, but he didn't look irritated. On the contrary, he appeared intrigued. His gaze, a glorious mix of golds and greens that reminded her of sunlight hitting a green lake, settled on her. There was definite interest there. It turned speculative. The sense of dangerous calculation she'd picked up on when she'd first made eye contact with him persisted. She had to remember that he had his own reasons for accepting her job offer, the foremost of which was taking down her father. Whatever potential attraction existed between Dev and her would come last—or not at all.

She shrugged. "Call it what you will, but Dad doesn't make idle threats."

His mouth tightened. "No, he doesn't. Did you say something to him about us working together?"

"I may have mentioned that I was looking for help dealing with the threats. But I didn't ask him to intervene. After you left last night, I had to talk to him. Your comment about him not liking Nathan bothered me." Eight years ago, the animosity between her father and David Wilson had been palpable. If her father had known just how close she and Nathan were to having a life together, away from the influence of their overbearing families, it would explain why he hadn't shed a tear at the Wilson funeral.

Dev's eyebrows went up. "I don't suppose he admitted to any wrongdoing in the Wilson tragedy."

"Of course not. But after I talked to him, he had his man, Archer, look through security tapes and they saw you with me last night, getting onto the elevator. Dad doesn't want you here."

"He's threatened by me." His attention shifted from her to the surveillance camera and a smug half-smile curved his beautiful mouth.

"You seem happy about that. He's probably about to chew you up and spit you out."

"Or maybe he has a game in mind."

She scoffed. "Poker? He'd take you for everything."

"More like chess. A game of strategy where only one king survives. I'm guessing he's playing for the highest stakes possible."

"What?"

"Not what. Who. *You.*" His gaze was back on her, sweeping over her face before traveling down her body. She might have resented the blatant perusal from any other man, but this man had a way of getting beneath her skin and into her head. And that he'd consider her worth gambling for—even if it was all part of his strategy to take down her father—sent pleasure coursing through her. If she weren't careful, she'd lose herself in Dev, as she had in Nathan. That had been a disaster she almost hadn't survived.

But there was no disguising the flare of heat between her and Dev. A tingle of something—anticipation, she realized with surprise—rippled over her body like a caress. It had been so long since she'd reacted that way to a man that she'd thought those parts of her were dead.

"This isn't about me," she said. "Games aren't my thing."

"I would have thought manipulation was in your

blood." At his insult, she inhaled sharply and he shook his head once. "I'm sorry, but you have to admit this whole kidnapping suggestion feels like a game."

She stiffened. "I assure you, it's not. It's my life, my future, at stake."

"And assurances mean nothing without trust."

"Not sure how we can get past that, other than to take a leap of faith. I know there's something here, between us. We can build on that, right?" She couldn't prevent the note of hopefulness that crept into her words.

"I don't know." With a curse, he shoved a hand through his dark hair. It looked soft and was just long enough to curl against his neck, the kind of style that beckoned for a woman to run her fingers through it. She gripped her tablet tighter. "Your family has been after me and my friends and family for months."

"What do you mean?" But he didn't answer her question, not with the question of trust still lingering between them. "If that's the case, Dad probably wants to use this time to find your weaknesses."

His expression softened a little at her warning, making her heart skip. When was the last time anyone had looked at her with caring and appreciation? She looked away to break the connection. She couldn't fall for this man. He was the key to obtaining her future, but he wasn't a part of it.

"You said you received more threats," Dev said. "Did you hear from your mysterious stalker again?"

Her brow furrowed. "No, but somehow I think it won't be long, even with Manny tailing me."

"I went by the Alpha Omega Theater last night."

That made her pause. "You did?"

"I even found a way inside. Probably the same way your stalker did."

"Inside?" She shook her head. "He didn't take me inside."

"There were signs someone had been sleeping in the attic. Though I suppose it could have been a squatter."

"*Had been?*"

"If it was your stalker, he must have decided to move on after confronting you. Returning to the scene of the crime might get him caught." He stood and picked up his jacket from where he'd draped it on the back of the barstool. The shift in position put him closer to her, so close she could breathe him in. Warm, musky male with a hint of caramel from the soda he'd been drinking. "Right now, there's only one thing I want more than taking down your father." He shocked her by bending down to touch his mouth to hers. The contact was brief and surprisingly soft, yet full of heat that shot straight through her. And it was over way too quickly. "I could do that all day," he murmured, his thumb brushing over her sensitized lips. His gaze traced the movement.

She was about to toss her electronic tablet aside, say to hell with her plans for the day and the lack of trust between them and thread her fingers through his hair when he took a step back.

He grinned up at the camera.

The kiss had been for her father's benefit, then. To rile him. The stab of disappointment made her scowl, and she fought the desire to slam her tablet over Dev's head.

Oblivious to her confused emotions, he laid some cash on the bar. "No matter what the danger, finding out what your father wants with me is too interesting to pass up, and might help me formulate a plan to kid— I mean, to *help* you."

As he started to walk away, she stopped him with a hand on his arm. "Be careful. My father's good at reading people and using their weaknesses to get what he wants." For some reason, though she'd intended to use Dev to suit her purposes and he clearly intended to use her as well, she didn't want him caught in her father's web. "Don't show him your hand."

Amusement and something else twinkled in his

eyes. "Poker face on. Got it. Any other tips?"

"He'll be out for revenge since you helped the task force build the case against him."

"Princess, he already made the first move."

"What did he do?"

"I'll share more later, and maybe you'll see why taking down the great Robert Stone is so important to me."

She nibbled on her lip, worried for him. But she'd been charmed by a handsome face and passionate kisses before. She wouldn't fall for it again. Not that it mattered. Dev was only a temporary part of her life. Besides, before this was over, he would come to hate her. She mustn't forget her plan, or she'd be trapped here forever, at the whims of dangerous and violent people. She had her own interests to protect.

His voice dropped to a low, husky tone. "I like that you're worried for me, but you should know I can handle myself. I've had a lot of practice." His grin faded, as did the light in his eyes. If she'd had to describe the transformation that came over him, it would be battle-ready.

But her father was out of Dev's league. He was out of everyone's league. Hell, he'd created his own league and the population there was exactly one. That was the way Robert Stone liked it—even if it meant making his daughter feel like a pawn or sometimes like a complete outsider.

She shifted away, giving herself a healthy bit of distance, though she could still taste Dev on her lips. "I have to get back to work. You know the way to his office?"

"I do."

"Right." Because he'd scoped the layout. How could she have forgotten how long Dev had waited for his revenge, too? Some might argue Dev and her father were cut from the same cloth. That thought alone should have been enough to scare her off.

Stone relaxed only marginally when he saw Devlin Grimm leave the bar area like an obedient lap dog. When Manny had called to alert him to Grimm's presence on Legacy grounds, Stone had used the app on his phone specially designed to view real-time footage from any security camera on any of his worldwide properties. But he'd nearly thrown the device against the wall when he saw the interloper lean in to kiss his daughter.

Worse, Ivy hadn't slapped the man or seemed to protest in any way, which meant she was not only openly disobeying his command to keep Grimm off the premises, but welcoming their enemy. The whole experience only fueled the doubts that had seized him lately.

Grimm wasn't the only one trying to get to Ivy and turn her against him. She'd been offered immunity to testify against him—which she'd apparently declined—but, according to what Archer had found on her email account this morning, she'd also been contacted by dozens of people, some more than once, who'd issued threats and demands, or sometimes pleas for her cooperation. And yet, this was the first he was hearing of it.

"What else has she been up to?" His question was rhetorical, but Archer looked up from the laptop he'd been working on in the corner of the office.

"Give me twenty-four hours and I'll find out," Archer assured him. A knock on the door had him sending Stone a questioning glance.

"Answer it and leave us," Stone ordered. Archer scooped up the laptop, opened the door to Grimm, then pushed past the man and left.

Grimm strode into Stone's office. "You wanted to see me?"

"*Wanted* isn't the word I'd use. I don't want you here, Mr. Grimm."

The man had the nerve to smile. "Call me Dev.

Ivy told me you issued an invitation I shouldn't refuse."

Stone grinned without humor. "It's pretty low to use a man's family to get to him. Faking an interest in Ivy won't get you far."

"You don't give her enough credit. I don't have to fake anything. She's attractive in so many ways." Dev's tone turned steely. "Besides, as you said, it's pretty low to use a man's family against him, and you began this little game."

"Pretend I know what you're talking about—"

"Curry Ranch, the things that have been going wrong there. Sabotage. You've made family members fair game. At least Ivy is a willing participant. *She* came to *me*. And I'd be crazy not to use that advantage."

Stone stiffened. "Ivy won't tell you anything that could help you build a case against me."

"No? Why else would I agree to work for her?"

Stone hadn't anticipated she'd go to the enemy for help. It was a blast to his pride and anger made him clutch the edge of his desk. "I have to say I'm surprised to see someone like you, who supposedly searches for justice through legal means, is willing to—"

"Stoop to your level?"

"—use below-the-belt means of intimidation. And let's also pretend I'm the horrible crime boss people believe me to be and that I have a legion of minions at my disposal via Redemption Club." Dev's gaze narrowed and Stone felt a moment of satisfaction, because yes, he was all of those things and had built an empire in both legal and illegal ways, and they both knew it. "If all of that's true, you'll never touch me. The outcome of that farce of a trial should have proven that much. And with those kinds of resources, I wouldn't even have begun to unleash hell on you or your family—if I weren't pretending, that is."

Dev stood and sent him a glare. "Leave my family out of it."

"Then leave *my* family out of it."

"Ivy asked for my help."

"She'd never do that, knowing how I feel about you. There has to be another reason." He could see the flicker of doubt in the other man's eyes and it made him smile. "And you've already considered that."

"Maybe your daughter's simply reached her limits with you. Or maybe you don't have as tight a leash on her as you think."

That hit too close to the mark, and Stone stood and strode to the door. "I've faced opposition stronger than you. When all is said and done, Ivy always comes back to me, because she knows she can trust me to always be there for her." He jerked open the door. "Leave, and never come back. There's nothing here for you." Archer had sent a security guard to wait outside, in case he was needed. Stone waved him forward and read the nametag. "Mr. Inverness, I'd consider it a great personal favor if you'd escort Mr. Grimm from the premises and ensure he leaves without talking to my daughter." With a final glare, Dev stalked out.

Stone called Archer. "Find out what my daughter's planning. There's some other reason she's insistent on involving Devlin Grimm in our lives."

"He kissed you," Emily said, sliding Ivy a glance across the bar they were stocking in one corner of Legacy's grand ballroom. The rest of the space was dedicated to making money for the charity, in the form of multiple tables set up to host games of chance— roulette, blackjack, and poker, mostly. Guests would be given play money, in amounts proportionate to what they donated, and they'd be able to use their winnings to bid on auction items such as stays in Stone Corp hotels around the world, a ten-day cruise in the Mediterranean, and even a small part in the next Stone Studios film.

Ivy looked up sharply at Emily's statement. "You saw that?"

Emily grinned. "I swear I wasn't spying. I was coming out of the stockroom. Not that there was anything to spy on. It was over in a second." She sighed regretfully.

Ivy was careful to keep her expression neutral under her friend's scrutiny. If anyone should be sighing regretfully, it was Ivy. She could still feel Dev's kiss on her lips, and her body wanted more. Her thoughts had strayed to him repeatedly throughout the afternoon. She wondered how he'd fared with her father, but he hadn't sought her out after the meeting. It was entirely possible her father had had him escorted from the building and she'd never see Dev again.

"The kiss was only to get Dad riled up," Ivy confessed. "And it probably worked."

Emily shook her head. "You're going to get caught in the middle of a war between those two."

"Maybe." But that was also part of her plan. "I'm well aware Dev's looking for a way to get to my father, so nothing will take me by surprise. Forewarned is forearmed."

"Or maybe Dev's looking for an angle to get to *you*."

"What?" She couldn't know about the kidnapping proposal, could she?

Emily's grin turned sly. "That kiss had quite a bit of heat."

A thrill shot through Ivy, and she ruthlessly squashed it. The dark promise in his eyes may have flashed more than a few times in her mind as she replayed his comment about her not knowing when or where he'd come for her, but she wasn't naive enough to think their attraction could lead anywhere. He was here because he wanted to take down her father—*take a number and stand in line*—but he wasn't here for her. Or, at least, he wouldn't be, once this job was complete.

"How's Adam?" Ivy asked to change the subject. Except for work, the couple had been nearly inseparable since they'd reunited last July.

Emily's smile brightened, as it always did when the topic of her fiancé came up. "Busy, but we've squeezed in time to plan the wedding. He works a lot." With Adam's involvement in the task force, Emily was guarded when she spoke of him to Ivy. She hated that her best friend felt the need to edit their conversations.

"It's okay," Ivy said. "If Adam or Dev—or anybody from the task force—finds anything against my father, I hope they pursue it. I want justice as much as anyone, and if my father's done the things people have accused him of, he should be punished. I certainly wouldn't hold you or anyone who's simply doing their job accountable."

Emily met her gaze and weighed Ivy's words before nodding. "I appreciate that. I know you're not like your brother or your father."

"At least someone does," she said, thinking of the disgust in Dev's gaze the previous evening, when he'd watched her from across the street as she'd dealt with the media circus. "And I think people like you, hardworking and dedicated to the success of the establishment, not with eyes on the power and wealth it can gain you, should be in charge someday. If Legacy was in your hands, I could leave happy."

Emily shot her a concerned glance. "You're not going to quit, are you? I mean, I enjoy running Legacy Lounge, but this whole place?" She laughed and shook her head. "It's more than I could handle."

Ivy glanced around the bustling activity of the ballroom. Everyone was doing his or her part like a well-choreographed dance. "It takes a team to make it come together. I only coordinate."

"But not everyone has that talent. You make it look so easy, though I know you work hard. I do wish you'd take some time for yourself." Emily glanced at her wristwatch. "In fact, go get ready. Soak in a hot bath or something. I'll hold down the fort."

"Thanks. I do need to get dressed for the event."

A minute later, Ivy's gaze moved left and right,

making sure all was in order as she made her way to the sky bridge that connected the conference and event center where the ballroom was located to the rest of the hotel. Manny stuck to her side but she ignored him. Did Dev still plan to kidnap her or had her father scared him off? She wished she knew the plan. She wasn't good at feeling out of control, and she definitely needed to at least say a few words at the charity event. If Dev tried to take her before then...

Tried.

Even if he were still working with her, maybe he wouldn't be able to get past her father's defenses. She glanced at Manny as they reached the elevator. She looked up at the camera in the corner of the lobby. There were almost always eyes on her, which is why she needed someone skilled to help her disappear.

After ordering Manny to remain in the hall, she let herself into her much-too-quiet suite. Her thoughts automatically shifted to Dev again, remembering how it had felt to have him here, filling up the empty spaces. She barely knew the man, but each time she was with him she felt... better. That was the only word she could come up with to describe the odd ball of feelings.

The cleaning lady had been here, as evidenced by the light scent of lemon that greeted her nose. Ivy hurried to her bedroom, conscious that time was ticking away. The event started in just an hour and she had to look her best tonight. And she had to look normal, as if she wasn't waiting to be kidnapped or attacked at any moment. People would be judging her, whether they meant to or not. It was human nature. But the joke was on all of them. Nobody could beat Ivy Stone up as much as she herself did.

After a quick shower, she donned a slinky silver dress and carefully applied makeup. As she swiped a deep red lipstick across her lips, the action had her thinking of Dev's kiss. Though brief, it had felt like he'd branded her as his. Her cells hummed with the memory as if they'd been imprinted. Or as if he'd awakened a desire that she'd lulled to sleep years ago. In fact, every brush of her hands across her skin had her thinking of him, wondering what his touch would feel like.

Suddenly, the quiet was too much. She jumped up to turn on the radio, finding a rock station that would jar her senses. She turned it up loud enough to echo off her bedroom walls. Returning to her makeup mirror, she noted the soft flush to her cheeks and hoped it was makeup and not her body's reaction to the thought of a certain perfect male specimen—perfect except that he considered himself her enemy. She ran a brush through her hair until the ebony shined like a slice of polished African blackwood, then pinned the sides back in an easy, but sophisticated, look.

Noting the time, she hurried to put on her shoes and switch off the music. She practically ran past the kitchen area toward the front door.

And stumbled to a stop as a face registered in her peripheral vision.

Clutching her hands to her chest as if she could push free the breath that had lodged there, it took her a moment to realize what she saw wasn't a face but a mask, hanging on the wall just inside her front door. At the perfect height to seem like a person was standing there at first glance.

She took a tentative step closer, examining the item. It was the classic tragedy-comedy drama mask, split down the middle into black and white. The mouth on the black half grimaced in a sad frown, the white half curved upward in a happy expression. But the alpha and omega symbols painted on the cheekbones made this mask different, and indicated who was responsible for the macabre gift.

She spun in a circle, her heart pounding. There was nobody there. She hadn't heard anyone, probably because she'd had AC/DC cranked to eleven. The suite was completely still and quiet now. Manny was theoretically posted outside the door, so had the mask been there when she'd arrived earlier, and in her hurry, she hadn't seen it?

She poked her head out into the hall, but there was no sign of Manny. She'd told him to wait for her on the first floor, by the elevators, since the penthouse elevator was exclusive and there was no way for someone to come up or down without him seeing, but he'd resisted her order earlier. It seemed he'd rethought his position.

A trickle of sweat dripped between her breasts and her breath came in short bursts. She closed and locked her door, then slumped against the wall and slid to the floor, a moan escaping her lips as she eyed the opposite wall.

Alpha and Omega. Another reference to the decrepit theater and a past that had come back to haunt her. The threat had to be from the man who'd been hired—supposedly by Nathan—to make her pay. But Nathan would never have tried to scare her like this, and the fact that someone would use his memory against her pissed her off. It gave her the strength to move.

Sliding back up the wall on shaky legs, she pulled the mask from its nail and turned it over. Another wave of nausea hit her as she saw the inside had four simple digits.

0512.

Someone out there knew her secret—and there was suddenly so much more to lose than her life.

CHAPTER EIGHT

Dev's target was cold, aloof, and stunningly beautiful as she played her part, greeting guests and charming them with her smile. Ivy could have been an actress or a model, but she was a businesswoman, following in her father's footsteps. Unlike Robert Stone, however, she avoided the limelight. Instead, she let everyone believe she was unapproachable. He had to wonder why.

But what bothered him most was his own reaction to her. Now that he'd seen one of Ivy's rare genuine smiles he yearned for another. And then there was the heat and passion in her eyes when he'd kissed her. He wouldn't mind putting that look on her face again, either.

Christ, those lips. He could still taste their sweetness. He'd only sampled them to make Stone angry—or so he liked to tell himself. And it had made the man angry, though Stone had tried hard to disguise it. So Dev couldn't even regret the kiss. It hadn't been far from his thoughts all afternoon after Stone's security guys had escorted him from the building. He'd glanced back at the lounge on his way past, but Ivy hadn't been there. Still, he'd gotten close enough to the enemy to see one of his weaknesses—Stone didn't like seeing Dev around his daughter, let alone kissing her. So no, he didn't regret the kiss one little bit.

His gaze swept the ballroom, assessing for threats. Beside him, Jared did the same. Part of his afternoon had been spent studying the blueprints for the convention center and ballroom annex to Legacy, locating the easy in-and-out access points. The ballroom they stood in had at least six double-door entrances, evenly spaced along opposite walls.

"Slow night," Jared muttered. "Stone's not even here." Jared had to be referring to the lack of criminal action, because there was enough of a crowd that they could get lost among the guests, who seemed to be engrossed in gambling and conversation. Dev was hoping to blend in and avoid another security escort to the parking lot.

"He's not here *yet*," Dev emphasized. "He will be. He needs to look charitable and humble."

Jared slid him a glance. "You sound like you know him."

"As if months of investigating him wasn't enough, he summoned me to his office today."

"Lucky you."

"It did give me some personal insight. The man's not above using his daughter to get what he wants, but gets angry if anyone else tries to get close to her. He views Ivy as his property, to control and do with as he pleases. And seeing her with me pushes his buttons."

Jared gave up surveying the crowd to face him, a grim expression darkening his face. "Don't get too involved in their warped family dynamics. We don't even know if Ivy's innocent."

"But if she is?" Then she was a victim like any other person in Stone's path. The thought stirred Dev's protective instincts.

"Skye likes her, and I know Emily does, too, but that doesn't mean we should interfere in Stone family business. Ivy can take care of herself. Forgive me, but you have a habit of riding to the rescue."

Dev bristled. "Look who's talking."

Jared grinned, his easy charm instantly lightening the mood. "It makes us the perfect team to run GSS."

That much was true. "It's good to have you back, man."

"And I've got your back." Jared's friendship meant everything, especially since the man had stood by Dev after the incident in Afghanistan, when people had blamed Dev for the deaths of a SEAL team and three civilians who'd been caught in the middle of an ambush Dev had tried to prevent. Only by fighting side by side with Jared, who'd been an MP stationed in the city at the time of the ambush, had they both survived that day—and managed to rescue a few other civilians who'd been in the wrong place at the wrong time. But people who hadn't been there and didn't know what they'd faced had focused on the negative and turned their backs on Dev.

"Any leads from interviewing the jurors?"

"Skye's still tracking down most of them. Of the ones we located, they're very tightlipped. I'm guessing they were paid well."

"Or they're scared. Redemption Club has been known to have a long reach."

"We won't let Stone, or the Club, touch any of your family," Jared insisted, reading the true concern beneath Dev's words.

"Not sure anybody can stop him now that he's free and clear. But it would be worth checking into this Archer guy who's always by Stone's side. Ivy said she didn't trust the men around her father."

Jared's gaze narrowed on Ivy as they spied her climbing the stairs to the stage at the other end of the large ballroom. "Man, I would have paid good money to see a Stone walk into our offices and beg for help, all disheveled and... human." Her job offer had been the main topic of discussion at the office meeting that morning. "I suppose it couldn't hurt to let her close enough to pick her brain about her father's activities."

"Unless she's setting me up for something." He'd seen a barrier in her eyes as if she was holding part of herself, or her story, back. "She's leaving some part of this equation out."

"Ah, the unknown variable that can make

everything go FUBAR in an instant."

Exactly what had happened in Afghanistan. Dev slammed the door shut on the memory of the violence they'd witnessed that day.

"But you'd risk everything when someone you care about is involved," Jared said, sending him a look of concern.

Dev assumed he was referring to his mother and brothers, and not to Ivy as he continued his visual sweep, eyeing the people who waited in line to peruse the silent auction items. A waiter plied guests with a tray of drinks to loosen their inhibitions—and their purse strings. "One thing is certain. One should never relax on Robert Stone's turf. Sitting across the desk from him was like staring into the mouth of a shark. I'm certain he wanted to rip me to bits."

The crowd around them quieted as the music ended, the lights dimmed, and Ivy approached the podium. Her dress clung to her body, the silvery material shimmering like waves in moonlight as her lithe body moved into position. One long, bare leg peeked out of a slit in the skirt that ran all the way up to mid-thigh. Unexpectedly, Dev's heart skipped a beat and he slammed back the rest of his champagne in annoyance. Planning to kidnap her was a job. He shouldn't be looking forward to it.

Ivy accepted the applause with a demure smile. She was beautiful. The dress's color contrasted with her long dark hair, which had been scooped up on the sides in an artful way, and left to cascade down her back. One sift of his fingers through that silk and the combs would come loose. Her vivid green eyes, accentuated with violet and silver eye shadow, tipped up slightly at the outer corners, inviting people to explore the mysterious depths.

She was a controlled, calculated threat in so many ways—and he wanted to muss her up, to throw her off-kilter, as she did to him.

"Thank you all for being here tonight," she said

into the microphone. Her words held just enough rasp and huskiness to both ruffle and stroke his skin. "Your support of Hope's Light Children's Foundation is much appreciated. The children need a voice, a protector." Her gaze moved across the crowd, carefully making eye contact with people here and there. Dev shifted closer to the pillar where he stood at the back of the room so that she wouldn't see him. "The kids served by the various agencies that are part of Hope's Light need the basics such as food, shelter, clothing, and so much more. Your donations tonight will show them that someone cares, that someone loves them. Enjoy yourselves, and thank you again for your generosity."

"An ice queen who cares about unwanted orphans?" Jared said, clearly as confused as Dev.

"Could be a smokescreen," Dev admitted.

"Maybe she's milking it to sink her claws further into you." Jared's suggestion made Dev go completely still.

"That would be truly insidious."

"And yet, not impossible for a Stone. How much does she know about your background?"

Dev's history as a foster kid who'd been passed around and unwanted until the age of fourteen wasn't well known, but wasn't exactly a secret either. Especially if someone had money and a decent private investigator.

He shoved aside the thought as ridiculous. If Ivy were going this far to get to him, using innocent children, she was indeed a cold bitch. He'd seen enough warmth in her that he had a hard time believing she was that evil. Besides, the event had to have been planned weeks ago... Then again, she'd first run into Dev three months ago.

The music from the DJ and the action at the gaming tables resumed as the lights went up again. Ivy moved through the crowd and stopped to chat with several people individually. He noted her guard dog Manny trailed her. Just one guard. Easy-peasy. He also noted that Manny was distracted whenever they passed one of the tables. A weakness for gambling, perhaps?

Dev scowled when a man grabbed Ivy's arm and pulled her close to speak with her. Her answering smile was automatic, but not warm. The suave, silver-haired guy looked familiar, and as he leaned in close to say something in her ear, as if he had the right to such intimacy, Ivy went completely still for several beats, shock registering on her face. Then, with practiced grace, her hospitable smile returned—a smile that didn't reach her eyes—and she took a step back. But the man tugged her back into him, wrapped an arm around her shoulders, and didn't let go. He bent down to brush his lips against her cheek and Ivy looked as if she might hit him. Meanwhile, Manny was keeping his distance, averting his eyes as if he'd been paid to look the other way.

A roaring sound filled Dev's head, and his feet were moving before he even knew his intention.

"Wait!" Jared hissed beside him.

The roar was growing like rapids, compelling Dev forward. Before he could reconsider his actions, he was standing in front of Ivy. Jared stopped beside him and heaved a sigh of resignation. Good, he might need backup—or bail—if this asshole didn't remove his mouth from beside Ivy's ear.

Her cheeks were too pale. To the crowd, it looked as if the older gentleman was embracing her in an affectionate way, perhaps leaning close so as to be heard over the music and noise. But the lines of strain around Ivy's lips told the truth.

Up close, Dev recognized the man as he pulled back enough to send her a wicked smile. Douglas Rains was the head hotshot lawyer from Stone's legal team. He'd given regular, brief statements to the media in defense of his client. Dev suspected the entire team had been paid well to ignore Stone's guilt and plunge forward with a strong defense, even if it meant borderline intimidation or out-and-out dirty tactics to discredit the witnesses who took the stand. Even more reason to dislike the man.

"Problem?" Dev asked Ivy, who looked relieved to see him.

"Um, no," her gaze moved from Dev to Rains. "Devlin Grimm, meet Douglas Rains. Doug was just saying how my family owed him." Her voice cooled several degrees as she spoke. "He mistakenly thought I could repay him."

"I'm certain we could come to some arrangement," Doug said. No doubt, Doug's suggestion for how Ivy could repay her father's debt fell into the nonmonetary category. The possessive way the man's eyes swept over Ivy's face, touching on her lips and hair as if he was physically caressing each feature, made Dev's fists clench. He was glad he'd found a passing tray to set his champagne flute on.

"Is Stone having trouble paying his legal fees?" Dev asked Rains.

"This is a family affair," Rains said, turning away from Dev as if he could dismiss him. "I have so much to offer, Ivy. Everything you want is right here in Vegas, and I can help you get it—and keep it safe."

Dev scowled at Manny, who lingered nearby, seemingly oblivious to the undercurrents of tension swirling around him. "I believe Robert Stone would want you to escort this man off the premises," he told Ivy's lax guard.

Rains smirked. "No need for that. Ivy, you know where to reach me when you're ready." With the confident swagger of a man who had argued away the prison sentences of many a criminal, Douglas Rains left.

"I'll follow him and make sure he leaves the event," Jared said at Dev's shoulder.

Dev gave a quick nod. "Are you okay?" he asked Ivy. He brushed a hand over her shoulder when she seemed preoccupied with watching Rains until he was out of sight. The gentle physical contact did the trick, recapturing her attention, and her gaze whipped to his.

"What?" Her lips were slicked with a deep red tonight, and his immediate thought was of cherries, ripe and juicy. Would she taste as good as he remembered if he kissed her again?

"I asked if you're okay."

"I'm fine."

A lie, but Dev figured it wasn't her first. Still, it irritated him that she continued to withhold the truth from him. "What did Rains want?"

"A trade. Information he supposedly has. He says it's worth a night with the *ice queen*. And, what's more, he had an extra-special bonus in mind if I please him." Her stunned gaze met his. "He wanted sex."

Dev would have laughed if the situation were even remotely funny. Did she have no clue how irresistible she was, or what some guys would risk for her? Dev would bet a million dollars that Rains would bring the full force of Stone's wrath down upon himself by propositioning his daughter. "Do you think he's working with your stalker?"

Surprise lit her expression. "It hadn't occurred to me, but no. He's not the subtle sort." A second later, a smug look crossed her face.

"What?" he asked, suspicious of that expression.

"You're here to kidnap me. I told you tonight would be perfect. I was right."

His lips twitched. "Sorry, princess, but I'm only checking on you. Besides, taking you in front of everyone, especially when you're the hostess, would be risky. Unless I could lure you away willingly." He hadn't meant that last part to sound so seductive, but at some point, his voice had lowered to a husky tone.

Her lips parted on a soft, "Oh." If he wasn't mistaken, that was heat and interest swirling together in her eyes.

A throat cleared behind him. Jared was back and Dev introduced him to Ivy.

"I remember you," Ivy told Jared. "From last spring." When Jared had been investigating her brother's possible involvement in some very bad things, he'd interviewed her briefly.

"Right," Jared said. "You look well."

"That's my job. Speaking of which, I need to get back to circulating among the guests." She smoothed her palms over her stomach. Her fingers were trembling, and Dev thought about snatching them up and kissing them—but then they'd both be trembling.

"You sure you're okay?" Dev asked her. "I could take you away from here if it would make you feel better."

A smile played about her lips. "Any time you're ready." Her gaze shifted to his mouth.

Jared, forgotten, cleared his throat again. "Be advised. Stone at three o'clock, closing in fast."

Ivy caught the look in her father's eye as he reached their group, and felt a chill creep over her skin. She took a step back at the same time Dev did, putting some distance between them. She wished she'd had time to ask Dev what had happened during their meeting earlier that afternoon. Whatever had been discussed, the two men were apparently still enemies—potentially even more so than before. She hadn't known it was possible for someone to go white with anger, but her father's jaw clenched so tightly that he must have cut off blood flow to parts of his head.

The fierce disappointment her father directed at her was soon smoothed over as an expression of crisp politeness overcame his features and he spoke to her companion. "Devlin Grimm, I didn't expect to see you here." He turned to her. "Lovely production. Of course, I'd expect nothing less from my talented daughter."

"Thank you," she said, bracing herself. There was a *but* in there.

"But did you have to let just anyone in?" He cast

a pointed glance at Dev and the chill in the air turned to frost. "I believe the fun should be reserved for friends of the family."

"You mean friends of the charity," Ivy corrected.

"I assure you I contributed like everyone else here," Dev said.

"If it was that important to you, you could have contributed without attending the event," her father said rudely. "I told you you're not welcome on the premises."

"The smart player knows when to fold and walk away." Dev's gaze shifted to Ivy. "And when to stay."

"Too bad your brother didn't abide by the same theory. That kind of lack of restraint was what landed him in prison—or so I heard."

At her father's comment, Dev went absolutely still. *Brother?* She dimly recalled, in her investigation into Dev weeks ago, a brother of his had gone to prison for aggravated assault. But why would her father know about it? Then again, he'd probably had Dev investigated months ago, when he realized GSS, along with other agencies, was coming after him.

Ivy had the urge to slip her hand into Dev's and comfort him. The hard line of his jaw tightened as he choked back whatever emotions had hit him after her father's callous comment. Protectiveness coursed through her, mingling with a sense of duty. She'd brought Dev here, invited him into her establishment. It was her job to break up this nonsense and shatter the tension that thickened the air surrounding their little group.

She took her father's arm and shot Dev an apologetic look. He still looked angry and a bit shaken. "Dad, I'd like you to meet some of the donors. If you'll excuse us, Dev?"

"Of course." Dev's words were stiff. Jared clapped a hand on his shoulder and leaned in to say something. A moment later, the pair headed in the opposite direction as her father propelled her, his hand at her elbow, toward one of the exits.

"Dad?" she asked, aware he was smiling but a darkness lurked beneath his expression.

"Not now," he bit out. He said a brief hello to an actress they passed. Anxiety rose up as Ivy realized the extent of her father's anger.

"I have to be here to take care of my—our—guests," she objected as they reached an exit. "You should be here, too. We're benefiting a lot of kids. I'm excited to see the good this money will do for them."

The moment they were outside of the ballroom, all semblance of amicability was gone. "Don't get too attached," he snapped.

Feeling the whiplash of his mood swing, and this time being unprepared for it, she struggled for words. Not that he wanted to hear what she had to say. He was already rushing onward.

"Have I taught you nothing?" he ground out as he dragged her farther down the hall that paralleled the length of the ballroom. "Never let personal feelings get in the way of family goals."

"Personal feelings?" Was he talking about Hope's Light or Dev? She nearly twisted her ankle as he veered toward an emergency exit stairwell.

"The charity is an institution. A means to an end. It doesn't deserve your full devotion. I do. Don't forget who's given you everything you have." Yanking her to a stop, he bent down so that he was in her face. "And I can take it away if I determine you no longer deserve my trust."

Suddenly, her breath was trapped in her lungs. What was he implying? "I can be trusted, Dad. Helping out Hope's Light achieves both family and personal interests."

He slammed open the door and pulled her toward the stairs, shutting the door and blocking out Manny, who'd followed their escape at a respectful distance. The harsh lights in the stairwell were bright in contrast to the softer lighting of the ballroom. She blinked, feeling off-balance and uncertain.

Her father grabbed her arms and shook her hard, taking her by surprise. For the first few seconds, she didn't even register the pain. "If you trust Devlin Grimm, you're an idiot," he said. "Why would you willingly bring that man into our lives?"

She tried to step back, but his grip only tightened. "You're hurting me." She glanced to her right, where a flight of a dozen or so stairs descended to the next cement landing. If he let go, or chose to shove her away, she could be seriously hurt. She stopped resisting, figuring he was at least anchoring her to the spot.

"And you hurt me with your deliberate defiance. How do you know that man's not behind the threats you've received?"

"I just do." She adopted her frosty demeanor, the one she relied on to insulate herself from the pain, both physical and mental. "Besides, you're the one who brought Dev into our lives. He was investigating your involvement in the Club. What did you mean about his brother back there? Did you have something to do with his imprisonment?" She'd lived in denial for so long, even as the evidence against her father mounted. But the thought of him intentionally harming others was starting to seem real. After all, if he could hurt her, the only family who'd stood by his side during all of this, what was to stop him from hurting the people who'd gone against him?

"You sound like you trust him more than your own father." With a sound of disgust, he let go of her so suddenly she stumbled. She grasped the railing as the edge of her spiked heel came close to the top stair. Her father seemed oblivious to the fact she'd almost taken a serious fall—because of him. Enveloped in a haze of anger, he paced back and forth on the landing. "You leave me no choice but to doubt you. That man would look for any reason to destroy our family."

"Forbidding him from being at Legacy would

only make us seem more guilty or suspicious. Or petty. It would undo everything we're trying to do to repair your image."

At the reminder that he'd damaged his supposedly good name, he shot her an angry look. "I was going to involve you in a very special project. Doug drew up the paperwork last week. It's all in my suite, ready for signatures. But I don't think you deserve it anymore."

Was he dangling a massive carrot, or was this another game? Maybe this had been the information Doug had sought to exchange. "Something about Legacy?"

"Yes. Something you've worked hard for."

The breath caught in her lungs. He was finally going to transfer ownership of the hotel and casino to her. Legacy had been one of the few bright spots that had allowed her to retain her sanity over the past several years. Her heart pounded against her breastbone, and then plummeted to her stomach as she recognized another sly move when she saw one. "You're holding my job over my head to make me fall in line." She regretted the accusation the moment it passed her lips.

"Watch yourself." He grabbed her again, squeezing her arm, and she clutched the railing, biting her lip against a moan.

She normally didn't raise her voice or give him trouble of any kind. She'd always strived to be the best daughter ever. As a young woman, deep down, she'd been afraid that if she disappointed him he'd leave her just like her mother had.

But she'd grown up. She wasn't going to be the compliant, unquestioning daughter he wanted her to be. She was going to be the woman she always wanted to be. She straightened her spine and kept her voice firm. "Let me go. You're hurting me."

He must have sensed her resolve hardening, because he released her. "I don't want to treat you like a child, Ivy, but your recent behavior worries me. You never would have turned to anyone but me before this."

"I never would have had to." She held his gaze despite the intimidation she felt, facing him down. "You've kept things from me. You and Ryan both did. I think I always sensed that you were doing things you shouldn't be, but I was content to be left in the dark. You were all I had and I didn't want to think the worst of you. Now that a light is shining on our family, illuminating the truth, I realize that, at some point, I have to protect my own interests. If I have to be a bad daughter in your eyes to be a good woman in mine, then so be it."

She was a means to an end, Victor reminded himself as he watched Ivy return to the ballroom. She moved with grace, stopping to play a round of blackjack or blow on the dice at the craps table.

Robert Stone didn't follow. In fact, he never reentered the room, which was just fine with Victor. He wasn't ready to play his trump card yet. The drama mask was only the beginning. Those were only steps to keep Ivy on edge. And then he'd push her over. He'd be quick about it. She wouldn't feel any pain. Not that Robert Stone had spared Victor or his loved ones pain when he'd gone after them using Redemption Club resources.

Yes, David Wilson had died that fateful day eight years ago in the car wreckage, along with his wife and child, but David's death had only been a spiritual one. It had only been the beginning of a painful, horrendous, lonely journey that had brought him to this point.

Unfortunately, Joanna and Nathan would never come back. After weeks of recovery for his broken body, David had emerged a new man, quite literally. He'd chosen the name Victor del Fuego, loosely translated to *victory over the fire.* He'd been thrown from the burning car that had consumed his entire family, but the fire had gotten him anyway.

It burned hot and furious in his gut. It demanded vengeance.

If fellow Club founder and friend Tom Hamilton hadn't found out what Robbie had planned and arrived at the crash scene first, then helped get Victor to safety and arranged the scene to make it look like there'd been a third body, Victor might not have survived.

But Victor hadn't exactly been an innocent. As a founder, he'd once wielded as much wealth and power via Redemption Club as Robbie or Tom had. Ivy was at least partially innocent. Her raw emotions, before she'd hidden them away, had been convincing enough in the car yesterday. Unfortunately, war often resulted in civilian casualties. Besides, killing her was the only way to take everything from Stone, just as Stone had taken from him. Victor intended to destroy anything related to Stone's so-called legacy.

Ivy. Redemption Club. Robbie himself.

He'd wipe any trace of them from this earth.

But not tonight. He'd swiped a housekeeping cart to deliver his little gift to Ivy earlier, a reminder of her past. His partner had told him to write *0512* on the mask as a message, but hadn't told him the significance of the number. Whatever it meant, it had worked. Ivy seemed shaken, as did her father, beneath his polished smoothness.

Damn, it was good to finally take pride in his work, in who he was, again. Robbie Stone wasn't the only one burning to leave a legacy behind.

CHAPTER NINE

"You failed to identify a threat," Robert Stone snarled at Archer the moment the man entered his penthouse suite. His private investigator, threat neutralizer, and troubleshooter all-in-one had failed in a big way. The charity event was still going on thirty floors below, but Stone couldn't stomach any more social interaction tonight. Not after his daughter had dared to throw her lack of trust and loyalty in his face.

"And which threat would that be?" Again, Archer moved around Stone's den as if he were at home. "Devlin Grimm is only a threat if you let him be. You said you'd handle Ivy and make it clear she couldn't hire Dev."

"I'm not talking about Devlin Grimm. What the devil did Douglas Rains intend by soliciting my daughter?"

Archer nodded. "Ah. Manny told you what he saw. I did see Rains chatting Ivy up downstairs, but he left. Did she say what their conversation was about?"

"No, but Manny overheard something that sounded like Rains was willing to exchange information for sexual favors. That's unacceptable, and a direct insult to my family."

"Since Rains is a close, personal friend of yours, Ivy probably didn't want to say anything. But she's not the timid type. She can stand up for herself."

"Or she's interested in whatever information he has to offer." Stone hated that he couldn't trust anyone, not even his own lawyer or daughter. "Did you find out why she wants to hire Grimm?"

"Not yet, but I will."

"What could Doug be thinking, going against me?"

"When I gave him back his Club card as you requested, he seemed a little smug. Maybe he's behind the threats to Ivy."

"Impossible." Except that it was entirely possible. Doug knew things about Stone that only a trusted legal advisor with a strict confidentiality policy and a debt owed to the Club should know. Now that Doug's debt had been cleared by helping Stone beat the charges against him, perhaps he'd gained a little too much confidence. Why was everyone around him so un-fucking-reliable?

Of course, Stone knew as well as any other businessman how easy it was to buy a person's loyalty. Greed was a powerful motivator. But fear of retribution should be just as motivating.

"You think Doug would cross me?" he asked Archer.

Archer shrugged. "Whether the man knows anything or not, he's overstepping his bounds with your daughter. He may need to be dealt with."

"And you're just the man for the job."

"That's why you keep me around. I don't mind dirty hands—in exchange for favors." Archer toasted him with his drink.

"Could it be Doug who turned the ledger pages over to the police?"

"And then defend you against the charges?" Archer laughed. "Until today, I wouldn't have said the guy had the balls, but after propositioning your daughter…"

"If he's our snitch, does he have more to offer them?" One of those missing pages detailed what he'd done to kill off his competition—David Wilson and his family. Perfect blackmail fodder for anyone wanting to tear him apart—or alienate his daughter.

"The emails in Ivy's account date back several weeks, and they appear to be from Nathan Wilson."

Stone froze. "Nathan Wilson can't be alive."

"No," Archer agreed. "And Ivy doesn't believe he's alive, either."

"Then who's sending her these emails?" Again, Stone had to wonder why Ivy hadn't come to him sooner. Stone counted on her to be the one steady thing in his life. Honest and devoted. Or maybe she hadn't given the emails any credibility.

Archer examined the liquid in his glass. "Judging by their content, someone wants to torture your daughter in a more emotional way. And it's definitely someone who knows the details of their relationship."

"Trace the IP address. I want to know who's posing as a dead man. And then I want him to *be* a dead man. And Ivy has to be taught a lesson—just enough to remind her of her place." He only wanted her scared enough to come to him, her father, begging on her knees for his help and guidance—as it should be. Somehow, over the past year, she'd lost sight of how important he was to her.

Ivy moved through the party with cheeks that ached from her ever-present false smile, watching for an opportunity to escape to her office and pop a headache pill to ease the tension of the night. Not that it would help her sort out the mess in her head. She needed time and space to think about all the strange interactions of the evening. Her father was his usual, controlling self, but he'd gone over the line. As had Rains. His odd offer to trade information for the use of her body had thrown off her equilibrium. What information could he possibly have that would warrant such a proposal? And was it the kind of information Dev was looking for, the kind that would take down her father? She'd wanted to avoid getting in the middle of that war, but the more time she spent around her father, and around Dev, the more she wanted to help Dev.

Her mind whirled with the possibilities, but the thought of calling Rains and asking him to clarify what kind of information he had made her shudder with revulsion. If he expected sexual favors for the information he supposedly had, she wasn't willing to trade. But there had to be some way to make an acceptable deal with him. Hell, maybe it would lead to the information Dev wanted, the information that would take down Redemption Club.

And then there was her father, who seemed threatened by her association with Dev. He had good reason to feel that way, but there'd been more than distrust in his eyes; there'd been barely controlled fury. She rubbed at her arms, where his fingers had left bruises. Good thing the marks were faint yet, or she'd have had to explain them away to her guests. Anger and hurt warred within. She'd never been anything but loyal to her father—until recently, anyway—but she did harbor a secret she'd protect to her grave.

Finally, there was Dev. He and Jared had disappeared quickly after her father had interrupted. Would they reappear this evening? More likely, Dev would return when she least expected it. But maybe she should cancel her contract with him. He would get caught in the middle, and very likely hurt, if she used him to make her escape.

She glanced at the noise and laughter around her, feeling both fatigued and amped up at the same time. The steady pounding against her skull amplified as a shout went up from the nearby roulette table.

She ignored her pain and reminded herself why she was doing this. A good cause. A great one, in fact. So many unclaimed children would benefit from this night. Children without the gift of unconditional love. She could relate. Her own parents' love had a high price tag.

Suddenly, her raging headache would no longer be denied. She could barely move without wincing. With a glance toward where Manny stood a few yards away, she judged the distance to the ladies room. She could excuse herself to go inside, then duck down the side hall instead. Manny would be left guarding the door to an empty restroom. A stab of unease was quickly erased by her need to be alone. She was surrounded by her hotel, by her employees, by people within shouting distance if she needed help.

A few minutes later, she'd done just that and was hurrying across the skywalk that led from the meeting center where the ballroom was located to the main hub of the Legacy complex. The rotunda was one of her favorite places, filled with light and color even at this time of night. During the day, the sunlight streamed through the twenty-foot diameter glass dome, with dark blue, magenta, and purple stained glass panels around the circumference. In the evening, colored lights created an ethereal effect across the white marble floor. Twelve white marble pillars, each one identical to the symbol of the hotel, stood like sentries on a clock face around the edge of the rotunda. It was impressive, but then her father never did anything halfway.

Tonight, even the soft lights were murder on her headache. Or maybe that was the noise from the casino on the other side of the hub. She needed to find a safe, quiet escape. A place to hide before Manny discovered she was missing. She didn't want an audience if she was about to break down.

She passed the entrance to the casino and moved toward the check-in counter. The main offices were hidden by a massive wall with *Legacy* written in giant, elegant, silver letters, and she made her way around the back. But instead of fleeing to her office, where Manny and anyone else was likely to look for her, on impulse, she took a sharp right into a wide hallway labeled Legacy Theater.

Like many of the larger casinos in Vegas, Legacy hosted a regular entertainment venue. At this late hour, the Saturday evening performance had wrapped, and the theater was empty except for the cleanup crew. She slid into a seat in the shadowy back row and massaged her temples, wishing she'd grabbed some medicine from her office first. But having a place to retreat, where nobody was watching her every move, was worth the pain.

"Keeping your shields in place must be exhausting," Dev's voice said.

She jumped in surprise and the pounding worsened. She shot a glare toward where he stood, observing her from the aisle beside her row. He was alone this time. "I thought you'd left for the evening."

"It pays to keep my eyes open, ready for anything. You should do the same." His hands were in his pockets, nonthreatening, but she was anything but relaxed. Besides, his stance made his dress shirt stretch across his wide shoulders in a way that had her swallowing hard. He'd removed his tuxedo jacket and tie, and even undone a button at his throat. How could a man's neck seem so sexy? And why was she tempted to press her nose to the skin there and breathe him in? But his next words were like a slap to the face. "Or maybe you're not really worried because there is no threat. Maybe you enjoy playing your father and me off each other. Are you using me, princess?"

Something in her chest lurched and tightened, but she swallowed it down and held his gaze. "I'm going to ignore that, because you have every right to distrust me."

He arched an ebony brow at that.

"Just as I have every right to distrust you," she added.

"You don't seem particularly worried."

"Help is only a shout away." She glanced at the two people sweeping the stage and aisles as if to prove her point, but they had their earbuds in and hadn't even seen her, let alone Dev, arrive.

Dev didn't look away. Of course, a man like him would be aware of his surroundings at all times. "They'd never get here in time." The promise in his eyes sent shivers of delight across her skin, making her seriously doubt her sanity. "And I'm not the only threat out there, at least, according to you. You should pay more attention."

"I was distracted," she admitted.

"Busy pretending everything's okay when your family is crumbling around you. Your brother dies, your father is arrested and nearly goes to prison for the rest of his life. And yet, not one civil case has been filed. Funny how he got out of that so easily."

She pressed her fingertips to her throbbing temples. "I don't need a trip down memory lane. If you're going to kidnap me, let's get on with it."

He grinned slyly. "I told you, I'm in charge. You don't get to set the schedule for your own abduction. That would be like organizing your own surprise party."

"Well, if you're not here to fulfill our agreement, why did you follow me?"

He came closer, filling her vision with his large frame before he dropped into the chair beside her, his muscles bunching and shifting with every movement. His biceps and long thigh aligned with her body, and heat flooded her. Even through their layers of clothing, she felt parts of her perk up with interest in a way that hadn't happened in nearly a decade.

Not since Nathan's death had she been interested in a man sexually. Oh, she'd tried, wanting to feel normal and whole again, but she'd eventually given up when she hadn't felt the spark, figuring she'd used up those hormones long ago. And figuring it was for the best. Nathan's death and all that came after had sucked the energy right out of her. Forming a relationship—or an attachment of any kind—took drive. Instead, she'd channeled her energy into earning a degree that could help her make her mark on the world—via Legacy.

After years of numbness and loneliness, she'd eventually realized her grief and depression had been mistaken for a bitchy disposition. It had been easier to nurture the image, as it served her well, protecting her, than to try to open herself to another intimate connection with someone. But now? Now, there was a definite thaw—at a most inconvenient time.

His body tightened as if he fought a similar reaction. "I don't know why I'm here, other than I had to find you. When I saw you head away from the ballroom, I was worried."

"Oh." That was sweet, and the tenderness tugged at more places inside that had been shut away. This time, it was her heart that opened.

He studied her carefully. "You still look a little shaken. Is it about the man who approached you, Douglas Rains? Or was it the way your father whisked you out of the ballroom so fast and furious that everyone was left in your dust?" Unconsciously, she rubbed her arms, feeling the soreness where her father's fingers had been. At her motion, Dev scowled. "Did he hurt you?"

Maybe someone *could* see past her defenses. Then again, Devlin Grimm had a reputation as a damn good investigator, as well as a security contractor who'd worked in some of the most dangerous places on earth. He ought to be able to see past any façade.

His scowl deepened as the silence between them stretched on. "I figured the man was capable of horrible things, but I never thought he'd harm his own daughter."

"I'm fine." Her voice was too brittle. "Do you think Dad had something to do with your brother's imprisonment?"

He eyed her carefully. "I have no idea, but I'll be looking into it, for sure."

"You said Dad's done things to your family

before?"

Dev shook his head. "Again, I have no proof, but my money's on Redemption Club thugs. There have been a few suspicious occurrences at the ranch."

As she frowned, her headache renewed its onslaught. She forced the muscles in her face to relax.

His brows drew together as he studied her. "You're hurting."

"I'm okay," she insisted, not wanting to share how disturbing she found his theories. More and more, it appeared she'd defended a guilty man for months. Years. "Just tired and I have a headache. I needed to unwind for a few moments."

"Here?"

She followed his gaze around the theater. "I like it here. It reminds me of happy times."

"You miss being an actress." The soft understanding in his voice nearly undid her.

"The theater is a part of my past, not my present or future."

"You sure about that? You would have made a great one."

He was probably right. Yet, she bristled at the subtle dig that she could use her skills to convince, pretend, and deceive.

"Hey," he said, breaking through her thoughts. "You don't have to act with me. You can be yourself."

Could she? Even while part of her yearned for him to understand her, to see her on a deeper level, it was hard to let down her defenses. She feared that if she let him in he wouldn't like what he saw. At the very least, she could fill him in on the less emotional details of her life. "Earlier, before I came down, I received another threat. Or maybe it was a message."

He straightened in his seat. "Another email?"

"Not this time." This time, the stalker had come physically close to her again. "Before I left my suite this evening, I saw a Greek players' style tragedy-comedy mask hanging on the wall, in my foyer. It rattled me."

And made her think of her time with Nathan, which stirred up a whole host of disturbing memories. "It also made me realize that this guy can get to me—anytime, anywhere. So why should I waste my time worrying?"

"Your stalker again? Inside your suite?" Obviously, Dev's thoughts had run the same path as hers.

"It must have been."

"Was there a message with it?"

She thought of the numbers written on the inside of the mask, but shook her head. That was a different type of message, a personal one, and she wasn't ready to share it with Dev. His fingers shifted from his thigh to hers, and he squeezed her hand where it rested there. The gesture was one of support, but it made her heart beat harder.

"I should give you my threats folder, too," she said.

He let out a soft laugh. "You have a threats folder?"

"In my office. I printed out every email or scrawled phone message and highlighted the dates they were received, as well as any names, if the sender gave one."

"Are you always so organized?"

"Always." She pressed her lips together to keep from defending herself. At least the look he was giving her was amused and intrigued, not judgmental. "Organization is what keeps me feeling like I'm not going to go completely insane on a regular basis. Besides, the police advised me to start documenting everything."

His amusement fled, replaced with concern. His fingers squeezed hers. "So, you did go to the police."

"Legacy has received more than its share of threats since Ryan's criminal behavior last year." Apparently, her brother's death didn't equal a pound of flesh in some people's eyes. "But after the first few times I reported the threats, I got the distinct impression nobody would help us."

"And the more personal threats? The ones that were supposedly from Nathan?"

"You had to have known Nathan—or our relationship—to know the subtle significance of these emails. Whoever sent them definitely knew one of us at that time."

He waited for her to continue, but to do so would bring up past hurts long buried. Still, it might help to have an unbiased opinion. She hadn't gone to her father with those emails because he would have either brushed them off as nonsense or railed about her indiscretions with Nathan, and how wrong she'd been. She'd definitely heard enough of that spiel. She'd thought it wiser to go to the police with the general threats. The ones supposedly from Nathan, she'd kept to herself—until yesterday.

"Have you replied to any of the emails?"

"No. I figured if I left it alone, whoever was doing this would just stop."

"But they didn't. From the emails you forwarded me, it appears they started arriving about six months ago."

"Yes. The first was on Nathan's birthday. But that date is a matter of public record. It wouldn't be difficult for someone to find that information."

"And the other emails? Were their dates significant?"

"Yes. One was on the date we first..." She looked away, feeling embarrassed with him.

"Made love?" he guessed, his voice softer. The heat of his hand against hers, so close to her inner thigh, suddenly intensified, though it was probably only in her mind.

She nodded. "Only he and I would have known the significance of that date." She frowned, considering the other ways someone might have known. "Or if one of our fathers had us followed. It happened at Alpha Omega. We'd been spending nearly all of our time at the theater that summer before senior year of college."

"You were both majoring in drama?"

"At the time, yes. After Nathan died, I decided to go the more practical route."

"Bet your father loved his daughter following in his footsteps." The sarcasm rang clear in his tone.

"He did, but there was more to it." She recalled the shock of learning nearly a year after Nathan's death, after she'd left home, that her infallible father needed help. "I got a call that Dad had had a heart attack. It scared me."

"Right into coming home."

"Yes. He was more supportive than he'd ever been, telling me I could take over Legacy one day. Maybe even inherit all of Stone Corp." Over the years, Ivy had come to recognize how her father had capitalized on her period of grief and confusion, steering her toward his dreams for her. She didn't regret what she'd learned and accomplished in the business realm, but in her heart, she missed the release that acting had provided. Her time at Alpha Omega had been the first and only time she'd felt free of family pressures.

But her father had felt threatened by her newfound freedom, Ivy now realized. Before Nathan's death, her father seemed to guard her like precious gold, questioning where she went, and with whom she spent her time. She'd been annoyed, had decided she was in college and didn't have to answer to her father or follow his rules, so she'd found ways to sneak around. Besides, her half-brother Ryan had been slyly disobeying their father for years without recrimination. She'd taken a few tips from his playbook.

Dev studied her a long moment, as if judging his next words. "Anybody Nathan may have bragged to would have known about the day you had sex, too."

"He wouldn't have bragged," Ivy said. "Our relationship wasn't like that. We both wanted to keep it secret."

"You're that certain you could trust him?"

"Yes."

"And you're certain he's not faking his death."

Dev suppressed a flinch as Ivy's eyes flashed. So, Nathan was still a sore spot for her, years later.

An unexpected jolt of jealousy snaked through him. She must have loved Nathan deeply. Or perhaps her young love had been glorified and amplified in her mind over the years. According to Dev's research, Nathan Wilson had been killed along with his parents, David and Joanna Wilson, in a car accident along California's Highway 1. The trip had been an opportunity for Nathan to audition for a big name director and his parents had come along for support. David Wilson had been one of Robert Stone's good friends for years, so close that they'd started Redemption Club together, along with the third in their trio, Tom Hamilton. Their fathers' friendship had to be why the two young lovers, Nathan and Ivy, had entered each other's orbits.

He watched her carefully as he posed his question. "You're sure these emails couldn't have been from Nathan? Maybe he's still alive, using wigs and makeup to disguise his identity."

A soft sound of distress emerged from deep within her throat. "He's gone. I'm sure of it." She pressed her fingers to her temples again.

"Got it." If he could save her the pain of recalling the details, perhaps going easy on her was acceptable at this time. Until he needed more pieces of the puzzle. "I've looked over the emails you forwarded, but I'd like to see that file so I can review the other threats." He pulled his hand away from hers as she stood. Funny, but he'd forgotten he'd been holding her hand. It had seemed so natural to comfort her.

He accompanied her to her office, where she pulled an accordion file from a desk drawer as he perused the room. There was a noted lack of clutter, but also few items to indicate her personality. It seemed Ivy actively cultivated that cold, untouchable image in her business dealings. The only splashes of color and personality were reserved for her home life— and, on the rare occasion, for him. The thought gave him a ridiculously smug satisfaction.

He flipped through the file, stopping at the pages she'd flagged with sticky notes. They were from Nathan—or at least, they claimed to be. He'd read them already, but perused them again as Ivy moved behind her desk and sifted through another drawer, coming up with a bottle of aspirin.

"Do these read like they're from Nathan?" he asked as he reread one of the more recent emails she'd forwarded him from *NWilson.* "Not saying he's still alive—I'm just wondering how close this person could have been to Nathan. This one mentions taking you away to start a new family, based on unconditional love, like you always wanted." A veiled threat, he supposed, but it could also be an admirer wanting to fill Nathan's shoes for her, to take Ivy for himself. A tug of protectiveness pulled at Dev.

Shutters came over her eyes, and for a moment, she looked like she wouldn't respond. "Yes, Nathan and I had discussed leaving town and starting fresh somewhere else, away from the pressures of our families." She tossed back the pills and chased them with a swallow from a glass of water.

"Did you two have any idea what your fathers were up to, that they'd been involved in Redemption Club?" He arched a brow, waiting for her to condemn herself. After all, why else would she want to *escape* her rich-kid life? In the media and with the police, she'd always claimed she didn't know anything about Redemption Club, or her family's involvement in it.

"It was more like a feeling that we were under someone else's control. My father can be..." She stopped and swallowed, clearly hesitant to condemn her father even after what he'd put her through. Dev's gaze moved to her arms, bared by the sleeveless dress, and his anger intensified as he spied the faint shadows, the beginnings of bruises, on her skin.

"He can be what?" He heard the dark danger in his tone but didn't temper it.

Her gaze flicked to his. "Domineering."

"I suppose that makes him a good businessman. And a lousy father."

"Yes, but I was young, going through a rebellious phase. Besides, that's his personality. He grew up with nothing, so accumulating wealth and protecting what he's built means everything to him."

"Don't make excuses, Ivy." He reached out and lightly traced a fingertip over the bruises. She shivered but didn't pull away. "He shouldn't be able to get away with being a bully."

"My mother left when I was young because she couldn't take it. She wanted a better life, and was willing to sell me out to get it."

"Sell you out?"

"I found out later, when my father found it convenient to throw it in my face, that my mother signed a contract with him, agreeing to leave me in his care. In exchange, she could pursue an acting career and Dad helped her land juicy roles." Disgust and hurt flashed in her eyes and his gut twisted in sympathy. "I was four years old."

He muttered a curse. She'd been so young when her mother had left. He knew what that felt like, and the kind of scars it could leave on one's soul. That burning in one's chest to make a mark on the world because one always felt less than enough.

She released a harsh laugh. "I was naïve, always hoping she'd come back. Then, when I was a barely a teen, my nanny was suddenly gone one day. My father said it was time for me to grow up and be more self-sufficient."

"That was Linda Castillo, the woman who's

house I saw you at?"

"We reconnected recently. Said my dad simply let her go one day and forbid her to have further contact with me."

"Bastard. She probably had a closer relationship with you than he did, and he was jealous. I hope you're starting to see how controlling he is. It's not healthy."

She looked away. "A couple years after Linda left, Ryan revealed his mother had been bought off when my mother came along and the great Robert Stone saw something he wanted more. Ryan realized earlier than I did that it was hopeless to try to win our father's love. He found ways to escape, sort of, until he embraced an alternative lifestyle."

"His partying?"

"Yes. And, I suppose, his revamping of the Club, behind my father's back, when my father had supposedly abandoned the idea years ago."

Dev didn't point out that she seemed to be coming around to the idea that her father was involved in Redemption Club. A spark of hope lit up inside him—hope that she'd finally see the truth.

"I went the other direction," Ivy continued, "doing whatever my father asked." A note of bitterness crept into her tone, though her features were still carefully composed. He had the urge to smash the marble façade she hid behind and see her true emotions. They were there, lurking beneath the surface, and they resonated with something deep inside of him.

But there were reasons they'd each developed their stone façades and he would allow her the defense—for now.

"Until you met Nathan," Dev said when her thoughts seemed to drift away. "Was your relationship a secret?"

"At first, but it was hard to keep anything from our fathers."

"And then?"

"They tried to keep us apart. I think that audition the day of Nathan's and his parents' deaths had been set up by his father. He was trying to get Nathan to leave Vegas and get out in the world more. Even made the trip into a sort of family vacation and gave him the sports car. Perhaps my father didn't approve of our relationship, but he wasn't the only one. Mr. Wilson went to great lengths to try to keep us apart, too." She hugged her arms around herself. He wondered if she even realized she was trying to comfort herself.

His lips twisted wryly. "But young love couldn't be denied, perhaps even beyond death."

Her sharp gaze cut him in two. "Something like that." She sighed, suddenly looking exhausted.

He worried about the fatigue in her eyes. "You need to rest. I'll escort you to your suite. I'd like to get a look at that mask, anyway. Is the charity event over?"

"Yes. At least, my part in it is done." She'd already said thank you to the crowd and personally said good night to the highest of the high rollers. A small smile tugged at her lips. "But no, thank you, on the personal escort. I'll bring the mask to you in the morning. Besides, it appears Manny's found me. He'll insist on escorting me." Her gaze moved past him to the doorway, where, sure enough, her bodyguard stood, glaring at him.

Dev reached out to tuck a strand of hair behind Ivy's ear, unable to resist brushing his fingers across the smooth, creamy skin of her cheek. Whether she realized it or not, she'd just told him everything he needed to know about how to get past her defenses.

CHAPTER TEN

Ivy jumped when the phone on her desk rang, and the notion of turning her cheek into Dev's warm fingers was quickly dismissed. He dropped his hand as she stepped away to reach for the phone.

"Three guesses who that is," Dev said, casting an accusatory look at Manny.

Dev was right. The caller ID listed her father's suite number. Her arms throbbed along with her headache at the memory of how he'd manhandled her just a couple hours ago. Still, she answered with a crisp hello.

"Join me for a cocktail," her father ordered. "Both you and Dev."

"No, thank you," she refused, the politeness in her tone so cold it could cause frostbite. "I've had quite enough excitement this evening."

"It's not a request."

She stiffened, every instinct in her demanding she scream and fight, but she couldn't let emotion rule her, especially with Dev watching her carefully. "Can whatever this is really about wait until morning?"

"No. There are some things we need to settle. Tonight."

She pulled the phone away from her ear to answer the question in Dev's eyes. "He wants us to come up for a night cap."

"I could use a drink," Dev said. She didn't trust the dark twinkle in his eye. It seemed the population in Power-struggle Town was about to increase by one.

Into the phone, she said, "We'll be right up," and

hung up without waiting for her father's response. "You've got your guard up, right?" she asked Dev as they breezed past Manny, who quickly fell in line behind them, and headed for the bank of elevators.

"Always," Dev said, shooting her an anticipatory grin.

"Masochist," she muttered under her breath as she slid her keycard into the slot. His soft chuckle surprised her, and sent warmth flooding through her body.

As they rode to the thirtieth floor, they didn't speak with Manny and his big ears—which were connected to a big mouth—listening in.

At the end of the long hall, she paused at the door to her father's suite. "You're sure?" she asked Dev again.

His gaze was steady. "I can handle myself."

Archer answered her knock. His expression was blatantly disapproving as it moved from her to Dev, and she squared her shoulders. She didn't owe Archer any explanation. She strode past him and found her father in the living room beyond, looking more jovial than she'd expected. What could he possibly want to say to her with Dev, Manny, and Archer in attendance? Her alert level shifted to DEFCON Four.

"Have a drink with us," her father said to Dev, pouring three whiskies without waiting for him to respond. Then again, most people did whatever Robert Stone wanted them to do. What's more, he had a way of making them believe their actions had been their choice all along.

Dev reached past her and claimed a drink, handing it to her before taking his own. His gaze warmed slightly when it landed on her. Maybe she'd imagined a new sense of camaraderie between them, but their awkward relationship seemed to have shifted over the last twenty-four hours. Perhaps there were even the beginnings of a foundation of trust.

Dev clearly didn't trust her father, though. He

didn't drink from the glass, he simply held it. It was probably wise not to indulge, anyway. They'd need to be on their toes around her father. Again, that prickle of forewarning raised the hairs on her scalp.

"Was there something specific you wanted to talk to me about?" she asked when several long seconds had passed without a word. "Because it's been a long night."

Her father pursed his lips. "I'm disappointed."

"So you told me earlier."

"That was before I knew what you were really up to."

More alarm bells clanged in her head. Her gaze shot to Dev. During their meeting earlier, had he told her father about her kidnapping plan? Dev only frowned.

"Disappointed in what, specifically?" she asked.

"Your recent choices. Some of your decisions have been rather questionable." His pointed gaze landed on Dev. "I know you hired him, just as I know what you hired him for." He reached into a drawer and pulled out a legal pad—*her* legal pad. The alarms in her head went quiet, replaced by a total silence that was so much more ominous. Her future, laid out in a step-by-step action list, was in her father's hands. And she knew then that he'd crush her dreams.

"You searched my suite?" Her fingers clenched around her glass. She wanted to slam it down on the coffee table, snatch her personal property away, and walk out, but she didn't dare. She aimed a glare at Archer, whom she was certain had violated her privacy. Had he been the one to leave the mask, too?

"You were planning to disappear," her father accused. "Forever, by the looks of this. You were going to contract new identity papers?" He clucked his tongue at her and she bristled. Thank God she'd hidden the documents she'd paid thousands of dollars for in another location, or he would have flaunted those, too. She breathed out slowly, taking a moment to relax in the knowledge that her options for the future were still open—until she realized that Dev had gone completely still beside her.

Damn. She'd been considering telling him about her plan to disappear, hoping Dev could help her, but none of that mattered now.

The truth was out, and the truth was damning. The delicate seedlings of trust were crushed beneath her father's boot. The list made it look like she was just as manipulative as her father. Explaining that she'd never intended to go through with that level of deception would only sound hollow.

Her father went back to the drawer to retrieve a manila folder. "I suppose it's a good thing I didn't give you this. Knowing what's inside here might have messed up all of your precious plans for a new life. As a reward for your loyalty and hard work, I'd decided to sign over Legacy's ownership to you years earlier than planned."

Her heart throbbed against her ribs. The organ seemed to have swelled to fill her body. She was caught between her old dreams and her new ones, neither of which seemed attainable now. Her independence, her inheritance, her legacy—all of it was at her father's fingertips. Always had been. He had the choice to extend his hand to her to offer help, or to curl his fingers and crush her in his fist.

He waved the folder and her eyes followed the movement, her heart sinking as he walked to the fireplace, where a fire was burning. Her entire body was frozen, only her eyes able to move. Was it just her, or was every occupant in the room holding their breaths? Even if she'd wanted to say something, she couldn't. Her throat wouldn't work. Her vocal chords had frozen with an internal, soundless scream of protest.

He tossed the folder into the fire as if it were kindling. The flames roared up, consuming her future.

No, not your future. You'd decided to leave.

Her father's grim expression was nearly

fanatical in the flickering light. He seemed to be waiting for her reaction to his cruel gesture. She wouldn't give him the satisfaction.

"With this," he said, thrusting the legal pad toward her, but keeping it just out of reach. She didn't grab for it, or even look at it. "You gave me the perfect way to get Devlin Grimm out of our lives. I knew there had to be a reason you were looking to hire Dev. Just as I suspected he didn't have the full story, either. You were going to use him." Without taking his eyes from her, he shoved the pad toward Dev.

Dev stood there a long moment before accepting the offering and scanning it. When she finally braved a look his way, his expression was unreadable.

She swallowed down a sudden wave of nausea and anger before she spoke to her father. "And you wonder why I can't come to you when I need anything."

"Your plans were a fantasy," her father said, his tone colder than she'd ever heard it. "You'll never leave. This man, our *enemy*, certainly isn't going to help you. Not after he realizes that you were manipulating him. Sorry to disappoint you, darling." His words twisted with bitterness and anger, and no small amount of disgust.

Disappointed? The word slammed through her skull until she thought she might vomit from the emotions it stirred. She'd spent her whole life trying to please Robert Stone—and had nothing to show for it. Not even a loving family. Disappointment was much too shallow a descriptor.

She glanced toward Dev, but he was staring at the evidence as if he might burn a hole through it. She wished it would go up in flames as much as the Legacy paperwork had.

She set her drink on the table and headed for the door. Archer and Manny hadn't moved a muscle, but they had to have heard every humiliating word.

"Don't you dare walk away from me," her father roared. She kept walking. "I'm not finished with you.

You won't get what you want by leaving me. You'll never be free of the Stone name. I keep what's mine."

That stopped her in her tracks. She gritted her teeth, shoved her anger down deep until she shook with the need to control it, and mentally counted to ten. Slowly, she turned back to him.

"You were never going to give me control of Legacy," she said. "It would have severed every bond you had that held me in my place, directly under your thumb. Now that I know where things stand, there's nothing keeping me here. You broke us just as effectively by calling me out as you would have by keeping your secrets. Besides, you're not the only one with resources. I know someone who knows your secrets and is willing to talk."

Her father's grin twisted her stomach. The bastard knew what he was doing to her, and apparently he hadn't played all of his cards yet. "If you're talking about Douglas Rains, he's been let go. You won't have to deal with him or his lascivious propositions anymore. You're welcome. I've freed you of all those things that distract you. You can go now, back to your suite. Think carefully about how you want to proceed, because no daughter of mine will walk away without consequences. There's a price for disloyalty."

She glanced toward Dev, but his scowl reminded her of last night, when she'd left the courthouse and seen only judgment and anger from his position across the street. Whether he was angry with her, or her father, or both, she didn't know. She didn't expect any sympathy from him.

"I'm leaving town tomorrow," her father continued, seemingly oblivious to the fury churning inside of her, "but Monday morning, I'll expect a plan as to how you're going to make this up to me."

She'd gone numb all over. Uncertain her legs would hold her, she took a step, then another, toward the door. Relieved when her knees didn't buckle, she took another few steps and grasped the knob.

I am secure in who I am. She mentally recited the mantra more as a reminder than to assert herself. No matter what the future brought, she had to be certain of her goal, and her ability to make it happen.

She kept her eyes forward as she made it into the hall, forcing herself not to break into a run as she heard Manny, the dutiful guard dog, following. She wouldn't show any weakness. She couldn't. Her pride was all she had left, and that was one thing she wouldn't let her father touch.

As the door to Stone's suite closed behind Manny, Dev's gut told him to go after Ivy, but she'd seemed so untouchable. No, not untouchable. Fragile. As if, had he approached her, she would have fractured. And she'd never forgive him if he watched her break, especially in front of her father.

The bastard had enjoyed posturing, manipulating her emotions to bring her to heel.

But if Stone wasn't lying—and Ivy's reaction suggested he wasn't—Dev had a lot to consider. He'd already suspected Ivy's request to be kidnapped had an ulterior motive, but to completely disappear? He couldn't say he blamed her for wanting to start a new life, but he was surprised by the extent of her desperation, and that she'd carry through with such a risky plan. She'd be giving up everything—the business, her legacy, her wealth and status. His gaze went to the fireplace, where all that remained of her claim to Legacy Hotel and Casino lay in ashes.

He gripped the legal pad tighter in his hand. The list was amateurish. It could have just been dreamy doodling. But she had a checkmark next to *obtain new identity documents.* So she must have taken steps at some point to make her dream a reality.

And Dev had fallen right into her trap. He'd become one of those steps she would check off and discard once she'd gotten what she needed from him.

Hell, perhaps she'd meant him to go to prison for her kidnapping, but somehow that didn't ring true.

He shifted his attention to Robert Stone, who was sitting back, enjoying his drink with one ankle resting on the opposite knee, watching the financial news with his buddy Archer as if he hadn't just wrecked his daughter's life, hadn't just hammered at Ivy's pride with everything he had.

"Was there even anything in that folder?" Dev asked Stone, stepping between the man and the television. Archer's smirk was his answer. "You made it up. There was no contract, signing over Legacy to her, was there?" And Dev had been made a witness to her humiliation to make the slap to her pride all the more painful. He'd been used by both father and daughter tonight. Anger simmered beneath the calm surface he fought to maintain, but he refused to let Stone see that he'd gotten to him.

Stone shrugged. "The end justifies the means. She won't go up against me again. And it would serve you well to learn that lesson, too. The minute you no longer served a purpose, she walked away."

"Feel better now that you've got her back on your leash?" Dev asked.

Stone's eyes narrowed. "I'm aware of the attributes my daughter brings to the table, but they're not worth going up against *me*. Not worth you or your family getting hurt."

"Not worth you hurting your family over, either, I would think. But I guess you and I don't think the same." Thank God.

Stone sat forward, elbows on knees, and eyed Dev. "I have the power to annihilate her. Remember that."

Hadn't the man just done that? Dev had seen Ivy at her most cold and broken, but somehow that didn't make him feel any better about the situation. She'd obviously been in pain, a hurt she couldn't hide behind her defenses. Why the hell would a father want to break his daughter? What more could he have in his arsenal? "You'd do that, just to win?"

"To win against both you and her? Yes." If Stone was going to lose his daughter, it was clear it was going to be by his own hands. Such was his twisted need to control everyone and everything.

"I suppose any parent has the power to do that to his or her child." But why the fuck would they?

"An occasional lesson in humility is healthy, don't you think?" Apparently, the same rules didn't apply to Robert Stone, who believed his place was right at the top, where he could step on everyone else.

Disgusted, Dev shook his head. "You're going to lose your daughter."

"Not to you, I won't. I've warned you before to stay out of our family business."

"Unfortunately, your business taints all of Las Vegas. I won't stop until you're behind bars." But he wouldn't be able to talk sense into a man who viewed an evil underground club as a way to power and notoriety. And why did he care if the monster destroyed his relationship with his daughter?

Because Dev cared about Ivy, apparently.

With a few long strides, he was out the door, anxious to get away from Stone and his perverse schemes. Manny stood in the hall, opposite Ivy's door.

Dev should find another way to take Stone down. He should walk on by and take the elevator to the main level, exit the casino, and never look back.

He really should.

But he'd never been a man to avoid risk. When it came to Ivy Stone, he was apparently a slow learner.

Ivy had locked herself in her suite after dismissing Manny for the night. The guard had only smirked, given her an insolent salute, and taken up residence in the hallway. He obviously held no more respect for her than her father did.

God, what a fool she'd been. Robert Stone was infamous for setting traps and manipulating people to get what he wanted, but she'd thought she was exempt from his machinations. She'd thought he loved her. She should have known better, but hadn't wanted to face the truth. Sometimes, he exhibited a flare for drama that rivaled her mother's. She'd seen it enough times to dislike his business methods and decide she wanted to do things differently when she'd taken the helm. So why had she assumed she was immune to his scheming?

Had the file really contained what she'd wanted? For years, Legacy had been her life. She'd made it her life, needing something positive to focus on after her life plans had taken a sharp, traumatic detour in college. But now she wasn't sure what would make her happy, except to be free of this life.

She leaned forward on the bathroom counter, pressing her palms into the cold marble surface as she studied herself in the mirror. Her eyes were watery and red from resisting the hard cry she wanted to indulge in. Her body was begging to release the emotions pent up inside, but she was afraid she couldn't recover if she let go. She'd already lost so much of herself.

She splashed water on her face, changed into her most comfortable, softest pajama bottoms and a T-shirt, and was crossing to the kitchen to make a cup of tea when she heard the knock at her door. Her father? She'd had enough of his torture games for the night. For a lifetime.

But as she peeked through the peephole, she saw, not her father's salt-and-pepper hair, but a familiar, dark head. *Dev.*

She leaned her forehead against the door with a soft *thunk*. Was he here to give her hell for lying?

"I heard you," he said. "And your lap dog is out here, so I know you're in there. Open up."

She cracked open the door.

"We need to talk." Dev's expression held a hint of

danger. But what hit her square in the breastbone was the disappointment she read in his eyes.

She struggled to maintain the appearance of nonchalance. "Don't bother. You're released from your contract. I'll send you a check for the time you've already put in." She moved to close the door but he slapped the legal pad—*her* legal pad, with the damning evidence—against the door and pressed, stopping her from closing it on his face. Behind him, Manny pushed away from the wall, suddenly alert.

"I'm not going to stand in the hall and argue when your father's front door is only yards away, and his eyes and ears are even closer," Dev growled in a low voice that held a quiet anger. "Besides, I didn't get what I was promised."

Goosebumps erupted on her arms. She stared, disbelieving that he'd still want her help. But this wasn't a discussion she wanted Manny overhearing, and Dev apparently wasn't going anywhere until he said his piece. She opened the door and allowed him inside, then shut the door in Manny's scowling face and headed to the side table, withdrawing her checkbook and a pen from her purse.

"What are you doing?" he asked.

"Paying what I owe you for the time you've wasted on me." She handed him the check, disturbed to see how much it shook in her trembling fingers.

He took the check and tore it up, tossing the pieces on the table. "I'm fine without your money, princess. Besides, that wasn't our agreement. I was to test your security, fake-kidnap you, and you were going to keep your eyes and ears open for any information that could take down your father. With him behind bars, my family and the entire Las Vegas community will finally be safe." Dev's gaze landed on the wall to his right, narrowing on the mask that her stalker had nailed there.

"I can't help you take him down." She pushed past him and into her living room.

"On the contrary, you're the only one who can."

"Why would you want to stay involved with me? If I were you, I'd run the other way."

He surprised her by stepping close. He studied her eyes for a long minute, and when she met his gaze, his anger had been banked, leaving only a surprising amount of empathy in their hazel depths. Thankfully, there was no tenderness, only understanding. Otherwise, she might have shattered.

"Of course you'd expect that," he said softly. "That's the way everyone else in your life behaved. Your mother, Nathan, your half-brother—they all left you. Why would you think anyone would stand by you?"

As if she'd been sucker-punched, her chest constricted so suddenly that all the air left her lungs in a whoosh. Moisture pricked at the back of her eyelids and she pressed them together for a long moment to reel in her emotions. What was it about this man that he could so easily get past her defenses, could damn well see right through her?

"You should go, too," she finally managed, shaking her head so that his hand fell away from her chin. "I wouldn't blame you. I lied to you. I was going to use you." She grabbed the legal pad from his other hand and waved it in his face. "I was going to be free of all of this, and you would have had to face my dad's wrath when I was gone."

His lips curved. "And I was going to allow myself to be used, because I wanted to use you, too." His gaze flicked to her lips for a moment, but then he stepped away. "But just so we're on the same page, how about you tell me what you had planned. What, exactly, does that list mean? After all, the original deal was only a measly kidnapping." There was an edge to his voice again.

"I have new identity papers—"

"I won't even ask how you found someone to do that for you."

"—and a friend who wants me to run a lodge up

in Idaho for her. I can also live there, and it's a fairly remote area."

"So you thought nobody would find you?" He shook his head. "This friend is willing to work with you as this new identity?"

"Look, I know disappearing is out of my skillset. I was going to tell you about the plan once I trusted you. Hell, I was willing to take your advice on how to go about this the right way. But I have nothing to offer you in exchange and I realize that trust is broken now—"

Dev tossed the legal pad to the coffee table, freeing both hands to cup her face. Though his eyes sparked with anger, his grip was firm, but gentle. It didn't allow her to retreat, and any further words stuck in her throat. "I'll help you."

"But I don't have anything to give in return," she whispered, mesmerized by his expression as his gaze tracked his thumbs, which were tracing the curve of her bottom lip. She bit back a moan at the intimacy of the gesture. Would he kiss her again? Her lips vibrated with the need to feel him again. "What do you want from me?"

"I want the truth. I want to take down your father. I want your help. I want..." His gaze held hers as he closed the gap and claimed her lips. He was surprisingly tender—for about two seconds, before his eyes closed and need swamped them both. Hunger, tinged with anger and frustration, ignited the kiss.

He devoured her. There was no other word for it. And she didn't mind one bit, because she ached to be devoured, to belong to someone who wanted her. She moaned and opened to him, clutching his shirt as she tasted him. His tongue slid past her teeth, possessing her. His hands skimmed from her cheeks to her hair, gripping her head as if she might disappear.

One of them groaned, and the spell was broken. He abruptly pulled away, releasing her.

She took a step back and sucked in air, her scalp

still tingling from where his fingers slipped away. Her lips, wet with him, went from hot to cold in an instant now that they were bare.

Holy hell, the man could kiss. This was nothing like the kiss in the bar, when he'd been marking her as his to get at her dad. This was him actually staking a real claim. Even if he didn't know it, her body responded as if it were made for him.

But his words turned her cold again. "You're not breaking our contract," he said. "You owe me even more now." He hastily moved to the kitchen and proceeded to open and close drawers and cupboards.

Did that mean he was going to keep his end and help her find a new life? "What are you doing?"

He came up with a paper bag and moved into the foyer, where he removed the tragedy-comedy drama mask from the wall. "I'm taking the mask to a lab I trust. Maybe they'll find prints. I'll be in touch."

He was gone before she could object further.

Her mind spun in confusion, trying to assess her options. She was at the mercy of two men who were at odds with one another. Her father wanted her on his side, firmly committed to him and the family business, at the cost of her individual needs and desires. Dev wanted her to use that connection to take down her father. The determined glint in his eyes had conveyed his purpose, and that he was unswerving in his mission.

She was caught between a Stone and a hard place.

CHAPTER ELEVEN

Despite it being a Sunday morning following a fitful night of sleep, Ivy was at her desk early. The memory of Dev's fingers firm but soft against her cheeks, and his lips hard with passion against hers, had her awake most of the night. And the horror of what her father might be capable of, even toward his daughter, haunted her. As did the significance of the mask, which Dev had thankfully taken with him.

Today, she began a new to-do list—this time in her head. At the top was figuring out how handle things with her father—long enough to survive until she decided how to handle the rest of her life. At least he was out of town until tomorrow.

She discovered a voicemail on her work phone from her mother. Damn. She'd missed one on her cell phone during the charity event last night, too.

"I need you to come to California right away," her mother said in her message, her voice sounding uncharacteristically uncertain and needy. It was unusual in and of itself for her mother to want to see her so badly. Their relationship had been populated with the occasional visit on a holiday, or to a set where her mother was filming, usually no more than twice a year. Gloria Westwood was a much-sought-after actress and had little time or room in her life for a child. Ivy had learned not to express—or to suppress—any need for a mother, especially since any mention of Gloria had upset her father. And vice versa.

And now that she had to make nice with her father, there was little chance she could get away from work. Manny was posted in the reception area again, waiting to document everything Ivy did and report it to her father.

Mentally, she noted item one on her new action list. *Temporarily appease Dad and develop a new plan of escape—with Dev's help.*

Gathering her courage, she dialed her father's cell phone.

He answered her gruffly. "Figured you'd call. The plane's about to take off."

"I'm sorry you were hurt by some of my recent choices," she began, "but that pad of paper was only a final exit strategy, should things have gotten too rough. It was a fantasy of sorts, during your trial. An escape hatch."

He grunted. "I don't know if I can believe anything you say anymore. Your decisions have certainly been questionable, especially when it comes to Grimm. Manny told me he was at your place last night. What am I supposed to think?"

And what was she supposed to think when her father grabbed her, shook her to the point of bruising, and basically manhandled her entire life. She took a deep breath, focusing more clinically on the goal and the best way to achieve it. "Where are you going?"

"I'm visiting one of the hotels." That could be anywhere, given Stone Corp owned hotels in over a dozen countries.

"When will you be back?"

"Tonight, late. Early tomorrow morning, at the latest. Why?"

"Can we postpone tomorrow's discussion? I need to take a couple days off. Mom's been asking me to visit, and apparently there's something urgent she wants to discuss."

"Absolutely not. She's just being melodramatic, as usual. There's too much to be done at Legacy. This is your chance to prove yourself to me again, Ivy. I expect excellence and dedication."

She bit back her frustration. He was going to get his way again. Demand what he wanted, no matter what the cost to others. She couldn't let him, but she didn't have the energy to fight him yet. She needed a plan in place first. There was too much at stake—and not only for herself.

"If you want time off, you'll have to prove yourself to me first," he said. "And you'll start by staying away from your mother."

Ivy bit her tongue until her father hung up a minute later after a lecture on loyalty. She crossed her office, slammed the door shut in Manny's face, and locked it with a satisfying click. Back at her desk, she used her hands as a cushion and lay her head down, fighting tears. She would not cry. That was weakness. Besides, she'd learned long ago that tears were a wasted currency, and could be used against her. They showed her hand. But her chest was so tight as the dam held back her emotions that she nearly whimpered.

A few minutes later, a light rap on the door told her Megan had arrived. It was Sunday, but her assistant had one task that needed to be done today. Ivy had set it up yesterday, anticipating she'd be leaving to start her new life soon, and there was something she had to finish first. In person.

Pressing her fingers to her moist eyes to be sure there was no trace of her momentary lapse, Ivy rose to unlock the door and then crossed back to the desk, taking the opportunity of having her back turned to further gather her composure.

"I have those reports you wanted," Megan said as she entered behind her. "And the final tally on last night's fundraiser, as well as the check. You said you wanted to hand-deliver it, right?"

Ivy nodded, using the pretense of signing a paper to keep her eyes averted as she regained control.

"Hey, are you okay?" Megan set the papers on Ivy's desk and examined her with concern. Ivy nearly released a hysterical laugh when she thought of how her father would disapprove of her letting *the help* see her emotions—not that she saw Megan as subservient. But hell, one never let anyone see one's emotions unless it strengthened your position.

Build the wall. Defend the wall to the death.

She tried a trick she'd learned as a kid, picturing stacking blocks of snow and ice like an igloo around her, the cooling sensation freezing her feelings into little ice cubes she could stack on a shelf in her mind. She'd gotten so good at the illusion that she could rebuild that invisible barrier within seconds.

She sent Megan a bright, if brittle smile. "I'm fine."

"You must be tired after last night, but at least it was a success. Everyone's raving about it." Megan frowned. "You should take a day off, get some rest. If you want a representative from Legacy to do it in person, I can deliver the check."

"No." Ivy was quick to refute the idea, but softened her tone when she realized she'd been snappish. "I really want to do this. I'm tired, but I'll catch up on rest soon."

"I hope so. Maybe you could even go out to California. Your mother asked me yesterday to have you call her, but I didn't catch you again. You've been working nonstop—"

A trip to California was out of the question, at least for a few days.

"That'll be all, Megan. Thank you," she added to soften the rejection. "Go and enjoy the rest of your day."

A small crease formed between Megan's brows as Ivy took a seat behind her desk. "But you were going to take the rest of today off, too, weren't you?"

"Plans change."

"Forgive me for saying so, but you should put yourself first sometimes."

"Thank you for your concern. That'll be all," Ivy said again.

But she wasn't going to have that moment of peace. Emily arrived at the tail end of their conversation. At least Megan figured it was finally safe to leave and returned to her desk.

"Concern about what?" Emily asked. The closest thing Ivy had to a best friend leaned across the desk to search her eyes. "I'm guessing Megan was concerned about *you*. She's not alone."

Ivy caved. "I want my life back. Is that too much to ask? I've been good. Except for a couple semi-rebellious years in college, I've done everything asked of me. I've been the model daughter and woman, and yet I can't seem to make up for one mistake years ago. No, it wasn't a mistake. The only mistake was not putting my own needs first then. I was too blind to see what I needed. Too confused and blinded by grief to know what I wanted."

"Hon, maybe you should sit down." Emily was watching her pace.

When had she stood up and come around her desk? God, she was losing it.

She sat and accepted the bottle of water Emily pulled from the minibar in the corner.

"I'm sorry," Ivy said. "I shouldn't have said any of that."

"It's okay. Do you want to talk about this mistake?"

"No. I mean I would if it would help. It would only make things worse." Feeling her eyes grow moist again, she looked away. Her gaze landed on the check. There was only one thing that would help right now. "I have to go out. Thanks for stopping by, though. You did a fabulous job with the bartending, and I appreciate everything."

Emily sent her an amused glance. "Are you getting rid of me? Dev warned me about that."

"Dev sent you?"

"He mentioned you might need some extra support today—and that you might refuse any help."

Ivy didn't know what to think about that. "I'm not refusing help, but I have to get out of here. I'll stop by later, okay?"

"Sure, if that works best for you." Emily watched her carefully, as if assessing her needs.

Ivy surprised her by grabbing her up in a hug. "I appreciate your friendship. And I promise I'll fill you in sometime." But not now. She had to figure out what was best first—not just for her, but for everyone involved.

She grabbed the check and a lightweight jacket off her coatrack. Megan's desk was empty, and the door to her father's office was closed. Manny tossed down the magazine he'd been flipping through and jumped to attention. Let him follow her. She had important things to do, and taking a guard was smart. There was still the matter of *Nathan's* champion antagonizing her. She was going to make a difference in this world, one for the better, and there was nothing her father or some stalker, bent on making her pay for her past, could do to stop her.

With Manny following in his own car—because she drew the line at letting him in hers—she drove ten minutes to her destination. The weight on her chest lessened as she pulled into the parking lot and stared at the building. Hope's Home, one of the benefactors of Hope's Light Children's Foundation, wasn't much more than a tidy two-story building with a playground out back, but being inside made her soul sing. Being with the kids reminded her what was important. Their simple joy as she read them a story or played piano gave her a sense of peace she never found in the business world.

As much as she enjoyed running Legacy, a part of her was missing and always would be: family, and unconditional love.

"Miss Ivy!" A cherub-faced girl with chocolate curls ran to embrace her legs the moment Ivy walked through the doors. "Are you here to read to us? Can I choose the book this time?"

"Sure, Caitlyn. Just give me a minute to get settled, okay?" The girl scampered off to the bookshelf in the community room. A couple of other kids noticed Caitlyn's excitement and settled on the rug in front of a rocking chair in anticipation of story time.

Another piece of Ivy's heart thawed. Being here would never make up for the things her family had done, but for today, it would be enough.

Hope's Home, a part of the Hope's Light Children's Foundation. And, apparently, a home for abandoned, unwanted children.

Dev sat behind the wheel of his SUV, which he'd considered throwing Ivy into—gently, of course, since she was paying him to help her escape her current life—but instead he sat, stunned. Angry, actually, and with no clue why.

Actually, he did have a clue. He'd spent most of his life growing up in a place very much like this one. Well, probably not anything like this one, since this one had a landscaped lawn, a fresh coat of paint, and a fenced-in play yard out back with a shiny new swing set, merry-go-round, and teeter-totter. He wondered if Ivy Stone had arranged for that. The charity event last night had been for the foundation, which benefited orphanages and children's hospitals throughout the state, but he hadn't expected her to take such a personal interest.

Was she using the kids as a pet project to improve the Stone family image? The thought made his chest tighten with anger.

As did the other reason he was burning to see her today. In his hurry to leave her suite last night before he did something stupid like kiss her again, he hadn't gotten a good look at the mask he'd taken from her wall. But the lab technician had turned it over while Dev had still been there and found *0512* scrawled on the backside. He had no clue what the number meant, and it could just be a numbered edition if the mask turned out to be some kind of art piece, but maybe Ivy knew more than she'd shared.

She'd seemed in a hurry to get inside the building, as if the hounds of hell were nipping at her backside. Manny was on her tail, watching her backside quite literally. She certainly hadn't been waiting for a camera crew, or any paparazzi that might capture her altruism and use the incident to her benefit. Manny was watchful, but she stopped him at the front door before he could follow her inside. Probably because the big hulk of a man would scare the children.

Dev phoned Jared and watched Manny light up a cigarette on the front porch of the building. "Did you talk to Douglas Rains yet?" he asked when Jared answered. They'd decided it was time to confront Stone's lawyer—or ex-lawyer—to see what the man knew that he thought was worthy of Ivy's sexual favors. The very thought of that man with his hands on her creamy skin had Dev's gut tightening.

"He's not answering calls," Jared replied, not in the least offended by Dev's abrupt manner.

"We need to talk to him," Dev nearly growled.

"Yeah, I know. What's up your ass?" Okay, maybe Jared had been a little offended.

"Nothing." A trip to the gym early this morning hadn't been enough to expel Dev's frustrations.

"Right." Jared always could see through him, just as Dev's brothers Aidan, Brady, and Colt could.

Thinking about Aidan had Dev gritting his teeth. He still needed to find time to stop by the prison during visitor hours and have a talk with his wayward brother, and see if Stone or Redemption Club could somehow have been involved in his brother's incident. The way Stone had referred to Aidan's prison sentence still bugged Dev. "Look, just keep me posted. And I think we should be looking more closely into the car accident that killed the Wilsons, too." Something didn't add up there. Why would someone want to pick up the Wilson banner after all this time and target Ivy?

He straightened as he spied a man with a cap pulled low over his eyes, bushy white hair sticking out underneath, getting out of a plain white van. He carried a vase of roses, which were so deep red they were nearly black, toward the building where Ivy had disappeared several minutes ago. He wore a deliveryman's outfit, with the name of a florist emblazoned on the back, but something didn't feel right. Who better to sneak a theater mask into Ivy's suite than a deliveryman?

The man detoured to a side door, possibly because he'd seen Manny standing by the front. Manny cast the man a glance, but didn't seem to think twice. Then again, Manny was probably some Club thug who was more muscle than expertise.

"I've got to go," Dev told Jared. "Call me when you've set up a meeting with Rains."

A moment later, Dev was also avoiding Manny's detection and entering the same door the deliveryman had gone through moments ago. There was no security here, but a pretty young woman looked up from where she was placing sliced apples onto a tray full of snack-sized bowls that already held cubes of cheese.

"Can I help you?" she asked, startled to see someone enter the kitchen from the outside door.

"Did a man just come through here?" Dev asked.

"Yes. He had a delivery for the front office, so I sent him through that way." She pointed to an archway that led down a short hall. "Beautiful roses. Unique. Said it was a surprise for Ivy Stone, to thank her for all she's done—"

Her voice trailed off behind him as he darted in the direction she pointed. He made a mental note to go back later and straighten the woman out on proper security techniques.

The hall led to a large gathering room that had

shelves of toys along one wall, books in another area, and several clusters of tables and chairs. The place was much cheerier, and larger, than where he'd spent much of his childhood.

He heard her voice before he saw her, and relief shot through him. Ivy's sultry voice had entered her upper register as she intoned a mouse's voice. A dozen kids were gathered around her as she sat cross-legged on the floor, showing them pictures in between reading pages. From the rocking chair behind her, Linda Castillo, Ivy's old nanny, watched it all with an amused expression.

"Please don't eat me, Mr. Cat," Ivy said, using expressions and voices that held the kids enthralled. "I can help you."

Like the call of a siren's song, she was mesmerizing, even as she mimicked a cartoon mouse. How did so many people overlook the natural charm in her? Of course, her acting skills deterred people from paying too close attention.

Avoiding Ivy's notice, he forced himself to move on, asking one of the staff members at the front desk, around the corner and out of sight of the community room, about the flower-delivery guy.

"Oh yes, he was here just a couple minutes ago," the woman replied. "I told him to put the vase in the music room, on the piano. She'll see it when she plays for the kids, which is just after reading time. Such a lovely thing she does each week."

That brought Dev up short. Ivy came here every week? "How long has she been doing this?"

"At least a couple years now. She and Linda are such a treat for the kids."

So Hope's Light hadn't simply been a smokescreen to improve the Stones' image. He hid his surprise and tamped down the admiration he felt for the woman. Perhaps it was Ivy's guilty conscience that prodded her to volunteer. And the kids were less likely to judge her, or understand what the Stone name stood for.

A quick examination of the music room and the rest of the rooms—mostly bedrooms, each clean, though cluttered with kids' stuff—showed the man was gone, probably through the rear exit that led to the playground. But nobody was out on the grounds, either. The gate to the side street was open.

What had the man intended? Had he seen Dev and decided to cut and run? Or perhaps the man was simply a deliveryman.

Dev put in a call to information as he returned to the piano room. "Beautiful Blooms, please," he told the woman, giving her the name listed on the back of the mystery deliveryman's shirt.

"I have no listing for that business, sir," the woman replied.

"Thank you." He hung up and examined the vase of roses. A card stuck out of the arrangement but no florist name was listed on it. Not surprising, since there was no florist. Without touching it, he read the message.

You can't get rid of me that easily. Soon, we'll be reunited—in death. Nathan.

Adrenaline was still coursing through him as he headed for the front of the building again. Reassured when he heard Ivy's voice coming from the main room, her baritone now apparently imitating the stern Mr. Cat, he again snuck by the opening to that room and continued to the front door. Manny's head swung toward him as he exited.

"What are you doing here?" Manny demanded, already pulling his phone from his pocket to report the enemy sighting to Mr. Stone.

"Side door," Dev said in answer to the unspoken question about how he'd gotten past the man. "Same way the man who probably tried to kidnap Ivy, the woman you're supposed to be guarding, came in. He's far away by now." Sure enough, the plain white van was gone.

CHAPTER TWELVE

Ivy had been stunned to look up from a dozen children's rapt expressions to glimpse Dev striding from the back hallway toward the front foyer as if he were a man on a mission. She finished the book, promising the eager kids she'd return after a quick break to play a song at the piano.

But as she rose to search for Dev, arms wrapped around her middle from behind. Little arms. Familiar, seven-year-old arms.

She turned within the hug and beamed down at Brandon, squeezing him back. "Hey, sweetie."

"I've missed you, Aunt Ivy," Brandon returned. She felt a pang of guilt. Usually, she saw him weekly, especially when Linda brought him here to volunteer, but with her father's trial, her outside activities had been limited.

Over Brandon's dark head, she met Linda's gaze. "I wasn't sure it was a good idea to see you guys today, but I couldn't stay away," Ivy said.

Linda sent her a gentle smile. "He missed you. We took a chance you'd be here today, after your fundraiser and all."

She grinned down at Brandon. "We raised a lot of money."

"And can help all these kids," he said excitedly. "Papa's going to donate and plant a tree in the yard for them, too." His papa was a landscaper who'd once worked at Robert Stone's mansion while Linda had served as Ivy's nanny. Linda and Miguel Castillo had taken on Brandon's guardianship from the time he was only a few month's old and raised him as their son. They hadn't been able to have kids of their own, and they'd been old enough to be grandparents when they'd adopted Brandon, but Linda's childcare business and the adoption—as well as keeping a maternal role in Ivy's life—had fulfilled Linda's desire for a family.

"That's wonderful. Where is your papa today?"

"He had some things to do at church," Linda replied for him.

As the tray of afternoon snacks arrived, Brandon's attention, along with the rest of the kids', shifted to food. "Can I?" he asked Linda.

"Sure," Linda replied. "You okay, *mija*?" she asked Ivy when the kids had migrated across the room. There was worry behind her gaze.

"Just tired." She glanced nervously toward the direction of the front entryway where she'd seen Dev disappear. Would he come back inside? Why had he come? "I have to get going soon."

"I wish you had more time. We've missed you."

"I've missed you guys, too. I'll call you later. Those changes I talked about may be happening soon."

Linda cupped her cheek. "For your sake, I hope so." After a quick hug, she moved to join the boisterous group enjoying their snacks.

Ivy headed to the front door, and it opened as she reached it. She didn't want to analyze the little leap her heart made when she saw Dev, though he looked frustrated. And dangerous.

"What are you doing here?" she asked.

"He was here," Dev murmured. Manny had entered behind him, and both of them were scowling.

She returned their frowns with a confused one of her own. "Who? Manny?"

"No. Your mystery man."

"You're sure?"

"So you didn't see him come through here about fifteen minutes ago?"

"No. Wait. There was a guy, but I couldn't see

him because of the flowers." Dark blooms. She remembered noticing that briefly, before the kids and the story pulled her back in. She glanced back toward the community room, from which the sounds of laughter still emanated. "Did I put the kids in danger?" She felt chilled to her marrow. If anything happened to those kids, especially because of her, she'd never forgive herself. "And how did you find me?"

"Emily told me you left Legacy, and where you were going. I waited in the parking lot, where I saw a deliveryman with a vase of flowers. Something didn't feel right." He described the man.

"He doesn't sound familiar," Ivy admitted.

"But your stalker has been known to use wigs and disguises."

"True. The flowers?"

"In the music room."

"If he left, maybe he really was a deliveryman."

"There's a note, supposedly from Nathan. And the flowers... well, they're unusual."

Again, she looked toward the children, who were rapidly finishing their snacks. "The kids..."

"He's gone now." He stroked a hand down her arm, making her aware that she was trembling. "I don't think he'd hurt them."

She headed for the music room, forcing a smile as several children followed her, clearly expecting her to play for them.

A sense of *déjà vu* hit her as she spied the bouquet. "These are Black Beauty roses," she whispered to Dev as she stepped forward to brush a fingertip along the velvety petals of one of the dozen blooms. "They look deep red when open like this, but they're nearly black when the petals are still furled." A couple sprigs of ivy complimented the bouquet, adding a touch of rich green.

"The color alone seems to be a threat."

"No." She smiled as a happy memory hit her.

At her denial, Dev looked surprised.

"Nathan used to get them for me after each performance," she explained. She reached for the card, but Dev stopped her.

"Don't touch it. There may be fingerprints, though I doubt it. The lab didn't find anything on the mask I took from your place last night."

"*Soon we'll be reunited—in death.*" She read the message in a whisper. It was signed from Nathan. The blood roared in her ears and she squeezed her eyes shut against the words.

"Hey, kids," Dev said, his voice sounding as if it came from a great distance. "How about you act out the story you just heard until we get back. Manny here will help you." He turned to Manny. "Give us a few minutes."

Dev's warm hand grabbed hers, making her realize her fingers had turned to ice. He tugged her into the hallway. Manny allowed them to move out of listening range, as if sensing Dev would physically remove him from the premises if he didn't give her some space, but kept an eye on them from the doorway.

"Who's doing this?" she asked. "Why do they want to scare me?"

"Could it be your father? Some sick game of his to get you to turn to him?"

"A test, maybe?" She was afraid that her father was all-too-capable of such a thing, but the messages had begun long before her father had found out her plans. "He doesn't know what I've sacrificed for him. I've had all kinds of people contact me over the past nine months. The LVPD wants me to answer questions about Ryan's Redemption Club activities—which, no, I don't know anything about. The FBI and DEA would like me to turn state's evidence against my father—again, I know nothing detailed or useful about his possible involvement in anything illegal. Even Club members have been trying to reach me for anything from stealing and returning their torn debt cards to them, to tearing out pages of the ledger and selling them to them, since, it appears, there's a market for that kind of thing. And no, I don't know anything about where the ledger is, either." She stopped, realizing she'd been rattling on, releasing the aggression pent up for months, and the volume of her voice had steadily increased until she was nearly shouting at him.

"Hey." He put his hands on her shoulders and stroked up and down her arms as if soothing a wild animal. "You're okay. You're safe. And I'm going to make sure you stay that way."

"Until you get what you want and take down my father."

He frowned, but didn't deny the accusation. His considering gaze went to the door of the music room, from which a man's low voice mimicked Mr. Cat. During her shouting spell, Manny had apparently given them the space they needed, and decided to go the extra mile besides. "Not sure why *Nathan* would bother coming inside if he wasn't going to approach you directly. Or maybe seeing all the kids around you deterred him."

Her blood ran cold. "If he thinks he can use the kids to get to me, I'll have to cut ties." Her heart broke a little, though she'd already been planning to do just that when she disappeared. She wouldn't be able to go back to even the most minuscule part of her previous life. Anything that could be traced to her new life would be disastrous.

"That would be difficult for you?" He scanned her face, searching out the truth.

"Contrary to what some believe, I fully support the charities I give my time to. I'm not a bad person. I wasn't back when Nathan was alive, and I'm not now. If only my stalker could see that."

He looked like he would say more, but she wasn't up for a discussion, or any further revelations on her part. She returned to the room and took a seat at the piano as Dev and Manny stood near the door. If she had to leave the kids, she was going to put on one hell of a final show.

Victor drove away from the children's home with his stomach churning. He'd been close enough to talk to her again, had intended to scare her, but there had been too many kids around, as well as a couple of adults. He'd have to wait his turn.

Surely, the roses had done the trick, though. Nathan used to give her roses like that—that very same variety. She had to be rattled by them.

Ivy could try to redeem herself by doing good deeds, but he knew the truth. Nothing she could do would change the past. Her posing as someone who cares was enough to make him want to kill her right then and there. But not in front of kids. The kids had saved her today.

As for Robbie, he'd fled town like a chicken shit. No matter. Victor would make the most of his absence.

He tried to call his partner to share the latest, but his call went to voicemail. Again. He should be relieved, but it had been the same story all day, and he was starting to worry. It wasn't like her not to pick up immediately, demanding the latest update, especially since her anxiety level seemed to be increasing hourly. The last message she'd left him had expressed her worry that Ivy was going to get hurt, and that she wanted her daughter in California for a few days, where Ivy wouldn't be in the middle of it all.

As the beep sounded, he took a risk and left a message. "Gloria, call me back ASAP."

CHAPTER THIRTEEN

While Ivy spoke with Linda, Dev made a call to GSS and arranged for an agent to pick up the bouquet and process it for evidence. Afterward, he'd felt Linda's eyes studying him as he waited for Ivy to say goodbye to the kids, but when he'd turned back, there'd been a small smile of approval on the woman's lips.

As he watched Ivy speak to and hug each of the kids, Dev's mind continually returned to the love that had shone in their eyes as they'd sung silly songs together. It seemed Ivy had found a way to bring unconditional love into her life despite being Robert Stone's daughter, and he had to admire her for it. The love that shone back at them through Ivy's beaming expression wasn't false. Nor did Dev think the moisture clinging to her long, thick eyelashes was acting.

"I'm taking you with me," Dev said after Ivy had said goodbye to the last child.

As they stepped into the parking lot, he scanned for threats. Behind them, Manny did the same, and he seemed to have accepted Dev's presence—for the moment.

"Taking me with you?" She laughed. "Oh, is *this* the part where you kidnap me? You're giving me a heads-up? What happened to 'you'll never know when or where'?"

Manny trailed after them, out of earshot. Dev leaned closer to her anyway. "This isn't a kidnapping."

"No?"

"No."

She glanced at Manny, who was inching closer,

trying to hear their conversation. "Then what exactly are you proposing?"

"A day off." The fact that the remaining concern in her gaze melted at the thought of a vacation day told him just how hard she'd been working. "An afternoon away from thoughts of the past, or a stalker. Or work. Or your father."

She sighed and sagged against his car. Her long hair brushed his hand where it rested on the roof, near her shoulder, and he resisted the urge to stroke it. "You have no idea how good that sounds. But," She bit her lip and her gaze shifted toward Manny.

He grinned. "I can ditch him. You just have to get in the car and lock the door. I'll do the rest. In fact, it would be my great pleasure." His grin widened as a mischievous light entered her emerald gaze and she reached behind her for the door handle.

What was she thinking, taking an afternoon off—with Devlin Grimm, of all people?

"Your family's ranch is thirty minutes north?" she asked as he passed another freeway exit. With Dev's expert driving, they'd lost Manny's tail in the city.

"You really didn't know?" From the driver's seat, he cast her a curious glance.

"No. Why would I?"

"You said you did your homework."

"About you, but this is your mother's place, right?"

"Yeah, but she's now involved." His jaw hardened and he looked out the window.

"Involved how?"

"Your father..." He shook his head. "Never mind."

She straightened in her seat. "What did my father do?"

"I'm not sure you'd believe me. My theory will

probably sound unfounded to you."

She stiffened. "I've heard rumblings about my family for much of the past year. And my best friend, Emily, was partially responsible for revealing what my brother had been up to. So yeah, I think reality's bitten me in the ass and I'm no longer turning a blind eye to it. But until I have hard proof my father's hurting people, I can't totally turn my back on him."

"Even after what he did to you." Dev stroked a finger along her upper arm, where the bruises beneath her shirt and jacket nearly throbbed in response. "Or is that part of your normal father-daughter relationship?" The light touch of his hands was in direct contrast to the steel beneath his words.

"It's not normal." She looked through the windshield to avoid the questions in his gaze. "I know that much. But it was all I had."

"At least you're talking in the past tense."

They rode in silence for the rest of the way, each lost in their thoughts. Ivy could only imagine what her father would say when he learned Manny had been outsmarted and she'd fled the scene to spend the day with Dev.

While Dev exited Highway 93 and took a few turns down gravel roads that ended at a gate about five miles from the freeway, Ivy's attention was captured by the landscape. The spring sun was warm through her window as he took a quick jaunt south and she gazed upon flat terrain covered with knee-high yellow grass that caught the sunlight and gleamed like gold. She was glad she'd gone casual today, knowing she'd be interacting with kids and wanting to be more on their level. The dark jeans and cotton blouse, as well as the low-heeled boots, were adaptable to the ranch.

Dev answered her questions about the size and function Curry Ranch as they drove another mile onto the property, pulling up at a sprawling house with a 1970s flare.

"My mother's house," Dev explained. "I built a

house down the road another half mile. My brothers have plots here, too, if they want them. So far, I'm the only one who built, but we all come back every Sunday, when we can. All but Aidan." Dev studied the house through the windshield. "Rose Curry adopted and raised four boys here on her own."

"She wasn't married?"

Dev shook his head and smiled regretfully. "She said she never did find a man who fit the bill." No father figure, then. A single woman who was already responsible for a large, working ranch had taken on a monumental task.

"She must be a strong woman."

"She is." Dev parked the car beside two other vehicles—a Corvette and a Harley. Neither were ranch material. "She reminds me of you, actually."

She shot him a glance, aware her cheeks were heating with pleasure. But he was out of the car before she could form a reply.

The ranch-style house had been updated. The roof was new, as was the porch with its freshly painted bench swing. A quilt that looked homemade was draped over the back of the swing. Ivy could envision an evening spent watching the colors of the sky change at sunset, cozied up beneath that blanket with a glass of cool wine and a warm man—Dev. She shook off the dream and followed him through the front door.

"Mom?" he called out. "I'm here, and I've brought a guest."

Rose Curry wiped her fingers on a dish towel as she emerged from the back of the house. "Dev!" She embraced her son and then shot a curious glance over his shoulder toward Ivy.

Ivy stepped forward and held out her hand. "I'm Ivy. I hope I'm not intruding on your family's afternoon." A myriad of emotions crossed the woman's face—anger, confusion, and surprisingly, acceptance— as she obviously recognized Ivy, despite leaving her last name out of the introduction.

"I heard Dev might be working with you," Rose acknowledged, accepting the handshake. "Come along to the kitchen and chat with me while I finish up. The pot roast is just about ready. Brady and Colt took a walk out to the stables, but they'll be back any moment." She headed back into the kitchen. The rich smells of roasted potatoes and vegetables and simmering meat made Ivy's mouth water.

Ivy shot Dev a look. "Working with you?" she leaned in to whisper.

Dev grinned. "Better than telling her you hired me to kidnap you, don't you think?" He slid an arm around her waist and squeezed lightly before releasing her to follow his mother.

Her body still tingled from the trail of his fingers across her waist when she joined them in the kitchen. A moment later, two rather handsome and imposing men entered through the back door. They had to be Brady and Colt. Though the brothers weren't of the same bloodlines, they were each tall and broad-shouldered. But their style of dress and taste in vehicles gave her an idea of their very different personalities.

Dev was casual in his jeans and a Henley, seeming to straddle the fashion choices of his brothers, but his dark good looks and reluctant smile indicated an underlying intensity that was quiet and potentially dangerous. The brother with dark brown hair, jeans, a plain tee, and a leather biker's jacket had to be the owner of the Harley. The other brother, the one with sandy blond hair cut in a professional style, wore a suit but, in deference to the casual occasion, had cast aside the tie and left the top button of his gray dress shirt undone.

Despite the difference in their DNA, each brother carried himself with a sexy, unmistakable confidence, for which Ivy gave Rose credit. So many of the kids Ivy had worked with through the Hope's Light had a variety of issues to work through, everything from abandonment to having a chip on their shoulders. Yet each of these men, who'd probably gone through similar circumstances, clearly felt confident within his realm.

But that didn't mean they gave trust easily. They were currently sending her suspicious looks. Just as she was about to pull on her icy persona to protect herself from their heated glares, Dev leaned down to speak in her ear. "Easy, Princess. Don't freeze up on me now. They won't bite."

She slowly released a breath and let her muscles relax. Her abdomen tightened again, this time with pleasure, as Dev's hand landed on the small of her back and he gestured to his brothers.

"Brady, Colt, meet Ivy Stone," Dev said. "She's nothing like her father."

"Glad to hear it." Colt's words were heavy with doubt, but he stepped forward to shake her hand, and then hugged Dev. "It's been too long."

Dev chuckled. "That happens when we're both putting out fires in the business world. Ivy, this is Colt Freeman."

"Brady Foster," the man in denim and leather said, not waiting for Dev to introduce him next. He didn't extend his hand, but he gave her a nod of greeting. His dark brown eyes assessed her, judging her worth.

"I let them each choose their own names when they came of age," Rose explained. "I encouraged each of them to be his own man, follow his passions."

"Dev mentioned that," Ivy said, recalling one of their early conversations. "He chose Grimm because he wanted a reminder of the grim world from which he came."

Rose chuckled. "That was part of it. His absentee father's last name started with G, and Dev wanted that as a reminder of his roots, and what he wanted to grow from instead of fester and die off."

"And there's one more of us," Colt added. "Aidan

Rock."

Brady nodded. "He was always the strongest. Even false imprisonment won't break him."

Ivy wondered how Brady and Colt had arrived at their last names, but she could guess, and their suspicious, hard expressions indicated they probably wouldn't be open to any sharing of personal stories.

"I saw him today," Rose said, scooping roasted potatoes and carrots beside the pot roast she'd laid on a pretty blue platter. As she worked, her sons moved around her, gathering plates and silverware, fetching a pitcher of iced tea from the refrigerator, and setting the table. "He asked how everyone was doing, especially after the verdict." She glanced up at Dev before resuming slicing the meat. "He hopes you're handling that okay."

"And I hope you lied to him," Dev said. "He can't be worried about what's going on here," Dev insisted when Rose didn't reply. "He needs to focus on survival in prison."

Ivy found she couldn't meet anyone's gazes, even though she wasn't responsible for her father's actions.

"He's doing okay," Rose said, but there was worry in her voice. "Besides, he only has another year on his sentence."

Brady grunted. "Unless someone stirs up more trouble for our family."

"Maybe Stone is done with his shenanigans now that he's been found not guilty. It would be stupid to tempt fate." She glanced at her sons, seemingly needing confirmation.

"We didn't see anything suspicious," Brady said. "No tire tracks anywhere close to the house or barn, anyway. Nothing disturbed. We can ride the fence line next."

"After you eat," Rose insisted. "Dinner's ready. Wash up." Ivy came forward to take the large tray of pot roast, surrounded by veggies, from her hands and Rose sent her a grateful look. "Thank you, dear. If you could put that on the table, through there."

"Suspicious?" Dev asked, his gaze moving from brother to brother before landing on Rose as everyone surrounded the table. Ivy took the spot beside Dev, as that seemed to be the only one left that wasn't one of the ends of the table. The two brothers sat opposite her and Dev. "What am I missing here? Did something else happen?"

Seated at the head of the table, Rose fluttered a hand, but kept her gaze on the platter as it was passed to her rather than look him in the eye. "Nothing for you to worry about. Thought I heard a noise during the night, is all. A truck. You know we don't get much traffic way out here. Was going to get my rifle and check it out, but figured it was safer to wait until daylight. And then I figured I'd wait until you all were here, what, with all the incidents in recent weeks. The ranch hands have Sunday off, so I didn't want to explore alone."

Incidents? The bite of potato in Ivy's mouth turned to glue as Dev's brothers shot her an accusing look. What, exactly, had her father done? She didn't realize she'd spoken the question aloud until Dev responded.

"We have no proof—"

"Of course," Colt muttered.

"—But there have been some strange things happening here," Dev continued. "At first, it was little sabotages like a stall door left open so that a prize mare that we were boarding for a neighbor was let run free overnight."

"Our staff is very careful about that," Rose added. "There are only a couple hands helping me out here, now that my boys have lives off the ranch, but they're very conscientious workers."

Ivy could see Dev was holding back. "What else?" she demanded.

"A cut in the fence line let a couple horses loose and they got onto the highway," Dev said. "We recovered them, but they were shaken."

"As were a couple of drivers," Colt added. "But that wasn't the worst of it. There was the rattlesnake in the barn."

"And just before that, the trough was contaminated," Brady said.

She gasped. "Are the horses okay?"

Rose nodded. "Luckily, the snake didn't do any damage except to frighten the horse whose stall we found it in. As for the contamination, it was enough to make several of them sick for a couple days, but they've recovered."

"Thank God," Ivy said. Her father's connection to a crime ring, putting her and the hotel in danger, was bad enough, but harming innocent people and animals was going way too far. "How long has this been going on?"

"A few months, but most of it was in recent weeks," Dev said.

"Started just about the time it became public knowledge that Dev was working to help the district attorney build a case against your father," Colt added.

If her father was capable of arranging such acts, it wasn't unthinkable that he'd had something to do with Aidan's predicament.

Ivy kept her concerns to herself, worried tossing unfounded theories out there would only earn her more accusatory looks from the brothers. The discussion turned toward the trial and the task force's plans to talk to jurors and witnesses to find evidence of tampering.

Eventually, the atmosphere became more casual as talk turned to family and dishes were cleared. Apparently, Brady owned a bike shop in Vegas that made specialty, custom Harleys. Colt was a defense lawyer. She wondered what career path Aidan had been on, and what had landed him in prison for eighteen months, but didn't want to bring up a sore subject.

Ivy did her part to help clean up after their meal, but she was distracted as thoughts of their conversation percolated in her brain.

"Take a ride with me?" Dev asked at her ear. Startled, she jumped and nearly dropped the platter she'd been drying. Dev caught it with an amused look.

"A ride?" she asked.

"Do you know how to ride a horse?"

"It's been a while, but yeah. When I was a teen, I spent a summer in Morocco while Dad oversaw the building of a hotel there. I took lessons at an Arabian horse farm."

Dev grinned. "You have any number of hidden talents."

"You'd think so." She frowned, remembering how she'd been hoping to impress her mother, who was arriving mid-summer to film a movie nearby. But her mother had never come to visit. The happy memory soured. There were countless examples of times Ivy had tried to be the best, the over-achiever, the perfect daughter in order to please her parents. And none of it had mattered. It had never been enough. *She'd* never been enough. And it had taken her thirty years to realize she never would be.

"Let's saddle up," Colt said from the doorway. He'd changed out of his suit and into more casual jeans. She recalled that they'd planned to ride the fence line.

The men donned jackets, hats and sunglasses and headed out into the early evening. Ivy stopped at Rose's side to hang up the drying towels. "Thank you so much for including me in your family dinner. It was truly wonderful."

Rose smiled. "I don't imagine you have many family meals."

"No. What you all have here is priceless. A real home." Something she wasn't sure she'd ever have.

Rose reached out and squeezed her hand. "Blood doesn't make a family. Bonds of unconditional love do. There's still hope."

"I'll try to remember that." Ivy squeezed her back before exiting by the back door. She smiled a little as the screen door slapped closed. Someday, maybe she'd have a squeaky, imperfect door and a house full of love.

The stables, the lifeblood of the ranch, were enormous, but Ivy had no trouble finding the brothers. The trio stood outside, saddling four majestic horses. Ivy felt a twist of disappointment in her gut. She couldn't imagine anyone wanting to harm such amazing animals.

Once they'd mounted, they rode for several minutes, heading east.

"Something dead or dying over there," Dev said. His body was fluid as he matched the gait of his horse, but there was tension in his voice. Ivy followed his gaze and spied the circling scavenger birds, their wings black against the bright blue sky. A chill ran over her skin, despite the heat of the late afternoon sun.

"All of the horses were accounted for," Brady said, but his mouth set in a hard line as if he expected to see the worst.

Dev swung his horse in that direction, his brothers and their horses flanking him. Their pace picked up to a gallop across the flat terrain as one of the birds swooped and dove. Ivy followed, but a tightening in her gut warned her to remain several yards behind.

A ditch lay between the fence that ran along the edge of the property and a dirt road beyond. The birds scattered as Dev and his brothers pulled their horses to a halt near the fence. They dismounted, looking grim. The wind changed and the horses began to prance nervously. Not a good sign. As Ivy dismounted, Dev held out a hand to halt her.

"Don't come any closer," he said. He released the reins of their mounts and gave them light swats on the behinds, letting them run toward a nearby pasture.

"Is it a horse?" Her hands were shaking as she

stepped closer, and she gripped them together tightly. They'd said all of the animals had been accounted for, but maybe someone had miscounted.

"Ivy, stop."

But she could already see what they were trying to keep out of her field of vision. Brady and Colt exchanged a grim look.

"Is he dead?" Her words must have sounded as shaky as she felt because Dev pulled her close against his chest, tucking her head down to shield her eyes. His heart beat against her cheek, and she focused on that, closing her eyes against the image now burned in her brain.

"Yes," Dev said.

"You recognized him, didn't you?" Brady asked, sounding far away.

"She knows him," Dev confirmed. "We both do."

Though the man couldn't have been dead more than a dozen hours, since they'd just seen him Saturday night. Still, his body had already been partially ravaged by animals—and not just birds. Or maybe his killer had mutilated him.

Ivy kept her gaze averted from the body, but straightened, preparing to face the condemnation in the brothers' eyes. She was surprised to find only open curiosity and concern in their expressions.

She stated the obvious, hoping hearing the words aloud would help her brain come to terms with what her eyes had seen. "That man was my father's lawyer, Douglas Rains."

CHAPTER FOURTEEN

"You really believe she had nothing to do with this?" Brady asked two hours later, after they'd collected and stabled their horses, returned to the main ranch house, and called the police, who currently filled their home. At the crime scene, Adam Wilde, the DEA agent coordinating the multi-agency organized crime task force formed nine months ago, had arrived soon after the officer from the LVMPD—Las Vegas Metropolitan Police Department, which combined the Las Vegas Police Department with the Clark County Sheriff's Department. Lights had been set up around the perimeter of the ditch where Rains's body had been discovered, in anticipation of a long night working the scene. The coroner's van had arrived just minutes ago.

From across his mother's living room, Dev's gaze was on Ivy. "She had nothing to do with his murder," he answered, knowing his brothers didn't share his view. They hadn't come to trust Ivy, hadn't had the opportunity to see her more vulnerable moments, or what conditions she was living under. "Look at her. She's in shock."

Just then, Ivy met his gaze. Over the past hour, her eyes had taken on a hollow expression, her cheeks pale against the dark hair that fell around her face in waves.

Dev had the urge to go to her side, to comfort her, but she was being questioned. The LVMPD officer's frustrated expression revealed he wasn't getting much from her. Or maybe she didn't have much to give.

"She could use a strong shoulder to lean on," Rose said as she stopped by Dev's side with a tray of coffees in one hand and a thermos in the other.

"You're not going out there, are you?" Dev jerked his head toward the thermos.

"I thought the boys at the scene could use a pick-me-up. It's going to be a long night." Adam wanted the scene processed by the book and with an extra eye out for anything that could be traced back to Robert Stone or Redemption Club. They needed something irrefutable to nail the guy on.

"Stay. I'll take it to them. I want to talk to Adam anyway and the officers are done with me."

"You don't want to stay for Ivy?"

Again, his eyes sought out the woman in question. Ivy was carefully composed, her back ramrod straight as she answered question after question about her relationship with Rains. "I'll be here when they're done. Just don't let her leave, okay?"

Rose smiled softly. "You care for her."

"She's a client." But there was a lot more to it, and the realization was slowly settling in. She'd tried to fire him, and he hadn't wanted to listen. And his desire to be with her was more than simply wanting to bring down her father, though that was certainly a strong motivation. "And she's alone," he admitted when Rose only shook her head and smiled.

As Dev took the thermos from her, freeing her hand, she patted his chest. "You always had a soft heart. Just see that you take care of it. I like her, and I don't want to be wrong, but she is a Stone."

"I know." He reminded himself at least once an hour.

Ten minutes later, he'd pulled his car into the dirt lane that ran the length of fence near where Rains's body had been discovered. He couldn't get closer than a hundred feet, with the police and Adam's vehicles filling the narrow road. He approached the man wearing the black cowboy hat and jeans.

Adam eyed the thermos with gratitude. "Good to see you, Dev. Wish it was under better circumstances."

Dev surrendered the coffee and surveyed the scene. The coroner was in the ditch with the corpse while a crime scene investigation technician stood watch. "How's it going?"

"Coroner confirmed there's a single gunshot wound to the head. Thinks Rains died around four a.m., but she'll need more time to process the victim before she can make an accurate assessment. I've got task force agent Mason Gray heading to Rains's home to see what he can find."

"I'm guessing it's not a suicide."

Adam looked down the lane. "I'm guessing you're right. No gun, for one thing. And why would he choose this place to draw his final breath? He had no ties to you, right?" His eyes zeroed in on Dev.

"I met him last night, at the charity event at Legacy. He was... talking to... Ivy." He'd almost said *antagonizing*, but he didn't think Ivy needed any more motive for the murder. "I showed up and the guy left."

Adam glanced up toward the house. "I need to talk to Ivy next. I assume she's still there?"

"Yeah. I think her interrogator could use a break." A grin tugged at his lips until he recalled her stoic demeanor. He hated seeing her shut her emotions down and was surprised at the possessive, protective feelings that reared up. "She could use a break, too."

"And Jared? Will he be here soon?"

"He's on his way. He was there last night, too, when we met Rains."

"And last you saw, the man was walking away, and he left the event immediately after?" Adam, once a detective, was in full-interrogation mode.

Dev could respect that. "Jared followed Rains to make sure he left without making more trouble, but Jared returned a minute later. The guy you should be looking at is Robert Stone."

Adam's eyes narrowed at the name. He and his

fiancée Emily had had enough experience with the Stone family to last a lifetime. "I've put in a call to the man, since Rains was his lawyer. Stone is apparently out of state and on his way back to town."

"Convenient that he was gone." They shared a look.

"He made it clear that his lawyer had just gotten him off some extremely serious charges, so he had no reason to kill the man."

"Except Douglas Rains told Ivy he had some information she might want. I have a feeling that information had the potential to hurt Stone, or at least his relationship with Ivy. And he's possessive of his daughter." Rains had wanted her to sell her body to him in exchange. The thought made Dev look away before Adam could read the fury there.

"Let's say Stone did have someone kill Rains," Adam began, "why would they dump him here?"

"Stone's had a personal vendetta against me since GSS was involved in unearthing the existence of Redemption Club. He's been trying to get me to stop cooperating with your task force for months now." He'd already told Adam about the suspicious occurrences, both to let the man in on what was going on at the ranch, but also to warn him Stone could come after Adam and other task force members, too. Or even Emily. "He's probably just trying to make problems for me. Or maybe he wants to frame me. I didn't like the way Rains was hitting on Ivy last night." Might as well be completely honest. Adam was a friend, but also a damn good investigator. He'd come across the information at some point.

The sound of an approaching vehicle drew their attention. From down the road, the bright headlights and dark form of an SUV emerged from the twilight purple horizon.

"That's probably Jared," Dev said.

"Let's meet him at the house," Adam suggested. "I need to talk to all of you, Ivy included."

Ivy breathed a little easier when Dev returned to Rose's home, even if his scowl was darker than ever. He trailed Adam, who wasn't exactly frowning, but gave off an intense vibe, too. Behind them, Jared and Skye entered.

"See? Told you he'd be back," Rose said from beside her on the couch. She patted Ivy's hand in reassurance before rising to greet the newcomers. Ivy resisted the urge to grab Rose's hand and squeeze, in a silent request for support. Rose's support belonged with Dev and his brothers. Besides, the woman herself had been through enough.

"You okay?" Dev scanned Ivy's face as he took a seat beside her.

She nodded, summoning a small smile. "There wasn't much I could tell them."

"Then this won't take long," Adam said, taking the chair the police officer had vacated only a moment ago. "I just have a few questions."

Hiding her disappointment, she shrugged. "Sure."

"It can't wait?" Dev asked, surprising both her and Adam. "The officer will have his report on your desk ASAP, I would imagine."

"And the officer doesn't know Stone like we do," Adam said. "He wouldn't ask all of the right questions."

"It's okay," Ivy said. "If it'll help resolve things, I can answer a few more questions. I'm just tired."

"How about some fresh air?" Adam asked, glancing toward where Dev's brothers were in the corner near the kitchen, standing like sentinels with crossed arms as they watched Ivy. Beyond the arch that joined the two rooms, Rose was bustling around the kitchen, making more coffee for a couple of Metro officers as they joined her there.

"That would be nice," Ivy said.

"I'm coming, too," Dev insisted.

Adam shrugged. "Suit yourself. But if you interfere, you're out of there."

Interfere? On her behalf? The thought was mindboggling, but sent a dangerous warmth—dangerous because she could easily become addicted to the feeling of being wanted, protected—through her body.

On the porch, Ivy could finally breathe. Adam had been thoughtful enough to give her the sense of space, and she was grateful, even if she had to answer still more questions. Perhaps it was an interrogation technique to make her trust him, but she already trusted him because Emily did, and her friend was the sharpest woman Ivy knew.

Whatever the reason for Adam's gesture, Ivy sank onto the swinging bench with a sigh of relief. She was surprised when Dev sat down next to her, so close that his thigh pressed against hers. Adam's brows rose for a second before he cleared his throat and reached for his notebook and pen.

"Ivy," Adam began, leaning on the porch railing across from them, "what can you tell me about Douglas Rains?"

She considered what she'd known of the attorney before this weekend. "He represented my father in any legal dealings for the past decade or so. Of course, that had been mostly business stuff until the past few months." She shot a glance toward Dev, but he was quietly encouraging. "Doug wasn't an expert in criminal law, so Dad brought in a couple other lawyers when the trial started."

"But your dad trusted Rains."

"Definitely. The man was by his side all the time, especially during the trial. That's why it came as such a shock when Doug approached me last night, at the casino event."

"Tell me about that incident."

She shook her head. "Not an incident so much as a very strange conversation. Doug had a proposition.

Said he had information he thought I'd be interested in."

"In exchange for?"

Beside her, Dev tensed, but there was nothing wrong with sharing the truth. "Me," she said. "He wanted a night with me. Or maybe more. I don't know because I didn't discuss it further with him."

Dev cursed beneath his breath and Adam shot him a warning look before asking his next question. "What was this information Rains wanted to bargain with related to?"

"I don't know. I wish I did." Something had been powerful enough to make the man behave out of character, to decide he could go up against her father.

Ivy looked up as a car came to a stop in the driveway. Emily emerged and, spying them on the porch, hurried to her side and squeezed her hand. "Are you okay? Adam told me the news." She swung to her fiancé. "Did you figure out who did this?"

"Working on it," Adam said, a softer note in his voice. Much softer than when he'd been questioning Ivy.

Emily picked up on the tension in the air. Her eyes narrowed on her husband. "You're interrogating Ivy? You can't seriously think she shot Rains, then dumped him on Dev's property."

"Just gathering information." Adam's tone was conciliatory now. He flipped his notebook closed. "And I think it's time for me to head back to the crime scene. The coroner should be about ready to move the body."

"Take a dinner break first," Emily said. "I brought your favorite. Figured it would be a long night."

Adam gave her a soft smile before turning to Ivy. "I assume I'll be able to talk to you later, if I need more."

She nodded, too numb to speak.

"I'll take you home," Dev told her, starting to get up as Emily and Adam headed down the driveway.

"No." Ivy put a hand on Dev's to stop him. "Stay."

"You don't have a car."

"I'll call a cab. Or, hell, I could call Manny."

"That's absurd."

"I mean it, Dev. I don't want you to drive me. You need to be here with your mother. She needs you tonight. She's a strong woman, but these sabotages, and now a murder, must be getting to her." She'd stumbled over the words, knowing her father was very likely connected to the *sabotages* and *murder* in question. "Besides, I don't want to antagonize Dad any further by having you spotted at Legacy again."

"I don't give a damn about antagonizing Robert Stone." On the contrary, he seemed to enjoy it. "I want—*need*—to see you home safely. Or, better yet, stay here with me." Dev's eyes darkened with unreadable emotions. "Or stay with my mother, if that's more comfortable."

"I think I'd better return to Legacy." But for once, it wasn't home. Not anymore. She wondered if it would ever again feel comfortable. "I don't want to put Rose, or you, in any more danger than you're already in. Besides, my father made it clear that he expects to meet with me in the morning. I'll see if I can get him to talk. Maybe if I apologize, and am appropriately contrite, he'll trust me again and reveal something important." She stood.

He reached for her. "Ivy—"

"Don't." She couldn't stay. Couldn't go farther down whatever road they were on. "I need some space, anyway. I think we both do." Dev dropped his hand.

On the driveway, Emily and Adam, having exchanged the bag with Adam's dinner, shared a quick kiss goodbye. As Ivy descended the porch steps, Emily came over. "I can take you back to Legacy. Adam's got a long night here, anyway."

"I would like that," Ivy said, relieved she wouldn't have to impose on Dev or rely on some stranger in a cab. She wasn't ready to accept another

kindness from Dev or his family. She already owed
them so much. But her suite would seem all the more
empty after being around Dev and his loving,
supportive family.

"Can I have a moment first?" Dev asked. At Ivy's
quick nod, Emily headed to the car.

Dev pulled Ivy to the side of the house, out of
view of the driveway. Before she could ask what he
intended, her chest was against his, her mouth caught
up in a hungry kiss. As the initial desire abated, the
kiss turned soft and sweet.

"I've been wanting to do that all day," he said as
he pulled away. "Especially as I watched them ask you
question after question. I wanted to get you the hell out
of there. It should have been your father facing the
firing squad."

"Interrogations are a turn-on?" she quipped
sarcastically, because it was the only defense she had
against the emotions he stirred. But her gaze dropped
to his lips, giving away her desire for another kiss. She
quickly met his gaze again, but not quick enough.

"Fuck space," he said.

Her eyes widened. "What?"

"You said *we need space*. I don't need it."

She looked away. "Maybe I do."

Victor took his time wandering Robert Stone's
empty Henderson mansion. The man was out of town,
and there was little security to bypass other than of the
electronic variety. Victor had always had a knack for
getting past such things.

He smoked a Cuban while indulging in a glass of
the oldest, finest whiskey known to mankind, and
tipped back in Robbie's office chair as he scanned the
den. Floor-to-ceiling bookcases housed thousands of
books and antiquities collected from travels around the
world. All of this could have been Victor's, had he not
been double-crossed years ago. The coil of anger in his

gut had tightened with every room he'd perused, every expensive bauble or framed photograph of Ivy or one of Stone Corp's many hotels that he'd passed. But now, in the den, he could relax and focus on the business at hand.

Unless Robbie had changed things—and he would have been too cocky to bother, thinking anyone who would cross him was dead—the oil painting of Zeus atop Mount Olympus hid the safe. There was a picture of Ivy on the desk, but nothing else of importance. The man was careful, but not careful enough. His ego would be his downfall.

He went to the painting and swung it outward on hinges that attached the left side of the frame to the wall. He smiled as his eyes landed on the safe hidden behind. It was the same as he remembered, but was the combination?

He spun the numbers, the birth date of Redemption Club, and pulled the handle down. A click sent twin thrills of satisfaction and anticipation chasing each other along Victor's nerves. He swung the door open and his smile bloomed even bigger. Robbie thought he was so smart but he was predictable. Most narcissists were.

He pulled the red leather-bound book from the depths of the safe, and then the box. Even that was the same, though a bit more tattered and worn. Inside, the number of torn playing cards with the names of the guilty on them had multiplied over the past eight years. More debts had been collected, more members added to the Club.

As he sat at Robbie's desk and poured another dram of whiskey, he flipped through the evidence that would bring Robbie to his knees. His phone rang from his pocket. Gloria was the only one who had the number for his burner phone.

"Finally," he snapped. "I've been trying to reach you all day."

"Yes, finally," a familiar—much too familiar—

male voice said.

Victor sat up suddenly. Robbie was the last person he'd expected on the other end of the phone. "How did you get this number?" he barked before he could recover his wits. Had Gloria double-crossed him, or had she been coerced into giving up the number?

Victor felt the urge to simply hang up. If he revealed any emotion, Robbie would scent blood in the water. Eyeing the ledger, Victor felt his confidence return. Let his enemy start putting pieces together. It was time for the monster's reckoning, and Victor finally had the upper hand.

"You had to know I'd trace the emails sooner or later," Robbie said. Victor could easily picture the smug sneer he heard in his voice. "Unfortunately, you chose a poor partner. My ex-wife isn't smart enough to launch a blackmail campaign. It'll only be a matter of time before I track you down, too. You should know Redemption Club deals with enemies swiftly and with finality. And when you harass my daughter..." He left the threat open-ended, assuming Victor would fill in the blank with any number of horrors.

Instead, Victor chuckled. "Oh, Robbie, you always did have a flare for the dramatic. And you thought Gloria was the only actor in your family. Then again, it was a skill that served us well in many of our con games. That's why I always let you be the face of the group."

There was a long pause on the other end. *"David?"*

Victor's grin spread until his cheeks hurt. Oh, this was fucking fantastic. Finally, he could let his existence—his goddamn *survival*—be known. "In response to your earlier, rather cocky statement, yes, I knew you'd find me eventually. But it's too late. Your whole house of cards is going to come tumbling down. What you did to my wife and son..." With effort, he swallowed past the sudden lump in his throat, choking down the rage as he always did. "You'll pay, just as your daughter will. This time, the game's not over until I say so, Robbie. And my name is Victor now. When I emerged from my near-death experience to find the rest of my family gone, I became a new man—one intent only on destroying *you*. I'll be the victor in the end. And you'll have lost everything."

"How will you proceed without your partner?" Stone asked, sounding smug, as if he had a dirty secret. "Poor Gloria won't be following through with her side of the bargain."

Victor froze.

"What's wrong, old buddy?" Stone said with a laugh. "Maybe you thought you could beat *Robbie* Stone, but *Robert* Stone is stronger than ever."

"Where are you?" Victor stood and whirled around as if he might see his nemesis standing right outside the window. Stone was supposed to be on a trip, but the man had always been full of surprises.

"If you check the flight log, my private plane made a quick trip to Malibu. I spent a lovely day on my yacht, deep sea fishing with a small, well-paid crew."

"You went to California."

"Haven't had time to have even a half-day off in months," Stone continued, "what with that pesky trial and all." His acquittal had been another win in the Stone column. His tone went from cheery to dangerous in the space of a sentence. "I know it was you and Gloria who turned over those ledger pages to the task force. She told me everything. She bought them on the Red Market, and you two were after the same thing—a way to bring me down—so you connected during the bidding war. Of course, you have less money than her, what with you being officially dead for the past eight years. Unfortunately, Gloria didn't share the little surprise about who you really were. The bitch will pay for that, too."

Victor tasted ash, and immediately, he was back at the site of the car crash, smelling burning rubber and gasoline. He'd been ejected from the car, and had just started crawling toward the wreckage for his family when the car exploded. Tom Hamilton had saved him that day, having discovered Robbie's plans and deciding it was going too far. Tom had taken a broken and battered David Wilson to a remote part of his northern Arizona ranch to recuperate before David decided to reinvent himself, become Victor, and disappear until he could exact his revenge.

But the scent of the wreckage still haunted Victor. He pinched the bridge of his nose hard, willing the sensory memories and the red haze of anger away so he could focus.

"So a day of sun and surf was just the ticket," Robbie was saying, vacillating back toward cheerfulness. "I enjoyed myself immensely. At least, that's what people will swear to. I pay my people well to say whatever I want them to say."

The small crew would, no doubt, swear Robbie had been with them the entire day. And the man was thorough enough to have spent a couple hours in a tanning bed to complete the effect. Yes, Robert Stone was a phenomenal actor—and an even better criminal.

Victor snatched up the ledger and the box of cards, still holding the phone to his ear as he beat a hasty retreat. It was time to get out of enemy territory. He could regain the upper hand and reconnect with Gloria later. They'd regroup.

"Your partner will no longer be participating in this childish game of yours. She's got other problems at the moment. I should have gotten rid of my traitorous ex-wife years ago."

Victor turned his barely restrained anger on Robbie. "If you've touched her, I'm going to destroy you."

"I beg your pardon? I'm certain I misheard you. The David Wilson I once knew would have taken the careful, logical path. The one that took weeks to plot. You're being careless."

But Victor was no longer David Wilson. And he'd

had eight torturously long years to plan his revenge. "I. Will. Destroy. You."

Robbie laughed. "You're so serious. What happened to the guy I met decades ago? The guy who could wield his power in business by day and party with the rest of us by night?"

"You know what happened."

"Ah yes. You died. Maybe if you hadn't let Nathan drive. Then again, that car was known to have some problems. That was unfortunate, but teenagers and sports cars don't mix. Not on those windy roads right next to extreme drop-offs—"

A dam inside him broke, and rage rushed through him. "You bastard. We both know you rigged the brakes. Tom told me everything."

"Too bad the proof went up in smoke—and that Tom's dead. Besides, why would I kill Nathan? My daughter said she loved him. Of course, I was there for her, able to help her move on—in the direction I approved of, of course."

"I'm going to take everything from you—your daughter, your business, your precious prestige. And then I'll take your life." He hurried out of the house and into the night, feeling like the world was pressing in on him.

"Come now, Nathan was trying to take my daughter away from me. You would have done the same had the roles been reversed."

Victor came to an abrupt stop on the sidewalk. His car was just down the quiet street, where he'd parked it in the darker shadows of the night. "They were just kids who thought they were in love." He might have hoped to lure Nathan into the big, wide world with a juicy part in a big production, but he would never have resorted to something so heartless and permanent as murder—until Robbie forced his hand, that is.

"He was a young man trying to steal my legacy. He deserved what he got. My only mistake was trusting a Club member to make sure the job was done. I should have handled it myself."

"You took everything from me," Victor said, setting the ledger and the box of cards in the passenger seat of his car and shutting the door harder than necessary as righteous anger flooded him. "Once I kill your daughter, spilling the last of your descendants' blood, I'll destroy the rest of your legacy."

"I don't think you'll do that."

"Have I not made myself clear?"

"You won't kill the mother of your grandson."

As if he'd been punched in the chest, Victor's breath whooshed out of him. "What?" This had to be a trick, another manipulative move intent on confusing and dissuading him.

"Now you know what else I learned from your traitorous partner tonight. Something she recently found out as she plotted her ridiculous blackmail scheme. Ivy had Nathan's baby eight months after his death. May twelfth, to be precise."

Victor swallowed hard. *0512.* The number Gloria had told him to put on the mask to scare Ivy, because she hadn't wanted her daughter killed, but wasn't above using her a bit to get what she wanted from Stone—control of his movie production company as well as a tidy sum of money that would keep her happy for many years to come. Plus, she'd have her revenge on her ex, who'd been so cold to her for decades.

"Congratulations, you're a grandpa. We both are. Too bad you'll never see the boy. You won't live long enough to bother my daughter, or any of *my* family, again. I'll make sure my grandson never knows about the Wilson part of him. He'll be all Stone."

Victor didn't realize his legs had given out until he felt the metal of the car slide against his back and his ass hit the sidewalk.

Somewhere out there in the big, cruel world, he had a grandson.

CHAPTER FIFTEEN

Ivy's body was exhausted, but her brain was revved up. A hot shower and slipping into fresh clothes helped, but the adrenaline highs and emotional lows of discovering Rains's dead body, then sitting patiently through question after question, then Dev's kiss and his surprisingly steady support, were enough to wear her out. Doing the right thing and walking away from Dev and his family to keep them safe from her father's possible warped schemes had been another loop on today's roller coaster.

So when a knock sounded at the door, she practically fell off the couch. A visitor was the last thing she expected once Emily had left her in her suite a half hour ago.

It wasn't Manny. He seemed to have disappeared after they'd ditched him while leaving the children's home earlier. Perhaps he was gone forever, worried what her father would do now that Manny had lost her a second time.

She peeked through the peephole and up went the roller coaster again. She was quick to undo the lock and fling open the door. "How did you get up here?"

Dev held up a key card. "I have an amazing guy on my staff who knows how to hack and program."

She'd figure out that breach of security later. "Okay, so *what* are you doing here?"

Dev's gaze made her heart beat hard against her breastbone. "I didn't like the way we left things. I don't believe *space* is what you need. In fact, I think you need someone to give a damn about you being so freaking scared of your current circumstances that you'd want to disappear and start over."

"It's not a good idea—"

"I came all this way. I'm at least getting some answers. Honest ones. You said you intend to get back into your father's good graces in order to gain information. What, exactly do you have planned?"

Not wanting to have this conversation with him standing in the hallway, Ivy stepped aside and gestured to him to enter. "It's not a plan. More of an idea."

"I don't like it already."

"It could get us the information you're looking for. If he thinks he has me in his pocket again, he might open up. I can convince him to trust me. " Dev might not want her to give in to her father, but he didn't know the extent to which she'd already sacrificed, and what she was willing to sacrifice to protect good people. Not that she knew for certain that her father was responsible for Rains's death, but that explanation made the most sense. She'd confront him tomorrow—about all of it.

He shoved a hand through his hair. "Don't."

"But if I can help—"

"You'd put yourself in danger for me?"

"For justice, yes. And for my future." She met his gaze. "And for you."

His gaze softened. "And if you can't fool him? You can never be what he wants you to be."

"Hopefully, I can try for just a little longer, until you get what you need."

"And you were going to do it alone." He shook his head. "I'd prefer if you let this go and stayed at the ranch. I can protect you there, and find another way to get Stone on my own. You can stay at my place until we figure out how to get you that new life you want, free of your father. If only you'd trust me."

"Ah, so this is about wounded male pride?" She

smiled, but the expression turned to surprise when he pulled her against him, and then pressed his mouth to hers. It was a hungry, frustrated kiss, but it had her lightheaded and pliant in a second.

Another roller coaster loop.

Unwilling to let him control her emotions, she gave as good as she got, letting her own passion have free rein as she sank into him. To have one night where she didn't have to think about losing everything, where she didn't have to think about the reality of her life— that would be heaven. Hadn't everyone been telling her to take something for herself?

His lips skirted her throat and pressed against the sensitive hollow near her collarbone. She gasped at the contact and felt him smile against her skin.

"You like that." His voice was cocky now.

"Too much," she admitted. She bit her lip as his hands skimmed up her waist, sliding beneath her tank top. She arched into him and wound her arms around his neck to pull him closer.

She'd find a way to have a future, free of the tainted Stone name, and the threats and danger that came with it. If it meant hanging tough a little longer before she could claim that future, Ivy would find the strength to do it, and to push Dev far away, if that's what was necessary to protect him.

But she had tonight. She'd be free tonight.

How could Dev have ever believed this woman was cold? Ivy was heat and energy and softness beneath his hands, and he didn't ever want to let her go.

He'd come here tonight with one purpose: to make sure she was okay. He was worried she was making plans of redemption on her own, plans that could put her in harm's way.

But deep down, where he had to be honest with himself, he'd wanted to continue the kiss he'd begun at the ranch. He'd wanted right then and there to take her back to his place like some kind of caveman claiming his woman, protecting her and keeping her close. Instead, he'd watched her and Emily drive away, and the lack of control over the situation had eaten at him.

His hands sifted into her hair, pulling it loose from the ponytail she'd put it in so that he could run his fingers through the silky length. He pulled her to the nearby couch, and into his lap, her mouth wet and hot as he delved into her depths.

When she pulled back, there was an uncertainty in her gaze that had him leaning his forehead against hers and backpedaling. "If you say stop, I stop," he said.

"I don't want to stop." Her lips curved and he nearly whimpered with relief.

"Then why do you look so worried? I won't hurt you."

"I know." Her hands cupped his face, but she looked away. "I haven't done this—let myself go like this—in a long time."

His entire body went rigid. "Since Nathan, you mean?" He fought to keep the incredulity from his voice. After all, a gorgeous, successful woman like Ivy Stone had to have men lined up for blocks. But the reports he'd read of her had only indicated the occasional series of dates, which never lasted long, or one or two long-distance relationships that he'd suspected were more for image purposes than romantic connections.

"I didn't want to." She finally met his gaze. "I was afraid to lose control. Until now. Now, I very much want to." There was a flicker of fear and self-doubt in her gaze that he longed to erase forever. Did she not realize how amazing she was?

But words weren't enough. He'd show her what she did to him, and what a gift her trust was. He pulled her close for a heated kiss, then wrapped his arms around her waist. As the kiss grew hungrier, he pulled her upright with him, picking her up so that she could wind her legs around his middle.

"God, what you do to me," he murmured against her lips. They curved against his mouth as her hands slid into his hair.

"It's definitely mutual," she said. She nipped at his bottom lip and he nearly dropped her back to the couch to have his way right then and there. Instead, he moved as quickly as possible to find a more suitable location.

He knew which bedroom was hers from when he'd searched her place Friday night. It had been the only one that had seemed lived in. Setting her on the bed, he went to work divesting himself of his shirt while she zeroed in on the button and zipper of his jeans. It seemed she wanted to see all of him just as much as he wanted to see her. He grabbed her legs and tugged her closer to the edge of the bed, then lifted a bare foot to his mouth, where he kissed the arch and delicate curve of her ankle. She propped up on her elbows to watch him. With a growl of impatience, he reached for her waistband so he could tug the material down. His breath caught. No panties.

She arched an eyebrow and sent him a wicked grin, then lifted her hips as he continued his quest. Her gaze was mesmerized by the caresses and kisses he strategically placed as he bared her skin—her inner thigh, the sensitive hollow behind her knee, her shin.

He crawled across her body to get to her top half. Her breath caught as his hands slid under the edge of her tank top to cup her unbound breasts. They were the perfect size for his hands—and his mouth. He couldn't wait to taste them. His thumbs brushed across tight nipples.

He wanted to make it good for her. She'd apparently waited a long time—and somehow she'd chosen him. The thought humbled him, and he forced himself to take it slow as he removed the final garments, kissing every inch of skin he bared until she was arching into his mouth and palms.

"Dev," she said, urgency in her words. "Please. Now. I need you."

He didn't need her to ask him twice. He pulled away long enough to find the condom in his pants pocket and sheath himself. Her arms reached for him and he fell against her, feeling uncertain for a moment. This felt too right.

But all thought fled as she wrapped her legs around his waist, urging him to fill her. He obliged, slowly sliding into her, her moist, tight heat welcoming him. Again, the feeling of rightness threatened to make him think too much. He shoved it aside and focused on the moment, on the physical sensations that flooded every nerve ending.

Her hands stroked down his back, then cupped his ass. He reached down between them to find the sensitive nub, swiping his thumb over it. Her little gasp of surprise, the tightening of her muscles as he nearly brought her to orgasm, filled him with satisfaction. With a final circle of his thumb, she found her release. She tossed her head back with a shout of pleasure.

Dev smiled against her throat. He couldn't help it. His ice queen was far from cold. He'd stoked the fire and he couldn't wait to do it again. He only hoped he didn't get burned.

But that was the last thought he had before she aimed a content smile at him, full of promise and joy, and helped him find his own release. This time, he followed her over the edge.

Ivy was still enjoying the bliss of a hard, warm body lying in her bed, heating all of her curves, when Dev spoke. His chest rumbled beneath her ear as she traced a fingertip around one of his bare pecs.

"I'm at a loss for words," he said with a self-deprecating laugh.

She propped her chin on his chest to look at him.

"Not sure we need any." She could think of a few, but none of them captured the entirety of what she was experiencing. Amazing. Sheet-scorching. Passionate. Special.

And then there was what was going on deeper inside her, the happiness swelling her chest until she thought she might burst and light would come pouring out of her. Soul-touching. Unforgettable.

"But I feel I need to say thank you," he added after a companionable moment of silence.

She frowned. "Thank you?"

His finger traced her downturned lips until she was relaxed. "This was out of the ordinary for you. I'm... honored."

Letting him this close was unusual, to say the least. More than he even knew. He'd restored her faith in men, and in her own sensuality. "Are you fishing for compliments, Mr. Grimm?"

"You're incredible, and you don't even know it." His gaze held an amount of wonder that made her squirm.

She pulled herself into a sitting position, clutching the sheet to her chest. This was going too deep, too fast. He didn't know her well enough to earn his admiration. And yet, a part of her wanted him to know her. If she could trust anyone with her deepest secrets, it was this man.

Dev pulled himself into a sitting position next to her. "Why did you stay so long, in this life with your father?"

"Other than the fact he's my father?" She couldn't hold back the defensiveness in her voice.

"I get that, but from what I've seen, he's treated you horribly. Why didn't you leave years ago?" Dev asked, confusion mixed with a hint of condemnation in his voice.

She didn't take offense. How could she, when she'd asked herself the same question so many times? "It wasn't always bad. And he travels a lot. Leaves me alone to run Legacy my way." And she'd mistaken that trust for love. "He needed me, especially after his heart attack several years ago. That's when I realized I was good at business, and found my place here at Legacy. And it's been a good place."

"Until this past year."

"Yeah. My suspicions were growing, but I didn't want to see the writing on the wall. And then the danger got too close. I was planning to leave, remember." She shot him a grin. "That's why I hired you."

"You could have just walked away." Dev's look was questioning. "Why a new identity?"

"It's not that easy."

"Explain it to me. Did your father threaten you? Would he have hunt you down?"

"Maybe. But there were others who could be at risk if I stayed any longer."

"Others?"

She found she didn't want to hold anything back from him anymore. If nothing else had proved to her she'd come to trust him, sleeping with him tonight did. She took a deep breath and took the plunge.

"I have a son," she said quietly. Quietly enough that she heard his sharp intake of breath. She couldn't look at him, though.

The mattress shifted as Dev turned to face her, insisting she meet his gaze. "A son?"

She picked nervously at the edge of the sheet. Despite the cover, she'd never felt so exposed. "Yes. He'll be eight next month, on May twelfth. I'm guessing the *0512* that had been written on the mask refers to that date, so someone knows my secret. I was only a few weeks pregnant when Nathan died. I didn't even know I was pregnant until several weeks after his funeral, when my fog-like grief lifted a bit. Nathan never knew he'd be a father." And that haunted her. If he hadn't died, if she hadn't felt so lost and alone at the time, perhaps her life would have taken a different path.

"There are no records—in the media or otherwise—of you having a son," he said, obviously trying to wrap his brain around it.

"I covered it up," she explained. "Pretended to go on a trip to Europe. I'd already been thinking of getting away, of trying to cope with my grief by running for a while. Instead, I went to a quiet town in Montana. I didn't tell anyone he existed. And then Dad had a heart attack, basically begged me to come home and help run the family business."

"He didn't know you'd had a baby?"

"No."

"Why hide your child? You said you didn't know what your father had done. Was that a lie?" The sudden coldness in Dev's voice surprised her.

"He'd said enough to make me wary of how he'd react if he knew I'd had Nathan Wilson's baby. I didn't know about the Club or anything illegal," she hastened to add when Dev's look turned hard. "I just knew how controlling my father could be, and how much he hated the Wilsons. And I wasn't ready to be a mother. Didn't know *how* to be one. With Dad's heart attack following soon after I gave birth, I knew I had to return to help."

"So you chose your father over your son." There was a definite chill to his words now. She tugged the sheet around her shoulders.

"I thought my son would have a better life with someone else, in a loving home." She'd done everything she could over the years to make certain of it. Her son would always have more love and happiness than she ever did. "Wait. Where are you going?"

He'd risen and was yanking on his clothing as if he couldn't get out of there fast enough. "You're as selfish as your father, taking what you want, discarding what—or *who*—you don't."

"You don't understand—"

When he spun to face her, fury darkened his expression and she flinched, though he never touched her. "*I* understand. I understand what it's like to be that little boy, the one whose parents found him to be a supreme inconvenience, so they threw him away like trash. What's the matter? Did a baby get in the way of your ambition?"

She pressed her hand to her forehead, not understanding what was going on. How had they jumped from pillow talk to an argument? "That's not—"

"You bought your own life, at the cost of a son. And you probably didn't bat an eyelash. Daddy says jump and you ask how high. My God. He manipulated you from the very beginning, and you let him."

"That's not how it was—"

"Stones can justify anything. Must be a family trait." With a look of raw disgust, he turned away and headed from her bedroom as if he couldn't get away from her fast enough.

Ivy was still in shock when, a few seconds later, she heard the door to her suite close and then utter quiet. The only man she'd ever risked opening up to—emotionally and physically—had rejected her. Judged and decimated her.

Shocked by how fast her world had flipped from bliss to misery, she could only sit on the bed and hug her knees to her chest.

Several minutes later, desolation gave way to anger. Rubbing a fist against the tight ball lodged against her breastbone, she took several steadying breaths and scrubbed at a tear that threatened to fall. She had no room for regrets.

Brandon. She'd done everything for Brandon's safety. For her son's wellbeing. Linda and Miguel had given him a loving, stable home.

And he was the sweetest, most confident kid she'd ever met because of her efforts. He was untainted by the machinations or controlling behavior of his grandfather.

Desperately needing to remind herself why she'd done this, and that she wasn't the horrible person Dev believed her to be, she rose and pulled on a robe, then went to her knees on the closet floor. Tucked into the pocket of a winter coat she rarely had occasion to use in Las Vegas, was the cell phone she'd hidden there. It was her lifeline, kept only for talking to the most special people in her life. Thankfully, Archer's search of her suite hadn't exposed it.

She pulled her legs into a cross-legged position and cleared the emotion from her throat as she dialed.

"Ivy?" Linda answered. Ivy nearly broke down at the sound of a friendly voice. "It's not our usual time."

"Am I interrupting anything?"

"No, *mija*. I was just reading Brandon his bedtime story."

"He's still up then?" She choked back a sob of relief.

"What's wrong?"

"Tough day. I could really use a dose of Brandon."

"You got it. Oh, and he has a part in the school's spring play, if you can make it. It's in two weeks."

While she wasn't a parental figure in Brandon's life, Ivy attended as many events as possible. She'd already missed so much of the day-to-day experiences, but that was a sacrifice she'd been willing to make for his sake. And she hadn't been lying to Dev when she'd said she'd been too immature to be a mother at twenty-one. Too sheltered and, in many ways, spoiled.

She didn't regret the decisions she'd made. How could she, given Brandon's loving family, and Linda and Miguel's happiness?

"And yes, I'm fishing for information," Linda added. "Have you made any plans yet?"

"I'm still hoping to leave town. Maybe, after the school year's over, you all could visit?" If it was safe.

"We're ready for any eventuality," Linda said, dropping her voice. "I hate that you have to disappear. But you know we'll be right behind you." In the months since Dev and Archer had shown up at Linda's home, they'd made plans to purchase and run a lodge in Idaho together. It wasn't anywhere near the same scale as running Legacy, but it was a prospect Ivy, Linda, and Miguel were excited about—especially if it gave Ivy a new start. Even Brandon had been told about the potential move, though he didn't know the details. He'd been excited at the prospect of an adventure with his parents and Aunt Ivy.

Ivy sniffed. "Thanks, Linda. I owe you so much."

"It's been my pleasure. There's nothing we wouldn't do for you. You've always been like a daughter to us."

"I love you."

"Love you too, *mija*. Brandon's right here." There was a shuffling sound. "Would you like to talk to Aunt Ivy?" Linda asked him.

"This late on a school night?" His voice was full of excitement. Ivy closed her eyes against the memory of Nathan's sense of adventure. His son carried the same personality trait.

"Special treat," Linda said, a smile in her voice.

"Aunt Ivy?" Brandon's voice came through the phone. After a hello, he launched into a description of what he'd done with his day since seeing her at Hope's Home, including a trip to the park and losing another tooth. He had Ivy laughing and wiping away happy tears within minutes.

This was what she needed. *This* was what she'd fought for. No matter what Dev thought, her child was in the best place possible. And Brandon's happiness was everything.

CHAPTER SIXTEEN

Ivy awoke on Monday morning with a feeling of foreboding. She'd spent most of the night tossing and turning. Dev's anger and accusations had slipped into her dreams, making restful sleep nearly impossible. But exhaustion had overcome her sometime near dawn.

When her phone chirped from the bedside table, she realized what had woken her this time. It was only six in the morning, yet she'd apparently missed numerous texts from her stepfather.

She stifled a stab of disappointment that it hadn't been Dev checking on her—or apologizing for leaving her without talking things out. He had a right to his anger, and part of her understood that she'd hit upon some raw nerves when she'd shared the news of her son. But he didn't know the whole story. He hadn't heard about Brandon, or how well adjusted the boy was, or how much Ivy wished she could have been what Brandon needed, but that Brandon had been exactly what Linda and Miguel needed.

None of that mattered now. Dev had walked away. And Ivy had to focus on rebooting her life.

Surprised to hear from her stepfather, especially with such urgency, she sat up, immediately alert. Like his wife, Albert Westwood rarely contacted Ivy. He was Gloria's second husband, and to the surprise of everyone in Hollywood, the union had survived nearly twenty-five years of marriage. Gloria had even opted to take his last name as her stage name early on in her career.

She scrolled through the log of texts, which had begun twenty minutes ago.

Call me.

We need to talk. Now. But I don't want to wake you. But then the messages became more urgent.

I'm serious, Ivy. This can't wait.

Don't punish your mother for things she had no control over. We need to talk.

What the hell did that mean? If it was so important, he should have tried to call her. And it wasn't like she hadn't tried to contact her mother.

Her stepfather was a tad dramatic and liked people to jump when he said jump. As a director whose works had repeatedly achieved critical acclaim, he'd chosen a profession that utilized those traits to perfection. He'd met Gloria on the set of one of her blockbuster movies.

The phone in her hand rang and she jumped, nearly dropping it.

"Hello?" she answered.

"Thank God," Albert said with obvious relief. "You got my texts? Why didn't you call? Why have you been ignoring your mother?" The questions spewed out of Albert, rapid-fire.

"I just read through them. I was about to call." After a shower and some coffee. She had planned to be at work in an hour, where her father would be expecting her to apologize. She was not looking forward to the day.

"Your mother's in the hospital."

"What? Why didn't you say so in the texts? I would have called right away. When? How?" Now she was the one shooting questions rapid-fire.

"I found her passed out on the couch in her acting studio late last night." Gloria had turned the guesthouse on their property into a private getaway where she could run lines and practice parts in peace. "The doctor suspects an overdose."

Overdose. Her blood seemed to thicken and slow, and spots danced in her field of vision. "I thought she was off those pain meds." It had been two years.

Everyone believed Gloria had kicked the habit that had started when a horse threw her during filming several years ago. She'd broken her collarbone and been laid up for weeks.

"The rehab clinic helped with the addiction but the depression came back, I guess." He bit out the words with anger, resignation and accusation. Whether the latter was directed toward Gloria or Ivy—or both—remained to be seen. He'd never understood why Ivy couldn't be there for them at the drop of a hat. Her father had warned her time and again not to get sucked into their world of extremes. Now, she was realizing just how many extremes she'd been pulled between.

Ivy stopped in the middle of pulling on her silk robe and sank onto her bed as the strength left her legs. "Depression? You're saying you don't think this was accidental, that this was an attempted suicide?"

"It wouldn't be the first time." Albert's voice grew shaky. The last time, Gloria had woken up and sworn it had been an accident. "But I didn't think she'd fallen into despair again. In fact, she'd seemed happier lately. She'd been talking about expanding our roles in the acting world, maybe into producing."

"Is she okay?"

"They pumped her stomach. She's stable, but unconscious. I think you should be here when she wakes up—if you think you can spare the time." His judgmental words were like darts to her chest.

Guilt swamped her. If only she'd made time to track down her mother yesterday. But how was she to know things were that serious? Her mother had often cried wolf with those around her, testing their loyalties almost as much as Ivy's father did. "Let me do some juggling and I'll be there as soon as I can."

"By tonight?" he pressed.

She sighed. "I'll do my best. Can I talk to her?"

"She's still unconscious, but the doctors are hopeful she'll wake up soon."

After hanging up, Ivy hurried to shower and

dress. She tried to ignore how her body was sensitive in places that reminded her of what she'd done with Dev. She strangled the fresh emotional pain it stirred up before it could take hold.

She called the airlines. Though her father had a private plane for his business travel, he wouldn't have let her use it for something as trivial as visiting her mother, even in this situation. In fact, he'd disapprove of her taking time off of work, especially if he learned Gloria might have tried to kill herself. He already had a litany of reasons he didn't want Ivy near her mother. Which gave Ivy one more reason to break free from his control over her.

Her hand shook as she had a vivid recollection of her father grabbing and shaking her in the stairwell, of him burning the envelope that supposedly would have given her Legacy, and she hung up without booking a ticket. She was going to California, but first, she'd need to speak to her father, or their relationship would only become more ugly and strained. And then she'd never get the answers that would help Dev.

The thought gave her pause. Was she still thinking of helping Dev, after he'd walked out on her? Recalling her conversation with her son last night, she knew it was the right thing to do. Brandon didn't deserve to grow up in a world where the bad guys got away. If her father had committed crime, especially murder, he needed to pay for what he'd done.

Ivy strode into the Legacy offices a half hour later. "Is he in?"

Megan looked up from her desk. "Yes. He wants to see you immediately."

Biting the inside of her cheek to keep her anxiety in check, Ivy rapped her knuckles sharply against his closed door. A moment later, Archer admitted her without a word. She cast him a sideways glance, but as her father made no move to dismiss his sidekick, she accepted that she'd have an audience this morning. Besides, it probably boosted her father's ego to have the head of his security witness her humiliation. Again. What she was realizing, more and more, was that it was a sick game her father played with her—a pattern that she'd recognized in her early twenties, with Nathan's help. She was more convinced than ever that keeping Brandon away from her father, and this warped legacy he insisted upon leaving, had been the right choice. The boy had everything he could need, but most important of all, he had loving parents.

"I need to talk to you in private," she said.

Her father didn't raise his gaze as he read through some document. "Anything you have to say can be said in front of Archer. You know that."

She waited quietly, demanding his full attention before she continued. A moment later, he looked up and removed his reading glasses. "Well? Am I going to get the apology I deserve?"

Dev was right about one thing. Her father had never gotten what he truly deserved.

"I'm sorry you feel I'm being disloyal to you," she said, avoiding admitting she'd done anything wrong.

Her father's gaze narrowed. "That's a half-assed sentiment."

She shrugged. "I don't feel I owe you anything. I kept Legacy running for the past year, fighting attack after attack on our reputation. And it seems it was all for nothing. Am I going to get the apology *I* deserve?"

"Watch your tone, girl."

"Did you kill Douglas Rains?" She huffed out a humorless laugh when he only stared at her, his expression carefully neutral. "Let me rephrase that. Did you *have someone* kill your lawyer? You told me before you left town that Doug wouldn't be bothering me again. I have to wonder exactly what you meant by that."

Her father rose from behind his desk, but she stood her ground as he came to a stop right in front of her. "Like I said, watch yourself. You've been treading on thin ice for a week now, and if you're not careful, you'll fall through."

"You'd kill me, too?" She taunted him with false bravado as a shiver of fear crept down her spine. She had no doubt that, if she became a big enough liability, he'd dispense with her.

His hands clenched and she could sense his struggle not to strike her. "I just found out last night about Doug's death."

"It was murder. And his body was dumped on Dev's ranch. I'm not clear whether you were trying to frame Dev or send him a message to back off. Are you really so threatened by him?"

A hiss of breath warned her a moment before he lashed out to slap her, but he stopped himself an inch from her cheek. She refused to flinch.

He withdrew his hand. "I'm not intimidated by anything or anyone. And if you were on my side, you wouldn't have to be, either."

"I'm not scared. I've been on your side my entire life. Maybe it's time for you to be on mine, to support what's best for me. I think a break from each other would do us good." And would give her time to plan her ultimate escape—in a way the Castillo family could join her, if they desired. Now that she didn't have Dev in her corner, or on her payroll, she'd need to regroup. She still had the necessary identity documents and plenty of money to start a new life stashed at Linda's home, but she'd have to proceed carefully or her father would find her, and she wasn't sure she'd ever be able to get away again. "I need to take a leave of absence for a couple days, anyway. It's important."

"No."

Her posture went rigid in defense. "You haven't even heard the circumstances."

"You're needed here. Numbers have been down the past few weeks. The hotel should be your focus."

And yours, she wanted to hurl at him. Numbers were down because of the connection to the illegal club *he'd* started and the trial that had made a mockery of them. She bit the inside of her cheek again before she could let the venom inside her spew forth. She wanted to scream at him, to demand that he hand over the ledger and face the consequences for what he'd done. If he was innocent, he would be trying hard to show that, and he shouldn't be afraid that Dev would find a damn book that proved otherwise.

Like a blindfold being removed, so much was becoming clear. Such as just how much she'd allowed herself to remain ignorant when it came to this man. And all because she valued his love and approval above her own.

"Get back to work," her father said. "There'll be no more talk of personal leave."

"Mom's in the hospital."

"So?" His lack of regard for her mother, while expected, still hurt. "There's not much you could do for her. If you leave, you forfeit your birthright, and all that comes with it. Choose—a woman who was no mother to you at all, or the father who holds your entire world in his hands. And by *entire world*, I'm including your dirty little secret."

Stomach churning, she swallowed in an attempt to wet her parched throat. "What are you talking about?"

"Archer told me we had a visitor in our hotel last night. I hope you've gotten Dev out of your system now, and are ready to recommit to our family's endeavors. Sleep with him, like you did with Nathan, and get your immature need to annoy me out of your system. Then get back to work."

She breathed a sigh of relief that the *dirty little secret* to which he referred had nothing to do with Brandon, but her reprieve was short-lived.

"Oh, and there's the matter of my grandson." This time, emotion did flash in her father's eyes. Anger, hot and then oh-so-cold.

Her stomach plummeted to the floor. How did he know about Brandon? *What* did he know about

Brandon?

Her father was watching her carefully, seeing every emotion that crossed her face. "That's right," he said now. "I know about my grandson. Doug revealed everything to me yesterday."

"Before you killed him?"

His cheeks flushed red with anger. "He was going to use the information against you. And sell it to me, too. Apparently, he'd already sold it to Gloria."

"What?"

"Doug was looking for a way to get me under his thumb. He tracked down your medical files from that year you were supposedly touring Europe, getting over Nathan's death. There's nothing you can keep secret from me, Ivy."

"He made everything up," she said, desperation making her spew any lie to protect her son. "I don't know how he forged medical files—" Her words were coming out in bursts of phrases as she panicked, her mind searching for a way out of this.

He held up a hand. "Please don't disrespect me with more lies." His mouth pressed into a tight line and she recognized the signs of an impending blow-up. "You had a son with Nathan. And you chose to hide my own flesh and blood from me. Where is he?"

Her flesh was chilled to the core at the moment. "I gave him up for adoption. It was sealed and private."

Thankfully, he seemed to accept this. "No matter. We'll find him. He's one of us."

Like hell. Brandon was happy where he was. She wasn't about to let anyone ruin his life.

"I'll let you visit your mother one last time and then you can cut her off for good," her father pronounced as if he were a king bestowing the greatest gift on one of his subjects. "You can take the private jet within an hour. I'll notify the captain to file a flight plan. Take the week to sort things out and then, when you return, commit fully to rebuilding this family." *Rebuilding.* With Brandon. He wouldn't hesitate to rip the boy from the loving, stable home that nurtured him.

"And in exchange?" There was always a cost to her father's so-called generosity.

"When you return, you'll bring my grandson to me, and all will be forgiven."

"A clean slate?" She couldn't keep the sarcasm from her voice. Her father never forgot an infraction against him. "I told you I don't know where he is."

His gaze turned hard again. "And I don't believe you. If you delay, I'll go looking for him myself. He should be living here, under our roof. And if you don't comply—or if you try to run—I'll find him."

As she walked away, Ivy knew only one thing with clarity. She needed to make sure her father never got his hands on her son. Her father had never admitted to killing Doug, and he never would, but she knew without a doubt he was involved.

As if he read her thoughts, her father made a parting comment as she walked past a smirking Archer. "I'll be sending some men to keep you safe while you're at your mother's, Ivy. After all, that stalker's still out there." What she needed protection from was her own father. "And if you consider running," he continued, "remember that I have resources everywhere. What's mine stays mine. That includes you *and* my grandson."

No matter how draining the physical exertion of a morning spent on ranch chores, Dev couldn't clear his mind of a certain woman. The flash of shock and hurt that had luminesced in Ivy's eyes as he'd shot accusations at her had turned his initial shock and anger to confusion. He'd ignored her hurt, hell-bent on expending the sudden fury that had taken hold at the thought of a child abandoned—and at his own memories, which her confession had brought to the surface like scum on a pond.

Now that he'd had time to cool down, he wasn't so certain he'd been right in his righteousness.

"You sure have a lot of energy today." Rose Curry shielded her eyes with a hand as she looked up at Dev where he perched on the roof of the stables, repairing loose shingles damaged in a spring hailstorm. Her jeans and sweatshirt were soft with wear, her long silvery hair pulled back into a ponytail that hung most of the way down her back. Sun and hard work had etched wrinkles around her eyes and mouth over the years, but her gaze twinkled with the same mixture of concern, good humor, and soft understanding that had eventually lured a fourteen-year-old Dev out of his perpetual sullenness and convinced him he'd found a home.

"Energy to burn," Dev agreed, not bothering to hide his frustrations. "And this needed to be done."

He'd rolled onto the ranch late last night. After leaving Ivy's bed, he hadn't wanted to stay in town, hadn't wanted to be within twenty miles of her.

She'd been right about them needing space after all.

Something about losing the sudden intimacy they'd developed over the past couple days was troubling. And the sex... He couldn't get the memories of their shared passion out of his head, either. She'd been so open, so honest in her reactions to his touch.

And then she'd confessed her secret, and Dev had seen red. It was probably better to walk away now, anyway, before getting in any deeper with a Stone. He should never have felt a connection with the daughter of a man who was evil, should never have agreed to get involved with her, even in a business sense, when she'd entered his office last week.

And yet, he'd seen the vulnerability in her eyes and he'd been lost.

It didn't help that the devil in him—the less scrupled part of him that had earned him his other nickname—had wanted her. Especially when she'd left the ranch, risking herself and walking straight back to hell to face her father, rather than put his family in danger.

If that was indeed what she'd done. Or maybe she'd lied.

From the barn's rooftop, he could see the flicker of yellow tape in the distance, where the crime scene remained cordoned off in case the task force needed to examine it further. Rains's body was at the coroner's office, being processed.

He climbed down the ladder and Rose handed him a thermos. "Stay and take a coffee break with me?" he asked, wanting a distraction.

"Of course," Rose said. "It's too beautiful a day to spend inside, especially since it's supposed to storm later this week."

"Then it's good I'm fixing the roof." He winked at her and slung an arm across her shoulders. But as they walked to the shade of a nearby tree and settled in the grass, a solemn chill fell over the warm spring day.

"Not that I'm complaining about all of your hard work, but I can see something's going on with you. Is it about the murder? Or about Stone, maybe? I know he must be linked to this somehow. And then there's Ivy. She must feel caught in the middle." She'd always had a knack for reading her sons' thoughts and emotions. "I know you have a need to be in control, to make sure the guilty pay for their crimes," she continued, then hesitated, searching for words. "I just wish you'd have a little more faith in people."

"I get the feeling you're talking about someone in particular."

She smiled softly. "I saw the way you looked at Ivy. And I know you think blood runs thick, and that a child must be like her—or his—father."

"Do I?"

She laughed. "Honey, why do you think you work so hard to prove yourself? You've always worried you'll be like your parents, that you'll end up in prison without a moral compass, abandoning anyone who needs help, like they did. But there's such a thing as overcompensating."

"Better than not even trying." So many times, he'd been tempted to give up and not care what the world thought of him. But Rose and his brothers had always brought him back on track.

She patted his hand. "Oh, I'm not complaining. I lucked out with all of you boys." She looked up at a cloud, thoughtfully. "Do you remember Roger Thomason?"

An image of a scrawny teen with spiked hair and a wicked smile came to mind. "Yeah. He was in the same children's home as me. A couple years older."

"I was told you guys hung out together, and the woman who ran the home said he was a bad influence."

Dev nodded. "He was." Roger would lead him into all manner of pranks and even some minor criminal activity. "He got caught for shoplifting, if I recall. Went to juvie for a bit."

She nodded. "He came to see you after he got out. You'd come to live with me during that time."

He recalled feeling intense guilt and self-preservation when Roger had approached him at school. His old friend had seemed different. Harder. Dev had stopped hanging out with him, despite Roger professing to have changed. "I didn't want to disappoint you by running with that crowd anymore."

"He did change, though. He's a mechanic up in Reno. Sends me Christmas cards of his family. Married and has two cute little girls."

"He does?"

"I spent some time talking with him, back then, when I was still mentoring at the children's home. He appreciated that."

Dev frowned, dismayed to realize that time of intense emotion had blinded him to a friend who'd been reaching out to him.

Rose smiled softly. "My point is, you have a

tendency to play white knight when someone's in need, but if that someone doesn't measure up..."

"I cut them off?"

"You tend to see them like your parents. That they'll either use or leave you. Because of them, you pick the most dangerous ways to prove yourself, almost as if you're tempting fate to come at you. You can trust some people, you know." She nudged his shoulder with hers. "And a little bit of faith can go a long way. Like with Roger. My gut says you can put your faith in Ivy. After all, I saw the way she looked at you, too."

He shot her a surprised glance. "Like what?"

"Like she wasn't happy unless you were in the room. That wasn't fake."

His mouth tightened. "Maybe it was. She had secrets." He met her gaze. "She gave away a son several years ago."

Rose's eyes went wide. "Did she have another option?"

"Keep him. Raise him. Don't we always have options?"

"She must have been, what, in her early twenties? Unmarried? Still under her father's roof?" And under his thumb.

"Yes, but she was smart. She could have found a way to provide for her son."

"Buying food and diapers doesn't equal a good parent. Perhaps giving her son up was the best way she could provide for him at the time." She patted his knee. "When you first came here, you had a mountain of anger on your shoulders, weighing you down, but now, looking back, can you imagine what your life would have been like had the state not taken you away from your parents?" They'd gone to prison for drug possession. When they'd been released months later, they hadn't bothered to come looking for Dev. And they'd soon landed in prison again. It was a vicious cycle that would have swallowed him whole. He wasn't sure they even remembered they'd had a son. He'd been immensely lucky to land on Rose Curry's doorstep.

He leaned forward to kiss her soft cheek and was hit with the smell he'd always associate with home—sunshine and lavender. "I don't know what I did to deserve you. You're an angel."

She laughed and cupped his face. "And I'm smart. Don't forget that." Her laughter faded and she grew serious. "Give Ivy a chance to explain. You might be surprised to learn that things aren't so black and white. Like with Roger. Or Aidan."

He looked away, and she dropped her hands. "That's different. Aidan nearly killed someone."

"Who was trying to kill him. It was self-defense."

"He could have asked for help for his situation before it got that bad." But Robert Stone's taunts came back to him. He'd implied he knew more about his brother's case than he should. Could the Club have been involved somehow?

She slid him a glance. "Unfortunately, we both know asking for help isn't Aidan's style. We all have our issues, and his is leaning on other people. That's always been tough for him. He'll come to realize he can count on others, just as you'll come to realize that a leap of faith can lead to incredible rewards." She put her hand on his arm. "He'll be okay. I think you blame yourself for not saving him, even without knowing what trouble he was in. You can't help when you don't know the problem."

He knew that. It was just hard to accept. He tried to clear the lump from his throat, but it wouldn't budge, so he simply nodded and stood. He brushed his hands on his jeans. "I should get back to work." But his phone rang in his pocket. Adam Wilde was calling. "This is probably about Rains," he told Rose before answering. "Hello?"

"I'm at Douglas Rains's home," Adam said.

"Did you find something that will lead us to the killer?" To Stone?

"I think you should see this for yourself."

CHAPTER SEVENTEEN

Ivy paced the waiting area at the airport, her gaze continually straying to her father's private jet on the tarmac. At least two men from the security detail he'd assigned her were out there, thoroughly checking the plane—for what, she didn't want to know, but she could guess any number of people would love to blow her father's plane into a billion bits, preferably with him inside it.

At least, while packing, she'd been able to make a quick call to Linda on her burner phone. The Castillos would take extra precautions with Brandon's safety, and their own, until Ivy could figure out what to do next to keep her father away from them.

She turned away from the window. Within the waiting area were another couple of men, one of them Archer. Thankfully, they'd given her a bit of space and were standing guard a few yards away.

She checked her phone for the hundredth time, wishing that Dev would contact her. More than ever, she wished she had him to bounce ideas around with, but it seemed he'd been able to walk away without looking back. That stung more than it should have. But the sting was mitigated by a numbness she'd finally achieved after confronting her father. She'd thought she was on her own before, but she hadn't known what loneliness was until she'd come to depend on someone's support, and then had it withdrawn. She'd only known Dev a few days, but she'd felt a bond she'd never had with anyone. Not even Nathan, whom she'd known her entire childhood. And maybe that was the crux of it. Their love had been a young one, relatively untested.

Her feelings for Dev were definitely being tested.

Her phone rang in her hands, startling her. Dread shot from her chest outward, through her limbs, making them heavy as she saw it was her stepfather. "Albert? How is she?"

"Dead. You're too late." His words were thick with emotion.

"Dead? You said she was stable. Unconscious, but I thought you said she'd be okay." Her heart went from her chest to her stomach, then up to her throat. How could things have gone from bad to so much worse in only a few hours? In her periphery, she saw Archer watching her and she turned away, not wanting him to intrude on such a personal moment. She gazed, unseeing, through the window to the plane.

"They were wrong." Albert laughed sharply. "Of course, when has your mother ever been totally *stable*? I should have known better."

"Did she... did she kill herself?"

"The jury's still out on that, but I'm guessing yes. The nurses had just come to tell me she'd woken up, and then all hell broke loose. All kinds of buzzers and alarms went off with another patient, so the staff was occupied there, and then the same thing happened in Gloria's room. They haven't told me what happened yet. I'm not sure the staff even knows. They're saying there might have been some kind of complication. A stroke, maybe. Or that she'd woken up and tried to harm herself again. You can bet I'll be demanding an investigation."

"Oh, God."

His voice became clogged with emotion. "Yeah, well, she's in His hands now."

"I'm at the airport. I was about to get on a plane to come out there."

"Good. You can handle the memorial. Gloria would have wanted that. Besides, you owe us that much."

Ivy bit back tears of frustration and grief. How could he be talking about what she owed at a time like this? Her loss was nearly as much as his. And what about the childhood, the *mother*, Ivy had been owed, yet denied? But Albert had to be just as angry about what had happened as Ivy was, so she swallowed her anger.

"You know how extravagant and dramatic Gloria likes—liked—to be," Albert said. "She once told me she wanted you to plan everything."

"Why me?" Why were they even talking about this so soon?

"I think she thought that having you handle it would be the perfect, final fuck-you from Gloria to your father." Albert understood how some ridiculous goodbye party, especially if Ivy organized it, would anger Robert Stone. And yet, Ivy couldn't say no to a final request.

"I'll be there."

"When?"

"A couple hours. The plane is almost ready. And then I'll be at your disposal for the next few days." Planning events was something she was good at, at least. Something she could offer that would also distract herself from the pain.

Albert's voice was thick with grief. "I'll see you soon."

She hung up and stared at the phone, trying to ignore the shaking of her hand. She sank down hard into one of the vinyl-covered waiting room chairs, dropping the phone to the seat next to her.

She buried her head in her hands, digging her fingertips into her scalp as she tried to cling to reality. Still numb from shock, she looked up as a chirp indicated she'd received another communication. An email popped up on her screen, and without even checking who had sent it, she embraced the distraction, scooping up the phone. And then she let out an involuntary gasp.

Your father is responsible for your mother's death.

She glanced at the sender, noting it was the fake Nathan—*NWilson*—who'd been contacting her for weeks via email, but had been quiet the last few days. She jumped up and spun in a circle, searching the area around her. The closest people were several rows away, a family of at least eight people awaiting another small jet's flight.

Had someone somehow heard her conversation, or was the timing a coincidence? How had the sender known about her mother's death? She'd only just now found out.

Archer looked over from his position near a pillar, where he could see people coming and going in this wing of the airport. "Something wrong?"

"My mother," Ivy said. "She's dead."

He raised a brow but there was no outward display of emotion. Of course, he was well paid to have the same opinions as her father. "Who called?"

"Her husband. And then I got a weird email."

He came over and tried to take the phone from her hands. She yanked it out of reach. He smirked. "I can access your account another way."

"Try it," she dared. "And I'll notify the police."

"And if you can find an honest cop, you might get somewhere. Good luck with that."

God, if *NWilson* was right and her father had something to do with her mother's death, then Robert Stone, and anyone on Redemption Club payroll, was capable of anything. Even killing his lawyer. His ex-wife. Where would that leave Brandon, if he got his hands on him?

She was shaking all over now, both furious and alarmed that her father's controlling reach extended so far. She glared at Archer. "I may have to put up with you and your crew for a few days, but I don't have to like it."

"Doesn't bother me if you hate me, sugar. My job

is to protect you, no matter what." His eyes glittered with a darkness that had always scared and intimidated her. He stepped closer, his gaze raking her face until she felt the urge to flinch. "As long as your father thinks you deserve protection, that is."

Victor merged with a large tourist group making its way past the waiting area. He'd bought a ticket for whatever small flight was going God-knows-where so that he could get through security and try to get close to Ivy. In his large-framed glasses and bushy white hair, he had been sitting just a couple rows away pretending he was part of a large family when she'd received the phone call.

Gloria had been silenced, just as Robbie had insinuated. But this time, it was definitely permanent. And all she'd wanted was to blackmail her ex-husband out of a ton of money and his film production company. She'd held back a page from the ledger that was to be the ultimate nail in Robbie's coffin—should he not pay up. Of course, she hadn't truly understood what she was undertaking when she and Victor had joined forces.

Victor, on the other hand, knew that violence was, ultimately, the only way to bring Robert Stone to his knees. He knew how the man thought because Victor—David—had always thought the same way.

He had no doubt some Redemption Club minion had committed the deed. Victor no longer had a partner to answer to, but he made a silent vow that he'd avenge Gloria along with his own family members who'd been terminated by Robbie. Even without his partner, the plan was still a go—Victor's plan, not Gloria's. It would be easier now. They'd always disagreed on the best path to taking down Robbie.

Victor was convinced Ivy was the key.

But not today. There was too much security around her today. It was time to make a getaway while he could. He maintained his hunched-over limp so as to appear like the tired old grandpa he'd dressed as, but inside he was fuming. He'd wanted to corner Ivy, to demand answers about his grandson, but that would have to wait, too.

While Robbie might think he was winning, he didn't have the ledger or the box of torn debt cards. Victor had tucked them away somewhere safe. Had Robbie even realized yet that they were missing?

He smiled, wishing he could see the monster's face when he discovered he'd been manipulated for a change. Victor had the ultimate tools to bring down the mighty Robert Stone for good, but he'd have to plan carefully. Underestimating Stone's power would be a rookie move. And if he simply turned over the evidence to the police, he risked it falling into the hands of someone on the Club's payroll—someone who could very well be listed in the ledger. Or, as history just showed, Robbie could buy the jury, intimidate witnesses, and escape punishment again.

That couldn't happen. When Victor brought Robbie down, it would be with finality.

He risked a quick look back at Ivy, who now stood at the window, her faraway expression seeming to indicate she wasn't seeing what was on the other side. Was she worried about her son, wherever he was?

The more Victor thought about it, the more certain he became that Ivy had hidden away Nathan's son from everyone—including, thank God, Robbie. Otherwise, Robert Stone would have been grooming the progeny—his precious legacy—to take over his empire one day. Until yesterday, Robbie hadn't known Victor was still alive, so he wouldn't have had a reason to hide the boy away from the world. He would have been actively molding the boy in his own image, giving him every advantage as his grandson.

After all, legacy was everything to a man like Robbie. Victor was counting on it.

Thirty minutes after leaving the ranch, Dev met Adam at the door to Douglas Rains's estate.

"What did you find?" he asked as Adam led him into the lawyer's living room, which looked like something out of a natural disaster movie.

Another member of the task force, DEA agent Mason Gray, emerged from a back room and sent him a nod of greeting. "Good to see you again, Dev."

"Looks like the place was worked over," Dev said, taking in his surroundings. What once must have been a luxuriously appointed room had been tossed, leather cushions and throw pillows sliced or ripped apart and cupboards hanging open. Items had been pulled or thrown from shelves, pottery shattered. Dev surveyed the damage and shook his head. "Are there signs of a struggle?"

"No," Adam said. "Not here, anyway. But someone was definitely looking for something."

"Was there anything left to find?"

"Actually, Rains was smart."

"No doubt. He did get Stone cleared of numerous charges." Dev would never underestimate someone Stone trusted to be on his payroll.

"He gave the most important documents to his assistant for safekeeping," Adam continued, leading Dev into the dining room—the only room that wasn't a disaster area, but only because there were few furnishings to tear apart or mutilate. On the table was a manila folder, fat with paperwork. "That assistant heard about Rains's death this morning, and showed up at the task force headquarters asking for me, head of the task force, as Rains had specifically directed in the event of his demise." Adam pulled the sheaths from inside and handed him one paper-clipped bunch.

Dev scanned Rains's last will and testament and a signed letter indicating they should look more closely at Stone and Archer, should anything happen to Rains. He arched a brow at Adam. "Sounds like the man expected to be killed, but this isn't exactly hard evidence against Stone."

Adam grunted an acknowledgment and handed over the next bundle of papers. Dev skimmed the thicker, older stack of paperwork. "You know anything about this?" Adam asked.

Dev's blood ran cold as he flipped through what appeared to be Ivy's medical file from some clinic in Montana. The photocopied paperwork dated back eight years and detailed her pregnancy and the birth of her son. Was her son still in Montana? Dev found he was inordinately curious about the boy. "She mentioned the son to me last night." Right before he'd walked out on her. "This must be the information Rains had planned to use to get Ivy into bed."

"Which gives her motive to kill him," Adam said grimly.

"It also gives Stone motive," Dev said, a strong wave of protectiveness coming over him on Ivy's behalf.

"How do you figure?"

"If he went after Rains for propositioning Ivy, he might have discovered this same information."

"That's a lot of ifs and mights." Adam scowled. "You don't think he already knew?"

"No. Ivy gave her son away." At the time she'd shared that information, Dev had locked onto the piece of the story that had hit him hardest. But now that he thought about it, in giving her son away, Ivy had kept the boy away from the influence of her father.

If Rains knew the truth, then it was possible Stone also knew about his grandson. How long ago had he found out? And where was the child now?

More importantly, how would Ivy's father use the child against her?

CHAPTER EIGHTEEN

Dev explained the situation to Adam before hurrying to Legacy to find Ivy. A sense of urgency told him he needed to be by her side, no matter how he'd walked out on her last night. Had her father already blindsided her with the information about her son? If so, she'd been left to take the blows alone, as usual.

And now, his calls were going straight to her voicemail. He couldn't blame her for ignoring him.

He never should have left her. He should have stayed to talk things out. He knew how hard it was when someone who was supposed to care about you judged you and walked away.

Asshole.

Regret weighed on his shoulders with each step he made through Legacy's rotunda, searching for the ebony curtain of Ivy's hair, reflecting magenta and blue in the sunlight streaming through the domed skylight in the ceiling. He didn't head straight for her office, aware that if Stone caught sight of him, he'd have Dev thrown off the property, and Dev desperately needed to make sure Ivy was okay first.

Instead, he headed for Legacy Lounge, aware that, if Ivy had gone to her friend for sympathy after the way he'd treated her, Emily might be just as dangerous as Stone at the moment. Emily was already there, serving the lunch crowd, and he moved over to the bar.

She greeted him with a warm smile but her eyes were coolly assessing. "Coffee?" she asked, taking in the dusty, wrinkled jeans and long-sleeved work shirt he hadn't bothered to change after working at the ranch. He'd been in too much of a hurry to see what Adam had found. "Or maybe something stronger?"

"No, thanks," he replied. "I'm looking for your boss."

"What do you want with Ivy now?"

That was a loaded question, and much too complicated for him to answer. His body wanted one thing, his mind another. "That's between me and her."

His impatient response sent both blonde eyebrows winging upward. Emily's loyalty to her friend and employer was further evidence that Ivy wasn't the icy bitch he'd assumed last week, or that he'd implied just the night before.

He sighed. "Look, have you seen her or not?"

"Not since I dropped her off at her place last night. She was really quiet on the ride home. I got the impression she needed some time alone, and that she specifically wanted some distance from you." So Ivy hadn't told Emily about their night together. He wasn't sure whether to be relieved or disappointed.

He ran a hand through his hair. "Look, we were both upset by Rains's murder. But you were there at the end. I didn't want her to leave and be alone last night, remember?"

"Yeah." There was a softening in her expression.

"I need to see her and make sure she's okay. She has plenty of reasons to be upset, especially since she planned to meet with her father this morning."

"Try the theater. She likes to retreat there to lick her wounds."

"Right." He should have thought of that after the last time he'd found her there.

Emily narrowed her gaze on him. "If you make things worse for her, I'll cut off your balls." She raised a paring knife from the cutting board where she'd been about to slice limes. "And I'll do the same to Stone if he does one more thing to hurt her. You two wouldn't be the first."

With a wry grin, Dev pushed away from the bar. "Got it." He intended to make things up to Ivy, starting with warning her—if she didn't already know—that her father likely knew about her child.

He crossed the rotunda again, heading for the theater's entrance. But the doors were locked and the lights inside were off. Circumventing the check-in desk, he pursued his final option and headed down the hall that led to the offices. His steps slowed as he approached the office assistant's desk. She was crying, on the phone with someone. He searched his memory for her name and finally recalled it was Megan.

"I just can't believe she's dead, you know?" Megan dabbed at her eyes with a tissue, not paying Dev any attention. "I admired her so much."

He stopped in his tracks. Surely, the woman wasn't talking about Ivy. After he'd left her, had she decided to go ahead with her plans to disappear, maybe even faking her death? Or worse... Could she actually be dead? Had Stone taken out his anger when he'd learned about his grandson? His heart stilled in his chest.

Megan caught sight of him. "I have to go," she said and hung up. "Can I help you?"

"Someone died?" Dev asked.

"You haven't heard?"

"No," he said, trying to bite back his impatience. "Obviously it was someone important to you."

"Gloria Westwood. So hard to believe. She's just such an icon. I grew up watching her movies."

Gloria. Not Ivy. *Ivy isn't dead.* Relief made Dev's knees weak and he was about to sink into a chair when he realized how Ivy must have taken the news about Gloria. He glanced through the open door to her office, but it was empty.

"Where's Ivy?" he asked.

Megan sniffled. "She left town. Even before the news hit, she was heading to California to be with her mom. Got a call early this morning that Gloria was in the hospital. But then..." She shook her head. "I can't imagine what Ivy's going through. She was trying to get there, but it was too late." As tears began to fall, Dev handed her another tissue from the box on her desk.

Stone's office door swung open and the man darkened the mood yet further with his scowl. "What the devil is all the noise about out here?" He stopped at the sight of Dev and smirked. "Ah. That devil. It'll be my pleasure to have Megan call security. *Again.*"

Dev scowled. "I would have thought the death of your ex-wife, the mother of your child, would be enough to alter your diatribe, but it's business as usual around here."

"Megan," he warned, ignoring Dev's barb. Stunned, Megan only looked between the two men. "Megan!" Stone barked. The woman jumped and reached for the phone, shooting Dev an apologetic look.

Dev raised his hand. "Don't bother. I'll show myself out."

He walked through the rotunda with its multitude of colors streaming through the stained glass dome. His thoughts and emotions were a maelstrom.

Ivy was alone and all the way in California. How could he best help her?

Or would she even let him? He'd left her alone to deal with a shitstorm of epic proportions, just when she'd needed his acceptance and comfort the most. He wouldn't make that mistake twice. He planned to offer his assistance until the proud, strong woman either accepted it or told him to go the hell away.

Stone took a drive to clear the anger from his system. The only way to deal with Devlin Grimm was to be rid of him forever. He swung into the gated driveway to his Henderson mansion, a sense of pride and purpose suffusing him as it always did when he came home. He'd bought the place years ago, with his first big windfall. The casino, and then his entertainment empire, had grown substantially from there. And he wasn't done yet. He expected his daughter, and now his grandson—his gut still constricted every time he thought about his flesh and blood being out there, raised by strangers—to continue the trend until Stones dominated the world. He'd already given them a great start. Not like his parents, who'd given him less than nothing.

The mansion was filled with things he'd collected over the years, but it was one thing in particular he sought this afternoon. He went directly to his den, with the French doors that overlooked a small, but spectacular garden. The greenhouse beyond held even more rarities in the form of specially imported blooms. A little hobby of his, to deal with the anger and disappointment. He'd even disposed of a problem or two out there, in the ashes that mixed with the soil. It was good for the plants. Good for his soul. He'd head out there next, after things were arranged.

Settling behind his desk with a drink, he dialed Archer. "It's done, then?" Stone asked. He'd seen Megan crying her eyes out at her desk a couple hours ago, so he assumed news was getting around.

"Gloria's dead," Archer confirmed. "Our Club connection in Hollywood came through. The news is trending worldwide."

"Good." Satisfaction that something, goddamn *something*, had gone right, flooded Stone's body.

"Not sure why we had to kill a public treasure." Archer was actually sounding a little pouty. "She told us how to contact her partner. If you wanted more from her, I could have tried threats first. I doubt she would have told anyone what she knew."

"The woman was coming after us. Don't tell me you've become soft in your old age."

"Hardly. But killing a high profile legend will raise questions."

"It was supposed to look like suicide."

"And it did, but she didn't die right away. Albert found her too soon. He got her to the hospital in time and then we had to have your third party deal with it."

"And he did."

"Disguised as an orderly, but if anyone remarks on how there was someone who shouldn't have been there, if anyone notices..."

"Aw, cheer up, Archer. It was easier this way." Snuffing out Gloria Westwood without drawing suspicion was almost too easy. The bitch always had been overdramatic and weak. But when she went directly against him, trying to blackmail him to take his hard-earned money and business, she went too far. He'd ordered the hit the moment Manny had informed him Ivy's stalker had tried to approach her again at some children's home, and then Archer had verified that the emails sent to Ivy, supposedly from Nathan, had originated from a junk account that could be traced to Albert Westwood's film studios. It had to be Gloria and David behind those threatening emails.

Besides, he was tired of dealing with the woman, and decided to nip that in bud right away. No more Gloria to mess up his plans. He should have done it years ago.

He set his drink down and came around his desk, swinging the painting of Zeus on Mount Olympus outward to reveal his personal safe. "I'll return the Club member's debt card, and compensate him handsomely to keep him quiet," he told Archer. "He'll disappear if I order him to." He turned the numbers to the combination. "And Ivy?"

"We just landed twenty minutes ago. Waiting on the luggage to be loaded into the car. First order of business when we get to the house is to disable her email account. I think David tried to contact her again."

"Good. Don't disable the account. It may be a way to get to him."

There was a pause on the other end. "You sure you want to use your daughter this way?"

"Gloria and David had to have something on me or they wouldn't have been so damn gutsy. Besides, I didn't get this far by being meek." If they had control of the bait—Ivy—that would lure David Wilson out of hiding, he'd damn well use it. Gloria had been looking for a way to best Stone for years, ever since he'd bought her daughter out from under her and used it against her every chance he could. And she'd thought she could blackmail him?

But how had Gloria known David Wilson was still alive? Stone had to assume the man had come to her. She hadn't been that smart. "We'll frustrate David's efforts and when he comes for her, you'll be ready to kill—" He froze as the safe swung open and revealed nothing.

"Robert?" As if from a great distance, Archer's voice was barely audible beyond the roaring in Stone's ears.

"They're gone."

"Gone? What's gone?"

"The ledger. And the box of debt cards." The records of all of everything Redemption Club had done, who'd done what, and who still owed a debt—the very foundation upon which the Club was built. Without them, Stone had nothing. And there was only one man who might have had the combination.

David Wilson had just signed his death warrant. Again.

Rage trembled through Stone's limbs. "Find David and kill him. Make it painful. But make sure you have the ledger and cards first."

"And if he doesn't take the bait?"

"If Ivy's not enough to trap him, we'll find something he'll want even more—our grandson."

CHAPTER NINETEEN

Wednesday afternoon came barreling at Ivy like a freight train, but she could slow life down when this was all over. Her mother had never done anything the usual way, so a mid-week memorial was the perfect tribute. Besides, Ivy was on borrowed time, feeling every hour she was away from Vegas might put Brandon more at risk. Was her father already looking for him? Linda had assured Ivy during their daily phone calls that their routine had not been disrupted and nobody seemed to be following them.

Pulling everything together in forty-eight hours hadn't been easy, but Gloria Westwood's name had opened many doors. While she'd wanted Ivy to make all of the arrangements, Gloria had laid out detailed plans for an extravagant memorial service, and left them with her lawyer years ago. Armed with her tablet, which displayed a checklist three pages long, Ivy had done what she did best—managed everyone around her—and that had kept the grief at bay.

The constant to-do list and phone calls from well-wishers and questions from the press had also kept her distracted from her breakup with Dev. He'd tried to call or text her several times over the past forty-eight hours, but she'd ignored his attempts. After all, what more could he say? Either he was still angry and hadn't finished berating her, or he was sorry. If it were the latter, she'd never know if his apology was due to guilt for walking out right before her mother died. He had to have heard the news about Gloria's death.

And then there was the last conversation she'd had with her father, who'd been oddly quiet for the past couple days, though his security guards remained close by her side. Another reason to leave Dev's calls and texts unanswered. Otherwise, attention would turn to him. The last thing she wanted was to put Dev, his family, or his ranch at risk again. Even after his hurtful words, she didn't want him hurt.

Ivy had managed to check in with Megan each day and confirmed that her father was working from his office, not off doing something that could harm anyone—something like finding his grandson. And with Archer here, part of the security crew, she had to hope Brandon was safe for the moment.

As she walked through her mother's home, she was relieved to see that the memorial was everything Gloria had requested. Lights. Cameras. People. Mostly, the people. Over a hundred of the most influential, rich and famous people in the industry filled the Westwood estate, attending the memorial as much to say they'd been there as to pay their respects to Gloria. Still, Ivy found a few friendly, recognizable faces in the crowd. She'd take whatever support she could get.

She and Gloria had been far from close, but losing a parent meant that anchor to the physical world was gone, and it was one more string cut that threatened to set Ivy adrift. She couldn't help but wonder if Brandon felt similarly. He knew he was adopted, especially since Linda and Miguel were in their fifties, old enough to be his grandparents.

And then there was the guilt that she felt for not having connected with her mother this weekend after the repeated phone calls. If she'd put more effort into getting in touch, or given in and made plans to come see her, would her mother still have been driven to overdose? Albert had seemed clueless as to what would have pushed Gloria over the edge.

The rest of the people gathered seemed just as confused and shocked.

"She died before her time."

"She was the image of class and beauty."

"Her work onscreen will be revered for decades to come. Such a role model."

Ivy tried not to cringe as she caught snatches of conversation and worked her way around the periphery of the room. A role model? Maybe in acting, but never as a parent. Ivy's lack of role models was one of the reason she'd felt so panicked at the thought of raising a baby as a single parent at age twenty-one.

It was obvious the mourners didn't know the truth of her demise, either, which was a relief. The news reported she'd been admitted to the hospital for a routine procedure. As if getting your stomach pumped to purge the pills was routine. Anger at Gloria's thoughtlessness and selfishness flooded her. Still, she made sure her smile was flawless despite the ache in her cheeks. Her lips curved as she greeted guests— smiling just enough to put them at ease, not too much or she'd look happy her mother was dead. And she wasn't. She wasn't horribly grief-stricken either. But the media wasn't her friend, so she had to remain even-keeled or she'd be slaughtered in the press again. The one good thing about having so much of her father's security around was they'd kept the reporters at bay.

But she wasn't sure she could take one more sympathetic squeeze of her hand or half-hug. Those were almost worse than no physical contact at all. Almost. Because a hug, a real embrace from someone genuine, like Linda, Rose or Dev, would break her right now.

"You did good," Albert said as he sidled up to her. Her stepfather's eyes were red-rimmed, but his white hair was neatly combed, his suit impeccable. "Your mother would have been very happy with this. As happy as she was with anything," he added, frowning into his drink. Despite his fondness for Gloria, her mother's judgmental side had impacted him, too. "You honor her today with this. I wish she could see it.

I know there were things that kept you apart—like your father—but she loved you, and she would have liked to see the love you put into this. I'm sure there's a cost to you, though. There's always a price with Robert Stone."

There was a high cost. Her father had demanded to meet Brandon.

Still, Ivy needed to do this for Gloria, not out of a sense of obligation, since there'd been little of the mother-daughter tenderness over the years, but because it would bring Ivy closure. She would no longer have to wonder if her mother would ever want her in her life. There would be no more opportunity for that kind of sentimentality, and Ivy would just have to learn to live with the regret. She vowed that, someday, when Brandon was old enough to understand, she'd make sure he understood his biological mother had never wanted to cast him aside. Ivy had only wanted what was best for him.

"I don't believe I've seen *him* before," Albert mumbled under his breath. "Some new actor, maybe?"

She followed his gaze to the other side of the room, near the front hall. Her eyes landed on broad shoulders, a dark head of hair, and intense hazel eyes and her body thrummed with awareness before he even made eye contact.

Dev.

Her heart stuttered for a second, then swelled against her ribs. Why was he here? He'd walked away from her, making it clear what he'd thought of her past and how she'd handled things with her son.

His lips curved in a soft smile that expressed both sympathy and tenderness. And something she'd never seen from him before—uncertainty.

The ache in her chest moved upward to her throat and she swallowed, scrambling to remind herself how this man had hurt her only a few days ago. Was she really going to let him destroy her defenses again?

"You know him?" Albert asked, seeing that Ivy's

and Dev's gazes hadn't wavered from each other.

"Devlin Grimm. He's a bodyguard, of sorts, from Las Vegas."

Albert glanced with distaste toward the four men, Archer included, who'd taken up various posts throughout the large living room. "Is he one of Stone's men?"

"No. Dev was on my payroll. I wasn't expecting him to show up." Wanting to change the subject, and not able to face Dev just yet when her emotions felt like they'd been in a blender, she looped her arm through Albert's and tugged him to the outside deck for some air.

But her thoughts went back to Dev. Why was he here? Her body ached at the memory of being cherished, even if just for the one night. He'd reawakened senses she'd long ago shut down, and then left her wanting so much more.

Yet another reason to be angry with him.

Dev knew Ivy was avoiding him, and gave her the space she apparently still needed. Despite their silent exchange from across the room, over an hour ago, she hadn't approached him. Hadn't done so much as looked at him again.

Coming to California had been an impulsive move, but Dev was through waiting for Ivy to return his messages. He suspected she'd soldier through this day alone, refusing to admit she could use a friend. He wasn't the most likely candidate, given how they'd left things, but he was determined to offer his shoulder—if she wanted one.

Watching her from afar as she hid her feelings behind a mask of polite grief was killing him. He'd seen her emotionally stripped bare, and now he could detect signs of raw pain beneath her carefully cultivated outer shell. Like a cool lake, there was much power, strength and activity beneath the glassy, pristine surface.

She was across the large deck now, talking with an elderly woman and laying a hand on her shoulder in a sympathetic gesture as they waited in the twilight for some kind of light display—or at least, that's what he'd heard. People should be comforting Ivy, and yet she moved through everything as if an angel of mercy imparting gentle smiles and kind gestures, hiding her heartache.

Close by, Archer and his fellow flunkies took turns scowling at him, as they had for the entire evening. He ignored the three of them. If Ivy wasn't kicking him out, he wasn't leaving. Not this time. This time, it would be her decision. He only hoped she'd stop ignoring him soon and let him talk to her. But he could bide his time. He'd prefer until it was just the two of them, anyway.

The twenty-minute fireworks display and light show was breathtaking, and the mourners were more like revelers by the end, which was, of course, the point. Things wound down in the half hour that followed, and Dev finally found Ivy in the front hall, saying goodbye to the last of the guests. Her stepfather had retreated to the living room with a few of his closest friends to swap stories, and Stone's guards were out on the grounds, sweeping the property for lingering threats, which left Dev and Ivy alone together for the first time in days.

Soft laughter trickled into the foyer from the small group gathered in the living room, as Ivy closed the door behind the last departing guest. Dev was about to announce his presence, as she had yet to notice he'd followed her, when she sank onto the hallway bench. Before his eyes, she seemed to fold inward on herself. Her elbows went to her knees, her head into her hands. She didn't make a sound, but the white in her knuckles as she gripped her scalp indicated she was trying hard to hold herself together—almost literally.

He took the seat next to her and her head shot

up. The green of her eyes turned from clouded to clear in an instant, her shields sliding into place. But not before he'd caught intense emotion. The ice queen wasn't so frozen on the inside as she'd like everyone to believe. Still, there was no sign of tears, which was a relief. He didn't think she'd forgive him if he saw her cry—not until she trusted him enough to let him past her barriers again. A woman like her probably saw emotional displays as a weakness. Or she'd been taught by her father not to show her hand. Which made it all the more precious that she'd let him in once. Dev was determined to earn her trust again.

She leaned back on the bench as if in retreat. Or to appear relaxed, though he sensed she was anything but. He brushed a thumb across one of the dark circles beneath her eyes.

"Did you need something?" she asked, jerking her head away from his touch. "Or maybe you're here to test my security while my defenses are down." She released a harsh laugh. "You're in luck, your timing superb. I may even agree to help you take down my father, damn all the consequences."

His lips curved slightly. "I don't think your defenses are ever down." But there was definitely a fragility underlying her barbed wire. "And I would never let you do anything to hurt yourself." Her willingness to put herself at risk to help him—especially after how he'd left her—undid something inside him, released the protector instinct he'd honed all these years in his security business. He glanced around. "Speaking of defenses, what happened to Manny? You've got a new crop of suits surrounding you."

"Courtesy of my father. No doubt, they've reported to him that you're here."

"I don't care. I'm here for you."

She eyed him a moment but didn't argue. "Manny never showed up again after we lost him in Vegas. "

"Pity." The insincerity of his statement pulled a small smile from her. "But I've had a couple GSS agents undercover at Legacy and around Gloria's neighborhood, watching out for you." Meyer and Duffy had sent him regular reports, and he'd been both relieved and concerned to hear that Ivy hadn't left Gloria's house except while making arrangements for the memorial.

"Oh." Her expression softened. "Why are you here, Dev?"

Damn, he liked the sound of his name on her lips. "I'm not leaving again. Not unless you ask me to."

She arched a brow at him. "When have you ever done anything I asked you to do? You haven't even done what I was willing to *pay* you to do."

He took her hand and raised it to his lips. "You've been through a lot, and I recognize my part in that. I'm sorry. I shouldn't have walked out on you." He caught her sharp intake of breath as his thumb moved over her hand. Would she accept his apology or kick him out? "I should have known better. Everyone in your life has walked out on you."

She turned her palm upward against his and interlaced their fingers. "At least you came back."

"Your father should be here for you, no matter what his feelings were for your mother."

She shook her head. "It's easier without him here."

"What did he say to you when you saw him Monday morning?"

Her tone turned bitter and angry. "He didn't confess to Rains's murder, if that's what you're asking."

He searched her face, certain he was missing something. Her anger at her father was a raw hurt she couldn't quite hide. "No. I'm asking what he said to you. Last I saw you two together, he was demanding some kind of tribute or symbol of your commitment, or other such nonsense."

"Oh, he's deciding to take my tribute in new and

particularly hurtful ways. That's what happens when the secret's out."

Dev stiffened. "Your son. So he does know about your child?"

She met his gaze and her shields slipped, revealing a crack of pain. "Yes. Dad's demanding to meet him."

"I'll kill him," Dev muttered.

She pulled her hand away and stood. "No. Stop stepping in for me. He can't know you think about me at all, or that you care in any way. He'll destroy you. More than ever, he's determined to bring me to heel, and he'll use whoever's close to me to do it."

Touched at the concern he heard in her voice, and surprised by the stab of need that raced through him at the thought that she cared that much, he stood, too, and pulled her into his arms. "I won't let him isolate you. Let me help you."

God help her, Ivy didn't have the strength to push Dev away. Not when his arms felt so good around her. His solid chest beneath her cheek was a rock she could cling to when the turbulent waters around her threatened to drown her.

But she was leaving tomorrow. For good. She didn't need Dev's help.

Once she returned to Vegas, she planned to stop by Linda's, pick up the cash and identity documents she'd stashed there, and go. She'd color her hair and hide her eyes behind glasses. She hoped the Castillos would follow with Brandon when it was safe and Ivy was settled in Idaho. She'd found a certain peacefulness to the area when she'd hidden out in Montana to give birth to Brandon, and now, she hoped to make a home for all of them.

So she couldn't get any closer to Dev. This time, it would be her leaving, and it wasn't to protect him so much as *her* heart. She was falling for him, and it was tempting her to take chances she shouldn't even consider. Like staying in Vegas and fighting to remain Ivy Stone.

As another chorus of laughter came from the direction of the living room, she stepped away, out of the circle of Dev's arms.

"Is there somewhere we can go that's more private?" he asked. "Just to talk."

She wouldn't mind having a private place to say goodbye to him. "There's a guesthouse out back. It was my mother's acting studio."

As Ivy stepped out through a side door off the kitchen and crossed the stone path to the guesthouse, she was conscious of Dev at her back and Archer off to the side, near the driveway. She ignored the other man, but was certain he'd be reporting every move she made—especially as they involved Dev—to her father. She didn't care, and the rebelliousness that filled her was glorious.

A raindrop fell and she turned her face up to the sky.

"I'm glad Gloria got her fireworks before the storm moved in," Dev said. "There wasn't even a cloud in the sky."

She smiled. "Gloria gets what Gloria wants. It's always been that way. But I'm glad I was able to pull it all together for her." She found the guesthouse unlocked and let them in just as the raindrops became a steady beat upon the windows.

Dev's phone chirped with an incoming text and Ivy stepped away to give him some privacy. She took in her surroundings, which hadn't changed over the years. Ivy remembered sitting on the white leather couch by the large window and watching butterflies dance in the garden while her mother ran lines in front of the floor-to-ceiling mirror that covered one entire wall. The place still held a trace of her mother's perfume, a delicate flowery scent she'd had specially made when she'd received her first major award. Years later, she'd begun selling the brand to the public.

"Any idea what this means?" Dev asked, holding out his phone. He'd been texted a picture. Recognizing it immediately, she grabbed it away and marched toward the guesthouse bedroom, with Dev following.

"Who sent this?" she demanded, heading straight to the dressing table in the photo. The window on this backside of the guesthouse was open and rain had spattered the curtains. They billowed as she passed by.

"That's the dresser in the photo," Dev said, realizing what she'd already discovered. He shoved her behind him as if pulling open the drawers might set off a bomb. "Wait. We don't know what this is about. Most likely, it's that stalker finding new ways to reach you. Stay by me." Evidently not convinced she'd obey, Dev dragged her with him as he shut the window, closed the curtains, and checked out the closets and the rest of the guesthouse.

When he was sure they were alone, they returned to the dresser. He pulled open the main drawer and there, sitting on top of her mother's makeup and boxes of costume jewelry, was a rolled up paper, tied with a red ribbon.

Dev untied the bow and carefully unfurled the paper, then laid it on the dressing table. Age had softened the edges of the page. Both sides were covered in names and dates.

Ivy's gaze flew to Dev's as recognition dawned. "That's from the Redemption Club ledger," she said.

"Unless it's a fake," Dev said. "Some criminals were looking to sell forgeries on the Red Market. Does any of this look like your father's handwriting?"

"Yes, several of the entries do." Her eye was drawn to a name. *Nathan.* Her finger shook as it pointed to the entry.

October 27, 2008—Nathan, Joanna, and David Wilson dead at the request of Robert Stone. Made to look like an accident. For David Wilson's attempts to extort money from a crime family, putting the entire club at risk.

Her father's signature was as real as the rest of the page, and had sealed the Wilsons' fate.

"One founder ordered the death of another," Dev said. But it wasn't only David Wilson's death warrant that had been signed by her father. It was Nathan's and Joanna's too. "I'm sorry, Ivy." Dev squeezed her hand.

Feeling sick, Ivy pulled away and stumbled from the room. Dev called out to her, but she couldn't stay there anymore.

He lied. Her father had lied again. And this time, it was unforgivable.

As she reached the yard, Ivy's legs suddenly felt rubbery. The lawn, now slick with rainwater, chilled her shins as she went to her knees. The silk of her black mourning dress clung to her skin like a shroud.

"Ivy!" Dev called. She heard other shouts and a few sets of footsteps, running toward her from the direction of the deck several yards away, but she could barely think beyond the howling of the rage inside of her.

Her father was a liar. The family image she'd fought so hard to preserve was a farce. And worse, she'd been a party to it all.

If Nathan hadn't fallen in love with her, if she hadn't planned to leave her father's side and start a new life eight years ago, would her father have ordered a hit on the Wilsons?

She was poison, tainted.

And Dev would be next if he came too close. He reached for her and she swatted his hand away.

Her breath rattled out of her lungs as the tiny remainder of her heart she'd kept open to the possibility that her father loved her shriveled up and died. Her father wasn't just the monster everyone claimed, he was a sadist, the devil himself. His techniques were ultra-cruel, stringing people along with the hope they'd achieve their goals, and then crushing them.

And he'd grouped her into that category along with the rest of the world. She was just as she'd feared—not special. Never enough. The realization that her father didn't view her as anything more than another pawn in his games stung.

And then there was the ledger page. Who had left it for her? Had it been her stalker, and was this how she was supposed to pay for her family's *past sins*?

Or had Gloria left the page for her? Perhaps her death hadn't been an accident, after all, but a way to silence her. If Robert Stone could kill one of his best friends and co-conspirators in a horrible car crash, what would he do to an ex-wife who had recently competed for Ivy's attention?

She whipped around, looking for the page, and saw Dev patting the pocket of his suit.

"It's safe," he said. "But we should get out of the rain." Already, his hair and clothes were soaked. Ivy looked down at herself. She was in even worse shape than him.

"What's wrong?" Archer asked, coming to a stop at her side, but aiming his question at Dev as he followed her gaze.

"None of your business," Ivy said.

Archer scowled and Ivy hung her head, welcoming the privacy that the curtain of her hair, now hanging loose and wet, provided. Her shock was becoming a burning anger. She was surprised steam wasn't rising from her bare arms. She would make her father pay. She owed Nathan—and Brandon—as much. Her father had stolen so much from all of them.

"What is it?" she heard Albert asking. "What's wrong? Is she okay?" Her stepfather's concerned questions broke through her haze. He didn't deserve anything that would further mar the bittersweet memory of this day.

Dev helped her to her feet, and this time she let him. Albert wrapped a trench coat around her soaked shoulders.

"I'm taking her home," Dev told Albert in a quiet voice. "Think you can keep these guys busy?" *Guys?* Archer and the rest of the security team, she realized. Albert nodded and she stepped forward to embrace him.

"I'm so sorry," she whispered in his ear. "Everything's going to be okay," she promised.

Dev managed to get her to his car and away from Gloria's home, but how, Ivy couldn't have said. She was just grateful he was there. His long, trim fingers gripped the wheel with confident ease. Despite the rain-slicked roads and fast driving, she felt safe and secure. She didn't care where he was taking her, as long as it was well away from the chaos her life had become.

CHAPTER TWENTY

I am invisible. I am untouchable. I am secure in who I am.

They were just words. Stupid, meaningless platitudes.

Hours away from Hollywood, safe in Dev's comfortable hand-hewn log cabin at Curry Ranch in the dead of night, Ivy was bundled in a blanket and sitting on a floor pillow, as close to the roaring fire as she could. Though she'd changed out of her wet clothes and into some sweats Rose had brought her, she couldn't get warm. Couldn't make the words, her mantra that had gotten her through so much, work.

She was broken.

Still, staring into the flames allowed her to lose focus, to stop thinking so hard for just a minute—just one damn minute when she didn't have to worry about her whole life caving in on her.

A mug was pressed into her hand and she sniffed. Hot chocolate laced with Irish cream. She took a sip and felt the heat enter her body. It didn't touch the coldness in her soul.

Her father had manipulated her as if she were a pawn. He'd always treated her as his doll to cart out and parade around when he wanted to impress others, but using her to stroke his ego and feed into his illusion of a legacy was one thing.

It was entirely different to kill in order to keep her in her place.

Her son was now at risk, after all of her efforts to

protect him, and if she couldn't get him beyond her father's wide reach soon, they might never get away. *God. Brandon.* Her heart squeezed. She hoped, one day, he'd come to understand the choices she'd made, and the ones she had yet to make.

The murmuring from the other room, where Dev and Rose were talking, quieted and a light weight settled on her shoulder. Rose's hand.

"I'm going to leave you in my son's very capable care," Rose said, then smoothed her hand down Ivy's arm. "Get some rest, honey."

Beyond Rose, Dev watched her with a fathomless expression. One look at his dark eyes and she saw concern, but also wariness. She wanted to scream at him to run while he still could. She was bad. Tainted by Stone evil.

"Thank you," Ivy murmured and Rose passed back through the A-frame cabin to the front door. It was a beautiful place with its warm wood and hand-wrought touches that made it both rustic and artistic. The furnishings were big, yet comfortable. Dev had great taste, and had clearly made a home for himself.

"You finally did your part," she said as Dev settled on the nearby couch behind her, his knee brushing her shoulder. She preferred the floor, where she could face the river stone fireplace and its warm fire. It was beyond time to face the fire.

"What?" he asked, confused.

"You kidnapped me."

His laugh surprised her and had her turning partway to look at him. "I suppose so, though it wasn't what I had planned."

"So you had planned something?"

"There's been little else on my mind since you walked into my office last week." His eyes darkened—not with judgment this time, but with desire. She was suddenly feeling very warm. Something deep in her belly tightened and lurched, as if trying to get to him, to grab him to her, but it was held on a very tight leash.

She took a gulp of the laced cocoa and set it aside so she could hug her knees to her chest, hoping it would contain her body's reaction to him. But she couldn't resist stoking the fire just a little bit. "What, exactly, had you planned?"

His gaze swept over her and he looked away, probably reminding himself that he didn't want a woman like her, one who could walk away from her child as his parents had walked away from him. Or a woman who could fool herself into believing the best in her father when the rest of the world was shouting at her to wake the hell up. But then he looked at her, trapping her with his gaze. "I was going to take you from your bed, in your penthouse suite."

Her mouth tilted upward on one side. "Like Rapunzel from her tower."

The five o'clock shadow that darkened his jaw was split by a flash of white teeth. "Yeah. I like that. But I didn't have a fiery steed."

"The SUV was perfect. Then again, I've never ridden a Harley before, especially one custom made by your brother."

He chuckled. "You've been spying on me again, Miss Stone."

She arched a brow imperiously, a force of habit, but her words were teasing. "I like to know whose hands I'm putting my life in." Damn. That had her looking at his hands where they were clasped together in front of him, between his knees. She imagined those large, ranch-roughened hands on her body again and swallowed hard.

His gaze twinkled as if he read her thoughts. "You're safe here," he said in a low tone. "You can trust me."

With her safety, yes. With her heart? She wasn't so sure. Or maybe she didn't trust herself. Her body was ready to surrender with just a look from him. Dev leaned forward and reached out to smooth a strand of damp hair away from her face, tucking it back behind her ear.

She grabbed his hand and pressed it to her cheek. "Thank you." She placed a kiss to his palm. She couldn't recall the last time someone had taken care of her, out of choice and not because they'd been paid to be her nanny or tutor or bodyguard.

"My pleasure." He looked like he meant it. "Unfortunately, there are things we need to talk about. Things you may not want to talk about."

She sighed and released him. "I know."

"Tell me about your son," he said. "Is he in danger?"

"While you were speaking with Rose in the kitchen, I called to check on him." Thankfully, before Dev had whisked her away from Gloria's home, he'd thought to grab her purse, and she'd had her burner phone inside. Linda had reported everything was still going smoothly at their home. "Brandon's sleeping soundly."

"His name is Brandon?"

She smiled, picturing her son. "Yes. He's a good kid."

"So you've remained in touch with them over the years?"

She nodded. "They're safe. His adoptive parents know what's at stake."

Dev's gaze raked her features. "You're sure."

"I wouldn't have left him with this couple if I hadn't trusted them implicitly. They know my father is aware of Brandon's existence. They'll be careful. I think they suspected what my father was capable of even before I fully did."

"You must have had hints, to go to all of this trouble to hide him from your father."

She looked away. "Remember the marks on my arms Saturday night?"

"The ones from when your father grabbed you? Yeah, I remember." His eyes narrowed. "You're saying that wasn't a one-time thing."

She shook her head. "It didn't happen often, but if he lost his temper, it was like he would just snap."

"So you learned to help him keep his temper by not displaying any of your own feelings."

"Or I avoided him. When Nathan came along and introduced me to theater life, it was like the windows were thrown wide open, and I could express myself. Nathan encouraged me to be who I really was."

"Easy to see why you fell in love."

"Yes. Young, tragic love."

She glanced at Dev's suit coat, now draped over a chair to dry. The ledger paper that had been tucked inside the pocket was spread out on a table to do the same. Thankfully, only the edges had gotten wet, so the ink hadn't smeared. Unfortunately, it still listed Nathan's name—that part hadn't been some warped nightmare. Their love, a threat to Stone's dominance, had been Nathan's downfall.

She swallowed hard before continuing. "One time, just a couple weeks after Nathan's funeral, when Dad had grown tired of seeing me mope around his mansion, he picked me up and threw me in the pool. I was fully clothed and it was the deep end. I remember breaking the surface, coughing and sputtering, and he laughed. Said it was a wake-up call. A week later, I'd come out of my grief enough to realize I was pregnant with Nathan's baby, and I knew I couldn't stay." She met Dev's piercing gaze. "I mean, what if instead of a pool, Dad had lost his temper at the top of a flight of stairs or something? Or if I hadn't been able to surface soon enough? And I had no doubt that me carrying Nathan's child would push my father into a rage. He'd always hated Nathan, and had railed about how his ex-partner, David Wilson, had backstabbed him. Bloodlines and legacies are everything to my father, who grew up much like you, without a family to anchor him. He obsesses about it. And here I was, carrying a child I was sure he wouldn't deem worthy enough to be a Stone. I had to protect my baby. Nathan's baby."

"And you did." It might have been her imagination, but it seemed there was a note of respect in Dev's words. "How much contact have you had with Brandon over the years?"

"As much as possible." At his arched brow, she shrugged. "You assumed I had given him away and never thought of him again, but I see him a couple times a month."

He straightened with surprise. "What? Wait. Was he at the children's home Sunday? Yes, the dark-haired boy who'd come with Linda. Linda is Brandon's adoptive mother?"

"Yes." She smiled. "Linda volunteers there, too, and often brings Brandon. Gives me more time with him, too. But he doesn't know the truth, only that Linda and Miguel adopted him."

"So you didn't abandon him." He scrubbed his hands down his face. "I'm sorry I jumped to conclusions."

She grimaced. "I'm sure you had your own issues to deal with. Being a foster kid can't have been easy, at least until a wonderful woman took you in."

"Perhaps we're more a product of our environment than our biological heritage."

She stood and advanced on him until he had to look up at her. "I'm not anything like my father."

"No, you're not. I may have lumped you in with Robert Stone once upon a time, but I was wrong."

She'd stopped close enough to see his hazel eyes sparkling with gold fire and a touch of humor and awe that soothed her pride. Damn right, he should be impressed. She was going to take charge and create the life she'd always dreamed of. "I have my own needs and desires, my own goals. And Brandon has always been a priority, even when I couldn't be with him. I know I can never be the mother I should have been, but I had hoped for some kind of relationship."

"I think you can do, or have, anything you set

your mind to." He took her hand and threaded their fingers.

The warmth that finally trickled into a tiny crack in her cold soul started a thaw around her heart. But the sudden feeling of vulnerability scared her.

She was untouchable—unless she asked to be touched. Or unless kindness obliterated her carefully constructed walls. She was very afraid there was nothing left of those walls.

She was afraid she'd fallen in love with Devlin Grimm.

Dev wanted to pull her to him—and not let her go until she admitted they were good for each other. Until she realized she wasn't alone anymore. But they'd both been through so much in the past few days, and grown close quickly. He was afraid to push her emotions too far, too fast. His own were still reeling from the rollercoaster they'd been on.

But the moment of softness between them stole the last of his resolve. She was strong enough to go up against the media, a mysterious stalker, and her own father, and yet there were glimpses of vulnerability that tugged at something inside him.

"What if what I want is you?" she murmured. "Can I have that?"

God, she unraveled him like nobody else. "For what? And be specific, Ivy. I want more than just one more night with you."

She surprised him by taking the final step toward him without hesitation. Her knees bumped his and she linked her free hand with his, so that they were also connected, palm-to-palm, fingers intertwined. Holding his gaze, she slid a knee onto the couch next to him, then the other onto the other side of him, straddling his lap.

"How about just a kiss?" She leaned forward and took his bottom lip between her teeth, nipping gently.

He groaned past the constriction of his throat. Hell, his whole body had gone tight with yearning.

The grin she gave him had him wanting to throw her down on the couch and cover her with his body. Screw asking. He'd have her *begging*.

She waited patiently while he fought his inner war, her hungry gaze scrambling his brain. What was she waiting for? Oh yeah, an answer to her question.

And that undid the last of his restraint. Despite the power struggles with her father, she was a woman used to being in control. And yet, she was giving up control to him. Not fully, since she was the one sitting on top and he could still feel the pleasure the sharp sting of her love bite had left on his lip, marking him as hers to take. But she was letting him in a bit more each time, showing she still trusted him after all he'd done, even if she didn't realize that was what her actions proved.

He untangled one hand from hers, and trailed it up her arm to cup the back of her neck. "A kiss is a good start." He melded her mouth to his. The heat exploded between them as teeth scraped and tongues delved. Lips slick with each other devoured.

Several moments later, she broke away to suck in air and slide her mouth down the side of his neck. With a moan, he tilted his head to give her better access, hissing as her hand moved between them and stroked him through his pants until the ache was nearly unbearable. She drove him wild, beyond endurance.

He flipped her so she was under him on the couch. His hands slid beneath the waistband of her sweatpants and she lifted her hips to help him slide them down. He hissed out a breath as his fingers brushed her bare ass. She wasn't wearing underwear. In a hurry to bare the rest of her, his hands slid over her hips and abdomen, and beneath the edge of her shirt. They soon discarded that, too.

Splayed out before him on his couch, naked, she

looked like a goddess, fallen from the heavens to land at his feet. Reverently, he cupped her breast, letting his thumb brush the nipple that was already pebbled. He took some satisfaction from the evidence that she was aching for him as much as he was for her. She rocked up into him, urging him to give her more.

All in good time.

They had all night, and he intended to make the most of it.

He intended to convince her to stay, to trust him, for much longer than one night.

He bent to press kisses across her collarbone, and trailed them down between her lush cleavage as his thumbs circled her nipples. She arched into his hands, releasing little pants of arousal. When he pulled away enough to look into her eyes, they were a smoky emerald.

He leaned his forehead to hers. "You undo me."

She grinned. "I was hoping for the opposite."

Dev's deep laugh was like a warm, soft blanket, warming Ivy from the outside in. She wasn't used to letting someone else have control, but this was the bedroom—well, technically, it was the living room—and in many ways, even at thirty years old, sex was still new territory for her. Lovemaking was even stranger still.

She trusted Dev. The thought shocked her. And yet, it was true. After all, how else could she give her body so easily and completely?

Reaching for his T-shirt, which he'd changed into when they'd arrived at his cabin, she tugged and lifted until the article of clothing was sailing across the room.

His lips curved. She wanted them on her bare skin in the worst way, wanted his hot mouth trailing kisses down her neck, across her nipples, which were so tight the ache bordered on pain.

The night in her Legacy suite had been passion

and flame. Tonight was for savoring. He'd said he wanted more than one night, but their paths would diverge soon enough. Tonight might be their last time together, and she drank him in with her gaze, memorized his angles and curves with her hands.

He settled between her thighs again and she moaned at the pleasure of full body contact. She sank her fingers into his hair, scraping his scalp gently and making him hiss in pleasure.

"I kind of like you telling me what to do," she said, her voice filled with a huskiness she didn't recognize. "I like you being in control. But if you tell anyone, I'll deny it."

"Oh no, princess. You're completely in control right now." His lips curved in a wicked smile that had her heart trying to leap out of her chest and flop onto his floor. The appropriate offering for a god, she supposed.

She ran her tongue over that smile, tasting it. The ridge of his desire grew harder and longer against her core and she rocked into him, wanting him inside her. He groaned and moved away briefly to retrieve a condom from somewhere. "Tell me what you like," he said.

She grinned. "So far, everything. But why don't you try it again just to make sure." He chuckled against her abdomen, sending waves of desire coursing through her.

Oh yes, she was in control—of him. Her own desires, however, were taking over her good sense. She should walk away, but Dev was too damn tempting. She wanted this one night for herself before she disappeared from his life forever.

CHAPTER TWENTY-ONE

They landed in Dev's bed at some point just before dawn, where he'd made love to her again. The feelings inside him had only grown stronger with each moment that passed, each soft sigh or laugh or moan that showed how she felt in return.

He stroked the hair from her face as she lay against his shoulder. Together, they watched the first rays of dawn shatter the black of the sky outside his window, and he couldn't help but think this wouldn't be the only time they'd lie like this. It felt too right. She belonged in his arms.

"I don't want this night to end," she said, a touch of melancholy to her tone as she echoed his thoughts. She had opened up so much to him, in so many ways, but Dev could see she was still holding back.

"You're planning something, aren't you?" he asked, his internal warning system belatedly going into alert mode.

She huffed out a laugh. "Yeah. Raid your kitchen for coffee."

He tipped his head to look at her. "You know what I mean. A plan for dealing with your father."

"I always have a plan." Green eyes glittered with secrets, and he hated that she still kept things from him. "It's how I've survived this long."

He kissed her forehead in an attempt to eliminate the defenses she'd just thrown in his path. "You and I are the same. It took me a while to realize it, but you and I both want to protect those we love, and leave behind those who weren't smart enough to love us."

"Yes, I have a specific plan in mind," she admitted after a moment of silence.

"Disappear?"

"Something like that."

"Truly?" His brows drew together as he realized what that would mean. "You'd leave Brandon?"

"Never," she said so fiercely that he smiled and nuzzled her hair. "I'll always be there for him, if he needs me."

How could Dev ever have thought she'd turn her back on her son? She wasn't anything like Dev's biological mother. Ivy would stay and fight, or flee if that was the stronger option, but she'd never act without consideration of those who counted on her. He admired that, admired *her*.

"So what's the plan?" he asked when it seemed she wasn't going to let him in.

"It wasn't ever supposed to be just me who disappeared after you kidnapped me," she replied, tracing a fingertip along the ridges in his abdomen. "Linda, Miguel and I have been prepping Brandon for the past few months—since that day you saw Archer outside Linda's home, actually—hinting that we might be exploring a new part of the world. I gave him a compass a few months ago, and he frequently wears it around his neck. Told him we would always find each other."

"Because you think you'll be apart?"

The smile that had curved her lips at that memory slowly slipped away. "For a little while. The plan was to get settled in a new location and make sure it's safe before Linda and Miguel follow with Brandon."

"Sounds like you've already got a place picked out."

"We do. And I'm leaving tomorrow."

His gut tightened. She was leaving? She actually planned to leave without him, probably without ever telling him goodbye. He was doubly glad he'd gone to

California to seek her out and make her listen. Was it too late to change her mind?

"Sounds like you have everything you need to start a new future as a big, happy family," Dev said, trying to ignore a stab of jealousy at the image she'd painted. This family could have been Dev's. That his thoughts had even made that leap, that he could easily imagine making room in his life for a future with Ivy and the son of hers he'd never officially met, as well as Brandon's adoptive parents, told him just how deep his feelings were for the brave, strong woman before him. An invitation to stay on his ranch was on his lips when she suddenly sat up.

"I should get going. There are a couple of things I need to do at Legacy before leaving."

"You can't go back there. Archer and your father will be watching for you."

"I can handle them, especially if I know it's the last time I'll have to." She scrambled off the bed, reaching for his phone, since hers was still in the living room. "Mind if I use your phone to call a cab?"

Dev fought a wave of frustration. Once she had all of her ducks in a row, she'd leave Dev in her rearview. But Ivy wasn't the only one in the room who knew how to fight for the future she wanted.

He stood and calmly took the phone from her hands. She grabbed for it, but he held it over his head.

"What are you doing?" she demanded.

"You're staying."

She huffed out a breath. "I can't stay here forever."

"In Vegas, I mean. I won't let you ditch your entire life because you're scared."

"I have to. Give me that phone, Dev." When she tried to punch him lightly in the chest, he looped his arm around her and pulled her in close.

"I'm in this with you now, and I promise your father won't touch you or Brandon. Or Linda or Miguel. You can stay with me, here at the ranch. My brothers and Rose will help watch over you. Hell, we'll build the Castillo family a cabin, too, or they can stay here with us."

"You have to be kidding." Her eyes were wide with disbelief as she pulled away to search his features for the truth, for signs he was joking, and found none. "We can't all move in here. You've already been in danger enough because of my family." As she spoke, she pulled farther and farther away, creating a physical distance to mirror the emotional distance growing between them.

"We'll be safe once your father's behind bars and the Club has been decimated. We have another ledger page."

"The prosecution had two pages before, and look where that got them." She shook her head. "No. This would never work out between us. Me being here tonight was our goodbye."

He stiffened. "This isn't goodbye."

"It has to be."

It couldn't be. He'd just found her.

"Archer's sure to have told my father about you showing up at Gloria's memorial and taking me away from there," she continued. "And Dad will rain hell down on you for interfering again. He's probably already got something planned." She glanced out the window as if she'd see a sharpshooter taking aim at him.

"I've been through worse." He stepped up behind her and gripped her hips, pulling her back against him. She tipped her head back against his chest and squeezed her eyes shut. He willed her to feel how his heart beat for her. "I'll keep you safe. How about we go see the Castillos and Brandon together after school today? I'd like to meet him." Dev remembered the kid from the children's home, but he'd been too focused on protecting Ivy to notice many details about the young crowd who surrounded her.

"I won't confuse him by telling him the truth—

not until he's ready, probably some day way off in the future. Linda and I agreed."

"I wasn't suggesting that. I just want to meet him."

She pressed a hand to her forehead and turned around within the circle of his arms. But the doubt in her eyes made his hopes sink. She couldn't see this opportunity, couldn't see how great they could be, if she'd give them the chance.

"You deserve to be in that boy's life—without hiding, without running, without leaving the life you built here," Dev said, kissing her fingertips until she peeled them from her forehead. "*Brandon* deserves to feel your love. Let's make that dream a reality together."

Ivy fought down defensiveness, knowing Dev was only trying to help. The fact that he was willing to offer protection to both her and her child—and included Linda and Miguel—meant the world to her.

"You really think you and I can get out from under my father's thumb if we stayed together?" Ivy asked, but she knew the answer. Look what her father had done to Nathan. She was hoping against hope that her father would let things go. Let her and Brandon go. But they were his legacy, which was everything to him. And anyone who threatened his dream would be dealt with swiftly and painfully.

"We have the ledger page," Dev said. He cupped her chin and looked her in the eyes. "It'll be enough. Even if it isn't, he'll never get you. Or anyone you love. He'll touch you again over my dead body."

That's what she was worried about. She'd never let it come to that. "This isn't your fight."

"Like hell. He's been coming at me and my family for months. It's time to end it."

"On that, at least, we agree."

"And I know there's something between us. Don't

you dare deny it." He kissed her then. One moment, he was looking her in the eyes as if he would argue more. The next, his hand slid from her chin to the back of her neck and he pulled her in close. And then the heat swamped her. She clung to him like a lifeline, letting herself belong with him, at least for a moment. When he pulled away a minute later, it was only an inch, and only to allow them both to catch their breaths.

"You can have the ledger page," she said, when she found her voice. "Turn it over to Adam." They would have done so last night, but Dev had been more concerned about clearing the shock from her eyes and getting them both warm, dry and safe. "Consider that my part of the contract paid. And you kidnapped me from Gloria's, so your part is done. Now we're free of each other."

But he didn't release her, didn't step away. "I'm not going anywhere. And it's not about a damn contract."

Her heart hurt with the effort of pushing him away. He'd lay down his own life to protect hers, and her son's, and not think twice of the sacrifice. The lack of strings was so unlike her father's kind of love that she was left confused.

A knock at the cabin's main door had him reluctantly backing away from her. "Don't go anywhere," he warned as he tugged on jeans from a drawer, not bothering with a T-shirt.

The sweats she'd borrowed were on the floor of the living room. Her dress was still hanging in his laundry room at the other side of the house. She was about to ransack Dev's drawers for something she could wear besides the bed sheet when he returned with a stack of folded clothing. Her purse sat on top.

"Mom thought you could use another change of clothes," he said. "Though I have to say I like you better this way."

"Bless her." She tugged on the pants and shirt as a defense against the man who was watching her.

Retrieving her cell phone, she briefly caught sight of
several messages from her father before tossing it back
into her purse. Thank goodness she'd put the phone on
vibrate last night. "I have to go."

He pushed away from the doorjamb where he'd
been leaning. "Don't."

When her other, burner phone rang, she
rummaged in her purse again. "Linda?" she answered,
immediately worried. "What's wrong?"

Linda released a strangled cry. "Brandon's
missing."

CHAPTER TWENTY-TWO

"Missing?" With the phone clutched to her ear, Ivy hurried to the living room and snatched up her shoes. "You don't have any idea where he is?" She struggled to keep the terror from her voice, fumbling with the straps of her sandals several times before Dev squeezed her shaking hand and took over the task for her. She met his gaze and saw her own worry mirrored there.

"I don't know." Linda sounded frightened. "Miguel and I were having our morning coffee early, like usual, before we had to wake Brandon up for school. Miguel wasn't sure he was going in to work. Said he suddenly felt like he was coming down with something. I told him to go lay down. I remember feeling dizzy and putting my head down on the kitchen table. After that, I guess everything went black. When I came to just now, an hour had passed. Miguel was sleeping in the bedroom and Brandon wasn't here."

Panic fluttered in Ivy's chest. "Are you and Miguel okay?"

"We're both a little woozy, but we'll be okay. Where could Brandon be? Did your dad take him?"

"That's the first place I'll look. You two call a cab and go get checked out at the hospital."

Dev shook his head and grabbed the phone. "Linda? This is Dev. I'll have someone come by right away and check you out, and someone from the task force, as well. Stay there in case Brandon comes back."

Ivy pressed a hand to her mouth. Why hadn't she thought of that? *Think, damn it.* Brandon could come back on his own, or the kidnappers could contact the Castillos. Of course they needed to be there. She stood and began to pace. Maybe it would help her clear her head and think.

"Keep your phone by you and call us if you hear anything," Dev told Linda and hung up, then eyed Ivy. "Sit for a second," he demanded. "We'll figure this out."

"No, I have to go."

"You don't have a car."

Right. She pressed her free hand to her forehead and sat down hard on the couch. Apparently, walking hadn't helped her thought process. "I'll call that cab." She tried to rise again, but Dev squatted in front of her, bracing his hands on her knees so that she couldn't get up without knocking him backward.

"You can't go straight to Legacy and confront your dad like this," Dev said in a tone one might use with someone who'd been through a trauma. "He'll eat you up. It's exactly what he wants, you begging for his mercy."

"I have to go. To get Brandon back, I'd give Dad whatever he wants."

"And he knows that."

Rose came out of the kitchen where she'd been preparing a plate of cinnamon rolls, now balanced in one hand, and a tray of coffee mugs in the other. In her state, Ivy hadn't even smelled the delicious scents or heard anyone else in the house.

"What's happened?" Rose asked, immediately sensing something was amiss. She set the rolls and coffee down on a side table and hurried over.

Nausea rolled through Ivy as she struggled to understand what Brandon must be going through. "I think Dad took my son."

Rose and Dev exchanged a look. "I'll take you into town," Rose said.

"She's not going to face her father without me,"

Dev said.

A new kind of chill rolled through her. She couldn't put him in the middle of this. Besides, she doubted he could do anything to persuade her father to act in any way he didn't want to.

Ivy bit her lip and looked away. "I can't involve you. The stakes are too high."

"The highest." Dev waited until she met his gaze. "Which is why you're not going in there alone."

"Listen to him, Ivy," Rose pleaded. "He can defend himself—and anyone else he loves."

Loves? Ivy opened her mouth to correct Rose, but Dev was already taking Ivy's hand and pulling her outside.

At the car, she spun to face him. "Don't you understand? I can't let you do this." She scanned the features that had become so precious to her—the scruff of his morning beard, the piercing, intelligent eyes, and the strong jaw—all of which were currently set in determination. "I'll tell you the same thing you told me at my mother's, when I was so upset I couldn't think straight. I would never let you do anything to hurt yourself. And if you follow me in there, hell-bent on helping but really just antagonizing my father further, you'll be making it worse for everyone, but mostly for yourself. For your family." She stepped into him and cupped his face gently. "I care enough to make you stay behind."

His arms came around her. "I'm not letting you go."

She squeezed him tighter. "Don't think of it as letting go. How about a head start? Take the ledger page to Adam and get a warrant, get the task force focused on finding the Redemption Club member who fulfilled Dad's order to kill the Wilsons. I'll find Brandon. We'll go after my dad from both sides and, together, we can catch him."

"A head start?" He looked away and shook his head, then met her gaze again. "I won't be far behind."

She placed a quick, soft kiss on his lips. "I'm counting on it."

Reluctantly, he handed her the keys to his car. "I'll come for you, Ivy. You and Brandon. And then I'm not letting go ever again."

"You're a handsome boy," Stone said to his grandson. *Brandon Castillo.* He'd get the last name changed the minute it was legally possible. Brandon Stone had a fine ring to it. He'd managed to look past the fact the boy was part Wilson.

"Thank you," Brandon replied. He wouldn't meet Stone's gaze. Of course, Brandon had been through a lot in the past few hours. Archer had had several days to consider where Ivy would have hidden away her son, or how she would have adopted him out to someone. By the time he'd returned from L.A., late last night, he'd narrowed down Ivy's moves over the past several years and realized that, if she'd stayed in touch with her son, her nanny might very likely know something. And, jackpot, he'd found the dark-haired, green-eyed boy named Brandon who admitted his birthday was May twelfth. Archer had managed to lace the Castillos' coffeepot with an undetectable drug that would knock the Castillos out for a little while. Long enough for Archer to take Brandon from his bed and bring him to Stone's office at Legacy. Stone would deal with the ex-nanny and her husband later.

"Come now, don't be meek. My flesh and blood will always stand tall and proud."

The boy's expression changed from wary to confused. "Flesh and blood?"

"We'll talk about that soon. Did Archer feed you?"

"Yes, sir. Pancakes in the restaurant." Brandon perked up a little at that memory. Soon, the boy would learn that everything within the Legacy complex would someday be his. He could have pancakes every damn day if he wanted.

Stone smiled with satisfaction at the boy's manners. "Good. You can have a swim in the hotel's pool a bit later, then I'll show you around."

"I shouldn't be here. You said Aunt Ivy would be here." The boy's voice was again much too small for Stone's liking. "I want to go home."

"You *are* home."

"To my parents, sir. I want them and Aunt Ivy."

Stone's rage threatened to boil over. "She's not your aunt, she's your mother. I'm your grandfather. We're family—the only *real* family you've got." The boy's eyes went round, right before they filled with tears. "For God's sake, don't cry." He couldn't keep the harshness from his voice.

Frustrated, he spun to face Archer, who remained near the closed door of his office. Stone had given the rest of the staff the day off, wanting privacy for this reunion—and what he planned for afterward. Brandon would be the ultimate bait to lure both his daughter and David Wilson, who still had the future of Redemption Club in his possession. Without that ledger and the debt cards, his legacy was at risk.

"She's not in her suite?" Stone asked Archer.

"No sign of her yet, sir," Archer replied.

"Then she's still with him." Damn Devlin Grimm. Archer had seen the man invade Gloria's memorial, lurk on the sidelines, and at the first opportunity, take Ivy away with him. He'd reported that she'd seemed extremely upset about something, but that he didn't know what.

"Brandon," he said, more calmly. "Listen to me." The silent tears stopped and the boy sniffed. "You're a Stone. Do you know what that means?"

"Like, a rock?"

"Sort of. We're family, boy, united under our last name."

"But my last name's Castillo."

"Not for long," Stone said, more fiercely than he

intended. The boy teared up again. Damn it. He took a breath and tried again. "Stones don't cry, right?"

He sniffed and seemed to think this over. "No, sir."

"And they don't break."

"They wear down from erosion." Brandon seemed pleased to have remembered this scientific fact. His little chest puffed out with pride. "The elements around it slowly, over time, cause cracks until the stone breaks apart."

Stone scowled. Not the image he was going for, unfortunately. "Stones are strong, though, right?"

"Sure, I guess." The boy seemed to retreat into himself again as he realized his explanation hadn't impressed Stone.

"She's on the premises," Archer interrupted to inform him. He held up his phone, where the security camera app showed Ivy at the main entrance. "Mr. Inverness, from security, is talking to her now."

"Make sure she's brought here immediately," Stone snapped. He was done waiting to claim his legacy. He only had a few more loose ends to tie up and then all would be right in his world again.

"She's being escorted to the offices by a guard," Skye informed Dev over the phone. While he'd promised Ivy a head start, he'd also told her he'd have GSS backup in place, should she need it. "I'll follow as much as I can without risking being stopped by security. Jared's got eyes on the rear exits in case anybody decides to go anywhere. No sign of the boy, but Emily said Stone dismissed his office staff for the day."

"Thanks for the update," Dev said, blowing out a breath and sending a hand through his hair in frustration. He'd wanted to be there himself by now, but the warrant was taking longer than he'd hoped. "We'll be there ASAP."

He'd always known that getting involved with

Ivy would put him through the wringer and leave him in worse shape than she'd found him. It's why his gut had screamed at him that first day she'd walked into his office, told him to run the other way and not look back. But winning, beating Robert Stone, especially after the man had just walked away from some serious charges without any punishment, had been too tempting.

And now Dev was paying the price. He was so anxious his chest hurt. He wanted to be there with her when she faced her father. But the fight wasn't over yet, and Dev suddenly had so much more to fight for, including a future with Ivy. Besides, few things worth having came without risk.

Ivy had conceded to having Emily, Skye, and Jared on the premises as a form of backup while she confronted her father, but she'd made them promise to remain discreet, knowing her father would have them thrown off the property—their backup rendered useless—if he knew they were there. She didn't want to do anything to put Brandon further at risk, and they all agreed on that point. Stone never did anything without an escape plan, and he was deadly dangerous, especially when cornered. Dev hated each second that ticked by without him there, within range of rescuing Ivy and Brandon should they need it.

First objective: recover Stone's bargaining chip— Brandon.

"Tell me the moment you have eyes on Brandon," he told Skye. "ETA for Adam and me, twenty minutes." He hoped. The judge was taking his sweet time perusing the ledger page from Gloria's guesthouse. Two previous pages had failed to provide enough evidence to convict Stone, but would the order of the hits on the Wilson family be enough? There were other entries, for lesser crimes, but none with Stone's name so conveniently attached to them. Thankfully, Adam and the task force had taken Dev's information on the Wilson crash seriously and begun researching it a few days ago. They'd found evidence that had added to the argument that the brakes might have been tampered with. And this morning, task force agent Mason Gray had immediately started investigating the Club member noted in the margin of the ledger, the man who might have committed triple homicide for Stone. Dev only hoped it was enough to bring Stone before a grand jury again.

"We got it," Adam said, holding up the signed warrant as he entered the judge's antechamber, where Dev had been forced to wait. "Ivy called the judge a short while ago, probably as she was driving to town. Apparently, she tried to explain everything and agreed to testify against her father. She laid the groundwork." Adam seemed surprised that Ivy would do such a thing, but Dev wasn't. He'd come to realize she wanted justice as much as anyone. She'd been one of Stone's victims, too.

"She'll always do the right thing," Dev argued. "She just needed to see the facts laid out for her. And for her father to push her to her limits."

Once in the driver's seat of Adam's SUV, Adam cast Dev an amused look. "You've got it bad for her."

"Just drive." Dev didn't want to talk about the feelings he was still sorting out. He'd been protective of Ivy, yes. Could envision the immediate future with her, yes. But more than that?

Yes. He could see even more than that—if they all survived the day.

Ivy's nerves were vibrating. The security guard who'd escorted her to her father's office didn't meet her gaze as he nudged her into the room and shut the door behind her. Her attention went from her father to Archer to the boy sitting at a corner table, coloring. Her throat closed over emotions that threatened to spill over.

Brandon was safe—for the moment.

That table in the corner was where, as a child, she'd sat and played quietly or did homework while she watched her father work, on the rare occasion when he'd allow her to remain close and didn't find her disruptive. That table was where she'd first learned to become invisible.

"Aunt Ivy!" Brandon dropped his crayon and raced to her.

"I told you, son, that's not your aunt," her father snapped.

Ivy cast her father a glare as Brandon froze against her side. The bastard had told her child the truth, without her or Linda there to explain things, to assure him they all loved him with all their hearts. Brandon's arms squeezed tighter around her waist as he buried his face against her.

"You're confusing him," she chastised her father.

Her father scoffed. "On the contrary, I'm setting the boy straight. For far too long, he's been denied his rightful place in the Stone family. And for that, I think you owe us each an apology."

She swallowed bile and bit back her pride. Her only regrets were that her dad was such a disappointment, that nothing she'd done in her life had been enough to earn an ounce of real love, and that she'd allowed herself to be duped and manipulated repeatedly. That was all she had to be sorry for.

"So you're really not my aunt?" Brandon asked, a combination of confusion, fear, and hope twisting a face that had become more precious to her than air.

She smoothed a fingertip over the crease in his brow. "No. I'm your biological mother. But there were reasons we were waiting to tell you."

"Excuses!" Her father roared, making both Ivy and Brandon jump. "They're for the weak. You made a mistake. Admit it."

"There was no mistake," she said. She sifted her fingers gently through Brandon's hair, trying to soothe while facing down her father. "I did what I thought was best for him, which included protecting him from you, from this lifestyle."

"This lifestyle gave you everything you could ever want." He ran a hand across the sleek, polished wood surface of his desk. "Do you know how I got this?" He'd told her the story many times, but she had the feeling the egotistical tirade was intended for Brandon's benefit this time.

"I won it from a billionaire tycoon," her father continued. "He was cocky and overplayed his hand. I swooped in and took it from him. It belonged with me, a man who could appreciate its fine craftsmanship and rare quality. Never fail to appreciate what's at your fingertips." His gaze shot from Brandon to Ivy, hammering home his point. "Because it could all be gone in an instant. That billionaire is in the poor house today." Probably because of her father. Ivy's gut twisted. Robert Stone didn't hesitate to teach his lessons to family and strangers alike. They were all less than equal in his eyes.

"Why bother with a legacy?" she asked, her words filled with bitterness. His entire existence was about building an empire that others would admire and ogle. That they would covet. "Nobody in this room wants your damn legacy. Except maybe Archer," she added, casting a hard glance toward the silent witness to their family meltdown. He didn't look away, didn't give away any of his thoughts in his expression. "Brandon and I don't want your name or an empire built on greed. All I ever wanted was your love and respect."

He laughed harshly. "Those are earned."

She replied with her own humorless laugh. "How? Nothing I did was ever enough. So why bother building something to leave behind when you never trusted me to handle it?"

"I was hopeful you wouldn't be the disappointment Ryan turned out to be. I recently learned I was wrong."

"Because you believe the evidence presented by outsiders."

"Archer isn't an outsider." This time, Archer shifted uncomfortably.

Ivy shook her head, sending her father a pitying glance. "What did your parents do to you that made it imperative to swindle, murder, and steal to get and keep what you have?"

"I won't dignify that with a response."

"What do you want from me?" she asked.

"The ledger. David Wilson has it, and you're going to get it."

She froze. "David Wilson?" Had her father finally gone totally off the deep end? "He's dead." Conscious that Brandon was next to her, listening to every word, she didn't confront her father about the fact that Redemption Club, and Stone's own orders, had been responsible for the murder of not just David Wilson, but the entire Wilson family.

"Apparently, I'm not as successful at scheming as you think," he said sarcastically. "I recently learned David is still alive."

Her jaw dropped. If David was alive, then maybe—

"Don't get your hopes up," he interrupted, apparently reading her expression. "Nobody else survived. And David Wilson..." His gaze went to Brandon before moving back to her. "Let's just say I always win in the end. Besides, you'll want vengeance just as much as me. He's the one who's been harassing you for weeks, pretending to be Nathan, or Nathan's emissary. Ridiculous. The David I knew would never have been so meek and passive-aggressive." Then maybe they hadn't seen the worst of her stalker yet.

As Brandon shifted nervously against her, another thought came to her. "Does he know about...?" *About his grandson.* She couldn't say the words aloud, didn't want Brandon even more confused. God, where was Dev and her backup? He had to have that warrant by now. She wanted them to take her son out of here, far, far away from this madness.

"He does. And I'm assuming it's only a matter of time before he learns where he can find you both." His eyes narrowed on her. "You're the first he'll come to. If you fail to get what I want, the boy's my backup bait."

She shivered. "He's your grandson." Did he have no compunction about involving a seven-year-old in what could be a bloody battle?

"Which is why he'll do what's necessary for the family." He grinned at Brandon. "Besides, I'm certain you'll have enough motivation now to do your part. There will be no need to involve your son. And you'll both be here, perfectly safe on Legacy property. David will meet us on our own turf."

"And getting him here will be enough for you?" she asked, already knowing her hope was pointless. Her father would squeeze her until she gave him everything that was important to her.

"Oh no, my dear. You have a lot to make up for. But getting my ex-partner, the ledger, and the box of half-cards here will be a good start. In the meantime, Archer will escort you to my suite to wait things out." He nodded to Archer, apparently signaling they were dismissed.

Archer sent her a significant glance and patted the waistline of his suit to indicate he had a gun and wouldn't hesitate to use it if she resisted. At the moment, Ivy was simply relieved to be out of her father's presence. She had to think, to plan. As they left her father's office, she hoped to catch Megan, maybe send her a silent message at her desk, but there was no sign of her there. In fact, none of the support staff were in their offices. Her father had probably given them the day off to get rid of any witnesses.

But she wouldn't give up hope. According to Dev, Emily, Skye and Jared would be nearby. At least one of them should be in the rotunda. She could send them some kind of signal when they reached the elevators, or even push Brandon toward them.

She bent down to speak in Brandon's ear, conscious Archer was watching them carefully from a few feet behind. "If I say run, follow the signs for Legacy Lounge and ask for Emily. She'll help."

"Stop talking," Archer ordered .

She straightened and squeezed Brandon's shoulder. He looked up at her and nodded that he'd understood her hasty, whispered message. She was relieved to see some measure of trust had returned to his eyes. They could sort out the rest of their confusing relationship later, and she'd do whatever it took, for however long necessary, to rebuild his trust. First, she had to see them both through this.

She craned her neck, trying to see toward the rotunda, and hoping help was nearby. The moment she spotted a friendly face, she'd give Brandon the signal to run. Just a few more yards and they'd be beyond the wall that separated the offices from the check-in desk, and then they'd enter the rotunda where she was sure Skye or Jared would be posted.

"Turn here," Archer said unexpectedly. To her left, a seldom-used back hall led away from the office area. The rotunda, and help, was straight ahead, just out of reach. The hallway was simply a side entrance to Legacy Theater and its backstage area.

"Why?" she asked.

"Just do it. No questions." To hell with that.

"This isn't the way to the elevators." A flutter of panic filled her chest, but she kept the emotion from her words, not wanting Brandon to pick up on her fear. "Dad said to take us to his suite. You're going against his wishes?" The imperious tone she'd used so many times in the past wasn't working on Archer.

"I said no questions."

She looked back at him, preparing to jump him and claw his eyes out if it would give Brandon a chance to run for safety. Instead, she was alarmed to see Archer had pulled his gun. She put an arm around

Brandon's shoulders to keep him facing forward as they turned down the hall Archer indicated. She didn't want her little boy any more scared than he already was. After all she'd done to protect him, the taint of her father's criminal activities and associations was still touching his life. She'd be damned if she'd let that continue.

"Why are you doing this?" she asked, Archer's *no-questions* decree be damned.

Archer grinned. "Maybe I like seeing the legendary ice queen obeying my orders. Soon, I'll have you on your knees." His tone had changed to something dark and dirty. She whipped her head back around to the path he'd directed them to take.

"This hall leads to Legacy Theater." Where she'd hidden away from the world for a few precious minutes, before Dev had found her. Would he find her again?

"I know." Just what was waiting for them in the theater?

That was one question she wouldn't dare ask.

CHAPTER TWENTY-THREE

Victor practically danced as he moved here and there, setting the stage. He hadn't felt this alive, this purposeful, in years. Finally, his moment was here. And nearly everything he'd needed had been in the prop room, or he'd been able to obtain it over the last couple days, with the help of his new partner in crime. Now all he lacked was his star actress and grandson.

When the side exit door of Legacy Theater swung open, Victor's pulse rate kicked in anticipation, his adrenaline shifting into overdrive as he spun to receive his guests. "This is for you, Nathan and Joanna," he whispered.

Ivy and Brandon entered first, with Archer behind them. Victor's mouth twisted grimly at the sight of the gun trained on his grandson, but he supposed it was necessary. At this time, Ivy's compliance was key. Soon, he and Brandon could be on their merry way and disappear forever, but first they had to avenge the boy's father.

Spying him on the stage, Ivy's eyes narrowed as if trying to make out the details in the dim lighting, then widened as he flipped the switch to turn on the spotlights that highlighted his display. She turned to Archer, and Victor imagined she was bargaining with him, but the man did his job, herding her toward the front row where several stairs led up to the stage.

"You really are looking to cross my father," she muttered to Archer as they grew close enough for

Victor to hear.

"Not just cross him, sweetheart," Archer said with a sly grin. "We aim to dethrone him."

"You've been with him for twenty-five years!"

Archer shrugged. "And as such a loyal servant, I deserved a bigger cut of the pie. It was becoming more and more evident that I wasn't going to get it."

"And, recognizing Archer's value, I offered it to him right away," Victor said. "He and I connected after Gloria's death. When he found out I still had a ledger page, as well as the actual ledger and the box of cards, he knew who really held the power. All I have to do is give him Redemption Club." As he spoke, he used his lighter at various points on the stage, and his props immediately added the eerie glow he wanted.

Ivy shook her head, watching his movements. "I don't understand what you get out of this, then."

What he would get was revenge. That would be enough. After all, he had more important things to think about after this was over, like raising his grandson. Unlike Robbie, Victor knew family came first.

The six torches he'd lit at intervals along the edge of the stage had come alive. The fire pit in the center, the focal point onto which Ivy's gaze had latched, now spewed two-foot flames.

"Come on up, my dear," Victor told Ivy, holding his hand out to help her up the four stairs that led from the first row of seats to the stage. She ignored his offering but, after a hesitant step and a glance back at Archer, who pointed the gun at the back of Brandon's head, obeyed his command. The boy was watching the flames, seemingly entranced.

"What's this?" she demanded, gesturing to the props.

"We're setting the scene. One of redemption and revenge." He smiled with satisfaction in his work. "I think Nathan would have liked the drama of it."

"Why are you doing this, Mr. Wilson?" Ivy eyed

the fire pit. The logs snapped and popped like jaws trying to devour prey. Maybe he'd added too much wood, but he'd wanted something big, something alive. The dancing flames were still only a taste of what his son and wife had faced. Ivy's wide, green eyes were everywhere and a look of shock crossed her face as her head tipped back and she took in the cage he'd suspended from the rafters.

Victor grinned. "I'm sure you and Mr. Grimm recovered the ledger page I had Archer leave for you at Gloria's? You must know by now what I truly want."

"Revenge." She took a step back, but Victor put his hand at her shoulder and dug his fingers in, preventing her retreat.

"Did you ever read Dante's *Inferno*? There's a special circle of hell for each type of sin, many layers populated with sinners suffering because they'd committed any manner of foul deeds. Your father could easily populate any one of those circles—greed, violence, and many more. More likely, he's the devil running the show. You can blame him for what's about to happen to you."

"You'll get no argument from me that my father's the devil," she said, surprising him by the way she spun to face him, breaking from his grip. "But why me? Why Brandon? Let him leave." Archer had nudged Brandon into a seat a few rows back from the stage.

"Oh, Brandon's going to stay here to make sure you behave. Besides, an actress is always better with an audience, is she not? And *you're* here to make sure your father behaves. Pretty simple, really."

"Dad will kill you if he has the chance."

"The good thing about rising from the dead is one has no illusions of grandeur. I know the worst that could happen, and I'm grateful every day simply to be alive—alive to pursue my interests. Unfortunately for you, the only interest I've had for eight years is avenging my family's death."

"I can help you find justice." The urgency in her

voice made her almost believable. But she was a Stone, and manipulation ran in her blood. "I've already got friends working on obtaining an arrest warrant for my father."

"Based on that ledger page?" Victor laughed. "He'll just slip out of the noose—again. No. That page was only meant to prompt you to confront your father. I wanted him to experience your disappointment, to see his hopes and dreams for a legacy crumble, before he dies. The only way justice will be served to Robbie Stone is red hot."

"Mr. Wilson—"

"I'm no longer David Wilson. Your father assassinated that man, his own partner, who perhaps understood him better than anybody. From the carnage rose a monster named Victor del Fuego. Do you know why I chose that name?"

She shook her head.

"I survived my trial by fire, and now I'll use flames to take down my opponents." He looked into the blaze and saw Stone's flesh charring, heard the man's screams in his head. "We just need the guest of honor." He moved to a side table where he'd covered the ledger and box of half-cards with a black cloth. He yanked it away with a magician's flair. "Let's see what your father values more: legacy by blood or legacy by Club."

Ivy had little doubt which her father would choose when presented the choice. The Club gave him power and prestige and didn't question his motives or agenda. He had absolute power there.

She, on the other hand, had disappointed him at every turn.

While she kept David talking so she could assess her options, she'd avoided looking at Brandon too often, not wanting to draw the man's attention to the boy or give away his importance to her, but now she sought her son's gaze. Even from ten yards away, she could see

Brandon was shaking, terrified. She tried to send him a reassuring smile, but what she needed was to get him out of here. Maybe, if she could throw herself on Archer and try to grab the gun, Brandon could run to the exit. But before she could push her way off the stage to get to him, there was another surprise.

David picked up a gun—probably the same one he'd used that day in the car—from one of the pedestals and aimed it at her. What scared her more, however, was the crazy glint in his eyes.

"Get in the cage," he ordered.

While she'd been considering her options for getting Brandon to safety, he'd moved to the side of the stage. He hit a button that lowered the tall, narrow cage. She'd be able to stand inside it, and the bars were wide enough she could reach between them, but she felt a moment of panic. Once she was inside, she'd be at a madman's mercy.

She looked at the pulley system and realized the cage could also move along another plane—which would put it just over the fire pit. Another wave of panic threatened to take her under but she was brought back to the present by Brandon's shout.

"No!" Brandon yelled. "Stop!"

From the seat behind him, Archer watched with soulless eyes as he lifted the gun to show he still had control over her son—which meant Archer and David controlled her. Bastards.

"Mr. Wilson's trying to put on a play," she said for Brandon's benefit, though even she could hear the quaver in her voice. "Remember how your school put on that play a couple months ago?"

"But they didn't have real fire. I don't like it."

She eyed the fire pit and shuddered. She didn't like it either.

"Get in," David said, in a voice low enough for only her to hear as he jabbed the muzzle of his gun into her side. "Or I'll make you watch as I put Brandon in that cage instead."

"You wouldn't," she said. "He's your grandson."

"And he should have had his father. At least this way I'd have control over Brandon's fate. Your father will never have a part in his life. Robbie can't taint Brandon if one of them is dead. I'd prefer it was Robbie rotting in the ground, but if it's not him, I'll have to settle for saving my grandson in other ways."

Swallowing hard, she climbed into the cage, which hung a couple feet off the floor. It swung a bit with her movement, and as Victor closed the door with a squeal of the hinges. He slid a padlock into place and she had to press her fingernails into her palms to distract herself from the terror that threatened to grip her.

"You got what you wanted, now get him out of here," Ivy pleaded with Victor. But the gleam in his eyes told her he wasn't listening. He was too wrapped up in his plot to torture her to realize his grandson was only forty feet away, crying and afraid.

Victor moved to the side to press a button and her cage began its ascent. She clutched the bars as the contraption shifted.

"He doesn't need to see this," she tried again. "Please." She crouched in her cage to get closer to the man's eye level. "In Nathan's memory, don't put his son through this."

That seemed to snap David out of it. He frowned, and looked out toward their audience. "Archer's about to take him somewhere else. Somewhere safe, away from Stone."

God, that was almost worse. She wouldn't know where Brandon was, or who he was with. But at least he wouldn't suffer the horror of watching her die.

And she *was* going to die. She was almost certain of it. Once David Wilson had what he wanted—her father—she'd be collateral damage.

Victor dipped a torch into the flames and waved it near her. Though her cage hung a couple feet off the ground, she flinched from the heat. Even the slightest movement set the cage to rocking, and she forced herself to be still, even as her tormentor inched closer.

"Get Brandon out of here," she bit out, inserting authority into her tone.

David grinned. "As you wish, my queen."

"Brandon, run!" she yelled, praying he'd at least have a fighting chance if he ran, and that he'd remember who to go to, who to trust.

But when she looked out into the darkened rows of seats, hoping to make eye contact with her son one last time and reassure him she loved him no matter what, he was gone.

Dev ran from the valet drop-off area where Adam had hastily parked, and into the rotunda at Legacy. The security guard at the door immediately recognized him and tried to stop them. Mr. Inverness was the same man who'd escorted Dev off the premises a couple days ago.

Adam pulled the warrant from his coat. "We're here to arrest Robert Stone. If you lay a hand on either of us, or if you radio him a warning so he can get away, you'll be charged with obstruction." Inverness scowled, but waved them on.

Skye emerged from her position along the periphery of the rotunda and joined their group as they crossed toward the check-in desk. "Emily's working in the lounge. Haven't seen Ivy since she headed to Stone's office. I couldn't get any closer without being recognized. Jared checked in a minute ago to say he hasn't seen any activity at the rear exits. I was about to head back to the offices to see if she's still there, even if I get kicked off the property because of it. I can always find a way to sneak back in, but it worries me how long she's been back there."

"Backup's still several minutes out," Adam reported.

"By all means, let's crash the party," Dev said,

unwilling to wait any longer. He hoped to find Ivy there, unharmed. And seeing Brandon by her side would be nice, too. But the office area was completely deserted except for Robert Stone, who sat behind his desk as if it were any ordinary workday.

Stone narrowed his eyes on the threesome as they entered his office. "What in the hell?" He looked beyond them, seeking his dutiful security guards, no doubt.

Adam handed him the warrant and began reading him his Miranda rights.

"This should be good," Skye said, a smile in her voice. "I've dreamt of this for a long time."

"You and me both," Jared said from the doorway. "Nobody's left the building by the rear," he reported.

"There's been no sign of Ivy or Brandon," Dev said.

"I'll head back to my post," Jared said. "I'm sure we'll catch sight of her."

"I'll try calling her suite again and see about getting a keycard to the penthouse level," Skye said, and she left with Jared.

Dev couldn't relax yet. He'd texted Ivy a few minutes ago to say they were close to Legacy, but she hadn't replied. "Where is she?" he demanded.

Stone grinned. "My daughter won't be on your side anymore," Stone said as Adam waved to him to rise from his chair so he could cuff him. "Like me, she'll do what's necessary to survive. You lose."

Dev only shook his head. "Too bad you killed your lawyer. You're going to need another good one willing to work for a scumbag like you to get you off these charges."

"Money can buy me anything." As could membership in Redemption Club. But once they had the ledger in their possession, Stone wouldn't have anything to bargain with. "And you'll never touch my daughter or grandson again."

Dev took a threatening step forward and Adam

shook his head once in warning. Right. No laying hands on the prisoner, or Adam would have to arrest Dev, too. Though it might be worth it.

But as Adam moved to cuff Stone, they were interrupted by the sound of an alarm, loud and fierce. It pierced the air and their eardrums. Adam and Dev exchanged a look.

"Could be a distraction." Dev stated what they both were thinking. But there were sounds of confusion and chaos from the direction of the rotunda.

"Fire!" someone shouted. "Everyone evacuate."

"Either way," Adam said, grabbing Stone's arm to pull him with them. "We need to get out of here. I won't cuff you until we get outside," he told Stone, "in case this is a survival situation. But I won't hesitate to shoot you in the back if you try to escape."

But as Adam nudged Stone through the office door, Mr. Inverness, the security guard from the front entrance, appeared—with his weapon aimed at them. The sounds of the alarms continued to echo off the walls, yet this man held steady.

"These men bothering you, Mr. Stone?" the guard asked.

"You don't want to do this," Dev said. "He's not worth it."

"I'm going to have to take a closer look at that warrant," Inverness replied. He jerked his gun toward Adam as Adam made a subtle move toward his holster. "Don't do it."

"There could be an active fire," Dev said, seeing the nerves beneath the steel in the guard's eyes. The loud noise was rattling him, but this man obviously had some sense of misguided loyalty toward Stone. "Let's sort this out outside." Where, hopefully, Dev would find that Ivy and Brandon had evacuated safely.

"We're not going anywhere," Stone said, sending Inverness a look. "Your loyalty will be well rewarded."

CHAPTER TWENTY-FOUR

Alarms shrieked in the distance as Ivy gripped the bars of the cage, which were surprisingly strong for what should have been a stage prop, and shook with all of her strength. That only succeeded in making her prison mobile. It swung on the chain from which it was suspended, and one end of the pendulum was too close to the fire for her comfort.

Swallowing a wail of frustration, she sank to the bottom of the cage and waited as the movement gradually stilled. The noise outside of the theater, however, continued. David or Archer must have disengaged the theater's portion of the system, because it was relatively quiet within these walls, especially given the amount of heat and smoke given off by the torches and fire pit.

At least Brandon was no longer forced to witness whatever David intended. But was Brandon safe? Was there a fire somewhere? *God, please don't let him be in danger.*

It was her job to protect her son from the evils of this world, and lately, she'd failed miserably.

"Let me out of here!" she yelled.

David sat at the edge of the stage, his gun in his hand, and ignored her. It was as if he couldn't hear the alarms. Instead, he was watching the doors, seemingly all of them at once, his head swiveling from one side of the theater to the other. But it wasn't anxiety on his face so much as anticipation. And the flickering of the flames at various points on the stage turned his expression into that of a maniacal demon.

"He won't come," she said. "My father doesn't care about me enough to put himself at risk. He'll find Brandon and they'll be out of your reach forever. The man knows how to cover his tracks. Set me free and I'll find him for you before it's too late."

"Oh, he'll come," David said. Her stomach clenched as he pushed to his feet and snatched a lit torch from its base, moving toward her again. But he passed her instead, heading for a box mounted on the wall. In that box was a button, and as he pushed it, her cage began moving on its other axis, shifting closer to the fire pit.

She tried a softer tone. "Please don't do this. I need to get out there. It's my job as manager of the hotel to make sure everyone's safe."

"You don't give a damn about anybody," David said, but some of the harshness had left his words as he scanned her face, finally seeming to notice her. And he'd taken his finger off the button, halting her progression toward the heat that nipped at her legs.

See me. See that I'm no threat to anyone.

"That's not true," she argued, "and you know it. Why else would I have protected Brandon from my father all these years? You and I are on the same side."

"Nathan should have been the one raising him."

"Agreed. And if he'd been here, we would have raised Brandon together." As if punctuating her statement, the alarms suddenly turned off, though the sound waves continued to bounce around in her skull.

David narrowed his gaze on her. "You really didn't have anything to do with Nathan's death?"

"I swear I didn't know."

His expression was conflicted for a few short seconds before it hardened. "Never trust a Stone."

"Or a Wilson," her father's voice called from somewhere off-stage.

Ivy and David spun in surprise and her cage

began swaying again.

Robert Stone walked toward them from the shadows until the spotlights hit him, illuminating him in red, orange, and white. "Looks like I'm late to the party," he said with a grin.

"Anything?" Dev asked Adam.

Stone had disappeared ten minutes ago, while the security guard with a misguided sense of loyalty held down the fort, keeping Dev and Adam detained at gunpoint until Stone could gain some distance. When Mr. Inverness deemed Stone had a decent head start, he'd fled, too.

Dev had immediately called Jared and Skye, and the foursome had split into pairs to search the busy rotunda and surrounding areas, but the press of mankind fleeing the noise and fire—a blaze which had yet to show itself—made moving more than a few inches at a time difficult. More than once, they'd had to stop a patron from running over his fellow man.

The atmosphere of constant noise, shouts of distress, and outright fear threatened to turn to full-fledged panic at any moment. And Stone had capitalized on the chaos.

Adam pressed his lips together grimly. "He's probably long gone by now. And when I get my hands on that security guard, there will be hell to pay."

Across the mass of people, Dev spied Emily standing near the Legacy Lounge archway. Adam seemed to see her at the same time. As they made their way toward her, Dev realized that she held a child behind her, her body shielding him from the press of guests heading for the front exit. Dev caught a glimpse of dark hair and worried green eyes that he remembered seeing at the children's home.

"You found Brandon," Dev said as they reached Emily. He glanced through the archway into the now-empty lounge, hoping to catch sight of Ivy. He wasn't that lucky.

Adam pulled Emily against him. "Thank God you're okay," he said against his fiancée's hair.

"Where's the fire?" Dev asked.

In answer, Emily glanced down at Brandon, nudging him. "No fire. This guy pulled the alarm to get help."

"I had to get away from the bad guy," Brandon said. "He was taking me somewhere, and I'm not supposed to go with strangers. Ivy told me to run when I could, to find her friend Emily. When I saw the alarm, I kicked the guy in the shin and ran to pull it."

Dev crouched down in front of him. "That was smart."

"But Aunt Ivy... I mean, my mom," Brandon began, uncertain. So, Stone had been spewing truth as much as lies lately, not letting Ivy and Linda handle things in a more tactful manner. Dev could punch Stone in the face for that alone. "She's still trapped. The other bad man's going to hurt her. And there really is a fire."

Dev's blood ran cold. "What? Where?"

"The stage."

"Alpha Omega Theater again?" Dev theorized aloud, glancing at Adam. "That's where her stalker took her the first time." But it didn't make sense that Brandon would be here, then.

Brandon tugged on his sleeve and pointed across the rotunda, toward Legacy Theater. "The fire's in there."

In the melee—and with the guard's help—Stone had broken away from the crowd—and, more importantly, from his captors. Inverness would be rewarded handsomely by Redemption Club—once Stone recovered the ledger.

Stone had ducked into a storeroom closet to regroup and shut out some of that blasted noise. There was no way he would face a damn judge and jury again. Besides, the task force's attempts to charge him with murder based solely on another page from the ledger were pathetic.

He'd tried calling his suite, where Archer was supposed to be guarding Ivy and Brandon. No answer there. Then he tried calling the man directly, but the call went to voicemail.

Stone had needed a way out, a clear path. He could have tried to blend in with the crowds streaming from the hotel, but it was a risk with several people looking for him. Besides, he wasn't exactly low profile in this town and there was bound to be media waiting outside.

Then he'd remembered the app Archer had developed for him and searched the live security camera shots from Legacy. He'd seen Archer heading toward a side entrance to the theater, but without Brandon. Unfortunately, there'd been no security cameras in the theater.

Stone had hurried to the backstage entrance and now, seeing the ledger and box of cards on their pedestals on the other side of the stage, he sneered at David. The idiot had gone through a lot of effort to stage something that could never work. There was no sign of Archer yet, but he had to be nearby somewhere, lurking. Hopefully, the man had his gun trained on David.

"You think you can best me?" Stone yelled.

"I have no doubt," David replied with a smirk, aiming his gun at Stone. "I have everything you want. Your daughter. Brandon. And your precious ledger."

Stone grinned. "I think you're mistaken about one of those."

David's face contorted in confusion. "Brandon?"

"Last I saw, Archer lost him."

Ivy gasped and Stone spared her a glance. She had proven herself less than useless. He wasn't sure how she'd fallen into David's hands so easily, but she was worthless to Stone now. "What do you mean, lost him?" she asked. Hearing the fear in her voice, he lost the last bit of respect he had for her.

"No worries," Stone said to David, ignoring Ivy. "I have no doubt Archer knows where the boy is and will return him to me."

"Dad, Archer isn't—" But Ivy's comment was interrupted when the man himself appeared, stepping forward from the same area where Stone had entered, his weapon raised.

Stone grinned. He was back in charge and David would finally die. The ledger and box of cards were within Stone's grasp. "Archer, show Mr. Wilson how we handle our opposition." But his triumph was short-lived.

"If only I were still on Team Stone," Archer said, smirking.

Stone's gaze narrowed on Archer as the man's aim turned on him. Fury shot through Stone. "You think you'll get a better deal working with *him?* I ousted him once before and I'll do it again. I *am* Redemption Club."

"We don't need you," Archer said. "We have the ledger. That's all we need to rebuild."

Stone laughed bitterly. "David doesn't want to rebuild. He wants to destroy. His actions eight years ago put the entire club at risk."

David shook his head. "Your actions are just as risky. Killing Gloria? That'll come back to bite you."

"You killed Mom?" Ivy's eyes grew round. "I didn't want to believe you had it in you, but I should have known better, after all the other lies."

Stone shrugged. Gloria had been a pain in his ass for decades, and he could have taken care of her long ago. "I kept her alive for your sake, but she was always pestering me for money, for better acting roles. And then, when she became famous but had squandered most of her money, she wanted more. She wanted Stone Studios, and was willing to blackmail me once she acquired the ledger page. Nobody gets away with that."

"And so you used the Club's resources to kill her." Ivy sank to her knees within the cage. "How could you?"

Stone waved a hand at David. "Ask him. It's not like he doesn't plan to do the same things with that ledger and those cards. Every member listed in that box still owes a debt. And they don't repay them without getting their own hands dirty."

David shook his head, denying the accusation. "There are more important things than the Club. Archer can have it. The important thing is Brandon's not in your hands anymore. He'll never be a part of your legacy. And I'll still be around to make certain of it." He looked behind him at the table where the ledger and box of cards lay, then waved a torch over the items. In his other hand, the gun lowered, but Archer still had his weapon trained on Stone.

"Don't you dare," Stone growled. "We both worked to start that club. We can make it great again." Until he could kill David—again.

"Over my dead body," Archer grumbled. "That power was promised to me."

"Choose," David ordered. "I torch your legacy tonight, as you torched mine eight years ago."

"Choose?"

David grinned. "Which piece of you I destroy first—the ledger or your daughter."

Dev's heart plummeted to his gut as he spied Ivy on the stage below, trapped in an iron cage. From his studies of Legacy's layout, he'd remembered this door and wanted to get a birds-eye view of what they'd be dealing with, but it put him way too far away from her. Even from this distance, on the balcony level, Dev could see she was shaking like a leaf.

The cage swung a little as she spun to face her

father, her hands gripping the bars as she watched him argue with two other men, Archer and some other man who fit the general description of her stalker. Archer and his cohort appeared to be armed with guns and a torch.

Before Dev had taken off for the theater, Brandon had told them the stalker was named David Wilson, according to the discussion he'd overheard between Ivy and Stone. So, one of the Wilsons had survived. Unfortunately, it was the one who'd helped start Redemption Club, and it looked as if he had an evil agenda of his own.

Dev's breath caught as Ivy shifted again and her cage swung close to the fire burning in some kind of pit in the middle of the stage. What had David done to her, and what did he plan to do?

Beside him, Adam signaled that they should move closer. *Hell, yeah,* Dev signaled back, impatient to get down there. Unfortunately, the only way down from here was to go over the railing and drop thirty feet or back out the rear door and around another way. Apparently, Adam realized the same thing and they moved in a crouch in the shadows back toward the door. Outside the theater, he filled Jared and Skye in on what they'd seen. They agreed to flank the audience area while Dev and Adam went through the backstage entrance.

"Take a breath, man," Adam hissed when Dev raced toward his entry point.

"Can't," he muttered. "Haven't had eyes on her in at least forty seconds." And anything could have happened in that time.

"Just be sure to wait until everyone's in place," Adam advised.

At the door to backstage, Dev signaled that he and Adam should split up. He chose the side that was closer to Ivy and her cage. He wanted her in his arms ASAP. Besides, Adam had a weapon, and would be the most effective against Archer and David.

But as Dev cautiously turned the corner that allowed him to see onto the stage, he had to force himself not to race in. Ivy nearly fell against the bars of the cage as David lunged toward her with a goddamn lit torch. But with weapons aimed at her from two hostiles, Dev bit back an oath and restrained himself, his body rippling with coiled tension.

"Choose," David shouted to Stone. Dev froze. Choose what? "I torch your legacy tonight, as you torched mine eight years ago."

"Choose?" Stone replied, taking a step closer to his nemesis.

As Dev peeked around the edge to see more while staying in the shadows, he caught David's answering grin. In the stage lighting, his face had twisted into a macabre mask of evil glee.

"Which piece of you I destroy first—the ledger or your daughter," David explained, waving the torch between the two choices.

"My daughter," Stone said without hesitation.

Dev froze, certain he had to have heard wrong. Even Archer appeared shocked. But when Dev saw Ivy's face, her stunned expression focused on her father, the pain expressed in the beautiful planes and curves accentuated by the shadows and light, he knew he'd heard right.

Stone had sacrificed his daughter for his precious Redemption Club.

Ivy didn't think her father could hurt her any more, but his choice had stolen her very breath as her entire chest squeezed. He'd written her off, but to choose to fight for possession of a book, rather than his daughter's life, was unthinkable.

Her gaze tracked her father as he lunged across the stage, intent on taking the ledger while David went after Ivy. Her father didn't look up at her, not even once. He'd made his decision, once more leaving her alone to deal with the consequences of his criminal actions. Did he not realize David would never let him get out of here alive—and certainly not with the ledger?

And Archer, who'd been promised the ledger and debt cards, was raising his gun. Her father would never get out of here with what he truly wanted.

But as he passed David, her father pivoted and shoved his whole weight into him, sending them both to the stage floor. The torch went rolling away. Archer seemed stunned and, while he aimed his gun at the grappling men, didn't take a shot. Of course, whoever he intended to shoot wasn't making himself an easy target because both David and her father struggled on the ground, rolling and punching and kicking. At times, they were dangerously close to the fire pit and the torches that rimmed the stage.

"Get me the key," she shouted to Archer. "I'll say you helped me if you get me out of here." While her words seemed to snap Archer out of his stunned trance, they had the wrong effect.

He picked up the fallen torch and touched it to one of the nearby thirty-foot-tall garnet-colored curtains hanging on the edges of the stage. The material caught fire immediately.

In her peripheral vision, Ivy was aware of shadows shifting as if figures moved in the darkness beyond the bright flames, but her gaze was locked on Archer, who grabbed the ledger and fired off several wild shots, causing the shadows to halt. He yanked open a trap door in the center of the stage floor, one that had been used for illusions. It now served as Archer's escape hatch.

But Ivy desperately needed an escape plan of her own. The flames from the burning curtain jumped higher toward the ceiling.

"Ivy!" Dev shouted from behind her.

She nearly wept with relief as he reached her cage. Through the flames and smoke, she recognized the other newcomers. Adam. And Skye and Jared.

"Oh, thank God," she said. "The button on the wall over there should move the cage away from the pit." Not that it mattered with the fire rapidly spreading across the stage. The heat seemed to come from all directions now. But Dev shifted direction toward the button.

"Archer has the ledger!" Ivy shouted. Neither of the men on the floor heard her over their grunts and groans as kicks and punches continued to fly. They seemed unaware of the chaos burning around them, or that there was nothing left to fight for. But Skye was already lifting the trap door and disappearing into the darkness beyond. Adam and Jared eyed the two men, approaching with caution.

As Dev found the button that moved her prison a few feet farther away from the central fire pit, and then pushed another button that lowered the cage to the ground, Ivy searched for a way out. The metal was solid, welded to the top and bottom panels. It seemed a losing battle.

When Dev returned to her side, she reached through the bars for him.

Ironically, now that a fire was rapidly growing, climbing the edges of the stage, there were no alarms or sprinklers. Her suspicion that David or Archer had disabled them seemed accurate.

"The firemen will be here soon," Dev assured her, again seeming to read her mind. "They'll respond to the other alarm."

"Brandon?" she asked as Dev circled her cage, searching for a weak spot. *Good luck.*

"Safe with Emily," Dev said.

"Oh, thank God." For the first time since she'd received the call from Linda that Brandon was missing, she breathed a sigh of relief. "There must be a key," she said, clutching at Dev's hands as he gripped the bars and tested their strength as she had. "There's no way out other than opening the door. I've tried. Ask David."

A gunshot echoed from the direction of the

thrashing men just as Dev made a step toward them. Adam and Jared joined the fray, working to separate the two Redemption Club founders. Adam picked up a pistol from the floor and tucked it into the back of his pants to keep it from the snarling men, who were still trying to tear each other apart.

"Fuck asking," Dev growled. "I'll beat it out of him."

But David already looked closer to death than she did. Jared held an arm, restraining the man from lunging at her father again, but one of David's hands clutched his gut, where blood practically poured from a wound and gushed between his fingers. He was already pale from the loss, and slipped in the puddle beneath him as he tried to struggle away from his captor. He must have been shot while wrestling with her father for the gun.

Her father, who was being placed in handcuffs by Adam, laughed. "Got anything else up your sleeve?" he taunted David. "Because so far, I'm not impressed. Then again, I shouldn't have expected anything but failure from you."

David made an attempt to lunge at her father, but he was weak and Jared still held onto him. With a groan of pain, he lost consciousness and sank to the floor.

"Jared," Dev called as he circled the stage, looking for a fire extinguisher. "Does David have a key on him? We need a key here, fast." His voice was calm and assertive, but she could see the alarm in his eyes as a piece of burning curtain fell nearby, catching the floor aflame only a few feet away. Jared patted the unconscious David down, but came up empty. Jared shook his head, and she caught the grimness in his expression.

"Go," Ivy pleaded with Dev. "If the fire gets much closer, promise me you'll just go."

He returned to her side and met her gaze, holding it as his fingers continued to uselessly work at the padlock. "I'll never leave you. I promise."

"Don't be stubborn. Please. I need to know you'll watch out for Brandon. He'll need your protection."

Dev's tone was dark with purpose. "Not without you. Brandon needs you. Linda and Miguel need you. I need you."

Her fingertips brushed his and she squeezed them. "I love you." She released a croaky laugh. "And I'm not just saying that because I might not have another chance. I should have realized it sooner." She swiped angrily at a tear, then gripped his hand again. "I was fighting it, fighting you."

He gave her a lopsided grin. "Well, I for one am glad you're a fighter, and it's part of what I love about you. I'm in love with you, Ivy Stone, and there's no way I'm letting you go now."

Her heart soared, even as her hopes plummeted. The fire and smoke were growing worse by the second.

"Get me out of here!" her father shouted, seeming to finally notice the encroaching danger. Adam had to grab the cuffed man to keep him from fleeing the stage by the only set of stairs that wasn't in flames. "It's your duty as an officer of the law to protect a citizen. Let's go!"

"What about your daughter?" she heard Adam shout, incredulous.

"She chose her fate."

"Get him out of here," Dev shouted. "Any luck, Jared?"

"No dice," Jared replied after patting down an unconscious David a second time. His fingers went to the man's neck, checking for a pulse. "He's fading."

"Where else could he have put the key?" Dev asked Ivy. But she was too panicked to think straight. She was going to die. Dev reached through the bars to hold her face, forcing her to focus only on him. "Ivy, think. Where else could David have put the key? It's got to be here somewhere."

She held his gaze, seeing the determination

there. He wasn't going to leave her and she wasn't going to let him die—not for her. She glanced around, the smoke making everything hazy now. Every breath made her lungs and throat itch. And then her gaze landed on the old box containing the torn debt cards. She suddenly remembered David opening the box after he'd locked her in the cage. "The box!"

Dev left her side, disappearing only a few feet away as he was engulfed in smoke. He returned with the entire box and threw the lid aside, digging until his fingers came up with the key.

CHAPTER TWENTY-FIVE

When the cage door swung open, Ivy practically tumbled into his arms. Dev gladly clutched her to him. He planned to never let her go again.

"Let's get out of here," Jared shouted. Seeing that Ivy was in Dev's capable hands, Jared hefted an unconscious David and made his way off the stage and down into the rows of seats.

Dev kissed Ivy hard on the lips and reluctantly pulled away. Words would have to wait for later. He grabbed her hand, pulling her behind him toward the stairs that Jared had descended just seconds before.

She resisted for a second, bending to scoop something off the ground with her free hand. He tugged and she picked up the pace, fleeing with him as the flames practically licked their heels.

They were both coughing as they raced up the aisle and out the exit door, just as a crash on the stage behind them told them the curtains had fallen and the flames had spread yet farther. Firefighters in full gear rushed past Dev and Ivy and into the theater.

Once outside the door, the relative quiet was eerie. The rotunda was abandoned, except for more firefighters who were now filtering through the front door. Only tendrils of smoke had made it this far, and Dev hoped the hotel could be saved, for Ivy's sake.

"Have the paramedics check you two out," Adam ordered. He'd waited in the rotunda to direct the firefighters to the fire. Beside him, Stone was cuffed, silent for once. Father and daughter faced off without a word, and Dev squeezed her hand in silent support.

"Skye?" Dev asked Adam.

"She just checked in," Adam said. She's got Archer pinned to the ground in a parking garage. She's got the ledger."

Dev sucked in a deep breath of relief, then searched the rotunda with his gaze. "And Jared?"

Adam pointed toward the rear doors. "I directed him to take David Wilson that way to one of the ambulances. Most of the crowd's out front. Figured he didn't need to face the media with a bleeding man on his shoulder. And David needs immediate attention."

"What he needs is to die," Stone bit out.

"Like Gloria, you mean?" Ivy said, her voice raspy from the smoke, but also from the emotion shimmering in her eyes. "Or me? You were going to leave me in that cage to burn or die from smoke inhalation." She held out the bundle she'd scooped off the floor. It shook in her hands. "Is this what you wanted more than life—more than *my* life?"

Stone eyed the offering. The box of torn half-cards, Dev realized. He wanted to run back into the theater and toss it in the fire.

"It's my life's work," Stone said with an unapologetic shrug. He eyed the box hungrily, and she shoved the thing toward Adam as if it were a snake.

"Please see that this is added to the evidence against Robert Stone," she said.

"Along with the ledger page, this'll help build the case against your father—" Adam began, but he was interrupted when Ivy held up her hand.

"My father's dead—at least to me."

Stone offered no reaction to her words. He only continued to eye the box Adam held as if it held all of life's secrets. Hell, it, along with the ledger, probably held all of Vegas's dirty little secrets.

"We're done here," Ivy said, turning toward the main doors. Dev wanted to scoop her up and carry her away, and not stop until she was tucked away safe and sound in his cabin on the ranch.

As they emerged into the bright, cheery afternoon sunlight, so incongruous with the fiery oranges and oppressive grays they'd just escaped, two figures rushed toward them from the crowd of guests and onlookers gathered in the parking lot.

"Ivy!"

Beside Dev, Ivy sank to her knees, a sob escaping her as she caught her son up to her and hugged him like she'd never let go.

After several long moments, in which Ivy inhaled deeply of Brandon's little-boy-and-sunshine scent and tried to control the shaking of her limbs, she pulled away, just far enough to look into his eyes.

"I always wanted to be part of your life," she whispered urgently. "Always. Don't ever doubt that. Someday, I'll explain everything."

Brandon grinned with easy acceptance. "Okay."

She laughed through her tears. Brandon's blind trust in her, his willingness to believe in her unconditional love, was everything. It's all she'd ever wanted for him.

Feeling a hand on her shoulder, she looked up at Dev. His face was soot-streaked and a couple small blisters had formed where the heat must have gotten too close, but he was beautiful to her. He always would be.

He jerked his head slightly to the side. "Just wanted you to know we have an audience, in case you want to take this somewhere more private."

She glanced toward the horde of reporters, even more in number than had been at her father's trial, and shakily got to her feet. "I'm not afraid of them. First, Brandon, I'd like you to meet a very good friend of mine, Devlin Grimm."

Dev grinned down at the boy and shook his hand. "Call me Dev. We met briefly. I've heard wonderful things about you." He winked at Ivy.

A few yards away, she heard the fire chief giving an impromptu press conference. "I'm happy to report everyone got out safely," the man said. "One casualty unrelated to the fire was rushed to the hospital, but we just received word he died on the way, the result of a gunshot wound." Ivy felt a tiny stab of regret for David's fate, but no good could come from a vengeful heart. She murmured a prayer that he would finally be at peace with Nathan and Joanna.

Ivy left Dev and Brandon long enough to go to Emily, who'd stood on the sidelines, watching Ivy's little family reunion with tears in her eyes.

"Adam's okay," Ivy said. "He should be out any second."

The relief made Emily's shoulders sag and she let out a shaky breath. "Good."

Ivy clutched her friend to her in a big hug. "I owe you so much for keeping Brandon safe. Thank you."

Emily squeezed her back. "Anytime. What are friends for? But I suspect we'll need a girl's night out to catch up. I want to know everything about your son."

She smiled. "You got it." She turned as she heard Brandon's shout. "Mama! Papa!" He ran to Linda and Miguel as they maneuvered to the front of the crowd. Miguel hoisted Brandon into his arms and carried him over to Ivy as Linda wrapped her in a big hug.

"Are you okay?" Ivy asked, pulling away to examine Linda.

"Me? Of course. That Dev of yours is a good guy."

"He is." Dev was the best kind of guy, the kind she'd thought only existed in fairy tales.

"The technician he sent over checked us out, and Agent Gray sat with us as we waited to see if we'd get a call, but the moment I saw the fire on television, I knew. Agent Gray was kind enough to drive us here with his sirens on."

"Cool!" Brandon added.

Linda smiled, but studied Ivy for a long moment.

She shook her head as if shaking off the fear. "I love you like family, *mija*. If anything had happened to you, I would have come after Stone myself."

Ivy squeezed Linda's hands. "I know you would have." She bit her lip. "Dad told Brandon the truth about my relationship to him."

"She's my biological mother," Brandon said, his tone so matter-of-fact that both women sent him a surprised glance.

"Then that means she's officially part of the family," Linda said, smoothing a hand over his cheek. "Think you can handle that?"

"Yeah."

Ivy's heart swelled in her chest. "You guys are amazing. If you hadn't been here, showing me what it's like to have real love, a real family, I might have given up the fight a long time ago."

"And we wouldn't have let you. You know we've always got your back." Her gaze moved beyond Ivy's shoulder. "But I have a feeling someone else wants the position now." She nudged her chin toward Dev, who still stood off to the side. He was conversing with authorities, but his gaze was on her.

Ivy grinned. "Yes, I think that position is filled." She trusted Dev would always be there to help her fight fires, battles, and whatever else came their way.

The shouts of reporters built to a crescendo and Ivy turned to see what the commotion was about. Adam had emerged from the building with her father in handcuffs. He didn't even look her way, instead shouting to anyone who'd listen that this was another travesty, another example of the task force's bumbling ways.

"He finally got him," Emily murmured, her eyes on her fiancé and a soft smile curving her lips as Adam sent her a wink. Emily cast Ivy an apologetic look. "I didn't mean to be insensitive."

Ivy shook her head. "Don't apologize. I'm glad so many people will finally find justice. Robert Stone is finally getting what he deserves."

"We all are," Dev said, sliding an arm around her waist as he came to her side. Brandon came to her other side to slip his hand in hers. Linda held his other hand. They were a solid unit that couldn't be broken by her father's schemes.

"Let me take you all home," he said.

Ivy blew out a breath. "I have a couple things left to do first." she said, her gaze going from Dev to the cameramen who were snapping shots of her father being put into the back of a police cruiser. At least she'd no longer have to do damage control for him. "I should deal with them, and then Legacy's guests. Wait for me?"

"Hell, no," Dev said softly. "I'm not waiting for you anymore. We're doing everything together from now on. I love you, remember?"

"I love you, too," she said against his smiling lips. "More than you'll ever know."

"I look forward to finding out."

Together, she faced the circus with Dev, Linda, Miguel and Brandon as a united family. She had a feeling she'd never have to be alone again.

EPILOGUE

One month later

Ivy's heart was so full that most days she thought it might burst out of her chest. The past two weeks had been full of celebrations—Brandon had invited her for a Mother's Day brunch along with him and Linda, a few days later had been Brandon's eighth birthday, and, just a few hours ago, Ivy had officially shed the Stone name forever.

She was now Ivy Grimm.

Ivy's gaze found Brandon dancing with Rose on the lawn in front of Dev's cabin, where their closest friends and family had gathered for a reception following their small wedding. Rose and Brandon had taken to each other immediately. Linda and Miguel danced next to them, smiling into each other's eyes.

Brandon seemed to have adapted well to suddenly having a large, supportive family who surrounded him with unconditional love. He'd spent some time getting to know Ivy and Dev better by visiting on weekends at the ranch. What's more, his visits had brought Rose and Linda together, and they'd discussed bringing the kids from Hope's Home out to do some horseback riding sometime soon. By the way Rose's eyes had lit up at the idea, Ivy had a hunch that might be a regular activity, and that more orphaned and foster children would soon be benefiting from the love at Curry Ranch.

Arms wrapped around her from behind and

Dev's mouth nuzzled her neck. "How much longer until I can get you alone?"

She'd never be alone, not truly. And she never wanted to be again. She turned in the circle of his arms and kissed him deeply, and then smiled against his mouth. "Will that tide you over?"

"One more should do it—for the moment."

A throat cleared behind her and she turned to greet Dev's brothers—two of them, at least. The case against Aidan had been reopened in light of evidence that showed someone in Redemption Club might have framed him, but he was still in prison until the review could be completed. Ivy would help Dev do everything they could to free him.

"Welcome to the family," Brady said, surprising her with a warm embrace.

Cody took a turn next, and then presented her with a black, three-ring binder wrapped in white ribbon. "I know it's not a traditional wedding present, but you've been working night and day on this for weeks."

"The foundation?" She glanced at Dev and he grinned.

"All of the nonprofit incorporation papers are in there," Cody assured her. "My friend rushed them through."

She'd decided to begin a new legacy for her son, and for any children she and Dev would be blessed with, by paying forward good deeds instead of criminal ones via a new non-profit called Forward. There was still a lot of evil in the world, but she hoped to counteract it with the good. "It's real?"

"Because of you, victims of crime, and their families, will receive the assistance they need. You're going to help a lot of people."

Her father was in a maximum-security prison, and while it would be months before his official trial began, there were enough agencies clamoring for his head that they'd ensure he didn't get away with anything this time. Besides, the remainder of his team of lawyers had disbursed now that his funds had dried up, his assets frozen by the IRS. Turned out he wasn't the social icon everyone believed, as everyone had abandoned him once the truth came out and he no longer had control of Redemption Club. The Club member mentioned in the ledger entry, the one who'd been contracted to commit the triple murder against the Wilsons, had also been located and arrested. So had the member who'd snuck into Gloria's hospital room and finished the job. And Archer was awaiting trial, as well.

While Ivy celebrated bringing Nathan's and Gloria's murderers to justice, she was too busy enjoying life to think about Robert Stone's fate. She had too many plans.

She wanted to restore Alpha Omega Theater and open it as a youth theater where kids of all ages and backgrounds could have a place to come together and use the arts as a means of communication and escape. Both Nathan and Gloria would have approved.

She was also rebuilding Legacy Hotel & Casino, which she also hoped to make hers once the IRS sorted things out at Stone Corp. The fire damage had been confined to the theater, some of the nearby casino, and the offices. The latter had actually come as an immense relief to Ivy. There were too many memories of her father there. She planned to renovate the offices completely.

"I can see she makes you happy," Brady told his brother. "You're a lucky man."

"You mean the man who melted the ice queen's heart," she said with a wink. She was well aware what his brothers had thought of her, but she was rapidly changing their minds.

Dev squeezed her waist. "There's no ice in your heart, or anywhere inside you."

"Not anymore." She thought her cheeks might shatter from smiling so much, but that was impossible.

She was no longer made of porcelain. Or ice. Or even stone. She was human flesh—the strongest, yet most malleable of any material she'd ever known.

"I love you," she murmured against Dev's lips. The flare of heat in his eyes never failed to reach inside and warm her.

"I love you, too." His hand smoothed over her back. There'd be a lifetime of caresses, hugs, and laughter. Their kids would fill the ranch, and Legacy hotel, and someday, Alpha Omega Theater, with energy, laughter, and light. And she would leave them a different kind of legacy.

"Can I kidnap you now?" Dev whispered in her ear as his brothers wisely moved away to give them some space.

"Yes, please."

I am visible. I am touchable. And she'd always have the security that only love—true, unconditional love—could provide.

ABOUT THE AUTHOR

Anne Marie has always been fascinated by people—inside and out—which led to degrees in Biology, Chemistry, Psychology, and Counseling. Her passion for understanding the human race is now satisfied by her roles as mother, wife, daughter, sister, and award-winning author of romantic suspense.

She writes to reclaim her sanity.

Find ways to connect with Anne Marie at www.AnneMarieBecker.com. There, sign up for her newsletter to receive the latest information regarding books, appearances, and giveaways.

Thank you for reading, and please consider leaving a review. If you'd like to learn more about my books and receive the latest news on upcoming releases and sales, please sign up for my newsletter or visit me on Facebook at "Anne Marie Becker, Author."

STACKING THE DECK
(Redemption Club, Book 1)

In a city built for sin, the Redemption Club is a secret society that exists to fulfill a person's darkest desires—including murder games—for a price.

Raised off the grid by an anti-government group, Skye Hamilton puts her resourcefulness and survival training to good use taking the dangerous tasks nobody else wants. When a job searching for a runaway teen brings Redemption Club members gunning for her, putting those she cares about in danger, she'll risk everything to fight the enemy. Including her heart.

Jared Bennigan, Las Vegas bodyguard to the elite, accepted his latest job hoping it would lead to his missing sister. All evidence points to his client as the last person to have seen her, but he's not the only one looking for a woman who disappeared. Skye's enticing blue eyes contradict her tough, distrusting exterior, revealing an intriguing combination of vulnerability and intelligence. But those eyes are watching his client—through her rifle's scope.

To find both missing women, Jared will need to convince Skye—who plays a wicked game of hard-to-get—to be his partner. And with the Redemption Club intent on making Skye the prey in a human hunting expedition, her skills, and her trust in Jared, will be put to the test. It's the ultimate game of survival of the fittest. But who will win?

ONLY FEAR
(The Mindhunters, Book 1)

After a violent incident with a patient leaves scars on both her mind and body, psychiatrist Dr. Maggie Levine craves isolation. A radio talk show host seems to be the perfect profession, a job where she can help people from a distance while staying safe. When a strange caller begins stalking her on the air and murdering people to get her attention, Maggie realizes she can no longer close herself off from the outside world.

A personal security expert, former Secret Service Agent Ethan Townsend is no stranger to tracking down the most violent monsters of society and bringing them to justice. Still, it will take all of Ethan's skills to protect his new assignment, the irresistible Maggie, from a man intent on teaching her the ultimate lesson in fear....